I0734155

# Genetic Soul Brothers

## Wayne E. Criss

To order additional copies of this book, contact:
Bookwhip
1-855-339-3589
https://www.bookwhip.com

# ACKNOWLEDGEMENTS

I wish to sincerely thank my Professor Historian Wife, Dr. Nur Bilge Criss, who taught me how to take a mountain rock and slowly, carefully change it into a lovely carved stone.

As with all writings many people contribute to make the final version a success. I sincerely thank the following for their assistance in giving of their time by reading, critiquing, and advising my first novel.

Jeremy Salt Alaeddin Yoruk Osman Oguz
Engin Ozgen Julie Aydinli James Smith Erin Johnson

A very special thanks to Mine Pinar Gozen for constructing the illustrations and images for the covers.

# PROLOGUE

Is it possible for a baby to be carried by and born to four different women in four different places in the world at the same time, and grow up as separate individual children, yet carry the exact same genes and share a common or multi-soul? It happened, and as these boys grow up they learn that they are one of four IDENTICALS. Therefore a difficult, frustrating twenty year long quest begins as they try to find each other. The life quest ends in unusual success for them, but their deaths produce a new quest for mankind – can souls be orchestrated?

* * *

Aaron is born into an aristocratic Irish Catholic family in Winchester, New Hampshire, is educated in Boston and New York City, becomes a physician and medical researcher, and establishes in NYC, the first Center for Cellular and Genetic Biology of Twinning in the world. Aaron's professional life is dedicated to collecting and documenting data on **nature** (genetics) versus **nurture** (environment) influence on a person's life decision making.

William (Bill) is born into a fifth generation German-Lutheran farm family in Iowa, is educated in Des Moines, and becomes a lawyer who specializes in litigation concerning Genetically Engineered (**GE**) food crops and Genetically Modified (**GM**) foods in the Midwest. Bill establishes new legal interpretations for molecular gene modification of plant crops and foods.

Charles is born to a middle-upper class 'southern' working couple in Atlanta, Georgia, is educated there in **Biology** and later in **Christian Theology**, and establishes a church and an environmental organization in southern Florida near the Everglades National Park. Charles brings Jesus to the Seminoles and, with his Animal Ecology Professor wife, places environmental pressures upon the polluters of the Everglades.

David (Dave) is born to a lower-middle class Caucasian couple in a Hispanic dominated area of San Diego, California, educated in the US Army, and becomes the Director of Intelligence for a major security firm in Washington, DC. Dave devises a **new security system** for foreign political officials and industrial VIPs, and the President of the USA.

During their early years each of the boys becomes suspicious of a multiple origin when each dreams of a 'look-a-like' male in various non-recognizable locations. Slowly the quest unfolds to discover possibly as many as four of them. Eventually, thwarted many times, but with persistent efforts, the four IDENTICALS finally find each other. The dreams now evolve into a spiritual two-way and eventually multi-way communications, again only at night when asleep.

And over the years, they each grow into very large men with bright red hair, jade green eyes, and a large cleft on the left ear, rather freak-like. So, this clandestine mode of night time communications helps maintain their anonymity. They each marry and have twins, boy and girl. The wives and children become acquainted before the men find each other. Genetically, each wife has four husbands, and each child has four fathers

Finally the gentlemen discover the culprit fertility clinic that brought this tragedy to life. They rendezvous with the clinic's management who admit a mistake might have happened. And now they must debate whether to sue this clinic for millions of dollars, lose their anonymity; become rich and famous, but disgrace their 'parents'; could they live with this? So they spend quality time as family units trying to make a decision that all four families could be comfortable with.

But if something should happen to cause one or more of the IDENTICALS to die or to be killed before that decision is implemented, and if they share a common or multi-soul, what will happen to the separation of their warm bodies and their soul, or partial souls. If partial souls, does each have to wait for the others? Is there a heaven, purgatory, or hell for partial souls? And can such relationships be orchestrated by medical theologians – soul maestros? Will such music continue after the IDENTICALS are...........where? Does this begin to happen after the first death or the second death or...............

Currently the ISSB's Multi Soul Company is running at a 92% success rate.

* * *

In the more than 25,000 years that more than 15 billion Homo sapiens have lived on this earth, such an occurrence has never happened. But now for the first time:

* * *

IT HAPPENED – SEPARATELY CARRIED – SEPARATELY
BORN -
SEPARATELY RAISED – GENETICALLY IDENTICAL
QUADRUPLETS -
SHARE THEIR LIVES AND SPIRIT/SOUL RELATIONSHIPS

# THE FAMILIES FOUR

Mary and James Armand Family – Boston, MA; New York City
  Aaron – MD, PhD, medical researcher and hospital director
  Josephine – PhD, medical researcher
  Hype – dinosaurs, intellectual, medicine
  Hope – tennis, social systems and management

Dorothy and Fred Bassinger Family – Des Moines, IA
  William – LLD, lawyer specializing in GE and GM systems
  Jenny – BS in Education, teacher of high school sciences
  Steve – football, baseball, medicine
  Stefennie – WWI airplanes, humanities and social sciences

Susan and William Collingswood Family – Everglades, FLA
  Charles – BS, Biology, Theology, minister and environmentalist
  Janice – PhD, environmentalist, animal ecologist
  Samuel –dinosaurs, intellectual, environmental engineering
  Sara – intellectual, doctor of veterinary medicine

Sylvia and Roy Dekker Family – Washington, DC
  David – military, director of intelligence for security firm
  Janet – orphan, middle school teacher in general science
  Action – tennis, kayaking, political science, law
  Alice – intellectual, computers and information sciences

# 1 – THE FERTILITY CLINIC

During the last week in July, 1975, there were four ladies sitting in the special lounge of the Jackson Fertility Clinic in McLean, Virginia, inside the Washington, DC metropolitan beltway. Each lady had visited the clinic several times during the past six months. They had been thoroughly tested and placed on special hormone protocols in anticipation of soon receiving a human pre-embryo implant. Each "soon to be mother" had her very personal reasons and badly wanted to carry and deliver her own baby. The Washington area fertility clinic was one of the most famous in the world. It had been in the business of helping unfertile couples have children for more than twenty five years. The clinic had even developed several fertility programs to deal with different types of sterility problems. It offered a 95% money back guarantee of success in case of failure to produce a child.

The clinic employed more than thirty six medical doctors, gynecologists and obstetricians specializing in fertility problems, endocrinologists, cell biologists, biochemists, molecular biologists, and nurses and laboratory technicians specially trained in endocrinology and reproductive biology. And it occupied more than thirty thousand square feet of clinic and laboratory space in a lovely modern building on Dolly Madison Road, a building designed just for such services. Professor Melvin Jackson was world renowned for being the first doctor to successfully develop the concept for and to implement the method of "test tube babies". More than two thousand unfertile couples now have children because of his pioneering efforts. Dr Jackson died one year ago. His Gynecologist-Obstetrician son, Dr William Jackson, now owns and runs the clinic. Unfortunately the second Dr Jackson is more interested in money than in helping such unfortunate couples have the babies of their dreams.

The four ladies ranged in age from twenty two to thirty five, the normal reproductive age range for successfully having such children. Each was found to be incapable of having a baby. For a variety of reasons, they and/or their husbands were sterile. Therefore each had sought out the Jackson Fertility Clinic in hopes of having a child of their own (even though the child's genes would not be theirs). They all understood that this was the only possible way that each could carry and have their own child. And their husbands agreed. The procedures guaranteed complete anonymity for both the couple and the oocyte and sperm donors. They would never meet nor ever know each other. Everyone involved signed a set of legal papers to negate any and all future rights or obligations to any offspring so produced at this time in this clinic with the selected fertility program. In fact the bookkeeping was such that both the donors' names and the recipient couple's names were coded and the codes were sealed away. Therefore, all four people and the clinic were completely protected from any future "changes of the mind" or additional obligations.

Mary Armand, at thirty two years, was the oldest of the waiting ladies. She was an intelligent and handsome woman, a little overweight, but in good physical health. She was from a New Hampshire Irish Catholic family, and was the first female of that family to have fertility difficulties. This was a major problem for her husband, James. He was a wealthy and famous New England aristocrat, also with an Irish Catholic background and was from a large family of four sisters and three brothers. Mrs. Armand had four sisters. Dr. Armand always assumed that they would have several children. And he planned accordingly by expanding their 40 year old family house on the two hundred and twenty acres of prime forest and agriculture land just outside of Manchester, New Hampshire, where his medical practice was located. Mary became an excellent estate manager and 'ran' the farm. James was almost ten years older and was an outstanding and very popular Family Doctor, so he continuously trained one-two other intern doctors in family medicine in his Armand Family Clinic. Dr Armand wrote several books on the subject of the need to have more family doctors especially in small communities. This was a medical specialty on the decline.

Mary and James had been married for twelve years without "offspring" success. Over a period of several years they had consulted with several gynecologists in Manchester and in nearby Boston. Various ideas, possibilities and options were discussed. They learned that several different types of fertility programs were available at the Jackson Fertility Clinic in McLean, Virginia. And since this fertility clinic was one of the best in the world, they finally decided to go there and "be tested out". They went to the Jackson Clinic and after three weeks of "testing and talking" they agreed to use the fertility program which seemed to have the best possibility of success. So Mrs. Armand was patiently waiting for her "child'.

Dorothy Bassinger was twenty five years old and already had three miscarriages during her few reproductive years. She was tall but due to her miscarriages she weighed less than she should and tended to slouch. She was not in good health but psychologically she badly needed a child. Dorothy and her husband, Fred lived in a small town about one half hour drive from Des Moines, Iowa. Fred was the fourth generation of German Lutheran descendents to live and work their land. They owned a two hundred and fifty acre tract of farm land and financially, were doing very well. However, after the third miscarriage they decided to go into the big city and ask for help from some gynecologists that specialize in fertility problems.

They met with Dr Jeremey Statson, a prominent gynecologist who recently moved to Des Moines after specialty training in female infertility problems in London. He ran a series of laboratory tests on both Bassingers. The results from the tests showed that Mrs. Bassinger did ovulate, she should have been able to carry a child, but it appeared that she showed an allergy to her husband's sperm cells. Therefore sex and/or fertilization of an oocyte or a growing embryo, resulting from Mr. Basssinger, would cause an allergic reaction in Mrs. Bassinger's womb, and a spontaneous abortion would occur. Thus she would not be able to carry her husband's child. She probably could carry a child from another man, an option that was quickly ruled out. They both did want a child very badly – the farm needed one. There were not many options that were available in Iowa. Dr Statson told them about the Jackson Fertility Clinic, so they decided to go there and seek other ideas. They went to McLean, were happy with what they saw and heard, and were promised a baby. So they were waiting for everything to begin.

Susan and William Collingswood met at Georgia Technical University while studying for their Master of Science Degrees in Business Management. They were both from 'Deep South' families. She was twenty six years old, he was twenty seven. Susan was in very good health and eagerly anticipated children to complete their dream lives. They were deeply in love, on their way to a great life together, and wanted "mountains" of children. After graduation and marriage they were both employed by the same large Sears Center in northern Atlanta, Georgia. They immediately bought a new car and a moderate house in Sandy Springs, an easy fifteen minute commute to work.

Life was good and they were ready to start that big family. Perhaps things were going too well, because three months later a truck ran a traffic light and bashed into the left side of their new car. Mr. Collingswood was driving and his left hip was crushed. He was in the hospital for several months before returning to work on crutches. Soon thereafter they again attempted to re-start their long awaited for new family. After more than one year of trying without a pregnancy, they knew something was wrong.

Over the next several months they went to three different gynecology clinics in Atlanta. Apparently the problem was that Mr. Collingswood had a very low sperm count, and some of the sperm were not "normal". Not having any pre-accident sperm data on him, the doctors concluded that the accident must have caused permanent damage to his reproductive tract. He was effectively sterile. They were referred to the Jackson Fertility Clinic in McLean for assistance with their "problem". So for two months they went up and down the east coast, spent much time with Dr Jackson and his staff, and were convinced that they should try to have a child using one of the Clinic's fertility programs. Therefore Mrs. Collingswood was now one of the four women also waiting for a pre-embryo transplant.

Sylvia Dekker was a small twenty seven year old woman with a variety of chronic health problems. She was currently in poor health and several pounds light for her height and bone structure. When she was a child she had developed ALL (acute lymphocytic leukemia). She underwent two rounds of chemotherapy, no radiotherapy. This was a successful effort because she has now been cancer free for eighteen years. During her teenage years she had menstrual problems and developed a treatable form of endometriosis (a disease which causes abnormal lining of the uterine endometrium). Even with these health problems, perhaps because of these problems, she desperately wanted to have a child. Her husband, Roy Dekker, was employed with the Water Commission of the City of San Diego, California. They lived in a predominately Hispanic area. And he loved children. He also had many buddies that had large families. So he was also willing to go the extra mile to try to have children.

The Dekkers talked with several of the gynecology clinics in the San Diego area which specialized in infertility problems. They ran a series of laboratory tests and concluded that it would be possible but extremely difficult for Mrs. Dekker to get pregnant and carry a baby through to birth. The first weeks of pregnancy would be very problematic. Given that the first month was successful, careful testing and additional but necessary hormonal therapy would be critical throughout the pregnancy. They highly recommended the Jackson Clinic in McLean, Virginia as the best clinic to attempt this difficult process. The Dekkers traveled across the USA, stayed with a cousin of hers in Falls Church, Virginia and consulted with the Jackson Clinic. After two weeks of testing, they decided to attempt one of the Clinic's fertility programs. So Mrs. Dekker was the fourth lady waiting for an opportunity to become a mother.

At precisely 9 o'clock on that morning the door to the special lounge at the Jackson Fertility Clinic opened. A secretary invited the four ladies down the hallway and into the large office of Dr William Jackson. With much apprehension and a variety of nervous gestures, they followed her. It was an impressive office with redwood paneling on all three interior walls, while the outer wall had five large floor-to-ceiling windows which opened onto a view of a beautiful Japanese garden.

Dr Jackson was forty four years of age, of medium height, small pot belly, a brown and receding hair line, and was wearing dark wire frame glasses and his doctors' white clinic-lab coat. Indeed he was quite average or rather normal for being the son of a famous doctor. However, he was more of a salesman than a physician. He immediately got up from his desk and went to meet them at the office door. He graciously welcomed each lady, one by one, using their complete names, their husband's names, and inquired about their health and his clinic's services. He offered a large armed chair to each, and took orders for coffee, tea, pastries, or other needs. The secretary had been waiting and listening. She immediately went to the wall on the left side of the office, opened two large doors to reveal a small kitchen area, poured coffee and tea and filled each order. After the ladies were thus comfortably seated and had been served their coffee or tea, he returned to his large red wood desk and sat behind it in his large swivel leather padded chair.

Next he asked, "Do any one of you have any questions concerning any phase of the procedures or techniques of your respective fertility program, role of the clinic personnel, time frames for embryo development, legal restrictions, or any other questions related to 'our future togetherness'".

Since no questions were forthcoming, he gave to each an envelope and asked them to open it and slowly and carefully read the contents. It said:

**0 – 00 – 000 – 0000**
**"Growth and Development of the Human Embryo"**
**When a (male) sperm carrying 23 chromosomes enters into a (female) egg cell (oocyte) carrying 23 chromosomes, fertilization occurs. A fertilized ovum or zygote is formed. A sudden electrostatic**

change takes place on the entire surface of this new ovum which results in a sealing of the ovum cell's outer membrane. Even though surrounded by millions of sperms, each trying to enter the oocyte, after fertilization, no single additional sperm can enter. Inside the ovum or zygote cell all of the chromosomes immediately fuse (#1 to #1, #2 to #2, #3 to #3, #4 to #4.........) which results in 23 pairs of chromosomes, or a total of 46 chromosomes in the zygote. One of each pair of the chromosomes came from the mother and one of each pair of the chromosomes came from the father. In this way a viable zygote is formed equally from both mother and father. For the next 12 to 14 days this zygote undergoes normal cell division ($1{\rightarrow}2{\rightarrow}4{\rightarrow}8{\rightarrow}16{\rightarrow}32{\rightarrow}64{\rightarrow}128{\rightarrow}256$ cells.......) as several million genetically identical cells form a maturing blastula.

This is a form of cloning and is called the blastula stage. <u>In vivo</u> <u>(normal man and woman reproduction)</u> the mature blastula implants itself into the uterine endometrium (womb membranes), begins growing, and begins the development of two protective membranes and an umbilical cord which will supply the future embryo with oxygen and nutrients. During <u>in vitro</u> <u>(test tube fertilization)</u> both the fertilization and early blastula formation take place in a special container, located outside of the womb, which contains a special growth media. Approximately ten to twelve days after fertilization the now maturing blastula is then directly injected or implanted into the uterine endometrium or womb of the potential mother.

So the two procedures, naturally within the uterus and controlled within the special container are almost exactly the same. In the first, God controls and in the second, we control. The mature blastula will continue to develop by making more pre-embryonic type cells; and the two protective membranes which will completely surround the mature blastula and an umbilical cord attachment to the endometrium or womb which will provide oxygen and nutrients to the growing and maturing blastula and subsequent embryo.

Around 15 days after fertilization, while the maturing blastula (a ball of identical cells) has begun growing within the endometrium/womb, a small dark area develops near the bottom of the maturing blastula. It is called Henson's node. Some of the cells of the blastula begin "soldier like" marching through this node. As they exit the node, from a down to up direction they are a darker color. This continues for next 13 to 14 days and is called the gastrula stage. [The blastula stage lasts the first 14 days and the gastrula stage lasts the second 14 days.] The darker cells which emerge from Henson's node eventually become the nerve cells which form the central nervous system in the head and the spinal cord in the back bone. They can be seen as a grey crescent or grey streak on the side of the gastrula. The remaining non-gray cells which are not part of this grey crescent now begin developing into many different types of cells of the skin, skeletal and heart muscle, bones, liver, lungs, digestive tract, and on and on.

After 6 – 7 weeks certain body areas such as head, arms, legs, and body shape begin to develop from these lighter cells. Eventually over 200 types of cells develop from that one fertilized ovum or zygote. And that one cell also becomes several billion cells, which is a baby, all in a matter of 7-9 months. It is a miracle in motion. And it all works perfectly 98% of the time.

In summary, with your specific pre-pregnancy program, the sperm and oocyte, which are taken from two anonymous donors, will be fused inside of a special container containing essential nutrients. Hence, fertilization will be accomplished in vitro (similar to test tube babies). At a selected time during the blastula stage, usually the 8 to 10 day old blastula, we will inject or implant the mature blastula (pre-embryo) into your uterus/womb.

You will feel no pain, only a little discomfort. Each of you will have a different mature blastula (pre-embryo) formed from different donors; so each of you will have your own unique child. It will grow by developing the two protective membranes and an umbilical cord connection to the uterus/womb and making millions of more cells. The cells will progress from a mature blastula to a gastrula to a mature gastrula to various stages of an embryo and on to a complete baby. Your body will do all of this for you. Within a short time you will begin to feel pregnant and will have the typical "side effects" of pregnancy.

After implantation you will remain with us for the next 3-4 weeks while we monitor your progress. You will remain longer if we foresee potential problems. If things go well, and we expect them to do so, we will coordinate the rest of your pregnancy with a gynecologist-obstetrician of your choice near your home. As long as your pregnancy continues well, and with our written permission, you may choose to have your baby delivered with your selected, but our approved, obstetrician and hospital.

**One other component of concern is the concept of a spirit or soul. Most types of Christianity believe that a spirit/soul enters the newly fertilized ovum or zygote soon after fertilization. It is the common Christian belief that somehow the soul comes from the genes related to the Mother and Father. They come from the genealogical or family 'tree'. You and your husband are not providing the genes for your future child, so his soul would not come from your family 'trees'. The child's genes and soul are from the two anonymous donors/providers of the oocyte and sperm. However, the child will be yours in every other way. Neither you nor we have any control over this; so there is nothing you or I can do about it. Therefore do no worry about something you have no control over.**

**And lastly, we suggest that you do not tell your new child about him or her coming from anonymous donors. The child is yours. Those donors will never see nor even know he/she exits. Never forget that! Love him/her, but keep his origin a secret.**

**0000 – 000 – 00 – 0**

After a few minutes had passed, and Dr. Jackson saw that each of the ladies was looking up at him, he again tried to open a conversation by saying, "Do you need more time to read and digest this important information concerning your program? If so, and please take your time, and allow me to answer any questions that you might have. If you need more time, please continue reading. We will wait."

Being the oldest, and also the one with the greatest need for a baby to make her husband and the relative families happy, Mrs. Armand responded first, "Why do we have to remain here in bed for several days or even weeks? Why can't we go home in two or three days like any other pregnancy?"

Dr. Jackson replied, "First of all this is not a normal pregnancy. I assume that you have never previously gotten pregnant from a needle and syringe."

They all smiled. And Mrs. Armand became very red in the face.

"It has been our long experience that extra and daily monitoring of the growing embryo and the new mother helps us identify any acute or future potential problems. One area that we very carefully monitor is the level of various hormones such as the three estrogens (estradiol, estrone, estriol), the progestins (progesterone especially), and luteinizing hormone in the blood of the mother. Specific levels of each of these hormones are necessary to maintain a normally developing embryo and prevent any type of abortion."

"If there are not normal levels of any one of these hormones we have the experience to make appropriate corrections. The corrective action does not just involve direct injections of a hormone if that hormone should be lower than normal. It requires a carefully coordinated alteration of all of the hormones involved in maintaining the pregnancy. Also there are several other blood and urine substances that we measure every day to help us monitor the health of both the embryo and mother. Diet and blood nutrients levels must be carefully controlled. The psychological state of the mother is continuously monitored. Several days of close control, during and immediately after implantation of the blastula, are essential."

Mrs. Collingswood asked, "Will we be put to sleep during the implantation procedure?"

Dr. Jackson responded, "Yes. With ladies having their first time implantations, like all of you, we will put each of you into a very light sleep during the procedure. This is routine and sort of guarantees no problems."

"Will it leave us with headaches or nausea afterward?" Mrs. Collingswood asked.

"Only for a few minutes," replied Dr. Jackson.

"I have a question," said Mrs. Dekker. "What is the difference between the oocyte, ovum, fertilized ovum, zygote, blastula, gastrula, embryo, and a baby?"

"That is a very good question!" exclaimed Dr. Jackson. "These are just medical or scientific terms to help us describe the general developmental periods between the fertilization of sperm and ovum and the birth of the baby. Before the cellular and chromosomal fusion, both the sperm and ovum are half cells. They each have only one half of the number of chromosomes so they cannot become growing cells. The ovum or 'half cell' must fuse with a sperm another 'half cell', in other words they each need each other to become a 'whole cell' that can grow. After these two half cells fuse, then their chromosomes must fuse to make a complete or whole cell with all of the chromosomes. This new whole cell is called a **fertilized ovum** or a **zygote**. Only a complete whole cell with a full set of chromosomes has the capacity to grow and make new cells. During each of these stages the physical and biochemical systems inside the cells continue to change."

"So the fertilized ovum or zygote is the cell that is formed at the time when the chromosomes of the sperm and ovum fuse. This new cell has the potential to become a baby (several months later). The cells that grow from the zygote form a round ball of cells."

"This ball of cells is called **blastula** or the blastula stage where every cell is genetically and physically identical (days 1 to 14). We often call the maturing blastula a pre-embryo."

"The next stage is the **gastrula** (days 15 to 28). It refers to the continuing development of the blastula as it begins to differentiate into various 'adult' cell types such as nerve cells. In early gastrula the grey crescent (pre-nerve cells) cells appear. In later gastrula several developing and changing cell types begin to occur."

"After these two weeks, nerve, muscle, bone, skin, fat, connective cells and tissues, and internal body organs such as liver, heart, kidney, and lungs, and then body appendages such as the head, arms and legs begin to form (beyond 30 days)

"Therefore, the word **embryo** refers to a mature gastrula (after one month) when the physical shape of the growing cell mass has begun to resemble a miniature child. We also divide the 9 months of pregnancy into three trimesters in order to follow the development of the embryo from a scientific viewpoint. We doctors use this terminology to help us describe biochemical and anatomical events which occur during the development of the baby. In this way we can identify, and try to correct, any potential problems before they lead to loss of the child. OK?"

Mrs. Dekker, "I think so. I will study this information that you gave to us some more. Can I come to you and ask more questions later?"

"Of course. We can discuss this later, any time that you want to do so. Your doctor is always available. And I am always available." replied Dr. Jackson.

Mrs. Dekker just smiled. Dr. Jackson turned to Mrs. Bassinger to ask her if she had any questions.

"I have several questions, if you please", said Mrs. Bassinger. "Will we have a boy or girl baby? Could we have twins? What if the child is abnormal? What happens if we lose the baby? If we should lose this one, what are the chances of trying again by using a different fertility program, and then carrying the second baby?"

"I will try to answer your questions in the order that you asked," Dr. Jackson responded. "We do not attempt to determine the sex of the potential baby at the time of fertilization. The sex can be determined during the very late gastrula stages, in a couple of months; but we do not do this unless there is a very special reason. Such attempts can damage the growing cells. So, like all pregnant women, you will have to wait until three to four months after fertilization to have an ultrasound test to determine the sex of your child. It is possible to have twins, but highly unlikely. A ten year analysis of our work shows that there is less than one percent chance of having more than one child using any of our fertility programs. If during the careful and extensive monitoring of your baby and your health status during your pregnancy we observe any life threatening problems, we will immediately inform you. Then you and your husband must make the choice of whether to continue or terminate the ongoing program."

"And to the last question, if the child is lost, and we do not expect this to happen, yes another attempt can be made. We had one lady who was unable to carry her first or second baby to birth. She had miscarriages twice, using two different fertility programs. However she did not give up. Using a third fertility program, she now has 2 beautiful children, a boy and a girl".

"Several years ago a friend of mine had a small skin cancer during her pregnancy," commented Mrs Dekker. "Is it possible for a baby to get a cancer from the mother?"

Dr. Jackson replied, "No. Cells of the Mother do not cross these protective membranes surrounding the growing embryo and enter into the embryo. I read your health history status. I know that you also had a type of blood cancer when you were very young which was cured, so I can understand your concern. But I would never recommend that you carry a baby if such a thing could occur."

"My problem involved an allergic response from the growing embryo when I got pregnant by my husband," said Mrs. Bassinger. "So I could get pregnant, but not carry the baby long enough to even have a C-section. How do I know that with this 'pre-embryo', which I will receive, will not cause an allergic response and I will lose it too."

'I am very sorry," answered Dr. Jackson. "We cannot know this in advance. This is one of the reasons that we need to keep you here for a few weeks and monitor both your health and the baby's health. We would observe an immune reaction very early in your pregnancy, and we would immediately notify you; then you and your husband would have to make the decision as to what to do. Do you understand?"

Mrs. Bassinger said, "If such a problem cannot be detected in advance of the implantation, I guess I have little choice but to take my chances."

"I will make special notations on your charts." He added. "We will monitor certain immune response cells and certain substances in your blood and determine if such a response is happening. I personally will watch you grow bigger with your pregnancy. It is one of the crazy pleasures that I have in my life, watching other peoples babies grow, and knowing I helped."

"All right. Are there any other questions? Again let me repeat. You have been given the office and cellular telephone numbers of your specific doctor, and the emergency telephone numbers for the laboratory personnel and secretary responsible for your specific program. I will now give to you my office and cellular phone numbers"

He hands out to each of them a card with his office and two cellular phone numbers, and his current weekly work schedule printed out on a day by day, hour by hour basis.

"If you have any questions at any time please contact your doctor or me, and we will answer them for you immediately. And now then we will see each of you here in the clinics on Wednesday: Mrs. Armand and Mrs. Bassinger at 9:00 AM, and Mrs. Collingswood and Mrs. Dekker at 2:00 PM. At those times we will put each of you into a light sleep, and implant your pre-embryo, and then we will assist you in the growth of your new baby."

Suddenly Dr. Jackson's desk telephone rang. He answered, listened for a minute, responded with an "OK" and "thank you" and hung up. After another minute of silence, he addressed the four ladies as follows.

"That was the Director of our Laboratories, Dr. Jackson explained. He just made a routine check of the four pre-embryos which are being prepared for you for Wednesday. He has made the judgment that they are not developed quite far enough for 100% successful implantation. He requested that the implantations be delayed two days, until Friday, to let them mature a little longer. He is the person that helped develop the methods that we use, and now has many years of experience in the use of the special growth techniques that we employ. In a situation like this I trust his judgment more than mine. So I concurred. Therefore, we will not see you ladies on Wednesday, but on Friday, the same times, and the same stations. Are there any questions?"

"We still expect that all will go well. It is even possible that your new one may come a few weeks early."

There were no questions now. But there would be many later.

# 2 – The Children

Aaron was born into the New England aristocratic family of Mary and James Armand on March 7, 1976. He was a beautiful baby with a head full of red hair, green eyes, and a slightly cleft left ear. His parents and numerous aunts, uncles, and cousins had been impatiently waiting for him for many years. He was worth the wait. He was a quiet, calm baby. He ate everything, easily played alone or with others, walked at ten months, and had a smile that melted everyone's heart. He obviously was a happy baby. As the only son of a very loving mother and physician father, he lived in the family chateau on three hundred acres of prime forested land and pastures: he lacked for nothing in the way of entertainment and playthings. As a boy he loved playing indoors and the outdoors. He even routinely went hiking, camping, hunting, boating, and fishing with his Father, relatives and friends.

When it came to choosing a school, Aaron's Father told him to never forget that one can either be a large frog in a small pond or a small frog in a large pond. Aaron never had much respect for his Father's advice. Why could he not be a large frog in a large pond? So, he bypassed his Father's school, the Whichworth Boys Academy. This school only had two hundred students and no really famous graduates over some seventy five years of existence. Instead he went to the large local public school (one thousand and five hundred students) which was very good academically and had every type of extra school activity, also girls.

Aaron excelled in school, academically number one or two in his class every year. He played many team sports during their year and season – baseball, soccer, basketball, and football. Later in his high school years he settled for football and baseball and won several school, conference and state athletic awards. Even though Aaron was the rich boy who always drove a Mercedes convertible, he was also the sports jock who helped win the school championships, set the curve on the science tests, sang in the choir, and performed in school stage drama events. For all of this he was not arrogant, and was indeed just "one of the guys". His social graces matched his intellectual and athletic prowess. During his senior year,

Aaron was elected King of the Senior Class, was fully expected to marry the elected Queen of the Senior Class, and go off to medical school and become a great and famous physician.

Actually Aaron did successfully complete four years of pre-med at Boston College and began medical studies at Harvard University Medical School in Boston, Mass. He did not do this because it was expected of him. From a young age he "understood" that he could not possibly be the son of Mary and James Armand. Physically there was no similarity whatsoever. Mrs. Armand was only 5 feet 2 inches tall, small boned with brown hair and brown eyes. Dr. Armand was 5 foot 8 inches, black hair, dark eyes, and a brownish complexion. While Aaron was 6 feet 6 inches tall, 210 pounds, large boned, and of course had a light complexion to go with his red hair and green eyes. It did not require much brain power to figure out that there was another mother and father out there somewhere. He never brought the subject up, and no one in the family unit even hinted such ideas. And he did love these two parents very much. He didn't want to hurt them. So his real reason for studying medicine was such that he could learn the concepts within biochemistry, cellular and molecular biology, genetics, human reproduction, ethics, and thus he could attempt to find his real mother and father, someday. He read about "test tube babies", cloning, stem cells and that sort of stuff.

Aaron was doing very well in his studies when one night during his second year at Boston College he had a very disturbing dream:

'He saw a young boy with red hair and green eyes (himself he assumed) running through a big cornfield. Directly behind followed two other boys, they both had brown hair and eyes. They were having a great time, laughing and shouting and tearing down and throwing ears of corn at each other. As they came to one end of the cornfield they climbed down a hill leading to a small creek. There was perhaps a foot or so of water running through the creek. They immediately striped off all of their clothes. And in all their nakedness they began making clay balls and damning up the creek. After a short time they had created a neat mud dam and the place started filling up with water until a small lake had formed. They swam, splashed themselves off, and laid down in the bright sunshine to dry off. One of the boys brought out a pack of cigarettes and each took one. They lit up and puffed and coughed their way until the pack was empty. The small pond was now really full, so now they could really swim. Then they proceeded to attach a rope to a tree overlooking the pond. All three boys took turns swinging and playing Tarzan and Cheta, singing dirty songs, and belly diving into the water from the rope above. After a while they began slowly crawling on their hands and knees up the creek in an area above the pond. They were looking for crawdads (crayfish). As they found one, they would rinse it off in the muddy water, pop it into their mouths and swallow it whole. These little guys were a challenge to eat before they pinched your tongue. Then suddenly a thunder and lightning storm hit.' And Aaron woke up.

This unusual dream left him very puzzled for many weeks. He assumed that the red haired-green eyed boy was himself. But he had never been in a cornfield, damned up creeks to make ponds, and never smoked a cigarette nor eaten raw crayfish. And that type of a thunder and lightning storm didn't happen in New Hampshire. Weird!

* * *

The state of Iowa was one state in the USA that was usually quiet and calm, where the land and the people were in reasonable control of their own fate. This meant their fate was only related to the weather to grow crops in the fields and the weekly fluctuation of futures prices in the stock markets. The capital city, Des Moines, was only a few hundred thousand in population, yet it was the largest city in the state. And the only time that there was major unrest (rioting?) was when the wrong high school girls basketball team won the state championship. Or a non-Iowan won the super load tractor pulling contest at the annual Iowa State Fair. There was an abundance of black rich soil which would grow just about any crop. And the soil was so maintained by many generations of family farms carefully rotating corn and soybeans every year. Iowa had basically three problems: 1) with the continuing increase in the size and capacity of the farming machinery, less human labor was needed to farm the large farms, so the farmers children started going the big cities, in state or out of state, for jobs; 2) economics dictated that each farm grow more and higher density crops which required higher quantities of toxic fertilizers and pesticides/herbicides; 3) and now the farmers were expected to use gene engineered crops (whatever that was) to be able to compete in the market place against foreign imports.

William (Bill) was born to Dorothy and Fred Bassinger on February 27, 1976. They had inherited over three hundred acres of rich Iowa farm land near Des Moines from Fred's Father, who died in 1979 from an overworked body, otherwise known as a stroke. Since then they had been working most of this land by rotating corn, wheat, and soy beans. However,

Mrs. Bassinger was not that strong, physically, so most of the hard field work fell on Mr. Bassinger's shoulders. A second pair of hands would be very welcome. However this little red haired, green eyed guy with a cleft in his left ear would have been welcome anyway. He was a beautiful and loving baby. And they just knew he came directly from God.

The Bassingers were sound Christian people and had Bill immediately baptized at the nearby Walltom Presbyterian Church which was just a couple of miles down the road. At church everyone who saw him fell in love with him and his smile. Also, that red hair certainly caught people's attention. Bill grew up rapidly. He was a good son and started routinely helping with the chores just as soon as he was big enough. Before long he was on that tractor most hours when he was not in school. He became a tall, 6 foot 8 inch strong young man, who was not only one of the top students in his class but also an outstanding tight end on the high school football team which won the Iowa State Football Championship in his senior year.

Over the years Bill had developed a special affection for Uncle Paul Bassinger, his Father's younger brother. His Uncle was an estates lawyer and lived near Des Moines. They all went to the same family church every Sunday. After church Paul and Jenny Bassinger, and their son, John, who was only one year younger than Bill, would come to the farm for Sunday dinner and often spend the afternoon playing ball, throwing horseshoes, or during the cold winter, they would play cards for hours. After graduation, he knew he did not want to spend the rest of his life on a farm, so he enrolled at nearby Iowa State University in pre-law. After his Bachelors degree, he entered Drake University Law School.

In January of his first year in law school, he was studying hard for his final exam in international law. He fell asleep at his desk. And he had a strange dream:

'He saw a young man, red haired and green eyed, riding high on a surfboard with giant waves all around him. As the waves lapped over his head his feet and the board shot up into the air and he appeared to go over backwards. The monstrous wave carried him under and for several seconds he disappeared from the world of air. Then suddenly he shot out from under the wave through a newly formed water tunnel, spun to his right and was immediately up near the top of the wave. He dipped his left hip, turned left and was again shooting down the side of the wave at nearly 80 miles per hour. The large crowd on the beach stood up and gave a roaring ovation. The young red headed man's maneuver received the highest judge's rating and the total in numbers from the days contest put him at the top of the leader board in the Tenth Pacific International Surfboard Le Granda (for under eighteen year olds). He slowly coasted on the board into the beach and his friends met him with cheering and shouting. His buddies picked him up, put him onto their shoulders. They carried him up to the grandstand area where the judges were sitting. After several minutes, he was placed upon a small podium, awarded $5,000 in prize money and a grand trophy. A beautiful young lady in a bikini appeared out of nowhere, took him by the arm and they walked alone together toward the sun which was sitting over the ocean. Catcalls and cheers followed them, but they paid no attention'.

Suddenly he woke up. Was that him in that dream? He had never seen an ocean let alone a surfboard. And to surf in waves like that. No way. The bikini was nice though. Weird!

* * *

Charles was born to Susan and William Collingswood on March 5, 1976. He first saw light in the large Selma Christopher Women's Health Center in Atlanta, Georgia. He had red hair, green eyes and a small cleft on his left ear. He was such a beautiful baby that even the nurses were regularly coming by to see him. His Mother and Father were ecstatic because they never thought they would see this day. Mrs. Collingswood had had an easy delivery and so they started thinking about having another child via the Jackson Clinic. But it was never to be. Apparently they were an accident prone family.

When Charles was four years of age, an electrical short circuit in the playroom started a fire. Several nearby plastic toys and coloring books caught fire. Charles was asleep in a corner of the room. When he smelled the toxic smoke he awoke, but he was trapped. The fire blazed and his Mother tried but could not enter the playroom from the hallway. After several minutes, being a very bright lad, he pushed a chair over to the open window and climbed out. Not knowing that Charles was out of danger, Mother panicked. She wrapped a wet towel around her head and ran into the playroom. She tripped over the rocking play horse and hit her head on the corner of a dresser. She was knocked out, and died later in the hospital of toxic fumes inhalation. Charles blamed himself for his Mother's death.

After that accident Charles matured very fast. He and Dad became fast buddies. They bought a yellow brown collie puppy and named him Bobby for the little brother he always wanted but would never have. Bobby and Charles went everywhere together. Often Charles would sneak into a jacket pocket a couple of the white mice, a guinea pig, his iguana ,or one of his spiders (in a jar of course). He had a room full of pets and he loved them all equally. And Dad chauffeured him around to his swimming lessons, boy scouts meetings, seasonal sport practices and games, and other extra-curricular events during his middle and high school years. He had top A's in all of his classes. He played first team in both basketball and baseball. But he remained a bit shy socially because he was still carrying the guilt of his Mother's accidental death. By the time he was a senior in high school he had reached 6 foot 4 inches in height, even though both Mom and Dad were well under 6 foot. He never asked himself why.

Several years after the accident, Charles began praying regularly. It seemed to help him accept something tragic that he really had no control over. By himself he began to regularly attend a nearby International Church of the Saint Peter. Dad did not go. The Pastor was a young man and the two of them "hit it off". Because of this new relationship, Charles considered becoming a "man of the cloth". But Father was against this and talked him into going to Atlanta University. Because of his love for animals he studied there in the Department of Biological Sciences. And after receiving his Bachelor of Science Degree, he entered the Anderson Theological Seminary to start his education for the ministry.

After beginning his seminary instruction he began sleeping better. When suddenly one night he had a very troublesome dream:

'He saw a young man who had red hair and green eyes wearing heavy winter clothes. He had snow skis on his feet and was riding in a chair lift up the side of a foggy snow covered mountain. It was snowing very hard and one could not see more that twenty or thirty feet. This did not seem to bother the young man as he hopped off of the ski lift when it neared the top of the mountain. He hesitated, looked around, got his bearings, determined which of the seven slopes he would go down, and immediately took off. At the beginning the slope was fairly gentle and he had little trouble. But as he descended the snow came down heavier and the fog got thicker. Visibility decreased to almost nothing. At some point the slope turned right and he went straight ahead. He entered a heavily treed area at high speed. He harshly brushed against two trees on his left and then bounced off of a low thick tree limb on his right. He flipped over and landed on his left side with his left ski smashed, his left leg wrapped under his body, and his left ankle hurting very badly. Slowly he was able to move his ankle and knew that it was not broken. But he was trapped under several tree branches and in deep snow. No matter how hard he tried he could not free himself. He could not be very far from the open ski slope, so he started to scream for help. His yells echoed. And then everything was silent. No one was skiing in this weather. After more than one hour of not being able to move in the freezing snow he was convinced he would die. He fell asleep. Sometime later he felt a warm wet tongue licking his face. His immediately reaction was this was God's angle welcoming him to heaven. Not yet. It was a dog angle named Tobby. And he was a St Bernard leading a small rescue team, which were following immediately behind him'.

Suddenly Charles woke up sweating. Was that him on that ski slope? Was he going to die? He had never ever been in such heavily snowed mountain forests. He did not know how to ski. What should he do! It certainly was crazy. Weird!

* * *

David Dekker was born to Sylvia and Roy Dekker in San Diego on February 28, 1976. Because of Mrs. Dekker's past health problems they decided to have the baby via the Jackson Fertility Clinic in McLean, Virginia. Everything went reasonably well. However she did not deliver naturally, but instead had a cesarean section. The baby was a beautiful boy with a head full of red hair, green eyes and a left ear cleft. The Dekkers knew that they would probably not be able to have another child, and even though they were simple middle class people living on a meager salary, they would try to give everything that they could to this little fellow. And they did.

Dave was a good baby, a typical playful little boy, and loved all the attention he got from the large families of his Father's work buddies. In San Diego most of Mr. Dekker's colleagues were of Mexican origin. So their families were large, and there was always with a wide range of ages of children. When the many families partied, which was almost every weekend, the handsome little red head with the green eyes was the prince of all the little girls. The little boys thought he was weird, until he started beating them in soccer, basketball, baseball, surfing and any other sport they wanted to play. As a teenager Dave was already over 6 feet tall and near 200 pounds. Thus he was wanted for every sports team, especially when his buddies were playing against outsiders. And every guy wanted him as a personal buddy. The public schools were below national standards so they were a breeze for him. He got A's without even trying. But the community social system in the area around Le Mesa, California was something else. He thought about college. But his Father had not gone, and he was doing OK. His Father's colleagues had not gone, and they were doing OK. And his buddies were all going to the military. So he would go military too.

After graduating from high school David Dekker joined the army. Because of his size, he was now 6 feet 7 inches tall and 225 pounds. Because of his excellent high school grades, he was sent for training for a combatant-commandos unit. After a couple of years of experience in actual combat, he would then be transferred for training in combatant-intelligence. The army was thinking long term for this young man. One night after a ten hour march with a fifty pound back pack, he showered and was asleep before he hit the bed. During the night a strange dream came to him:

'He dreamed of a young man with red hair and green eyes dressed like a female clown. He was riding on a single wheel cycle beside a parade float which was going down Martin Luther King Jr. Avenue on the annual Peach Blossom Day celebration in Atlanta. He was surrounded by several other males who were also dressed as female clowns. As they came down the street on this beautiful bright sunshiny day they tossed candies to the children along the route. They had developed some gymnastic and special formation maneuvers such as weaving in and out on their cycles, performing backward and forward antics, racing each other, chasing little "kids", playing musical instruments, and singing cheers for the Hawks, Falcons, Braves, and Thrashers. All of the clowns, except one, seemed to be thoroughly enjoying themselves. Only the red head appeared to more or less be just going through the routine procedures by rote. He was not "into" the celebrations taking place around him. As the clown group reached the termination of the parade route it started to break up. Of the dozen or so clowns most of them headed down a side street to a tavern. Two or three went their separate ways. The red head went with the large group.'

'They entered the tavern and pulled together a couple of tables near the back of the large single room. Everyone in the group appeared to be familiar with the tavern and the tavern was familiar with them. Before they sat down one of the "male waitresses" was bringing nine beers toward them, one for each of them. Members of the group began to sort of pair off as they drank the beers from the bottles. The red head looked around, became disgusted, took his opened beer and sat it directly on the counter by the door and he exited from the tavern. At the door he looked right and left, the street was empty. He turned right and walked several blocks and turned up Simpson Street. A short time later he entered into a Lutheran church, walked down the center aisle to the altar, kneeled, and started praying'.

Dave suddenly woke up. He was thoroughly puzzled. That could not have been him. But the red headed guy with green eyes sure looked like him, only he was little smaller. And he had never been to Atlanta, Georgia. He certainly did not like the Falcons. Even though most of his childhood buddies were Catholic and went to church often, his parents were Methodist. So he assumed he must be Methodist also, but he had not been in a church in years. Plus homosexuality! Weird!

# 3 –REAL TIME HIGH TECH SCIENCE MYSTERIES

Professor Criss lived his entire professional life in the high technology of biological and medical sciences. He has now begun a series of novels which are adventurous, historical, ethnic, family oriented mysteries that are based on current high technology. These books create human stories which focus on today and tomorrow's research efforts, not yesterdays nor science fiction, but what is happening now and tomorrow in the medical/science world.

The first book ***Genetic Soul Brothers*** looks at relationships between genes, spirits/souls versus environment in the growth, development, and behavior of separately carried, separately born, and separately raised genetically identical quadruplets.

The second book is entitled ***Nanomedicine – Cure or Kill***; it focuses on the constructive and destructive use of nano-targeting body units to give or take human life in the highly competitive and rapidly changing world of high technology.

The third book is entitled ***Hydra*** which is a story about a cave lake microscopic organism which causes multi-century longevity in humans, stimulates conversion of stem cells into new human body parts, and destroys the Last Empire on Earth.

In each novel, the people and stories, and the events and locations are fictional or are used in a fictional way. However, the science is real.

# 4 – The Gentlemen

It was a gorgeous sunshiny day in early October and Aaron was studying in the library for an exam in his favorite course *Molecular Systems and Ethics* next week. His mind started to daydream about his current roommate. This relationship had been progressing rapidly for the past 8 months. Her name was Gabriela Longenstein. She was an only child from an old Jewish family of Boston. Her Father was a wealthy businessman who imported and exported rare gems and select gold jewelry. She was the apple, peach, orange, and all the fruits put together of his eye. Gabriela was much more world savvy than Aaron. Her Mother died early in Gabriela's child hood; so she had traveled abroad regularly with her Father. Because of such travel she was much more conscious of world events. Aaron was jealous of this. He had only been to Europe one time, and that was just for two weeks. Jenifer had been to Europe, the Middle East, and South East Asia several times. Also he was jealous of her being the academic number one in their medical class, while he was number two.

Gabriela was very tall, 6 foot 2 inches, pretty, not beautiful, dark hair and a radiant smile. Give her five minutes and she could have anyone eating out of her hand. Because of her brain power and travel experiences she was hard "to get the best of" in a discussion of almost anything. He fully liked being with her and was openly proud of this relationship. This intellectual jealously, respect for her ideas and judgments, was beginning to turn into a want-need-love for him.

He remembered their heart to heart conversations over a period of several weeks. More than once they had gotten down to a serious discussion about life values. It had all began with their expressing their loss about not having any brothers or sisters. How different their childhoods might have been if they had had someone their age to share the goods and the bads. Their memories today would be very different and much more complete.

Gabriela was sitting beside Aaron and, having already prepared for the same exam, started daydreaming out loud, "I always wanted a younger brother or sister to play with, but Father said he could only love one woman. And that woman was gone; there would not be another for him.

I tried to talk him into adopting a little sister for me, but he said his travels were too much, he was getting older, and it just would not be the same as having your own child."

Aaron flinched at that and looked up. He replied, "Maybe your Father should have considered a 'test tube baby' arrangement. In that way it would be his genetic child. Surrogate mothers are readily available. And they give up all legal obligations and restrictions on such children. In fact, his sperm could be used to fertilize an autonomous female donor and carried by a second autonomous surrogate mother. He would not see nor ever know who they were. And all legal aspects would be taken care of in advance. At least the baby would have been genetically one half of you, your half sister."

Gabriela gave him a puzzled look. "How do you know so much about test tube babies, surrogate mothers, half sisters and all?"

In an attempt to quickly change the subject Aaron swallowed, "Are you about ready for your final exam in orthopedic surgery of the hand and wrist?" He knew that this small part of the body had more than 100 bones, muscles, arteries, veins, ligaments, and tendons, and he had not done very well on the same exam last month.

She gave him a dirty look because she knew he was changing the subject. "One only has to memorize to pass any test concerning anatomy!"

Aaron responded with, "OK, OK, how about you. Do you want more than one child?"

Gabriela never hesitated. She replied, "I want two children, one boy and one girl, in that sequence, but I would have a full time nanny and housekeeper. I plan to become an excellent Orthopedic Surgeon specializing on children. And to save those little damaged bodies or hands I will need to study and train many hours in pediatric surgery. I want the love, experiences, and memories of my own children, but I will not have time for the daily wiping of noses and tails. And I would hope to find a man to share these ideas."

"I have not given it much thought," he responded. "I certainly plan to be an outstanding physician and researcher in Human Cellular and Molecular Genetics. I too want more than one child. But I do not care which sex nor any sequence. And I too would put my career co-equal with my children and my wife. So I guess we are not too far apart from a general agreement concerning what we expect from future life efforts."

She gave him that "you are a great guy" smile. Learned over, kissed him and said, "Then when am I going to meet your parents? You have already met my Father."

And when that week end came, and she would meet his Father.

However, his mind had turned to his meeting with the other Father. Gabriela's Father was a wealthy sixtyish typical Jewish-American male. He was a very highly respected leader in the Jewish community in the Boston area. He was not "completely" kosher, but had lived in Israel twice during his life, met his only wife there, and was therefore conscious of the modern versus the conservative Jewish way of life. He did believe in the concept that the Jewish female carried the genetics of Jews. If a Jewish male wanted to have Jewish children he must mate with a Jewish woman. While a Jewish woman could mate with a non-Jewish male, produce offspring which, via certain rituals, could become Jewish.

One of their recent conversations went as follows:

Mr. Longenstein asked, "What do you know about the history of the Jews?"

Aaron responded, "I know that they have one of the longest histories on earth."

Mr. Longenstein asked, "Do you know why the Jews are called Israelis and now live in their ancestral homeland?"

Aaron responded. "I think it was because of the Nazi slaughtering of the Jews in World War II, and America giving this land back to them"

Mr. Longenstein asked, "Do you know why there are black African Jews and yellow Oriental Jews, and that they all now live together in harmony?"

Aaron responded, "No."

Mr. Longenstein asked, "Would you allow any children that you and Gabriela might have become a Jew and be raised in Israel?"

Aaron responded, "I don't think so."

Mr. Longenstein asked, "Have you heard of the Torah, Tanakh, or Talmud?"

Aaron responded, "No."

Mr. Longenstein asked. "Would you consider a kosher lifestyle?"

And Aaron could not answer that question because he was not exactly sure what all was involved in a kosher life style.

It was obvious that Mr. Longenstein really wanted his little Jewish Princess to marry a Jewish male. He did not exactly say this to Aaron when they recently had spent some time alone together. But Aaron was left with idea that any future marriage with Gabriela, especially if it involved children, might not be so easy.

So on that week-end Aaron and Gabriela took off for Manchester, New Hampshire to meet his parents. Early afternoon they turned into the half mile long tree lined asphalt driveway up to the five acre knoll near the upper part of the two hundred and twenty five acre Armand estate. The small knoll was surrounded by an eight foot high perimeter stone wall which was entered via a large iron gate. The gate was on the north side so one drove south to enter the seven thousand square foot main house. The farm employee housing and farm buildings were located outside the stone wall and to the lower southwest side of the estate. They had a separate access road. A major portion of the estate was being farmed. The old English Manor House was located near the center of the knoll, and was surrounded by lawns filled with lovely old trees and shrubbery.

As they drove up to the old house Gabriela could see that this three story structure was built almost entirely of stone and hand cut oak timbers. From the front there was a large central three floor octagonal turret and the two side wings that were composed of three floors units with front facing gables. The front entry turret had a double columned porch which projected forward and had a small matching gable roof covering it. All roofing was of a blue-gray slate which matched the brown-gray stone on the building's stone walls. This five hundred year old English Manor house was obtained for the family only eighty years ago by Dr. Armand's Grandfather who had purchased, renovated and expanded it over several years.

They parked the car in the circular driveway. The family valet was there to greet them, took their luggage and led them into the house. Aaron's Mother met them on the entry porch just in front of the large hand carved four inch thick wooden front door.

She beamed and smiled, "Welcome, welcome, welcome. I hope that you had a pleasant drive. The weather is lovely for this time of the year. God promised that it will be a beautiful weekend. And here it is."

Gabriela glanced at Aaron; Aaron avoided her look and simply confirmed "Yes, the drive and weather were good. We had no difficulties on the roads once we were outside the Boston metropolitan area. We are happy to be here as Gabriela really wanted to meet you."

She kissed both of the 'children' and looked them up and down. After checking out the new 'girlfriend', and apparently approving she said, "Again, welcome to our small castle or old manor house, which ever you want to call it. It is several hundred years old, we don't know exactly when the first construction began; and we are the third family to live in it. Aaron's Grandfather purchased it and we have been continuously renovating it ever since. Aaron, you help take the luggage upstairs and refresh yourself, I will give Gabriela the short grand tour of house."

Aaron responded, "That is a good idea. I have seen the house before."

And Mother gave him a harsh look. That was all she could do as he was more than one foot taller than her. He winked at Gabriela and said, 'Be careful. She can sell one half a peanut at a time to an elephant for a dollar a bite."

And a second harsh look was received by Aaron, who just chuckled and headed inside.

Gabriela replied, "Thank you very much. I have wanted to meet you and Aaron's Father for a very long time. But as you know, Aaron is very stubborn. He had to meet my Father first. Unfortunately my Mother died many years ago."

"I am very sorry. Nothing can replace a Mother. All right. Let us stroll around for a few minutes and then Aaron can join us on the terrace. It faces the south and there are still a couple of hours remaining of nice autumn sunshine. Do you drink tea?"

Gabriela noticed the old style dress that Mrs. Armand was wearing and answered, "Yes that would be nice. This is a large lovely foyer."

The foyer-entry in the octagonal turret was large, with two opposing semi-circular stairways going up and around. At the top they emptied into a long open corridor/balcony on the second floor where the six family bedrooms were located. The third floor contained additional bedrooms and living space for the servants. The turret foyer was also two floors high inside with a domed ceiling that was decorated with outdoor scenes of trees, flowers, streams, and mountain peaks and valleys. Hanging on the staircase walls were four large landscape paintings of Ireland by the famous Irish landscape artist, Johnny O'Hara.

She noticed that there were four doors in the foyer. The wooden entry door; the door to the right led into the dining room which had capacity to seat sixteen people around a beautiful antique mahogany table and chairs. The central interior door in the foyer continued directly under the two stairways and allowed entry into a very large salon. While the door on the left side of the foyer led into the games room which contained a pool table, cards table, and several arm chairs as it was the conversation room for the men.

The salon had two large conversation areas and contained several antique couches and wing tipped arm chairs, many of which had been brought from Ireland when Irish immigrant families came to the Boston area. On both ends of the salon were large four foot tall see-through fireplaces connecting the salon to the dining room on the right side and the salon to the games room on the left side. And of course there were access doors between the salon-dining room and the salon-games room.

All of the walls on the ground floor were twelve foot tall with eight foot tall windows. The floor to ceiling curtains were a light cranberry in color. All of the floors were hand carved oak planking covered with large and very old Turkish carpets. The carpets were a deep red in color. All of this warm color in this old stone house, setting on a cold and snowy knoll in New Hampshire, helped to keep the interior atmosphere psychologically warm during the long winter months. Whiles several portraits of family members hung on various walls in the salon, dining room, and games room.

Going directly through and between and the two conversation areas in the salon, Gabriel noticed that you had to walk down several steps into a large enclosed veranda which had numerous hanging and standing plants. The salon connected in all four directions, via a door to each of the foyer, dining room, games room, and the veranda. The veranda was in the back of the house and was thus entered from the salon; therefore this room faced the south and looked down into the Handers Valley. The veranda was one and one half stories high and had a glass roof and floor to ceiling glass exterior walls/doors which could be opened in the summer. They were open today. This room was the ladies conversation room. It was designed to be a special New England style of conservatory.

So, Aaron's Mother had received Gabriela very warmly and had given her the brief grand tour of the house. She was only not taken into the kitchen which was an addition attached behind the dining room and to the side of the veranda. Gabriela was amazed by the size of such a house for basically two people, now that Aaron was gone. She was familiar with the Catholic mindset that a family needs many children because they are all gifts from God. In fact it was obvious that she was awed by what she saw because she sort of visualized a point in time when it would be handed down to the only son, and his wife and family. She was now properly introduced to the major domo, valet, head chef and assistant chef, two heavy duty cleaning maids, a general purpose servant, and two gardeners.

The two of them went outdoors, sat on the terrace, an extension of the enclosed veranda, and drank their tea. As Gabriela looked down into the lower valley she was fascinated at the beautifully landscaped scene. First she saw large flower gardens at the end of their blooming season. Next was the large swimming pool, below it was the tennis court, more flower gardens, and then the lower stone wall. It was probably one hundred meters from the terrace to the wall. Beyond the wall she could enjoy the massive multicolored forest and valley beyond. If she married Aaron she would have to 'suffer' this view every day.

As Gabriela, Aaron and Mrs. Armand sat on their white rot-iron chairs at the glass topped white rot-iron table sipping their tea and surrounded by beautiful smelling flowers, Gabriel's Mother asked, "What do you think of our lovely mountains with all these trees and this beautiful nature?"

Gabriela replied, "I love nature. We live in an area in Boston where there are trees. But Aaron and I see them only between 6:00 and 6:30 o'clock in the morning when we are going to the medical school; and that is only in the summer. In the evenings we study until 9:00 or 10:00 o'clock and all of nature has already gone to sleep when we go home. And of course in the winter we only see nature on Sunday afternoons, when we look through the library windows, as that is also study time."

Mrs. Armand replied, "Then you will just have to come up here during your school vacation periods. Thanksgiving and Christmas are coming. Let us plan for a lovely several days here for Christmas and New Years."

She really did not understand that the Jewish people do not celebrate Christmas and they do have a different Jewish New Years. Being from several generations of Catholic families she just assumed that all Americans were Christians. No one worked on those two days. Everyone celebrated on those two days. So it was logical that her son and potential daughter-in-law should join them on those two holidays.

Fortunately, or unfortunately, Dr. James Armand came out onto the veranda and the subject became less sensitive. He welcomed, hugged, and kissed his son's current girl friend and began with his questions:

"How to you like medical school? Do you plan to continue on to a residency? What kind of residency do you want to study? Do you want to try General Practice? I would be happy to have you train in my clinics. When you do finish, where do you want to set up medical practice? In the big cities doctors fight doctors for patients because there are too many doctors; while the smaller cities are crying out for more doctors. The place to start any medical practice is in the smaller communities where there is no rush hour traffic and you can actually recognize and remember a patient's name when you see them later in the supermarket. And when you have children they can walk to school and not have to fight buses, taxies, and commuter cars to get to school. You can even live on the true ground and have some trees of your own, and not live on the fortieth floor, which is above all trees................"

They had a formal evening dinner in the dining room table at 8 o'clock sharp. The meal was delicious and included grouse and ham, cheese-cauliflower soufflé, asparagus, candied yams, fresh cooked-hot rye bread, and for desert they had a special strawberry-chocolate cake with Gabriela written on the top using twenty five candles. Her birthday had been the week before. And did she give her "future" Mother-in-law a big winning smile. Obviously they were going to get along just fine.

Gabriela responded, "My Mother died when I was seven years old so I have grown up all these years without female guidance. I miss her very much. My Father tried to take her place but that was not possible. He has whiskers and they are rough on a little girl's face when she is kissed. I remember my Mother's face being beautiful and smooth. And she certainly smelled different, if you know what I mean."

A round of chuckles followed.

She continued, "My Father was, is, a beautiful man, but a man nevertheless. He gave me everything, whether I wanted it or not. Many a times he would give to me a beautiful gift, for which I would politely thank him. Then when he left I would carefully dispose of it. A good example is when he gave to me a beautiful green and yellow dress, perfect for a twelve year old, but I was eighteen years old. I hope that you can meet him in the near future."

Dr. Armand inquired, "We have a small hunting lodge up near the Canadian border. Aaron and I, and our friends go there for hunting, fishing, or just relaxing during summer and winter vacations, or when we can get away from school and the clinic. Maybe you and your Father could join us sometime this winter. Because of my clinic, we have our vacations sort of in the area. We haven't travelled abroad very much. I understand that you have travelled to Europe and beyond."

"Yes. I have traveled with my Father to Europe, the Middle East, and Southeast Asia."

The Armands had only been to England one time, so they switched into a more "casual" conversation and moved into the salon to have coffee and liquors. The ladies entered into a discussion of flowers and gardens, something that Gabriela always had an interest in but no time to pursue. She hoped to do so someday. While the men entered into a discussion about the need for modernization of community medicine.

They all turned in early that night as tomorrow was Sunday and most of the relatives were coming to a large after Sunday church dinner. It was to be a welcome to the possible next Mrs. Armand dinner. Only Mr. and Mrs. Armand were expected at church, because Aaron was in Boston in school. He usually did not go anyway.

So on Sunday morning Gabriela and Aaron got up late. His parents had already gone to early mass and were expected back in about an hour. The "students" had a light brunch below the veranda, on the patio beside the pool and as they chatted, Aaron explained, "In the afternoon a mass of my relatives will descend upon the House. I guess there will be twenty or twenty five in total, mostly brothers and sisters of my parents, and their families. We have a large extended family and many live within an hour drive of Manchester or within the Boston area. They all try to get together at the House during major holiday periods such as Thanksgiving and Christmas. So everyone is sort of up to date as to what the others were doing. And they know about us. That is why they all want to meet and get to know you. Are you ready?"

Gabriela looked at him and said, "Have I ever taken a difficult exam before now?"

Some family members began arriving around noon. They were each introduced to Gabriela and then drifted into the salon, called the Great Room in ancient English parlance, and out onto the veranda. Everyone tried to single Gabriela out and sniff out her interests in life and in Aaron and in Manchester. It was a rather stiff/formal affair. Everyone seemed to be happy to meet her and sort of welcome her into the family unit.

Around 1:00 PM, Dr. and Mrs. Armand returned and everyone they took seats in the dining room for a five course Sunday dinner. The table was set for eighteen people and a small table in the corner was set for the three children. Dr. Armand sat at one end of the table and Mrs. Armand sat at the other end. Gabriela and Aaron sat in the exact center, across from each other. On each side of them were the more senior members of the enlarged family. The seating arrangement alone told everyone that this meal was going to be more serious than usual. In other words Gabriela was being considered as a possible future family member, and was being tested.

Mr. Harry Armand, Dr. Armand's Uncle asked Gabriela, "Do you want children someday? Even many professional ladies can work and have children. The world has changed and now accepts this sort of thing."

Gabriela answered, "A real family must have children such that the family image, intellectually and socially, is carried forward."

Mr. Raymond Herschel, Mrs. Armand's older brother, asked Gabriela, "Don't you think that small communities are better for raising children that the violent city streets?"

Gabriela answered, "Street crime seems to get worst every year in most cities."

Mrs. Anne Roundtree, Mrs. Armand's sister asked Gabriela, "Don't you think the church should do more to help the many underfed children in South Africa?"

Gabriela answered, "I think everyone should help in any way they can to help the underfed children everywhere."

The conversations and the meal lasted for nearly three hours. They began with a cheese-broccoli soufflé, and then went directly into servings of both deer and wild boar, followed by a choice of a half dozen types of vegetables and casseroles, three types of fresh hot bread and a choice of pumpkin and apple pies and angel food cake. Red wine, coffee and teas made their rounds. Aaron received his share of questions but the focus was definitely on Gabriela. Finally all were stuffed, especially with multiple desserts. And it appeared that the "important" family members had their opportunity to judge the new young lady; so the ladies retired to the veranda for another round of tea and coffee. While the men first went into the games room for a smoke and only one round of brandy, they would all be driving later. Then they went outdoors to look at a new horse that Dr. Armand had just acquired.

There were several riding trails which circled through many of the nearby estates. The horses were only for gentle country riding. As the sun began setting the individual families said their goodbyes and gave their blessings to Gabriela, and Aaron. All expressed their hope to see her again, soon. Aaron was very proud of the acceptance and positive interactions of Gabriela with all family members. After all, she was a young Jewish lady, and as Catholics they knew about the genetic importance of the woman in Judaism. Certain older family members were more concerned about the genetics of Aaron. However, that Pandora's Box was not opened. The day certainly left Gabriela with the feeling that she would be very welcome into Aaron's family.

Because Boston was only a little more than an hour drive, Gabriela and Aaron remained for another couple of hours with his parents and chatted. They took turns answering some of Gabriela's many questions about various family members. Whose child belonged to which couple? Which family lived in Boston? Who was the lady who was a free lance reporter for the New York Times? Did Uncle Howard really get a Purple Heart in the Vietnam War? How did Aunt Selma break her leg? Are any of the children thinking about going to medical school? Where did Uncle George practice medicine? Obviously Gabriela was really enjoying this large extended family. She only had her Father and they lived very much to themselves in a small house in Saugus, north Boston. They had no relatives living nearby, and had just a few Jewish friends.

On the way back to school, conversation in the car was rather subdued for the first half hour. Then Gabriela could not contain herself any longer.

She began. "I want to thank you for allowing me to meet your family. They are really beautiful and a lot of fun. I am certain that anyone who you take to the House will be loved and cherished, just as I feel loved and cherished right now. While we are alone, may I ask some personal family related questions?"

"Of course," Aaron responded.

Gabriela continued. "Those beautiful people are not your genetic family, are they? You do not resemble any single one of them. Every man and woman was less than six foot tall. No one had red or even auburn hair. No one had green or even blue eyes. Everyone was of average body size and bone structure. You are much bigger and have a larger bone structure. Also I did not find your personality within anyone. I just couldn't find you among them. I'm sorry. In my opinion you are not genetically of them."

Aaron was stunned and could not respond. Conservation stopped for several minutes.

Finally, Aaron said, "I have been suspicious, perhaps even certain of this for many years. But no one in the family will respond to me when I question my genetic origin. It is like the worst kept family secret which no one fully understands. So they are reluctant to give to me just the piece of the secret that they know, or think they know. Only Mary and James Armand, my parents, know the entire true story. I have not been able to get them to tell me. And I am afraid of hurting them if I press too hard. I have seen the birth certificate, and I believe it to be authentic. So I know where and when I was born, I just do not know where, when, how and by whom that I was conceived. I guess that is one of the reasons why I have a special interest in germ cells and cloning, human cellular and molecular genetics, and human clinical genetics."

They were both quiet for the rest of the trip. The subject was too sensitive, and now was not the time or the place to continue this discussion.

That night Aaron did not sleep well. And yes, he had another dream about this look-alike guy. This was his fourth such dream during the past couple of years.

'The scene opened in a sandy desert area loaded with prickly cactus. The red haired, green eyed fellow was digging a trench in the hard ground. He was working with several other people who had darker hair and skin than he had. He was also several inches taller than any one. Because of his light skin and the harsh sun he was now quite red skinned. They all wore large brimmed hats that looked like what he would call sombreros. It looked like they had begun building some kind of structure. Probably they were working on the footings for a building. Piled off to the side were bags of cement, concrete blocks, and a cement mixer. In the distance were tall bare mountains. They were difficult to see because the sun was very hot and it blurred any long distance vision. It appeared to be about mid day. Suddenly over the horizon came a small beat up old truck. Riding in the back of the truck were four ladies of varying ages. An older man was driving. As they arrived the workers dropped their tools and began hollering and shouting. It was lunch time and the food, and girls, had arrived. The truck came to a stop. The girls, all dark skinned, hopped out and immediately began unloading the food, cold water, and beer. All of the men gathered around the food, and the girls, took paper plates and started helping themselves to the sandwiches, baked beans, potatoes, and corn on the cob. The beer appeared to have a Mexican label. Apparently the food was not very good as the conversation continued very loudly and there were many complaints about the food. There was much joking and playing around. Some of the jokes focused upon the big, red haired, green eyed fellow. Basically the jokes seemed to focus on whether he was as big downstairs as upstairs. And they were challenging one of the girls to experiment for them. So after they finished eating, she took up the challenge. She took the big guy by the hand and started toward a large mound of sand. As the two of them disappeared behind the sand dune, with lots of catcalls from the other workers, Aaron woke up in a sweat. Just what did all of these dreams mean?'

* * *

William (Bill) Bassinger liked his home in Iowa and thought both Iowa State University at Ames and Drake University in Des Moines to be really good. He had no other schools with which to compare, so it was logical he thought that these were the best schools. And both universities were close to home. So he could attend classes and regularly help Dad on the farm. Plus the two schools would give him the education as he really wanted to focus on legal problems in intellectual property rights. Drake U. had an Intellectual Property Rights Center where he could do research and eventually get his Masters or even his PhD. This area of law dealt with the cutting edge issues of legal problems in biotechnology, agriculture, food technology, and health sciences.

One day after a plant biology class Bill started thinking, 'If I understand correctly, there are two concepts here. There are GE (genetic engineered) and GM (genetic modified) systems. GE crops involved a single gene transfer into seeds such that the subsequent growing of crops would be more disease resistant, reliant on less fertilizer, more susceptible to shorter half life herbicides and pesticides, have increased product yield, improve and/shorten growth periods, improve growth on dryer and more "difficult" soils, and improve cultivation technology, and more.'

'And GM foods involve single gene transfers into "hybrid" food crops (for animals) and foods (for people). GM modification of foods was used to increase protein content, decrease fat content, lower cholesterol levels, increase vitamin, mineral, and fiber content, change the color, flavor, ripening time, need for less preservatives and flavor enhancers, and more.'

'I know that currently there are major problems in the interpretation of the laws for GE and GM agriculture and foods. And there is the problem of social acceptance which makes everything become political.'

Bill thought back to his youth, 'Several times over the years my Father tested out different GE modified corn seeds. I remember that they usually gave 95%+ sprouting, grew very well, and had excellent yields. But there many legal problems concerning the gene, it source or origin, its transfer methodology, marketing techniques, and liability of failure, which prevented Father's continued use of these GE seeds.'

'Therefore I simply need to carefully learn the current laws, as they change every year, their judicial interpretations, and the limitations of the patents and patent rights in this area. Legal problems concerning single gene transfer in crops and foods are here to stay and I think that these problems will expand exponentially in the near future.'

He still liked his high school sweet heart, Jenny. At 6 foot, 120 pounds, and a former high school star basketball player, she was smaller than Bill. But everyone was smaller than Bill. They would probably get married. She was currently finishing her fourth year in the School of Education at Drake University. In the Des Moines area she had begun looking for a high school where she could teach mathematics and science. She wanted to remain near Des Moines such that they could continue see each until he finished law school in one more year. Then they would have to make that really hard decision about with whom to spend the rest of their life. As they say, you can't chose your parents or children, but you can chose (and unchose) your spouse. They were being careful. HA! HA! They had only been thinking about marriage for the past five or six years.

Bill had to choose between going to college or playing professional football immediately after high school. He accepted a scholarship to ISU. Because during his senior year in high school he had been selected as the outstanding tight end in the state of Iowa, he was also considered for the NFL draft. Usually high school graduates are not so drafted. First there is a minimum of a few years in college. Basically this is because most young men have not yet reached the peak of their physical growth by eighteen years of age. Twenty one or twenty two is better. After all, the NFL has many guys who are two hundred fifty to three hundred pounds and are very physical. Most recruiting occurs after three to four years of college football. However, it is not uncommon during the post high school season to offer try-outs to special players. And William was a corn fed six foot 9 inch, 265 pound Iowa boy. These athletes could not directly accept money or they could lose their amateur status and not be able to play college ball. But there were ways to deal with that problem. Bill had been so chosen by the Minnesota Vikings. The spring and summer immediately after high school graduation he joined the Viking camp. After six weeks of very heavy exercise, six hours a day for six days each week, he lost all interest in American football. So he entered ISU pre-law with the full intention of becoming a professional lawyer someday, not a professional football player. And as it turned out the pay was better, and so was the longevity of employment.

During the second year of law school Bill had been chosen as an editor of the ISU Law Review. He was really looking forward to that because he did have the knack of putting words on paper. He had never taken any grammar or writing courses, it just came to him naturally. As an undergraduate he had written a couple of short stories, one had even been published. He did have an interest in journalism but had heard that it was a difficult field in which to get established. And because of his athletic reputation he had already been approached about future employment by one of the best law firms in Des Moines.

Yet he kept having these dreams about this redheaded, green eyed guy playing around in the ocean, which he had never seen. 'The most recent dream had this guy, even though it looked like him he knew it was not him, playing with his friends on a nice yacht on the beautiful dark blue water. The yacht was not large, maybe thirty five feet. It was trawling slowly and it seemed that everyone had a fishing rod and reel in his hands. Suddenly the red headed guy gave a jerk of his rod and started shouting, "I've got one." His buddies quickly gathered around and started cheering for him. He pulled the rod up, reeled like mad, and let it down, up and down, up and down, again and again. Finally after what seemed like a long time he brought up a big beautiful marlin. It was a lovely platinum blue with a white streak on the side. It must have been more than one hundred pounds. One of his friends managed to get a grapple hook into it and brought it aboard. Now that was the kind of story that would be fun to write about and try to publish in an Outdoors magazine.'

As he woke up he said out loud, "Iowans would drool over that, especially if there were also some neat colored pictures of that fabulous water. But that guy must be my twin."

* * *

Charles Collingswood completed his certificate at the Dawson Seminary and was assigned to a small town called Indian Nest in southern Florida. He seemed to have stopped growing early in life. This small community was on the northern edge of the Florida everglades. In fact he was less than one half hour in hiking time to a main body of the water. Some of the members of his new congregation were hikers and they had encouraged the Reverend Charles Collingswood to join them whenever he had time. After all, at the age of 24, he was younger than many of them. Two very fine members of the hiking group were William (Osecola) Johnson and Samel (Abiaka) Black. They were ethnically Seminole Indians. Charles had wanted to be involved with a mixture of native and white (European) Americans.

As Charles thought about his new opportunity he speculated, 'This new church location here in the middle of native Americans provides me with an excellent opportunity. I fully believe in God. And I understand how European immigrants, who have had extensive exposure to one God for many generations, and the European immigrant's children within America who have had extensive exposure to only one God throughout their lifetimes, would believe in only that one God.'

'However, belief in one God is not automatic; it is taught by people like me. And it appears to be true, or is it, that people who have not been exposed during early in their life time cannot understand the concept of this one God. And if God is omnipotent, why does not one just directly accept his presence and not have to be taught. One does not have to be taught to enjoy the beauty of the white clouds in a bright blue sky, the sound of rippling water in a rocky stream, of a beautiful eagle in flight, of a new born baby kitty, and the smile of a new born baby. Why does the presence of God have to be taught? Or does it? I have these questions and I want to try to test these ideas with people, who had not been "exposed" through several generations to the *only one God* is present concept.'

'And then there is the accompanying punishment that if you do not so believe in this one God, your spirit or soul will never be allowed in heaven. Heaven is described as some ultimate place up there. Certainly it must be the ultimate place because my very innocent Mother is up there. She was never baptized, did not go to church, but if anyone ever deserved heaven it is Mother. It could not have been refused to her. She must be up there.'

And if one examines the Peoples of the Books, Jews, Christians, and Muslims, there are similarities and differences. The major similarities involve accepting the one God and the existence of both a Heaven and a Hell. Correct living, as defined by "official" representatives, allows access to heaven. Incorrect living, as defined by these same "official' representatives, guarantees entry into Hell. The presence of a waiting time frame called Purgatory varies between the three groups. And we are not talking about places where our bodies can go when we die, obviously the dead flesh remains for us to properly bury, even as nature will reclaim it from anyplace. It is this spirit or soul that is allowed travel to the proposed Heaven, Purgatory, or Hell.'

'Now, for the newly converted aborigines (American Indians) of southern Florida, this new generation should be compared to the older generation. Does the new generation understand and believe in all of this new faith? Does the older generation still believe in their Fathers spiritual beliefs? Do they think that their non-Christian ancestors went to the Christian Heaven or to another Place? Is it not possible to go to the Christian Heaven unless you are learned (or trained) in Christianity? If their ancestors' spirits went elsewhere (another Heaven?), how can they ever meet their ancestor's spirits when they leave this life? If a Father was from the old ways and was not baptized as a Christian, and his son is from the new ways and is baptized as a Christian, will their souls ever meet after they die? If there is more than one Heaven, are there linkages between them to allow "spiritual talking". But there is always the overriding question. Do the three Peoples of the Book have the same God, Heaven, or Hell; or does each have a different one? They do not share their followers. Do they share their God?'

These questions had been at the forefront of Charles's mind for many years. He had always badgered his religious superiors with these questions, but had not yet found satisfactory answers.

One evening, after Charles and his friends had returned home from an all day hike down into the glades, he showered, ate a light dinner, turned on Bach's Brandenburg Concerto number one, sipped a glass of red wine, and drifted nicely into sleep in his recliner. And another dream began:

'There were several cars, filled with young people, driving down an off track old dirt road. It was early in the evening and the sun was brightly shining through the corn picked cornfields. They drove through a broken gate and entered an old abandoned farmstead. Each car parked near the old barn. The unloading from the cars of ice chests filled with soft drinks and beer, mostly Budweiser, began in earnest. And picnic baskets filled with sandwiches, cold vegetables such as carrots, celery, and cauliflower, potato and corn chips were placed onto a large blanket near the cars. Several yards from the cars a large portable music/CD player was set up and turned on to the maximum volume. Within five minutes of arrival the music blasted and the teenagers were in vigorous motion. All types of dancing were allowed. It appeared that the boys and girls were from the same high school as they all knew each other and some were obviously paired. Among the group was a very big red headed, green eyed fellow. This guy certainly looked a lot like Charles, but he was physically much bigger. He watched the big guy dance with the smoothness of a predator cat. He had partnered up with a small pretty blond wearing a pink halter, pink shorts, and pink tennis shoes. Interesting!? Most of the girls were also wearing only the accepted minimum (what their boyfriends allowed?). Guys were with or without T-shirts and Levis. Everyone was having a blast.

The party went on for half hour to forty five minutes when the sky suddenly grew very dark. Off to the western horizon a large grey cloud appeared. This cloud came at them very fast. When the bottom of the now black cloud reached to the ground and the winds began to pick up they all knew what it was. It was a tornado. And here they were completely exposed with no shelter anywhere. The old house and barn were falling apart. As the wind increased, panic set in. Some tried to collect the blown away food, empty beer cans, and papers. Others ran to the cars for shelter as it now started to rain very hard. Screams of fear were everywhere as the wind blew people against the buildings and rocked the cars. One of the small SUVs flipped over and rolled down a small incline. The old barn collapsed. Bigger people locked arms with smaller people to try to protect them from the ferocious storm. And then suddenly, as quickly as it came, it left. The wind was gone. The rain trailed off. The sun returned. And everyone breathed a sigh of relief. A general accounting was quickly made and, other than scratches, no major injuries were found.'

Charles woke in a sweat. Again his dream had violence and near death, and that red headed, green eyed fellow was there. What saved them? Luck, God, or both.

* * *

Afghanistan was a country that was bypassed when the earth was formed. It is two thirds desolate mountains and one third desolate low lands. The mountains are the Hindu Kush Mountains, a branch of the Himalaya Mountains. The land increases to 8000 feet in the north at Nowshak, to 5000 feet in the middle near the capital, Kabul, and to a few hundred feet along the Helmand River in the southwest. The winters are cold, snowy, and very harsh. The summers are tolerable if you are a strong formidable people, are born here, and lived here all of your life. As you can imagine, immigration out of Afghanistan is greater than into Afghanistan. However, because of it geographical location between the Middle East, China, and India, foreign armies have fought over this desolate rocky mountain region throughout history. Currently the military arm of the North Atlantic Treaty Organization was there. That included the United States of America.

David Dekker was now 6 foot 10 inches tall and 267 pounds. He had survived more than two years leading NATO commando units in the mountains of Afghanistan They had been somewhat successful at hunting and killing lots of insurgents. But there were a lot of mountains and a lot of caves to hide in. It was their land and they knew it better than did any foreign soldier. Successful raids were not common. This was now his second year in commando intelligence when he usually remained in

Kabul or at a nearby specific command post. His role had changed from direct identification with the eyes, hunt, and kill by guns, to electronic identification by air, hunt, and kill by missiles. He now controlled missile loaded drones and not rifles. This method of warfare was certainly less dangerous for the NATO forces, but not necessarily more successful than direct action. Obviously the decision makers thought both methods were important. Therefore both methods were used. At least he was having experience with each. Such experience would be an important asset later in life.

But another experience changed his life sooner than expected. He was working at a command post within a NATO base in Qandahar in southern Afghanistan when he received a high priority signal. There was a report coming in that a group of heavily armed men, determined not to be Afghan nor Pakistan military, were driving east toward what had been an old Al Khaddar command post and munitions cave network. They were in three covered and three uncovered pickups, and were now east of Qalat and approaching the Toba Kakar Ro mountain range on the Afghan-Pakistan border. They had been sighted an hour ago by a nomadic Pushtur tribe of Afghans which was moving north to south in the area. The tribal chief was known to be on NATO payroll to do just that, spy and report any suspicious movement of armed men. NATO did have one missile carrying drone in the area, but no ground troops and no satellites were in position to confirm these reported sightings. David notified his superiors and they ordered him to move the drone closer and try to confirm the on-the-ground sighting. As he moved the drone closer to the column of trucks he calculated that they were only a few miles from the Pakistan border. They certainly would reach it within fifteen to twenty minutes.

Pakistan and Afghanistan were currently very unhappy about American missiles being used inside their border areas. Many local villagers had recently been killed "by American missiles". They had vigorously protested to the United Nations. So some kind of decision was going to have to be made about this convey, immediately. From the drone's cameras there were indeed several, perhaps fifteen or more armed men in six covered and uncovered trucks. He could see no women or children. This was later confirmed on the photographs. He reported what he saw to his superiors, and was given permission to fire two missiles at the trucks and take out as many as he could. He did. The missiles hit their targets. The next day a helicopter reconnaissance of the strike confirmed the worst. The truck column was a group of Pakistan villagers returning to Pakistan. They had been attending a three day wedding festival in a village outside of Qalat. There was much intermarrying along this border region. And such extended celebrations were common. Eleven children, seven women, and ten men were killed. No enemy combatants were found.

That night Dave had his next dream. 'He saw a beautiful green and yellow grove of trees and red and blue flowers with the morning sun slicing its way through the branches. It reflected from the nearby pond which was fed by a small almost silent waterfall. The pond had been created by a beaver dam at a narrow point in a slow flowing stream which had emerged from the nearby snow capped mountain. It was a lovely spring day and the creatures of the forest were all out shopping.

A small female rabbit complained, "What is the terrible smell in the air? Let us move to another place for lunch."

Her friend replied, "There is a human on the other side of that tree. That is where the disgusting smell originates. I agree, let us go down the stream."

And sure enough, sitting up against a tree was a large red headed man who was fast asleep. Upon seeing this, Dave knew immediately that this person had green eyes and looked exactly like him.

Before the rabbits could leave, a beautiful red breasted robin spoke up, "Why do humans have to come here and bring their smells and leave toxic papers and plastics? And their pollution of the air is becoming so bad that we birds are having more and more trouble breathing. We are going to have to mutate and develop a chemical filter for our lungs to survive these humans."

A little brown mouse, hiding behind a toad stool, suddenly shouted out, "And they not only pollute the air but also destroy the earth. Try living inside a house that is constantly bombarded by rusty water one day and liquid garbage the next."

Then two kissing fish jumped up out of the lake, kissed and called out, "Humans complain about not having enough of us to eat. Yet they don't seem to understand that we cannot live in stinking polluted water, let alone have and raise large families in such water."

Suddenly several butterflies and dragonflies flew down and also started complaining about the chemical pesticides and fertilizers that humans sprayed into the air over their fields, but which was always blown into their forest. "Many of our friends are killed every spring by such stupidity," they shouted. "These pesticides kill us and our friends, but we are not pests!"

From a nearby ant mound the queen ant stood at the top and agreed with the other creatures that lived in the forest. She hissed, "Why don't we make war on any humans who come onto our land without our permission. By human or animal law this forest does not belong to us. But we have squatters' rights. We have been here for millions of years. Let us make an example out of this human who is asleep here."

A vote was taken of all the creatures in the vicinity of the tree where the red headed human was sleeping. The vote was unanimous to attack. Several thousand tiny creatures advanced toward the tree. From a tree branch directly above the red haired man's cleft left ear a small spider started descending; the spider was singing the Star Spangled Banner.'

Suddenly Dave woke up screaming. He was dripping wet. He looked around everywhere. He checked under the blankets, around the bed, throughout the room, outside the door, and even walked around the barracks. Macho Solider, huh?

How could a dream start as a Walt Disney special and quickly turn into an Edgar Allen Poe special?

# 5 - The Professionals

Graduation from Harvard University Medical School was the start of a life time career of: 1) helping to prevent people from dying, 2) making a lot of money, 3) performing medical research and developing new drugs, new medical techniques and new theories about diseases. Most new doctors would excel in number 1; all doctors would excel in number 2. And only a very few doctors would excel in number 3. But for number 3, several additional years of training, internship and special residency, were required. Gabriela Longenstein and Aaron Armand graduated with all the pomp and ceremony expected and deserved. That night the parties celebrated to the gods of alcohol more than the gods of food or medicine. And Gabriela and Aaron made their final decision. Gabriela had been accepted into the residency program at Boston General Hospital in pediatric orthopedics. She would follow her dream of operating on and saving the smashed/cut/ blown up little hands and little feet of children, especially in war torn areas of the world. She would also be living near her aging Father for a few more years during her advanced training program. Aaron was going to New York City to Columbia University Medical School and the Presbyterian Hospital. He would study for a PhD in Cellular and Molecular Biology and also take up residency training in Molecular Pathology. This program would require several more years of his life. Their last supper took place in a private booth in the Boars Head Inn, where they had originally met.

They looked each other in the eye and Gabriela spoke first, "It has been a fantastic period of our lives, these last three years. We always knew that we would get to this day, but there are no guarantees in life. I have loved you, and I still do love you. But I guess it is not enough for either of us. You follow your gene quest to New York, and I follow my knife and needle, eventually to the Middle East. Head wins over heart. Not a common ending. But for us it is the best, perhaps the only ending possible."

Aaron took both of her hands in his and responded, "Yes, I will always love you too. We do have super memories which will last forever. I'm certain that I will never find another woman that will be able to put me in my place like you do, at least not so easily."

Gabriela blushed, "That is the straight talk of my Father. As a Jew who survived the War and lost both parents, he never had time for trivia or stupid stuttering, as he called it."

"He is a very proud Father; his daughter is number one at the best medical school in the world. And what she has chosen to do with the rest of her life also must make him very happy. I too congratulate you. I tried like mad to catch you, but I am proud to be number two behind you. Your way of thinking and approach to problem solving, both social and medical, have helped me in my personal quest. If you ever need anything, from anywhere, at any time, I will come immediately. I will never forget you."

"And I am certain that your Mother is looking down from up there. I know that she will be happy when you do finally return to Israel and help children who are trying to survive in the middle of continuous wars. I hate the words 'collateral damage'. This is just a way that intelligent grown men try to hide the fact that many women and children are mutilated by their bullets and explosive devises."

And with tears beginning to form in both of their eyes they quickly changed the subject and began to discuss the new pride in the Armand family at having another doctor in the House.

That night, as usual, whenever the day was filled with high stress, Aaron had another dream:

'It began in a small square room with four men sitting around a four sided card table. Each man was red headed, green eyed, and had a cleft left ear. They had identical faces and bodies. They each wore blue shirts, blue trousers, blue socks, and blue shoes. Each man had four cards in his hands; all of the other cards were on a four separate stacks in the center of the table. They were not playing. They were looking at each other and talking, but Aaron could not hear any voices so he did not know what they were talking about. Beside each man sat a golden colored, full grown Great Dane dog. In one corner of the room there were four white cats playing together. In the other three corners sat, respectively, four little girls with platinum hair, four red headed little boys, and four blond, blue eyed ladies. Four lights directly above the table served to light up the room, even though there was one window on each of the four walls. However the room had no doors. The music filling the air was Beethoven's Fourth Symphony, The King. The setting was strange but very peaceful. It did not change during the entire duration of Aaron's dream.'

* * *

Law School had been really great. Bill Bassinger had made the correct decision to not go toward professional football, but to take up law. He was now William Bassinger, Esquire. And Dorothy and Fred Bassinger were very proud of him. After the graduation ceremony they threw a gigantic party for all of their friends and family. And just as great, he would start his career in Des Moines with Johnson, Krebs, Jansen, Peterson, Birmingham, and Associates. He obviously was an Associate, a beginning Associate as he would find out.

At the family farm house the Bar-B-Q party was well underway. His lawyer Uncle Paul munched on a foot long hot dog and congratulated Bill. "I am pleased that you chose law as you will find it more stimulating during your lifetime. You are bright, a very good writer, and you enjoy working with people, so it is the perfect profession for you. You can help the rich and the poor. It is your choice. And you can make as much money as you want. You don't need to specialize immediately. Let it happen. Just take the given assignments, do well on all of them and you will probably be given a choice of specialization later. If not, strike out on your own. You have a good Iowa name, so people will trust you and come to you for help."

Bill responded with his winning smile and said nothing. He knew he wanted to focus on intellectual property rights in crops and foods, but that would take more schooling and he was not ready to go back to the grind.

He finally said, "I do want to make some money for a while. Being a farmer's son I have never had more than an old broken down used car and pocket change. Also Jenny and I plan to get married on her parents wedding anniversary this July 4."

Uncle Paul chuckled. He smiled. "Are you sure that dating for six or seven years is long enough for the two of you to make this decision toward such a long term commitment?"

Bill reached over and grabbed Uncle Paul around the neck and they started one of their famous wrestling matches. Uncle Paul was only six foot tall but he was almost three hundred pounds and had won the Iowa State Wrestling Championship a 'few' years ago. So they were a pretty good match. When they did wrestle, people just sort got out of the way and let them go to it. Actually no one dared interfere with the little boy's fun.

Suddenly a tall, very pretty, slim, blonde haired, blue eyed young lady took a big glass of water and threw it on both of them. They looked up and realized it was the new bride-to-be. So they looked each other in the eye, winked, turned toward this lady, charged at her, picked her up, put her onto their shoulders, and marched around the crowd singing "Here comes the bride….." Everyone joined in. Jenny was so embarrassed. It is said that she never threw water at her (future) husband ever again.

After the impromptu parade around the yard, they put Jenny down. Then the guys quickly dragged Bill over to the horse shoe pitching area. This game involved throwing (pitching) horse shoes toward and around a steel stake. If one threw it around the stake it was a ringer and counted two points. If the shoe lit such that it was one shoe width from the stake, it counted one point. If it lit further away from the stake no points were given. Games were routinely played to twenty one points. The horse shoes ranged from one to five pounds in size. And the stakes were from fifteen to thirty feet apart. With this variety of weights and distances, big and little contestants could more fairly compete. However, today was special and only the five pound horse shoes and the thirty feet distance would be challenged. Thus only the bigger men would play. The ten biggest men each challenged Bill. He did not understand why they all wanted to challenge him, but he took them on, one by one. And he beat each of them, one by one. But after an hour and one-half of throwing that five pound piece of steel thirty feet a couple hundred times, he was exhausted. He only learned a few days later that the entire contest was contrived to try to wear him out so he would not be able to properly celebrate his graduation with Jenny that night. In the long run who really won?

After the horse shoe contest, Jenny dragged the winner over to the corner of the yard where they could be alone. She excitedly exclaimed, "I found the perfect house for us yesterday. It is in Windsor on a cul-de-sac, three bedroom, two baths, living and family room with fireplace, big open kitchen, lovely patio in back with privacy fence, and several nice big shade trees. I talked to the realtor and she said that we could probably work out a meager down payment and she would help arrange a thirty year standard loan at six percent. When mortgage interest rates come down we can re-finance. She knows all about us, that I am teaching mathematics at the Briarwood High School, and that you will be going downtown to work at the law firm on Walnut Avenue. So this location is close to both of our work places. Can we go look at it in the morning?"

What could he say except, "Of course, my darling."

A few days later they placed a down payment on the house of their choice. They began to buy and move some furniture to the house. And Bill started to work at the downtown office. The wedding was only one month away, so he decided to try to put in as many hours of work as possible to be able to have some honeymoon money. He billed each of his clients by the hour for work on their case or problem. The billing ranged from $100 to $500 an hour. The specific amount was determined by the Partners. And he quickly learned that the cases with the higher billing rates were given to the Partners and the Associates who had been with the firm for longer periods of time. Nevertheless, he had never made $100 an hour at any job he had during his lifetime. And working sixty to seventy hours a week allowed him to save up honeymoon money. He might even have enough to buy a new car.

One night Bill arrived at home at 3:00 AM. Exhausted, he was asleep when he hit the bed. And his next dream began:

'Before him appeared a large football stadium with an exciting game in progress. The scoreboard read twenty to seventeen, visiting team in the lead. There was fifty seven seconds left on the clock in the fourth quarter. The home team had the ball on the visitor's thirty five yard line. A quarterback roll out to the right and a quick pass completion to the wide receiver and out of bounds on that side of the field was good for nine yards. The clock stopped at fifty seconds. This time the quarterback used a draw play and the running back carried the ball off to the left side, headed toward the sideline and went out of bounds on the visitor's seven yard line. Twenty seconds were left on the clock. On the next play the quarterback ran a quarterback keeper up the center. It fooled no one. He made a one yard gain. With four seconds remaining, he quickly called time out. The home team could not settle for a three point field goal, they needed a seven point touchdown to win. And ties were for lilies. He took off his helmet and walked to the sidelined to talk with the coach. Bill looked more closely and saw that the quarterback was red haired and green eyed. He looked at the coach and he was red haired and green eyed. He glanced at the players on sideline of the home team and they were all red haired and green eyed. All of the fans on the home side of the stadium were red haired and green eyed. All of the policemen on the field were red haired and green eyed............'

* * *

Charles Collingswood was the fifth member of the hiking group that was preparing to enter the Florida Everglades. He knew all of the others very well as they were all members of his little church there in Indian Nest. Dr. Janice Stryker was tall and slim, blond hair, blue eyes, and a couple of years older than Charles. She was an Assistant Professor in the Department of Environmental Studies at the University of Miami. Her permanent residence was in Miami, more than one hour away. But since her research specialty was marsh and swamp wildlife, she rented a small apartment next door to the church. Then she usually "jumped off" from this area into the Everglades for her data collecting expeditions.

Dr. Stryker and Reverend Collingswood had become rather close as they spent many evenings on his lovely screened "mosquito free" back porch. Her Father was a naturalist and had been employed for thirty five years by the US government to work in the Okefenokee National Wildlife Refuge and Wilderness Area in Georgia. So Dr. Stryker grew up as a swamp girl and was very comfortable in this very dangerous environment. She had made all of the arrangements for this one day excursion. In fact it really was not going to be a hike. The group would ride on marsh land during the morning in a swamp buggy. Then they would switch to an Everglades airboat for the afternoon water venture.

The other members of the group included: Fern Wilson was a dark skinned twenty four year old student of Dr Stryker's who lived in a neighboring village and was currently going to school at UM. She came from Miami just for the day, and stop and see her parents on the way back. She was beginning her Master of Science research project in Environmental Studies. They would discuss research options during the voyage.

Harry Johnson was a sixty three year old, bald, paunchy and cigar smoking new resident to the little community. One month ago he moved to Florida from Canada. He was not yet very well liked, but peace was one of the products that ministers sell. So as a favor to the Reverend, he was invited along. And Mr. Johnson really did want to see an alligator. He would.

And the last hiker was Delwine Gaston who was a forty six years old weather beaten captain of a small cabin cruiser. He made his living by chartering his boat to "Yankees" to fish for the big ones – marlin. He chartered out of Naples, Florida. Dr. Stryker was a long time friend and had promised to take him along on this trip to see this small inner sea called by some as the Florida Inner-glades.

They were to meet at 8:30 AM sharp at the Heron House where the swamp buggy was kept. Everyone was on time. All had followed orders which included wearing long light pants, long sleeve light shirts, brimmed hats or some kind of head and neck covers, thick sun glasses, tennis shoes, and an excess application of mosquito repellent and sun screen lotion. Dr. Stryker had brought along snacks, and plenty of soft drinks and drinking water. They took two ice chests filled with ice. It could be needed today.

The weather was expected to be beautiful, no clouds but more than 100 degrees. In the late afternoon the mosquitoes would be very hungry.

The group of five climbed into the four wheel drive swamp buggy. They would both ride and walk during the morning tour, but only ride in the airboat during the afternoon tour.

So they were off into the Everglades where only the American Indians called Seminoles had ever lived. Soon they would understand why. The nature was beautiful – multiple varieties of swamp grasses everywhere, palmettos, small and large palm trees, numerous cypress, pines, and oaks, berries of all kinds, vegetation everywhere. Obviously water meant life for numerous types of plants and animals. From the latter category they saw a wild boar, numerous deer, many species of birds, several snakes, a couple of raccoons, maybe a bobcat, and hundreds of frogs.

The ground was reasonably dry in many places at this time of the year. However Dr. Stryker explained that if you started walking you would quickly learn that there are small areas of dry and small areas of wet; and in trying to travel any distance on foot you would soon get lost in trying to negotiate around the small areas of wet. They did hit some very rough dry areas and plowed through water pockets in some low marsh and swamp areas. But there existed a trail only because Dr. Stryker called it a trail. No one else recognized it as a trail, let alone a road. If fact if she had not been driving the swamp buggy they would have been continuously lost.

Around 11:00 AM they had returned to the Indian Nest. No one realized that they had made a three hour circle until they saw the familiar buildings. It all went so fast, and each was left with a kaleidoscope of images of nature frozen in his mind. There was so much to see. But there was a sign of relief because everyone had indeed been lost, except the Professor of course. Lunch time!

Two hours later, cooled off, relaxed, tummies full, rehydrated, they climbed aboard the Everglades airboat. It was located at the small fishing pier next to the Heron House, which sold fishing and hunting supplies. They blasted off. Dr Stryker was again in the driver's seat. This time they were water bound. And water there was. But with all of the floating vegetation, even floating islands with full grown trees; it was very difficult to really know where water was and where water was not. You just knew that you did not want to step out of the airboat whether moving or sitting still.

There were beautiful water lilies of many colors everywhere. They saw numerous herons including many of the great white heron, thousands of birds including several many ospreys and eagles, a few ducks, more snakes, a manatee family, two dolphins, and hundreds of alligators. The scary green guys were of all sizes and they were given plenty of room. The afternoon also went very fast and they returned "home" around 5:00 PM. It had been a fascinating day and very educational. For four of the five travelers this was the first such experience. And they unanimously agreed that they would never go into the glades again without Dr. Stryker leading them. It was fun but dangerous.

They thanked her again and again. Everyone kissed and hugged and then walked to their cars. Everyone headed for a different home at the end of a day; each was filled with new and fascinating memories.

Two of the group lived next door to each other; and that was the Reverend Charles Collingswood and Dr. Janice Stryker. Charles was very pleased that Janice had accepted his invitation to join him on his mosquito free porch for a cool glass of white wine and to listen to Vivaldi's Four Seasons. A couple days ago at their last mosquito free porch evening "exchange of ideas", they had been discussing the concept of spirits and souls. Because Janice was a Professor of Swamp "Life", she did not agree that God gave souls only to homo-sapiens (humans). Science had documented at least a dozen other homo-types to have existed on this earth. And chimpanzees have 98% of the same genes that homo-sapiens have. Why should it bother humans if other animals have their own god, heaven, and hell? She was certain that other animals, humans were animals also, did not care if there were gods other than their own. Because he had a special and strong love for animals he could understand her "desire" to let animals have souls and heavens. However there was no such passage in the Bible that could be so interpreted. 'God made man in his own image.' Simple. He had developed a new argument and was ready to try it out on her. He wanted desperately to bring her into full belief of the Christian God. And it was not just because he thought she would be a beautiful wife and mother for his children.

As Janice sat in one of the two arm chairs on the small porch she asked, "So what did you think of my children today?"

Charles answered, "I enjoyed them tremendously. You must remember that I have my only university degree in biology. But like most biology students I have never seen so many and such a variety of plants and animals in one day in my entire life; not even in the Atlanta zoo. There are so many I am sure you cannot give personal names even to your favorite animals."

"Of course not," she replied, "but you would be surprised that in some places where I go often, certain little guys do sort of adopt me and show up to just say hello. I do not feed them so they must come for the curiosity. And I currently do have a couple of favorites such as two young deer on the Button Bay Pennsulia which I call rammy and rippy. The even hear me coming and wait for me. But this has happened in the past. Young deer are curious; but as they get older they become family oriented I think and stop coming. Then I have to wait for the next year to see their new young. The hunting is very restricted in the Everglades; so many of the animals, like the deer, are not afraid of humans."

Charles said, "I would like to get to know some of them better. Is it possible that I could join you sometimes when you are making your rounds and doing your counting?"

Janice responded, "Why not? You were a biologist before you became a minister."

He replied, "I think I am a little of both. If you love mankind you have to love animals."

"I am going out next Tuesday. If you are free you can join me and I can teach you about my family and show you why I am trying to protect them just like any mother would do."

"Next Tuesday is a date, "Charles responded.

And somehow, tonight, he had lost his nerve to have a serious religious discussion; he would try another time. He really did not know her well enough, yet.

Later that night he had another dream:

'He saw Janice Stryker swimming out in open water. She was beautiful even when swimming. She was swimming slowly on her back and seemed totally relaxed, just staring up into the star filled sky. He thought that she must be in communication with God. He looked more closely and saw that she was as naked as a new born baby. Four ospreys went flying overhead. Each osprey had a human head which had red hair and green eyes. Four islands started drifting toward her from four different directions. As they got closer four alligators, one from each island, slowly eased into the water. Each alligator had a human head which had red hair and green eyes. They started slowly swimming toward her. From the sky above four eagles circled downward toward the alligators. Each eagle had a human head which had red hair and green eyes. The alligators got closer and closer. They opened their mouths. Janet did not see them or hear their presence. Each of the four alligators clamped their mouths onto Janet's arms or legs.

One alligator was on each arm and each leg. They started to back up as if to tear her arms and legs off. Suddenly four great white herons dived from the sky. Each heron attacked the head of an alligator. Each heron had a human head which had red hair and green eyes. Four ospreys – Four alligators – Four eagles – Four herons – and all had human heads which had red hair and green eyes.'

Charles woke up screaming – "NO – NO – NO – NO!"

* * *

David Dekker was resigning from the military after only four years. The colossal mistake of killing eleven children and seven women never left his mind. He enjoyed the camaraderie, the excitement, and the guns, but he could not stay where he might have to be involved with such decisions again. Security, yes – unneeded killing – no!

While on an R&R in Kabul, he met an old buddy, Jimmy Caffey sitting in a bar. Sergeant Caffey could have been Dave's older brother because he was 6 foot 10 inches tall and well over 260 pounds of solid muscle. Jimmy was an African American from Chicago. He had been the instructor who had trained Dave on the drone system. Several months ago Jimmy had left the army and joined a private American security company.

Dave sat down beside him and said, "So how is the world outside of the military?"

Jimmy responded, "Come buy me a beer and I will tell you."

Dave sat and Jimmy hollered for four more beers, he planned to talk for a while. He started, "As you know I quit the army two months ago and went private sector. I joined the Blue Ravens Security Firm in Washington, DC. They are a very impressive group. They really screen their new hires. There are a lot of men coming out of the army which have gun training and combat action from both the mountains and the deserted city streets. So they have a lot of young ex-military guys to choose from. That experience is not good enough. They also give you some intelligence tests, some psychology tests, and check out your physical health. And then, so I heard, they hire about one in ten applicants."

Dave replied, "That sounds pretty rough. But you did make it."

"Yeah,' Jimmy replied. "By the skin of my teeth; but after a couple of months I can see why they do that. Protecting people in the middle of New York City or Washington, DC is not the same as Saigon City, Bagdad, or Kabul. You wear nice clothes, usually suits. You carry hidden guns. You walk on normal sidewalks and ride in not normal (armored) cars. You protect one or two key people at a time. And it is usually protection in the middle of crowds who look and are normal like you. You watch people's eyes, looking for a sigh that he has a small gun or knife and has designs on the people you are supposed to protect. No big bang; but little bangs can kill too."

"So it is security control; but in a different way. American streets are very different streets than those of the warring areas of Middle East, Africa, and South East Asia. Collateral damage of an 'unknown' in Bagdad is not the same as collateral damage to an 'unknown' in Washington, DC. In DC it will most likely be an American citizen. In Iraq or Afghanistan it was just an 'unknown'. The police place a different interpretation on a shooting incidence in American cities. Wearing an army uniform usually gave you immunity to shooting someone in a 'battle zone'. Wearing civilian clothing here does not give such immunity in the USA – different type of battle zones!" And he laughed.

Dave asked, "Have you had any violent action then?"

"No, none," answered Jimmy. "We get paid better; the working environment is not hostile; and we usually get to sleep at night in a real bed. You can't beat that."

"It sounds like something that I should try," said Dave. "Ever since I was involved in the 'accidental' killing of that group of Pakistanis in Afghanistan, I have trouble sleeping because I am afraid that it could happen again. That is why I am getting out. I am looking for a good job, but not abroad again. I assume that most of the work with the Blue Ravens is within the USA. Is that right?"

Jimmy answered, "They have a group that goes abroad, but I think that most of their work is on the East Coast. If you are interested just say so and I will put in a good word for you."

Dave said, "I am interested."

So, David Dekker, who had two years experience leading commando units and more than one year in commando intelligence operations in the mountains of Afghanistan, applied for a job with the Blue Ravens Security Firm. All of the reports by his military superiors showed Dave to be outstanding in personal character and to have performed in a superior way in all assignments. One requirement for joining the Blue Ravens was that the applicant must have had recent army combat experience and knowledge of army intelligence. He was also required to take a two day examination. The first day was an extensive knowledge examination and a 'morals' test. The second day was a field test evaluating his commando skills. He scored the highest ever of any recruit in the thirty seven years of Blue Ravens history, or at least for as long as they had been giving such exams. They were pleased. He was pleased. He became a Blue Raven. And he felt as if he might have found a profession in which he could excel and also do something important, protect "important" people.

The Blue Ravens were indeed a special private security company. Most of their funds came from contracts with the American government. Frequently America would host a large international conference in a major city. Such three to four day long conferences would be attended by twenty, maybe thirty heads of state, many of whom would stay at some location other than the conference site and had to be chauffeured back and forth. During these short travel intervals security problems were maximal. The Federal Bureau of Investigation did not have enough agents to cover all such events, and by law the military could not be used to assist. So private security companies were called in to assist, or occasionally take the lead.

One such example was the annual January meeting of the United Nations in New York City. At that meeting more than one hundred and fifty heads of state attended, coming and going over a period of five days. And each head of state would have his security people and come and go on different days. In addition there were numerous smaller critical meetings with special government and non-government VIPs that required special security concerns.

And with the newly increased threat from foreign terrorists, private security had become a rapidly expanding employment profession. If you were a policeman and didn't like your job or your boss, you could quit the government job and go private; better work for better pay was the motto. During the past twenty to thirty years America had grown from five thousand to more than fifty thousand registered private security agents.

Because the Blue Ravens were the number one security company in America, located in Washington, and with excellent political contacts "in the House" and "on the Hill', their agents went through some extra special training. Dave was tapped for this. He spent several weeks in Quantico, Virginia learning CQBD (close quarter body defense) mechanisms from a select marine unit. He then received one month of special weapons training at Fort Benning, Georgia. Also they were in continuous contact with key people in the Department of Homeland Security. And Dave spent a few days in briefing conferences with these 'latter' people at least once a month, or more often if the need so required. In addition there was always a high ranking military officer from the Department of Defense in attendance at the briefings. So he was being trained up to the level where, after a couple of years of experience, he would be able to have his own security unit and handle his own special security assignments. That was just what he wanted, a worthwhile challenge.

The headquarters of the Blue Raven Security Firm was on Dolly Madison Boulevard, near Tyson's Corner, McLean, Virginia. They also owned a fifty acre farm-ranch near Frederick, Maryland. It was at this latter location where they had their practice target shooting ranges. Here they also tested out and trained with new maximum high tech weapon systems. They had a fully equipped physical exercise center where every agent worked out two mornings a week. All five buildings were one hundred percent sound proofed such that the neighbors did not even know that their neighbors were "dangerous" people. The property sign at the controlled entry booth declared the land belonged to the Potomac Gun and Hunting Club, Private. The structure closest to the road was designed, inside and out, to look like a private hunting club headquarters building. It contained a large lounge, bar, large and small high tech conference rooms, lunch facilities, four bed rooms and a secure holding facility for six people. Most of the brain work took place in McLean. But sometimes special brain work required additional security of its own.

For several years he successfully completed a variety of security assignments such as:

-for seven days they chauffeured three Arab sheikhs, their associates, and translators, all of who met with high level officials in the Department of Commerce and in the Department of Energy, in Washington, DC, as they lodged in the Hyatt Regency Hotel at Dulles Airport;

-for three days the Blue Raven Firm escorted the CEO and his advisors of the Santaray Steel Corporation of India who met for three days with officials in the Department of Labor in Washington, for two days they went to the Bethlehem Steel Corporation in Allentown, Pennsylvania to meet with their Board of Directors, and then they returned to Washington to spend two more days with high level officials in the Department of Treasury, each stop was at a different hotel;

-for eleven days his team of agents chauffeured the United Nation's Chairman of UNICEF and several of his colleagues to various locations in Canada, USA, Mexico, and Nicaragua.

-for four days a small team of officials from the Toyota Automobile Corporation of Tokyo held a conference with officials in the Department of Commerce, then for three days they went to Detroit, Michigan and talked with the CEO and CFO and key automobile engine all electric design engineers of General Motors, next they traveled to Selma, Georgia to visit their new Toyota automobile assembly plant, Dave and the Blue Ravens managed the security during the entire time;

- for six days the President of the Boar Diamond Mining Company, from South Africa, visited with senior personnel in the Department of Treasury and select Directors of the Washington Division of the PNC Bank by utilizing Blue Raven security.

There was no end to the number of governments and large corporations who wanted their senior people to have the best in security when they were traveling, even in the United States. And that was just what the Blue Ravens were all about. Within five years David Dekker was Captain of his own 5 to 10 agent team. Life was good and he felt he was doing something with his life. And then he met her.

Dave had purchased a small townhouse just off Carlin Springs Road near Baileys Crossroads in Arlington, Virginia. It was ten minutes to his office in McLean, fifteen minutes to downtown DC, and less than an hour to the Frederick ranch.

One Friday morning he had given his Navigator to the Lincoln Dealership on the corner of Columbia Pike and Glebe Road to have the breaks re-adjusted, and was having a cup of coffee at a nearby Starbucks. As he was quietly sitting, reading the Washington Post and enjoying his coffee, suddenly a cup of very hot coffee was dumped onto his lap. He was up out of his chair and automatically started a harsh CQBD take down of the stupid idiot who had just tried to cook his legs. In mid motion he stopped, looked into the most beautiful blue eyes he had ever seen, and fell in love. She was slightly over 6 feet tall, nearly 110 pounds, and had a light complexion with long blonde hair. She was wearing a short red skirt, blue green sweater and a bright red jacket which matched her bright red lipstick. Her lips looked very kissable. This was a moment he would never forget. After five minutes of apologies and re-apologies, the embarrassed and careful blotting of his pants, a re-purchase of another cup of coffee, the occupation of another table in the sun so his pants would dry faster, introductions began.

Because the accident was her fault the tall blond began the conversation. "My name is Janet Simpson. I live and work nearby. I come to Starbucks regularly to have some real coffee. Again I am very sorry. "

"And I'm David Dekker. It's nice to meet you, I think," he said while using his biggest and best smile. I live close by and I am waiting for my car which is being repaired across the street. I work for the Blue Raven Security Firm which is located just up the road in McLean."

She continued, "I work at the Dorothy Walker Summers Orphans Home which is just down the street. About six months ago I moved to Washington from St Louis, Missouri where I was born and raised."

David jumped in, "Gee, the St Louis Cardinals are my favorite baseball team."

Janet continued as if not interrupted. "My Father left my Mother when I was a baby. I have no memories of him. And my Mother died from pneumonia when I was three years of age. So I grew up in a government sponsored orphans home in St. Louis. In most orphan homes children are adopted or placed into foster homes before they reach their teens. I was not so lucky, or I was very lucky, however one wants to judge the past. I lived my childhood and teenage years in that home. But I not only helped to raise "my children," I also completed high school and two years of college. With a government scholarship I studied for two years at Washington University in St Louis and received an Associates Degree in Social Studies and Family Affairs. After graduation I was immediately hired as Director of the Dorothy Walker Summers Orphans Home, and began work here six months ago."

There were a couple of minutes of silence. Dave did not know how to respond. What a handicap to overcome. No parents and yet she had lifted herself to become more than a just productive member of society. She will spend her life helping other children, like her, who were not lucky enough to be born to loving parents. If anyone could understand and help these children, she could.

Finally Dave said, "You certainly turned your nightmare into a dream. I feel that you will be great with your "new children" and you will have more love from them than even a mother and father could give. I envy you."

And then he went on and described his loving home and buddy oriented military life, always surrounded by many friends and men who placed their lives into each other's hands. On the battlefield a close colleague was often the difference between life and death. And now he was working as a security agent protecting people he did not know, and even getting paid a lot of money to do this. He did have a small team of security agents, and they did work together, but they did not live together, play together, or sleep together in one room barracks like in the military. So there was friendship, yes, but there was not the warm family friendship found in the military. He missed that a lot.

David remembered a recent past event. "I have already played with your "new children'. Last year at Halloween the orphans at the Dorothy Walker Summers Home for Orphans had a Halloween festival. They dressed up in Halloween costumes and had tables and booths for sports and games, such as throwing darts at balloons, pitching pennies onto elevated plates, shooting rubber tipped arrows at a target, shooting a basketball at a low basket, bobbing for apples, snacks and candies for sale, and more. It was organized by a local NGO I think. I spent the entire day there and had a great time. Do you plan to have this Orphans Halloween Day again this year?"

Janet responded, "Yes, it is my understanding that the local Arlington Rotary Club wants to again organize and sponsor the event. It is very popular, and the children love it. It sort of gives the children a special standing in the neighborhood and at school too. We are planning it again this year."

"Can I be of some help?" he asked.

Janet looked him in the eye and replied, "I'm sure that we can find something for you to do, but I insist that you wear clean, dry pants and no mask."

He wasn't sure just how to interpret that clean, dry pants and no mask bit. But he knew a yes came next.

So they talked away for the next three hours, exchanged telephone numbers, promised to get together for dinner immediately after Dave's next out-of-Washington assignment which began tomorrow, said reluctant good-byes, exited Starbucks, and went in different directions.

A week later Dave called Janet and she invited him to her apartment at the Orphanage for dinner. The Orphanage was a very large old European manor house situated on more than two acres of prime property in Arlington, Virginia. When Dorothy Walker Summers died, ten years ago, she endowed the entire estate to the City of Arlington under conditions that it be supported as an orphanage for a minimum of 50 years. The main building had two large living rooms; one had two walls of filled book shelves. There was a large kitchen, ten bedrooms, and several baths, upstairs and down. The full basement, other than the heating area, had been renovated into a large play room. And of course the large yard had a mixture of play structures in the back.

There were two additional buildings. A garage-storage shed was located in the back right corner of the property. And a rather large carriage house sat near the front gate. Janet lived in a small two bedroom apartment within the carriage house. This building had been nicely renovated two years ago. The entire estate was completely surrounded by an eight foot high stone fence. There were currently twenty eight children, ages three to thirteen, staying in the big house. And "escape" was not so easy, so control was not so difficult.

Janet invited Dave into her small but uniquely furnished in a European style salon. He sat in the large arm chair. She immediately said, "I hope you like cold raw vegetables."

And then she placed in front of him a glass of white wine and a plate of cut celery, carrots, broccoli, and cauliflower. They were cold and directly from the refrigerator. She did eat meat occasionally, but was basically a vegetarian, so Dave was being tested already.

Dave looked at the plate, then up at Janet, she was waiting for a response, and he said, "My Mother was a vegetarian, so I recognize these as uncooked and cold vegetables, and containing approximately forty three percent more vitamins and minerals than when cooked. In fact the broccoli contains seventy eight percent more vitamin C when uncooked. It is not too critical with carrots, as they do not lose significant amounts of vitamin D when cooked. So cooked or uncooked they can........."

Dave glanced up at Janet and she was smiling from ear to ear. He saw right threw her test. She leaned over and gave him his first kiss, but it was not to be his last. So their relationship continued smoothly onward from last week's tragic encounter at Starbucks. They engaged in small talk for a while. Then they moved into a small dining area which was located within a glass enclosed projection protruding into the gardens on the big house side. It was early enough that most of the big house lights were still turned on; it was a lovely view of a lovely old house providing much love for little ones who desperately needed it. It gave both of them a nice warm feeling. Dave had told Janet of the accidental killing of the women and children in Afghanistan and his role in it. It seemed as if this big house was trying to tell him something.

Janet served a substantial dinner which was heavy on the carbohydrates. But she fully understood that Dave was a big guy and had lived in the army for many years. So she had purchased one and a half pounds of Bar-B-Q ribs, assuming she could sneak a couple of them onto her plate before he had a chance to take inventory. A large baked potato with yogurt plus red and yellow squash completed the carbs. It worked out perfectly. She actually got three ribs from the batch of fifteen ribs. And desert was a small chocolate pudding made with fat free milk. It was enough for him, as his mind was not food-focused. And they were both comfortably happy. It was a very new beginning, dry clean pants and all.

And after the meal he managed, "You sure know how to feed a big guy."

And he smiled. She smiled back. And they just sort of sat there looking at each other and smiled for several moments. There were invisible but noisy fireworks in the air.

When Dave returned home he was in the most relaxed mode that he had been in for a very long time. He could not remember being happier. And his dream started:

'A big red headed fellow with green eyes was dressed in a blue trench coat and was walking up Connecticut Avenue toward DuPont Circle in downtown DC. It was early evening and there was a cold fog in the area. One could not see more than 100 feet. The man turned west onto Massachusetts Avenue and continued walking. There were no people anywhere. In the distance, he could hear the sirens of police cars coming down Massachusetts Avenue. It was small caravan of four cars. Leading was a police car containing four policemen in full body armor. The next two cars were large bullet proof limousines each containing an Ambassador, two body guards and chauffer all in full body armor. And last was another police car containing four policemen in full body armor. After going through the Sheridan Circle the caravan slowed and turned into the short circular driveway of the Cosmos Club on Massachusetts Avenue. The Cosmos Club was a very elite club in which most of it members were Nobel Laureates, Pulitzer Prize winners, very high ranking members of the Executive, Legislative, or the Judicial Branches of the American Government, presidents of certain corporations, and VIPs with appropriate friends. Apparently the two Ambassadors had been invited for a special dinner party.

Suddenly from four directions four motorcycles appeared. Each motorcycle had a driver and a rider. From two of the cycles two of the riders quickly hopped off of their cycles and each shot a rocket propelled grenade into the windows of each of the two police cars. The two police cars immediately exploded and burst into flames. The two riders from the other two motorcycles had already jumped onto the top of the two limousines. They quickly attached 2 pounds of plastic explosives onto the top of each limousine. The latter two terrorists then hopped down, remounted their cycles, and they all fled away. Within five seconds the two bombs exploded. The tops of each limousine were ripped off and the limousines were on fire. The entire attack lasted less than fifteen seconds. As the eight terrors escaped they tore off their helmets and shouted slogans of freedom. And each terrorist had red hair and green eyes.

A siren went off. Suddenly all of the "dead" guys got up. They brushed off their clothes, sheepishly smiled at each, shook hands, and walked around. The four motorcycles came back down the street and entered the Cosmos Club's driveway. The riders took off their helmets. They were not red haired and green eyed, but they had various shades of brown and blonde hair and a mixture of light and dark colored eyes. The door of the Club opened and out came four older men dressed in black suites. They looked grim faced and went around and spoke to several of the "live" and "dead" men. It had been fast and bloody.'

When David woke up and he suddenly understood that the entire scene had been orchestrated to illustrate a terrorist attack for four members of the Congressional Armed Services Committee from the House of Representatives. But he was still sweating a little.

# 6 – The Families

New York City is a very unique city. Frank Sinatra was correct, it never sleeps. Somewhat similar to London, there are more foreigners living in NYC than American citizens. At least in London, most of the foreigners are citizens of countries that are members of the British Commonwealth. This does give them some legitimacy to London which cannot be transferred to NYC's foreigners. The USA does not have foreign colonies, or does it? Nearly eight million American citizens work in New York City but live in the suburbs and commute. The nine million plus people live in the city can be divided into two general groups. In Manhattan, higher income working and retired-wealthy American citizens occupy the upper floors in most of the skyscrapers; the other skyscrapers contain businesses, offices, and factories of soft industry such as textile manufacturing. The lower income citizens and foreigners live on the lower levels or on the streets. The other four boroughs are Bronx, Brooklyn, Queens, and Staten Island. These districts and Upper Manhattan have many high rise buildings and a few skyscrapers. Middle and lower income American citizens and foreigners make up the majority population. However the populations in all regions of New York City have continuously changed over the decades with microcosms of some twenty or thirty different ethnic groups coming and going.

Long Island and the area now called the New York Metropolitan Area was first settled in 1524 by the Dutch and other white Europeans. It was then called New Amsterdam. When the British took over in 1625, it became New York. It had a population of less than one thousand in 1625, which continuously increased every year for almost four hundred years until today it is approaching twenty million people of numerous ethnic groups. It is appropriate that it houses the home of the world's United Nations. New York City itself is a united nations-city.

As the various ethnic groups settled-in and settled-out of the five boroughs, the Upper West Side Manhattan was first settled by Jews. This is the region in Manhattan between Central Park and the Harlem River on the east, the Hudson River on the west, and 70 to 80th Streets on the south.

Over the years it became a famous intellectual and a cultural center of its own. The intellectualism was exceptionally high in the areas of science and medicine. Eventually bright young non-Jews moved in and slowly the cultural atmosphere broadened; while the intellectual atmosphere continued to blossom.

And that is why Dr Aaron Armand loved it. Even though Boston had an excellent intellectual atmosphere, he was ready for some cultural re-adaptation, and Boston had only about three million people. He needed a larger population research base for his future research studies. As far as he was concerned the Upper West Side Manhattan had the specific science and medicine he wanted and needed, and a cultural atmosphere loaded with young, in-motion intellectuals. Life was concentrated. And if you wanted to extend your social atmosphere to Lower Manhattan, it was but 15-20 minutes. Presbyterian Hospital and Medical Center with the Columbia University Medical School and affiliated hospitals had given to Aaron an almost unlimited opportunity to finish his education and training. He would then establish at that location the first Center for Cellular and Genetic Biology of Twinning (CCGBT) in the world, and pursue his genetic quest.

Today, in medicine there are basically two general types of medical researchers, clinical and laboratory. Both require a doctorate plus additional specialty training. To become a clinical researcher it requires four years of undergraduate college for the Bachelor of Science degree, four years of medical school to receive the Medical Doctorate degree, and three to five years of special residency training (such as for Obstetrics, Pediatrics, etc) to be board certified. These doctors now can see patients in the clinics and partner-up with laboratory doctors for laboratory research studies. To become a laboratory researcher requires four years of undergraduate college for the Bachelor of Science degree, two years for the Master of Science degree, four years for the PhD degree, and two to three years of post-doctoral laboratory training. These doctors can perform research in the laboratory with animals or tissue culture systems, and partner-up with clinical doctors for research with human systems.

Hence medical research qualification requires from ten to twelve years of study and training beyond high school. And to be qualified to do research in both the clinic and laboratory, one must complete all of the training for both clinical and laboratory as listed above. However one does not require twenty years of direct study to reach this level of qualification. If one has the brainpower and energy, dual MD-PhD medical research qualification programs are available in which one can take double course loads and also double up on clinic/laboratory training requirements. One would then be eligible to perform and direct teams of medical researchers which required both clinical and laboratory analysis and methodologies, and to use both human tissues and animals in research studies. This latter program can be accomplished in twelve to fifteen years beyond high school.

Dr Aaron Armand would settle for nothing less than maximum qualifications. In order to ask his questions about twinning, his genetic quest, he was certain that he would require all the knowledge that he could jam into his brain. And now he only had another year to finish his dual program at Columbia University Medical School. He was constantly thinking, organizing, recruiting faculty researchers, making equipment lists, identifying first research projects, and seeking more start up money for his new CCGBT. It would officially begin in eighteen months.

Columbia University Medical School had several dormitories nearby for students and researchers. Aaron had been settled into one of them, the Ft. Washington Residence House, for the past three years. This building was only for postdoctoral fellows and required less than ten minutes to walk to his research building on campus. He continued to maintain a good relationship with his parents; he did love them, even though he fully believed they were wrong in their silence to him about his true parenthood. In addition, he was still in training so his salary was rather small. Thus Dad's support money allowed him to rent a top floor suite with three bedrooms, living room, two baths and a kitchen.

His apartment mate for the past two and one half years was a very intelligent, tall, slim, blonde, blue eyed post doctoral fellow who was born and raised in Denver, Colorado. Her name was Josephine Christianson. She always went by Jos. She was the third child in a middle class family, so she had to fight her educational way with scholarships supporting her for the BS, MS, and PhD degrees at Stanford University in Palo Alto, California. Her doctorate was in Molecular Biology and Genetics and she was now doing her postdoctoral studies with a team of doctors (two with MDs, three with PhDs, and two with MD-PhD) and two other postdoctoral fellows and two PhD candidate students at Columbia U. Her research team won the coveted Jacobson Johnston Prize in Diabetes last year; and she had made a significant contribution in the project. She loved her research and she also loved Aaron. She just had to figure out how to have both, and not pay a gigantic emotional price.

Large research oriented medical schools and hospital complexes, today, have a common entrenched hierarchy. From top down are Professors, Associate Professors, Assistant Professors, Postdoctoral fellows, and PhD students. Their responsibilities were as follows:

- Professors – faculty – much administration, some teaching, some research, responsibility for obtaining funds for and control of research projects, writing of research publications and books,
- Associate Professors – faculty – some administration, much teaching, some research, responsibility for obtaining funds for and control of research projects, writing of research publications,
- Assistant Professors – faculty – much teaching, much research, responsibility for obtaining funds for and control of research projects, writing of research publications,
- Postdoctoral fellows – non faculty – 100% time doing research and writing of research publications, and focusing day and night on the research project, no other responsibilities.
- PhD Students – non faculty – classroom and laboratory courses, and laboratory research.

Only faculty level professors have a full salary, retirement benefits, health, disability, and life insurance which cover the entire family, annual vacation allowance, and other benefits that all full time staff and employees of universities and hospitals have.

Postdoctoral fellows are not faculty. Therefore they have none of the benefits of the faculty. They only have a salary and some insurance coverage; and this money is coming from the research funds, not from the university medical school nor the from hospital income. So, no research project, no money, no salary, no bread. And to have that research project continue every year requires high quality research and writing research papers about the project so the world will know the latest new knowledge about that disease that you are studying. The unwritten slogan of all researchers is Publish or Perish – translated it means that if your work is not excellent, or if you do not publish it, your research and you will disappear from the medical research world. Postdoctoral fellows are the true foot soldiers in the war against human diseases. It is expected that they will work 10 to 12 hours a day 6 to 7 days a week, vacations do not exist. Usually the research for the entire research team progresses at a rate directly related to the laboratory efforts by the postdoctoral fellows on the team. And the competition for discovery is always maximal for two reasons: 1- people are suffering and perhaps dying from whatever disease they are studying, 2- the egos of the researchers are at such a level that each wants to be the FIRST to make that discovery and become famous. Money is just not that important.

Both Aaron and Jos held doctor's degrees so they were postdoctoral fellows. Therefore, their free time really did not exist. A typical day was to get up at 6:00 AM. They would eat a quick breakfast of cereal and milk, fruit, and musli-bars, and take a powerful multiple vitamin-mineral complex; stick a couple of musli-bars in their briefcases and make a quick walk to their respective laboratories; work straight through until noon; have a good respectable lunch (their only real meal of the day) in one of the university cafeterias, plus a big cup of coffee – sometimes together and sometimes with members of their own lab team or just friends; work straight through until 5:00 or 6:00 PM and then have a light dinner (soup, salad, sandwich) usually at a local café or at university food service location, plus a big cup of coffee; work straight through until 8:00 or 9:00 PM; and then go back to the apartment, nibble on something, maybe have another cup of coffee, open their laptops and analyze the day's data and plan tomorrow's research effort. They went to bed either when they finished or became too sleepy to work. Play was sort of forgotten.

They would try to find an hour or so in the late evening to exchange, "Hello, how was your day? Good, how was your day? Fine. How will tomorrow be? Good! Will you make your projected research deadline? That's good. Goodnight. Goodnight. See you tomorrow".

Routine daily work was defined as standing or sitting at a laboratory bench and performing biological and chemical experiments with micro-pipettes, micro-flasks, mini-centrifuge tubes, micro-syringes, micro-test tubes of many sizes, tissue culture flasks, microscopes, and a wide variety of special machines and equipment which would help convert the biology to mathematics. Most of science was based, not on subjective judgments, but on objective numbers. That was what the special equipment was all about. Human Biology to Mathematics!

Therefore it was very difficult for postdoctoral fellows to find time to develop a private social relationship such as in man and woman. Occasionally the two of them would leave work early, 6:00 or 7:00PM and go have a good dinner, see a movie, enjoy the symphony or an opera at the Lincoln Center. They would also sometimes not work on Sunday and instead stroll through Central Park, or play in the tourism areas in Lower Manhattan. Twice they had driven up to see his parents in New Hampshire. But Aaron had never met Jos's parents in Denver.

Today they had made into an annual no work special day. It was March 7, their birthdays. They were born on the same day. Aaron was thirty one and Jos was twenty nine. So they drove across the George Washington Bridge and headed up along the west side of the Hudson River on the Palisades Parkway to the Black Bear Restaurant. It was a lovely two hour drive and was located on a mountain ridge which projected out from Bear Mountain and provided a spectacular view down the Hudson River Valley. It was a favorite of the Columbia University faculty. And it served only Canadian French food.

Aaron and Jos arrived about 6:30 PM. They entered an authentic Swiss Chalet style restaurant which would seat about one hundred guests, most of them in front of large two floor tall windows with a lovely view. They first went into the library, a large den with numerous book shelves filled with books and a roaring wood burning fireplace. They ordered a round of cocktails as the weather had turned cooler and the fire was physically and psychologically correct for this evening.

At 7:30 PM they entered their exclusive little dining nook, screened off to give privacy. Aaron had made special reservations. They looked at the table setting. There were Dutch hand crafted linen table cloth and napkins, Belgian ceramic plates, French silver ware, two French silver candle holders containing red candles with flame, and Swiss crystal glasses with a bottle of Canadian Bordeaux's Chateau Gruaud Larose wine on the dining room table. The waiter seated them and then opened the wine, asked Aaron to sample it, and after receiving an affirmative node, with a bon appétit he left. They had pre-ordered their dinner while enjoying the library fireplace. Dinner would be served in half hour.

Aaron and Jos looked at each other, smiled, giggled, and immediately sat down. They had never eaten in an atmosphere such as this. They made small talk and then the food arrived. It was delivered on hot plates in silver covered containers. When the covers were removed they suddenly found that they were hungry, and the food smelled too good to delay any longer. So they began the richest (calories and money) meal of their lives. It was fun, and it was:

- chestnut soup with crème fraiche
- Quebec salad vinaigrette
- caribou and mushrooms crepe
- white asparagus tips in a crème-blanc wine sauce
- fresh hot French bread
- grand marnier soufflé

And they finished the meal with French Remy Martin cognac in large crystal sniffer glasses. What a super meal. With all of that alcohol they were feeling very good. Not being regular connoisseurs of alcohol their liver alcohol dehydrogenase enzymes did not rapidly detoxify the toxic stuff, so they needed to sit a while to clear their heads. A half an hour later Jos broke the ice and spoke.

She said, "I love you very much, Aaron."

Aaron responded, "And I love you very much, Jos." as he reached into his jacket pocket.

She continued, "But I am not sure that I could live my entire life with you."

Aaron slowly eased his empty hand out of his pocket and said, "Why do you say that?"

Jos responded, "I have busted my tail for the past fifteen years to become a very good medical laboratory researcher. My family and friends have sacrificed for me and I am the only member of my family to attain this level of achievement. I owe them and myself to dedicate as much of my life as possible to medical research pursuits. I will not settle for just being a wife and a mother! I have been watching the older female researchers at the University."

"I have counted five types. 1) Those who remain single, dedicate their lives to research and have occasional flings with males; 2) Those who get married and dedicate their lives to research and share that life with a similar dedicated male and do not have children; 3) Those who get married and try to maximize their research efforts while at the same time being responsible for a husband and growing children; 4) Those who get married and try to maximize their research efforts while sharing the responsibility of raising children with their husband; 5) And there are those, who I know about, who completely gave up all of their research for that 'special' male."

Aaron was stunned! He did not know how to respond. But he knew she was right.

Jos continued, "I know that you have not thought about us like this. Males are always given the green light when two professional people marry and both pursue their careers. Please think about it. I have no problem with that. I am not into equal opportunity. But I will have my career also."

Aaron smiled and said, "I have thought about us and our duel careers, perhaps not in the depth that you have. I do want both of our research careers to continue at maximum. I want you and I want our children, two of them, one boy and one girl, maybe twins. For my own peace of mind, I need to have children. I need to find out where I came from and if I will continue. And I need to re-grow up with them. So from your numbers I chose number four."

Then he went on to explain his suspicions about his as yet not understood genetic relationship with his 'parents'.

"I know that I have more than one unidentified, but genetically identical brother out there. I am even guessing that there are four 'of we' males. All of my dreams and extrasensory systems are telling me so. Obviously, just comparing the physical characteristics of my Mother and Father with myself one would be suspicious of a genetic or possible hospital mistake, such as a baby name labeling mistake in the new babies unit of the hospital. However I am told that did not happen. Once I can get the CCGBT up and running I will perform some sophisticated DNA analysis on cells from my parents and myself. That will at least tell me if we are genetically the same, only physically different. But beyond that, can I even have children? I really do not know."

"If so, will there be twins? Twins or not I want to monitor their growth processes, decision making efforts, personalities, physical abilities, innate habits, etc. All of this lies at the heart of twinning concepts. Can we identify specific genes which code for personality and decision making, and not just give credit or blame to environmental modifications? I will dedicate my life to this effort. So again, I want you to continue your research career, you are already much better in the laboratory than I will ever be. I am more comfortable with patients. I might even try to recruit you into my CCGBT. Yes, I know, generally husband and wives do not work well together, especially on the same research project, but the exceptions to this are highly synergistic. And I want my, our children which I, we can raise together. You, children, and sharing all of life, is my wish. Will you marry me?"

And he withdrew from his pocket a small gift. He gave it to her and said, "Happy Birthday!"

Jos took the gift, tears forming in her eyes. By the size and shape she knew what it was. She opened it and started crying. She could not find her voice. Aaron quickly got up, came around the table, kissed her, and put the ring on her third finger left hand. He had tears in his eyes. By then her face was very wet and bright red. She got up. They passionately kissed. He laid two 100 dollar bills on the table, picked her up, carried her through the entire length of the restaurant, received a nice applause by the diners, placed her in the car and headed back to the City. She never did say yes or no.

And during his sleep that night his dream began:

'From a mountain top he looked down into a beautiful valley filled with golden wheat. It was surrounded on all sides by snow capped mountains colored yellow by the bright noonday sun. His eyes began to focus down, down, and millions of lovely shrubs appeared. They were green, like the color of his eyes, with numerous red berries, like the color of his hair. As his eyes continued to focus he saw a bubbling stream flowing toward a small lake. Near where the water entered the lake a small group of animals appeared. He looked closely and counted eight animals all lying down and dozing, or so it appeared. There were four golden colored, shaggy manned male lions, and four beautiful small white goats. Each had human heads with red hair and jade green eyes. They were all at peace.'

* * *

William Bassinger, Esq. was sailing through life. He now had two children and a Master of Science in Property Rights from Drake University Law School. And Jenny Bassinger had completed her Master of Science in Education and very much enjoyed her teaching.

Jenny had given birth to fraternal twins one and a half years ago. The oldest by five minutes was a little boy who had red hair and almond colored eyes. For a twin he was big at seven and one half pounds. And he was very active. They named him Steven. The second to arrive was a little girl who had straw blond hair and jade blue eyes. She was also big at seven pounds, but quite docile. She was named Stefannie. So they had a new Steve and Stef in their now new four bedroom house, also in Winsor Heights. Jenny's Mother was a young sixty six year old widow, not working and was thrilled to temporarily move into her daughter's house and play nanny. So life was good for the Bassinger family.

William was not yet a partner in the law firm. Partnership usually took many years, unless you hit upon some moneyed clients at the large corporation level who might help your upward movement. But he was now Chief Counselor of a legal team which had begun to specialize in property rights and legal problems concerning GE crops and GM foods. His Father had had experience with GE crops, and he was old enough to remember and to partially understand what had happened. They would use a certain type of seed corn one year, but in the second year it was now suddenly illegal, so they could not use it even if it gave a more profitable harvest than others that they had been using. It was explained as infringement of patent rights. So during his Master's program he also audited courses in Molecular Biology, Molecular Genetics, and Plant Genetics. He was beginning to understand the science. So during preparation for his next court case his mind started to review what science he had learned:

'Until the late twentieth century, new crops and new animals were produced by alterations in hybridizing and breeding with whole plants and intact animals. One plant would be cross pollinated to a second plant to yield a new plant which did not naturally exist; for example this new plant could be resistant to a specific fungus or could grow better on poor and dryer soils or could yield quantitatively a much larger harvest or….. The methodology involved adding pollen (equivalent to animal sperm) to the stigma (equivalent to animal ovary containing oocytes) of a growing fertile plant (equivalent a fertile female animal). This controlled sexual fertilization in plants (or animals) was accomplished by the fusion of whole cells with whole cells. Each of these cells contained many genes on many chromosomes. The intent was to transfer only one gene, yet the methodology transferred that one gene and several thousand additional genes which were not needed and perhaps not wanted. Yet this was the only methodology available, until recently when single gene transfer became available.'

'Cross pollination and interbreeding was the universal method that was used for thousands of years to create new crops and new animal products for the dining room table. Today all plant crops are very non-natural as they have been artificially cross-pollinated numerous times. During the latter part of the twentieth century the chemical (DNA), its structure (double stranded alpha helix), its linear sequence of A-G-T-Cs (inside the chromosomes) were determined to be the basis of genes. It was where all genetic inheritance (microorganisms, plants, and animals) originated. Hence genes, their chemistries and physical structures had now been discovered and carefully detailed. When a specific gene was proven to code for special characteristics (such as disease resistance), that specific gene could be isolated or synthesized and directly inserted into the food crop or animal. Sexual transmission of thousands of genes was no longer necessary. The single gene could even be transferred directly into a single cell.'

'To summarize the science - A single gene is called a double helix because of its corkscrew shape and is like a sentence in a book. It is composed of an alphabet of only four letters: A-G-T-C. And every word is composed of three letters: AGC-CAG-TAT-GGC-TTA------. One gene could have one thousand words which would code for a sentence which would give the cell a new protein called jfds; that new jfds protein could tell the cell to start growing. Another gene could have three thousand words which could code a sentence which would give the cell a new protein called pjmn; that new pjmn protein could be part of the cell wall or cell membrane around the nucleus. If each chromosome in a plant or an animal contains from fifty or one thousand or more genes (sentences); then each chromosome contains from ten thousand to ten million DNA letters.'

'Plants differ from other plants, and animals differ from other animals because of: 1) different genes, 2) same genes located on different chromosomes, and 3) because of changes in the functional or non-functional DNA letter sequences within any single gene. All genes contain functional and non-functional DNA letter sequences (sequences of the gene DNA codes).'

'If a non-functional DNA letter sequence is changed or lost and the functional DNA letter sequence is unchanged, the gene will code for normal functioning. However, if a functional DNA letter sequence is changed or lost, this may cause the gene code to be lost, and the gene's function to be lost to the cell.'

'Many diseases result from the loss of an entire gene or from the mutation (negative change) or loss of a specific DNA letter in a functional DNA letter sequence within a gene, such as A changes to C, or A is lost. Several cancers are caused by the change in a single DNA letter in a functional DNA letter sequence. The latter types of change are very common in the functional DNA letter sequences and can result in new non-functional genes – the gene is present but it does not function, or a new function results from this new gene.'

'So today medical laboratories do not just measure the presence or absence of a gene, but they also measure the functional versus non-functional DNA letter sequences of the key genes that are present. Scientifically, presence or absence of a gene may not be enough; it does not give adequate information about the functional DNA letter sequences of the gene.'

'Therefore, in simple genetic science, the concept of functional and non functional DNA letter sequences within a gene is the basis for the legal problems in GE crops and GM foods. For example, if one wants to transfer a gene into a plant to modify that plant you need only to transfer the DNA letter sequence that allows for a functional gene, not one hundred percent of the gene; maybe less than half of the original gene is necessary for functionality. Therefore an unlimited number of **functional partial genes** could be manufactured as long as the functional DNA letter sequences are present; **several nonfunctional DNA letter sequences could be added** to one end of the gene or to the other end of the gene, and then it would not interfere with the gene's function or code. --- **Therefore many similar genes could all code for the same function in the target cell as long as they have the correct functional DNA letter sequence. So the legal problem is --- because of different nonfunctional DNA letter sequence additions to one or both ends of a functional DNA letter sequence, are these all the same gene?** --- You now have potentially many different genes having the same function! Different companies use such similar but different genes in their GE or GM products. Each similar-different gene could have its own patent. This is where patent law interpretations are critical in trying to solve the multi-billion dollar problems related to genetic changes for the dining room table.'


'I like to think of it as the same Christmas gift just wrapped in different Christmas wrappings. Do different wrappings make it a different gift?' Examples;

## DNA SEQUENCING IN A NORMAL-ALTERED GENE

**NON-FUNCTIONAL     FUNCTIONAL     NON-FUNCTIONAL**

1-2-3-4-5-6-7-8-9-10++++++++++++++++++145-146-147-148-149-150

41     42     43     44     45     46     47

Natural gene:     ++++*AAA*-*GTA*-*GGT*-**TCA**-**TAG**-**GGG**-**CTT**++++

New gene #333:  ++++*GAG*-*GTA*-*GGT*-**TCA**-**TAG**-**GGG**-**CTT**++++

New gene #666:  ++++*AAA*-*GTA*-*GGT*-**TCA**-**TAG**-**CGC**-**CTT**++++

'In this above example, for the natural gene has the DNA letter sequences of 1 to 150. The DNA letter sequences 1-43 and 92-150 are non-functional DNA letter sequences, the functional DNA letter sequence is 44-91. Only the DNA letter sequence 44-91 is necessary for the gene to code for a functional message (sentence) to the cell; the DNA letter sequences 1-43 and 92-150 are extra and unnecessary information. These latter are wrappings on the gift.'

'In this above example, for the new gene #333 there is a change in gene code 41, from AAA to GAG. This change occurred within the non-functional DNA letter sequence, 1-43 is not in the functional DNA letter sequence; so #333 is a new gene but it should act as a normal natural gene and code for the correct message. This is a new wrapping.'

'In the above example, for new gene #666 there is a change in gene code 46, from GGG to CGC. This change occurred within the functional DNA letter sequence, 44-92; so #666 is a new gene but it will not work because the mutation is in a functional DNA letter sequence, hence a critical region. #666 cannot be decoded into the correct special protein, or it may not even be decoded into any functional protein. This is a new gift.'

'When life becomes organs, tissues, cells, nuclei, mitochondria, chromosomes, genes, gene codes, DNA letter sequences, and mutations, how is any lawyer supposed to defend or defeat court cases involving GE crops and GM foods. I guess I just keep learning.'

On Monday morning William had a court case involving GE crops in which he must argue this science. He better get it right.

William Bassinger's client was National Genetics of Indianapolis. For the past 5 years they had been successfully marketing a gene which prevented a deadly corn borer disease in corn. They had a patent on this gene. Two years ago Sunshine Genetics of Chicago began marketing the "same" gene but in a "modified" state - same gift but in a different wrapping. They had applied for a patent on this "modified" gene but had not yet received it. However the patent was pending. National Genetics was suing Sunshine Genetics for ten billion dollars for patent rights infringement.

On Monday morning Bill was up and out of the house before 7:00 AM. He wanted to re-review several components of the case before court time at 9:00AM, so he stopped at his office for an hour of study and a second cup of coffee. He arrived at the United States District Court, Southern District of Iowa on Walnut Street in Des Moines at 8:45AM and entered the court room. It was a modern, typical government quality room which would hold about fifty people. The case would be decided only by the judge. And Bill had been in this room defending clients many times.

Mr. Harry Robertson, Esq. from Green, Dunningham, Roberts, Miller, and Associates arrived. He would represent this law firm who were handling the defendant, Sunshine Genetics Corporation. Bill did not know Mr. Robertson; but of course, he went over and introduced himself, shook hands and wished him luck ('he would need it'). His associate, Mr. John Gelman, Esq. arrived, late as usual.

They barely had time to exchange greetings as the court room began filling up with people. Two of the arrivals were Mr. Gary Melton and Dr. Karl Oldoni from National Genetics Corporation. Mr. Melton was a 'front office man.' Dr. Oldoni held a PhD in Molecular Genetics, had assisted in the development of the anti-corn borer gene, and would serve as scientific advisor if needed.

Bill welcomed each of them and assured them that everything was under control and he felt positive about the case. But he warned that the case would probably not be decided today because this particular judge usually took some time to make his decisions. By law there was no deadline imposed upon the judge. Bill glanced around the court room and noted several people from the Iowa State Department of Agriculture and from the Department of Food and Drug Control. He also noted several local farmers, representatives of two local law firms, members of several farm products manufacturers and their salesmen, and reporters from the Des Moines Register and Chicago Tribune.

At 9:00 AM the Clerk of the District Court stood and announced the arrival of His Honor Judge Stanton Bellingview. Everyone stood; the judge entered; he sat; everyone else sat; the judge pounded the gavel and the court officially began.

The Clerk read out the case, "The plaintiff, National Genetics Corporation, is suing the defendant, Sunshine Genetics Corporation, for ten billion dollars for patent rights infringement on gene ACB-3528, an anti-corn borer treatment. Mr. Johnson, Krebs, Jansen, Peterson, Birmingham, and Associates will represent National Genetics Corporation; Mr. William Bassinger will give the charges. Mr. Green, Cunningham, Roberts, and Miller and Associates will represent Sunshine Genetics Corporation; Mr. Harry Robertson will contest those charges."

The judge asked, "Are there any comments from the general floor? No, then let us proceed. Mr. Bassinger you may begin."

Mr. Bassinger began. He stood and began walking around the front of the courtroom and in general was looking at all of the people in the room. "Ten years ago the National Genetics Corporation began the development of a new genetic modification technique in an attempt to produce a preventive anti-corn bore treatment in corn. These attempts required two and one half years and cost National Genetics more than one million dollars. The treatment procedure was case tested in 12 different farm areas in Iowa, Illinois, and Indiana over the next two corn growing seasons. This testing cost National Genetics more than three million dollars. The treatment was successful to the extent that today more than one thousand two hundred farmers are using ACB-2538 treatment on more than twenty two million acres of corn in these three states."

William looked directly at the judge to be certain he had his attention, he did.

So he continued. "Adult corn borers are moths. They have a four stage cycle: egg, larva, pupa, and air born. In the larval stage they feed on corn leaves and can destroy a field of corn in three to four days. The Bt toxin gene codes for the Bt toxin which can kill corn borers in the egg or larva stage. Corn cells which carry this gene produce the toxin and directly kill the corn borers before they can become destructive. No other herbicides are needed. This gene is introduced into growing corn via placing the gene into a virus which infects a bacterium, Agrobacterium, and then the bacterium is infected into corn cells. This technique is called micro-projectile bombardment carrier procedure. The bacterium carries the virus, which contains the Bt toxin gene named ACB-2538, into the growing corn cell. National Genetics has also developed and patented this technique. Sunshine Genetics is trying to market a look-alike treatment gene and procedure."

William looked at Mr. Robinson, who only looked back and did not comment.

He continued again. "The Bt toxin gene is 2,489 DNA letters long. Only the middle 1,750 DNA letters are in the sequence that is necessary to provide a functional code to produce an active Bt toxin within the corn cells. Hence the entire gene is not necessary to accomplish this treatment. National Genetics currently have patent rights and is marketing a disease prevention procedure with the entire Bt toxin gene, again named ACB-2538.

Sunshine Genetics have produced a Bt toxin gene which is 1,995 DNA letters long and it includes the middle 1,750 bps that carries the code for the functionally active or essential region of the Bt toxin. They have named their gene ACBM-428. Technically the ACBM-428 gene is the same as the ACB-2538 gene, only that it is a little smaller due to a small portion of the non-essential part of the Bt toxin gene having been removed. Essentially and functionally ACBM-428 is a look-a-like of ACB-2538. It is not a new gene, and in addition Sunshine Genetics does not have a patent for ACBM-428."

Again William looked around again to see if he was being "heard" by Judge Bellingview. The judge nodded for him to continue.

"A second problem is included in this patent rights infringement case. And that is the problem of the gene carrier mechanism that Sunshine Genetics developed and is using. A gene carrier mechanism is necessary to deliver any gene into any cell because as that cell grows the gene and its carrier must also grow. The two major types of gene carriers are bacteria and viruses. Before a cell undergoes cell division into two identical cells, all the genes in that cell must make new identical genes such that each new cell has all of the same genes. However all genes live within chromosomes. So as the chromosomes double in number, so do the contained genes double in number. The Bt toxin gene will not reproduce itself unless it is within a chromosome. So one cannot just inject this gene into a cell and expect that when that cell undergoes cell division into ten million identical cells that the Bt toxin gene will also reproduce itself into ten million new Bt toxin genes, it must be within a chromosome. Hence a gene carrier mechanism is necessary to deliver any gene into the plant cell. We use a bacterium."

"In the treatment procedure that National Genetics has developed and patented the Bt toxin gene is placed into Agrobacterium and enters into the chromosomes of the Agrobacterium. When this Agrobacterium is then infected into all of the growing corn cells, the bacterium carries the Bt toxin gene into the plant cells. The bacterium does not harm the growing corn cells or the corn in general. So, as the corn cells grow, the bacterium grows, and the Bt toxin genes grow. Overall the continued presence of Bt toxin in growing corn is because of the presence of the growing bacterium whose chromosomes contain the Bt toxin."

"Again Sunshine Genetics have attempted to mimic or to do a look-a-like micro-projectile bombardment methodology. They use a cousin bacterium in attempts to accomplish the gene transfer. They use Agro-bacillious-B. This is a synthetically created bacterium. It is a slightly different bacterium, but all of the procedures and methodology are a direct copy of the treatment system that National Genetics have been using for the past eight to ten years."

"In conclusion, we submit to you that the Sunshine Genetics Corporation has infringed twice on the patent rights of the National Genetic Corporation: 1) producing and marketing a look-a-like gene of ACB-2538 currently under patent number 4973018 held by National Genetics, 2) producing and marketing a copy of the gene carrier methodology entitled, micro-projectile bombardment methodology, currently under patent number 8603006, both filed at the United States Patent Office in Washington, DC."

"Your Honor, do you have any questions?"

Judge Bellingview responded with, "not yet."

William Bassinger, Esq. sat down and thought to himself, 'That was well done, I think.'

The court room was silent for a couple of minutes as the judge was making some additional notes. He had been taking notes all through Bill's presentation.

Judge Bellingview called out, "May we hear your rebuttal now, Mr. Robertson."

Harry Robertson, Esq. stood up and approached the judge's bench. He said, "If it pleases your honor, I will try to be concise because my colleague has done a marvelous job of elucidating the science involved in this wrongful law suit."

He stopped and looked up at the judge for a response. He received none.

So he continued. "We fully agree that the transfer of a Bt-toxin gene by the microprojectile bombardment technique has been successfully accomplished by the National Genetics Corporation. However, the question is whether or not the Sunshine Genetics Corporation, in making another Bt-toxin gene and transferring it by the same gene transfer technology, but using a different carrier, results in an infringement on the patents held by the National Genetics Corporation. The answer to that question is no. Gene ACBM-428 is simply a smaller version of the Bt-toxin gene which National Genetics Corporation named ACB-2538. One can produce numerous smaller or larger Bt-toxin genes as long as the final gene product has that middle region of 1,750 DNA letters. Nature does this all of the time. The gene which codes for an enzyme called glucose-6-phosphate dehydrogenase (G6PDH), a critical molecule in the metabolism of glucose especially in diabetics, is found in every living organism. There are more than 150 'different' G6PDH genes, including 3 in man. In all of these genes the critical region or functional DNA letter sequences which code for the functional product are always there, it is the noncritical or non-functional region of DNA letters which are missing or are variable. Therefore all 150 genes throughout nature are similar but different. Gene ACBM-428 is but one of many versions of ACB-2538 that can be prepared and used in anti-corn borer procedures."

"He looked up and he had the judge's full attention, so he continued, "With regard to the gene transfer technology. There are many types of gene transfer procedures currently being used by many groups around the world. Placing a gene into a biological agent which is known to infect certain cells is not new nor is it patentable. Such technology has become commonplace today. The entire effort of gene therapy in human cancers is based upon placing an anti-cancer gene or genes into a virus which infects only the cancer cells and thus delivers the gene or genes specifically into the cancer. Therefore, the National Genetics patent number 8603006 is no longer a legally sustainable patent."

Mr. Robertson finished. "I conclude that utilization of any variations of the Bt-toxin gene and the micro-projectile bombardment technique are not an infringement on the two patents in question – patent number 4973018 and patent number 8603006. Does your Honor have any questions?"

The Judge paused for a moment and carefully looked over his notes. He asked. "What percent of the Bt-toxin gene (ACB-2538) was removed or excluded to yield the smaller version of the gene (ACBM-428)?"

He looked first at Mr. Robertson, who appeared at a loss for words. He then turned to Mr. Bassinger.

William immediately responded, "Less than 20%."

The Judge again checked his notes and asked, "Have plant viruses been used in the transfer of the Bt-toxin gene or its variations in corn plants?"

Again William immediately responded, "No. The plant viruses that have been used in attempts to transfer the Bt-toxin gene are usually lethal to the plants. Only plant bacteria have been successfully used for this transfer."

Judge Bellingview addressed the lawyers and the other people in the court room. "We are seeing and hearing more about this gene transfer in GE and GM situations. And I see several people here from the government and private sector which are involved in this new science. I highly recommend that you people explain this technology to the news media so that in the future my law cases do not turn into science classrooms."

Everyone had a good laugh. Even the judge smiled and said. "I want you news people to learn about this new gene transfer technology for GE crops and GM foods. There will be many more problems with regard to these synthetic genes which are patented, non-patented, patentable, and non-patentable. We Iowans are going to have to learn to live with this new science. And it also points out the numerous possibilities in molecular genetics for foods which are coming down the road right now. How do the Greens know which supermarket food to boycott and which not to boycott?"

And again the courtroom crowd had another good round of smiles and chuckles.

Judge Bellingview continued, "In fact I hope that I am not around to have to solve the legal interpretations, ramifications and disputes which will immediately parallel this new science; the new confusing laws will be a gift from our brilliant politicians, of that I am certain. Thank you, gentlemen for the excellent and succinct presentations. And I thank the rest of you for your kind courtesy during this past hour. We will resume this case of the National Genetics Corporation versus the Sunshine Genetics Corporation in the afternoon at 2:00. Court is adjourned."

Bill left the courthouse not sure whether it was win, lose, or draw. He was not expecting such a technically oriented response from Mr.

Robertson. He thought he was one up on the technology. Yet he had never heard about anti-cancer carrying genes in viruses used in cancer patient therapy! And he probably would not even know the outcome of this case for several weeks!

The afternoon and evening went by in a daze. What more did he need to know to strengthen his argument, to lessen their argument, to project a waste in research expenditures, to document a loss of profits, to prove copy cat status....... With this state of mind he almost expected a dream and was not disappointed:

'It began with a pretty little mouse scampering along a narrow forest trail. She had white fur, pink feet, pink ears, pink eyes, and a cute pink button nose. She was very happy because she was finding little pieces of cheese every few feet. As she nibbled her way away along she got too close to a little shrub when – Bang. A mouse trap suddenly closed and caught her by the tip of her tail. The little mouse started screaming for help. It hurt. Suddenly four big white rats heard her and started toward her. Two approached from up the trail and two approached from down the trail. They were handsome animals as they each had grey-white fur, white feet and ears, and blue eyes. As they got closer to the little mouse they saw that she needed a doctor's help. Suddenly they were wearing white doctor's coats and carrying small baskets. When they reached the little mouse they calmed her down. And then they took from their baskets some needles, thread, and what looked like several tiny beads. The many beads were beautiful as they were composed of every color of the rainbow. The "doctor" rats proceeded to sew the beads onto the little mouse's fur. They sewed them everywhere – legs, sides, front, tummy. As the beads were sowed onto the little mouse the little mouse felt less pain and became happy. When they finished the little mouse looked like she was ready for Christmas. After the rats were satisfied, they walked away, two going up the trail and two going down the trail. Suddenly the beads turned into four only colors – A-G-T-C. The tip of the little tail just fell off, painlessly. The beads started moving and dancing. And then they turned into little birds, flew up in the air above the little mouse, and started singing. The little mouse jumped up and she started dancing while the birds whirled around her singing. The departing rats looked at each other and smiled. Suddenly they had human heads with red hair and jade green eyes.'

* * *

After the startling nightmare several months ago of Janice and the alligators, Charles Collingswood was more determined than ever to join Dr. Janice Stryker's life to his own. He was too late and not able to save his Mother. He would not let that happen to his only other love. She was a very special person and in motion. She could never become just a minister's wife in a small church. And her current focus was on saving the Everglades of Florida. They were being destroyed by urbanization, agriculture development, pollution, hunters, and the annual flooding from hurricanes. He had a special love for plants and animals. He did have a university degree in biology and was very familiar with both plants and animals of the wild. It was obvious to him that if he wanted Janice he would have to join his life to hers. So one night when they were sitting on his mosquito free porch, drinking a California Chardonnay and listening to Tchaikovsky's Swan Lake, Charles brought up the subject of "the joining of their lives."

Charles opened the conversation. "Are you still thinking about using a canoe, instead of the air boat, to sit your traps? I know you have complained in the past about the noise and disruption when you take the noisy critter everywhere."

Janice responded. 'Yes. For some time now I have wanted to switch to a quiet canoe to use for my research. The air boat destroys near-water nests and in-water nests. I'm sure it also kills tadpoles, fish, shrimp, and crabs. And what effects it has on growing shelled animals such as clams, oysters, and muscles, I do not know. Setting and checking my research "live catch" traps would be better if I had a silent water vehicle. But I am not strong enough to paddle a canoe for several hours a day over several days. And I cannot afford to hire a full time helper."

Nonchalantly looking out the window he returned, "I know of a 6 foot 6 inch 220 pound guy that might be available if the compensation was appropriate."

She looked him in the eye, smiled, and said, "Do I know him?"

Charles swallowed twice and responded. "When I was in high school I had always had high grades and I played several sports. In the university I majored in Biology, was on the Dean's list every semester, and continued to play tennis, street basketball, and weekly lap swimming in a nearby pool. I went directly to the seminary. In the seminary I did occasional jogging. But since then, for the past several years, I have performed no exercise, even fast walking. I badly need to build some real exercise into my life style before I get fat and flaccid, and no woman will have me."

Janice smiled and nodded, "I agree."

He continued. "Also I am finding that the ministry, while it is very rewarding from the spiritual and cultural point of view, and I know that I have helped many people, intellectually it is not very challenging. I would like more. I have been reading a variety of environmental magazines. It seems to me that the slow destruction of the Everglades is similar to what is happening around the world – excess environmental carbon dioxide levels, global warming, melting of polar ice regions, increased desertification, increased destruction of forests, always more plants and animals on the disappearing species list, increased factory and city sewage, increased farming pollutants in streams, rivers, and oceans, more and increased ferocity of storms, and on and on."

"Even here in America, the only country in the world which washes cars with drinking water, is in trouble. We can no longer routinely drink out of any faucet or fountain. We now buy and drink water from plastic bottles like the Europeans have been doing for many years. More common people need to organize, stand up, and be heard. The world's life styles must be modified to become less destructive and more protective for all of God's beasts, including mankind."

He stopped and looked at her. She was not sure how to respond. She debated to herself, 'I have always thought this way. I did not know he was of such a similar mind. I had not considered him to be an action man. He is not aggressive, but indeed a big, very bright, gentle person. And I know that if he starts a project it will be done correctly with vigor. Where was this new logic going?'

Charles continued. "I want us to get involved with several of the environmental groups such as the Greens, Save the Everglades, Animal Chaplains, the Wildlife Society for Protection of Animals, and the Wildlife Rehabilitation of the World. I want you to come here and live with me. You can still make your two days a week commute to the UM to teach your classes. We can get married. I can paddle your canoe. And we can have a several children that I will teach to paddle the big canoe such that as I get older and retire from paddling there will be someone to take my place in the canoe, or we can just get a bigger family canoe. OK? And you can believe in a God for animals and I will believe in the Lord. OK?"

Janice was shocked but said, "I think I heard, somewhere between the canoes, a marriage proposal. Did I?"

Charles looked at the floor and muttered, "I guess I heard one too."

Janice replied. "Get up and come over here. Kiss me. How many children do you want?"

Assuming that was a yes and not a no, Charles responded, "More than one but less than ten."

He had a gentle no dream night.

* * *

David Dekker was a happy family man but a not very satisfied professional man. Janet and he had married. David bought a large three bedroom condominium in Arlington which was only a few blocks from the "House". Janet continued to be part of the management of the orphanage, but in a part time role. They now had two babies, fraternal twins. First a boy named Action, and then a girl named Alice. Action had red hair and almond colored eyes: and his personality matched his name. Alice had straw hair and jade blue eyes and made you work to get a smile. She was going to be a serious one. They were beautiful children and she thoroughly enjoyed them. So Janet chose to work part time, and stay at home with the little ones part time.

In Arlington County, only orphanage children over the age of 5 were allowed to go to the local schools, first grade and up. About one half of the current children in the orphanage were over 5, so they were gone from the "House" to the county schools during the day. While the other half remained. Janet had developed a pre-school program for those under five who were capable of learning. So she taught the pre-school children on Monday, Wednesday, and Friday.

A university student in the social sciences, named Isabel Brockly, lived nearby and attended Georgetown University. So Ms Brockly took care of the Dekker children on the three days when Janet taught. While she could be with her children two work week days and all weekend.

David was gone a lot, sometimes a week or more at a time, so it was essential that she have complete command of the home unit of the family when they were both out of the house. It allowed Janet to be with both her home babies and "House" babies. She could have her cake and eat it too, so to speak. She loved the "military" approach to problem solving. And she was a very happy wife, mother, and professional.

David, however, was not entirely satisfied with the Blue Ravens. Over the past several years he and his security team had been very successful, except for one contract, which had been a disaster. In general, the FBI and also the CIA provided necessary security for official American government employees from the President to the Members of Congress to Supreme Court Justices to Heads of Departments to any government official to whom they were assigned. They were also responsible for foreign Heads of State or foreign government officials in the USA on "official" business. In other words they were responsible for the government sector. Therefore most of the private sector, whether they needed or thought they needed security, sought out private security firms such as the Blue Ravens. The Blue Ravens were in demand seven days a week in Washington and frequently elsewhere in the country. And the security was rarely for one person; it was usually for that one person and his accompanying secretaries, assistants, specialists, and sometimes even his family.

Over the years the Blue Ravens and their clients were frequently sitting ducks for well organized attacks on their clients. They needed an intelligence unit which maintained a personal contact and current data base about potential enemies of their clients, in advance of the assignments. After a very bad encounter in which two of his men were killed, Dave threatened to resign if such a data base on current and future clients was not established within the Blue Ravens Security Firm. The Board of Directors agreed and gave Dave one year away from the field to do just that. He became very successful at selected risk analysis for each client or group of clients.

With the assistance of the FBI, CIA, and the Pentagon, David was able to establish a liaison relationship which would allow the Blue Ravens to utilize certain data within certain data bases upon the basis of need to know. Need to know was generally defined as current and immediate future security contract relationships. Whenever a contract was signed by a client it gave the Blue Ravens permission to undertake select research into the background of that client with the purpose of identifying any potential security risk to that client. So they began to build up a data base of their own for use in identifying, in advance, specific risk factors such as a business background with any adverse competition, negative family relationships, general health status, political relationships, interactions with dissident groups, known enemies, etc. The contract also included complete legal non-disclosure rights for the client, such as to encourage the client to assist in the accumulation of such information. After all, it was his life that they were trying to protect. For those who would not cooperate, no contract would be signed.

A couple of years earlier the Blue Ravens Security Firm's Board of Directors implemented a new Division of Intelligence (BRDI). They appointed David Dekker as the first Director. This would turn out to be a major improvement in their operations. It also made Dave very happy since now he had a real challenge that he felt positive about. Would knowledge before the fact prevent the fact from happening? He did not have long to wait.

A few months later, Mr. Cousino Azocar, President of the Antofagasta Copper and Minerals Company, from Santiago, Chile, signed a contract with the Blue Ravens Security Firm to provide security for himself and three business colleagues for a five day tour in the USA. They would spend two days in Atlanta and three days in Los Angeles. While accumulating the background information on Mr. Azocar, Dave noticed that Mr. Azocar had recently divorced his wife after twenty six years of marriage. The ex-Mrs. Azocar had an older brother who was at a "senior level" in the Bolivian drug cartel; and he was unhappy with the slight to his family. However Dave found no public threats in any direction in the local newspapers. But this was certainly a direction from which to watch for trouble.

David called up a friend who had lived many years in Chile and was currently Assistant Director in the State Department and was responsible for South American Affairs. He wanted some advice concerning family affairs.

"Hi Dan," David spoke up. "How are you doing with the latest uprising in Venezuela? Is it finally coming under some control? Will you have some time to have a beer some evening this week?"

Dan answered, "Hi Dave. Good to hear from you. Yes, things will be quiet for a few weeks maybe. With the increased drug movement through that area conflicts will probably pop up again soon. I'm sorry but I am leaving for Brazil in two days and cannot get free before that. When I return I will give you a call and we can try a beer on for size; but I promise not to try to match you in mug numbers. So what can I do for you right not?"

"I can limit it to a couple of quick questions," Dave replied. "Have you heard of Cousino Azocar?"

Dan answered, "Yes, he is President of Antofagusta Copper and Minerals in Santiago, Chile. He is a big man in the minerals world and close friends of the current President of Chile. Why?"

Dave explained, "We have a contract to protect him while he is here in DC for a few days and I was looking around for personal or professional enemies that he might have picked up over the years. He recently divorced his wife who has family involved in some of the drug cartels. Should I look for any personal problems from such family relationships?"

"Very definitely yes," Dan answered. "These people consider their families number one. So if Mr. Azocar has insulted a cartel member's family, he needs extra protection until that insult has been 'taken care of'."

We have pictures of her family members who are in the two cartels, said Dave. "I guess our best bet is to watch for any illegal entries from Chile and watch the crowd for family-cartel members. Do you recommend anything else?'

"Yes," replied Dan. "Monitor flights out of Chile for cartel members. And have a couple of Spanish-Americans on your team such that you can better monitor faces and overhear Spanish speakers in the immediate vicinity of your boy as you move around the city."

Dave finished, "Good ideas. We will follow up on everything. I admit that I am nervous on this one because family revenge is more difficult than a simple professional hit. Thank you for taking time to share your excellent advice, as always. When you return from Brazil give me a call. We can have a beer and I promise no more than a two to one mug advantage."

Dan responded, "I have a better idea. You use the quart size mug and I will use a pint size mug. OK?"

Dave said, "Whatever will make you happy."

They both laughed and hung up

Mr. Azocar and his group arrived at the Hartsfield Atlanta International Airport at 11 AM, where the Blue Ravens' team led by John Boston met them. They picked the Chileans up in two large land rovers and took them to the Hilton Hotel on Hill Street. They escorted them to scheduled appointments all afternoon, evening and the next morning.

In the afternoon of the second day they all returned to Atlanta International and flew by first class on Southwest Airlines to Los Angeles. After arriving at Los Angeles International Airport, John had again arranged for two large land rovers to use to escort Mr. Azocar and his associates through the downtown area and on to the Four Seasons Hotel in Buena Park. They rested for the remainder of the day and ate in the hotel that night. The group had not yet fully recovered from the Santiago to Atlanta trip.

The next morning the Blue Raven's team picked them up from the hotel when Jim Riley, who had grown up in the San Diego-Los Angeles area, thought he recognized a familiar face in the lounge area of the hotel. He was specifically on the team to monitor Spanish looking faces. They climbed into the cars and took off. During the ride Jim opened his lap top and scanned through the more than 100 pictures that he had previously down loaded. These were pictures of Mr. Azocar's family, family members of his associates, cartel members and any other "high risk" people that might be a potential problem during this assignment. Yes, he had recognized a face. It was Anjo Garcia. Anjo Garcia was a Chilean and a friend of the brother of the recent ex-Mrs. Azocar. He would be someone to watch out for. Jim made copies of Anjo Garcia and gave to all of the Blue Raven team members.

The last appointment in the afternoon was at the Delgado Copper Mining Company building off of Hawthorn Avenue. As the group was leaving the building they spotted Anjo Garcia walking toward them. When he got close he drew from his coat pocket an Uzi machine pistol and pointed it at Mr. Azocar. The Blue Raven team was ready. As Anjo Garcia had been slowly approaching the group, Jerry Green of the team had slipped around behind. When Mr. Garcia made his move, Jerry quickly wrestled him to the ground before Anjo could get a shot off. They cell phoned a nearby police unit, had him arrested and placed under police custody until Mr. Azocar and his associates left the country two days later. It turned out that Anjo Garcia had a green card and was legally working in San Diego. He was charged with carrying a concealed weapon and attempted murder. Indeed, knowledge before the fact probably saved at least one man's life, possibly several.

A couple of weeks later there was an almost repeat performance. Mr. Tasila de Caminha, CEO and President of Companhia Siderurgica de Tubarao, from Fortalaza, Brazil, contracted with the Blue Raven Security Firm for three days of security in New York City. This company was one of the world's largest steel manufacturing companies. Mr. Caminha and two of his company executives were attending a private meeting of CEOs from seven other major steel manufacturers located in Europe, Asia, and the USA. The entire three day meeting would take place in a private conference room in the Hyatt Regency Hotel on the Avenue of the Americas in Manhattan. There was reason to believe of a possible assassination by the Brazil Freedom Saviors. They were an anti-capitalist terrorist gang.

The Blue Ravens' team, lead by Dick Atkinson, picked the three Brazilians up from JF Kennedy Airport at 5:00 PM on Wednesday evening. They were taken in an explosion proof limousine, escorted in front and in back by two bullet proof Landrovers with two agents in each. While one agent rode shotgun in the limousine. They slowly worked their way through rush hour traffic to the Hotel. Everyone checked in. One 3 bedroom suite was reserved for Mr. Carminha and his people, and an adjacent-connecting room was for the team members. Everything went smoothly.

Usually for a hotel meeting such as this one, where there are many important foreigners, the hotel brings on board extra security people. However they also allow and cooperate with private security people hired by the guests. Thus the cooperation included showing the guest's security people the location of the security control room, the security camera and voice recorder units, introduction to hotel security staff that were assigned to the meeting, routes of secure and non-secure entry to the hotel, elevator control keys, and emergency exits. They did not anticipate any problems but would appreciate being informed of any unusual happenings and the sharing of any changes in schedules. It looked to be well organized and the Blue Raven team relaxed down a notch.

The conference began at 9:00 AM on Thursday morning with a general introduction of each of the CEOs from the eight largest steel manufacturing companies in the world; in turn each CEO introduced his key associates. The purpose was to discuss ideas concerning the establishment of a new organization to be called the International Steel Manufacturers Cooperative (ISMC). Such an organization would be patterned after the Oil Producing Exporters Cooperative (OPEC) with similar types of goals, to influence the international steel prices. Over the next two days each CEO had an opportunity to express his feeling concerning such organizational efforts. The talk was quite positive.

Mr. Carminha was the last speaker on Saturday morning. His English was not very good and he was very nervous. He had not slept for the last two nights. He was seventy three years old, rather badly overweight, and looked forward to retirement in a couple of years. His overall general health was not great. He was on medication but in the excitement he forgot his medicine and left it at home. He would replenish it when he returned home. When the invitation to attend this conference arrived, he attempted to send a substitute, but the President of Brazil called him and said he would attend. So he came.

As Mr. Carminha got up to speak he broke out in a heavy sweat. He started hyperventilating; his eyes rolled back into his head; he took off his coat and tried to loosen his tie. He then stumbled down off of the podium and ran out the conference room door. He pulled open a nearby hallway door and headed down a back steel stairway which was used only by hotel service staff. Riggins Holms, a member of the Blue Ravens, was one step behind. As Mr. Carminha lost his balance and started to fall down the stairs, Riggins caught him, pulled him back, and wrestled him to the floor. Mr. Carminha started thrashing around, jerking his arms and legs in all directions, striking the stairway's steel railing, hitting his head on the wall, twisting and turning. Within a few seconds Dick Atkinson arrived and the two of them put Dick's coat under the man's head, placed a billfold between his teeth, and simply lay down on top of him.

Dave was running down the hallway with the hotel's emergency medic and they arrived just as Mr. Carminha had stopped moving. David was afraid he had died of a heart attack.

Finally Mr. Carminha's breathing slowed, and suddenly his eyes closed and he started snoring. He had gone to sleep. About ten minutes later Mr. Carminha slowly woke up and asked the gentlemen lying on top of him what happened. He did not remember and had a migraine headache. He asked them if they would kindly get off of him as he had a speech to give. They helped him recover. And then the two Blue Ravens' members, and Mr. Carminha and his associates went into a nearby office and David explained to him what happened

Several days ago, after David Dekker finished preparing the background information on Mr. Carminha, business associates, family, and certain friends, he started reviewing the information looking for a weak unit. The key to better security was to identify potential problems before the fact. The man was old, not healthy, and with his weak English he would be hyper-stressed in front of a group of 'equals'. In addition he had epilepsy. His medical history referred to approximately one epileptic seizure every year or two. As long as he stayed on his medicine and was not overly stressed he would be OK. Potential danger! So David assigned Riggins Holms to the team for these three days. Riggins had been a medic for six years in the army. And he had experience with epileptic seizures. So he was assigned to stay close to Mr. Carminha, especially if a stressful situation should appear. It appeared, he stayed close, the correct therapy was applied, and again, knowledge before fact probably saved a man's life.

A few months later on the third anniversary of the BRDI, a big in-house party was held to celebrate the successful utilization of "knowledge before the fact". The BRDI was given credit for ten 'special take-downs' and the saving of thirty five lives including the lives of several Blue Raven agents. David and Janet were ecstatic that evening. Rightfully David was a new conquering hero, for a while. Until he went to sleep:

'His dream opened and he found himself walking beside a tall red headed, jade green eyed man. They entered a gate which said Welcome to the Garden of Fours. A large thick overgrown garden-forest opened out in front them. Numerous evergreen and deciduous trees, shrubs of all shades of green, and flowers of many different colors were everywhere. As they strolled through the garden they spotted many unusual things. Trees grew in clusters of four. Each of the trees had only 4 branches, each branch had 4 leaves. Shrubs grew in clusters of four. The shrubs also had only 4 branches each and 4 leaves on each branch. All of the flowers were in clusters of 4. And each flower had only 4 petals. When they began looking for animals they spotted a family of rabbits. Examining each closely they saw that each rabbit had 4 eyes and 4 ears. They turned around and saw a deer running by. The deer had 4 eyes and 4 ears. This was also true for a pair of nearby raccoons who had 4 eyes and 4 ears. As they went deeper into the garden they heard loud noises off to their right. They went in that direction. Soon they saw the cause of the noise. A large bear and a mountain lion were growling at each other; they were at a standoff. Both the bear and the mountain lion each had 4 eyes and 4 ears. David did not understand any of this and began to think himself as going crazy. Then they heard some people talking. They went toward the people hoping to obtain an explanation for all of this craziness. When they arrived, David looked at the people. They each had 4 eyes and 4 ears. He turned back to his friend. His friend had disappeared. And he woke up. He hyperventilated for several moments and simply could not get back to sleep.'

# 7 – There Are Two of Us

Doctor Aaron and Doctor Josephine Armand had twins nine months and one day after they were married. They named the two minute older boy, Hype; and the two minute younger girl, Hope. Hype had red hair and almond colored eyes. Hope had straw blond hair and jade blue eyes. They were about the same size when born. But Hype was a voracious eater, quickly gained weight, and became the larger of the two. The rest of their lives he was always the bigger and more physical. Hope was not small; she was aggressive, always just one half step behind her brother, and it was obvious from her eating and playing habits that she would match him in many areas of life. But Hype was simply not capable of slowing down. He was "stopped" only when he was asleep. Hope liked her hugs. While one was lucky if they could get Hype to sit on their lap longer that thirty seconds and only then if he was occupied by eating a candy sucker or playing with a new "thing." Both were going to be very active kids.

The four Armands purchased and moved into a house across the Hudson River in Ridgefield Park, New Jersey. The George Washington Bridge was nearby and made the commute to the Columbia University Medical Campus only twenty to thirty minutes. The new Center for Cellular and Genetic Biology of Twinning was in motion. Columbia University had temporarily assigned three laboratories in an affiliated laboratory research building, fifteen beds, and some office space in an affiliated hospital to Aaron to start his research projects and to begin the foundation work for the Center.

He identified both private and government funding sources. Several NGOs including the American Twinning Association, the International Diabetes Society, and the International Association of Behavior and Change, and the American Cancer Society had provided start up monies. Two private foundations, the Fanderback Trust Fund and the Laurence and Constance Lenningear Foundation gave substantial amounts of research funds. The Eastern Biotech Laboratories and the Gen-Bio Corporation (GBC), both private sector high tech labs, were assisting by providing money for equipment and were interested in sharing future projects.

And they had a three year core establishment grant from the National Institutes of Health to provide salaries for key researchers, secretaries, and administrative staff.

Columbia U. had identified approximately an acre of land on the medical campus for a new twelve floor CCGBT hospital and laboratory building. They currently were trying to identify a large donation near seventy to eighty million dollars to construct the new building and thus establish the first molecular oriented research program on human behavior in the world. They were actively talking with Mr. James Stevenson and Mr. John Stevenson, both New York bankers, about a building construction donation. The Stevensons were from a long family line of twins. Every generation for more than one hundred and twenty years had at least one set of twins per generation, so obviously they had a strong interest in such a research center.

Aaron sat back in his desk chair and began thinking of the future research questions that needed answers. He thought, 'My research people have already identified twenty eight pairs of identical twins and more than forty pairs of fraternal twins. Most of these voluntary research participants have already undergone a variety of behavior testing procedures; and most live in the New York Metropolitan area therefore they can come to an appointment upon short notice. This makes it really excellent for research purposes as the research teams do not have to arrange their scheduling weeks in advance. When certain gene patterns or DNA sequences are identified from a set of identical or paternal twins which are thought to be related to a specific behavioral characteristic or characteristics, such as hostility or language fluidity, this can be quickly checked with other identical twins and with paternal twins which are known to have similar behavioral characteristics. Such experiments can be completed in a two or three weeks instead of two or three months.'

'And what kinds of questions will the CCGBT investigate over the years? We will seek gene patterns and DNA sequence relationships, using cells taken from identical and paternal twins; and we will try to relate this genetic data to a wide variety of unknowns:'

'1) domestic or general behavioral characteristics such as: alpha versus beta personalities, aggressiveness versus passivity, mental aggression versus physical aggression, high basal energy versus low basal energy levels, controlled versus uncontrolled emotions, controlled versus uncontrolled environments, control of versus loss of temper, high versus low intelligence (IQ), high versus low mathematics and science skills, rapid versus slow problem solving, computer literacy, high tech interests, capacity for language learning, susceptibility to common diseases, winter colds, preferences or choice for wives, children, male friends, female friends, same sex, specific tastes in foods, type of pets, style of houses, colors-style of clothes, color-type of car, gifts for friends, city life, country life, vacations, sports, recreational activities, challenges, occupations, groups, emotional linkages.'

'2) criminal relationships such as physical violence with hands, knives, guns, or explosives, rape, murder, sadistic behavior, torture.'

'3) and diseases such as certain cancers, cystic fibrosis, Prader-Willi syndrome, Angelman syndrome, hemophilia, muscular dystrophy, Huntington's disease, sickle cell anemia, Alzheimer's disease, Parkinson's disease, and spinal cerebrellar ataxias.'

'This extensive type of data gathering requires that the CCGBT must have the capacity to measure and evaluate chromosomes, genes, internal gene sequences, segmental DNA analysis, single DNA-letter alterations, etc. To perform any such analysis, first live cells must be taken from the research participant, usually by cheek swabs, and then the genes have to be separated from their chromosomes. After separation, they have to be cut into small segments to be able to analyze. Cutting into small segments is easily accomplished using a molecule called an enzyme-scissors.'

'There are more than one hundred enzyme-scissors that can be used. Each enzyme-scissors cuts in a different place, such as: enzyme-scissors #1 could cut between the two Gs in the following DNA-letter sequence – T-G-G-A-C-G-A-T-C-....; enzyme-scissors #2 could cut between the two As in the following DNA-letter sequence – G-A-A-G-C-C-T-G-..... ; enzyme-scissors #3 could cut between an A-T when surrounded by Cs as in the following DNA-letter sequence – G-C-C-A-T-C-C-G-...., etc. The cut group sequences (3 to 12 DNA-letters long) are then separated by various laboratory instruments, each of which focuses on different chemical characteristics of the individual DNA-letters. Different combinations of DNA-letters allow for different separation characteristics. Hence G-G-T-T-T can be easily separated from G-G-T-G-T. So by using different enzyme-scissors and different instruments of separation a researcher can obtain several different DNA fingerprints or DNA profiles from the same research participant. All senior technicians will learn how to do this as it is the key to understanding the genetic basis of human behavior.'

'The Center must have the capacity to use the following different DNA and protein analysis procedures: PRC thermocycler (for polymerase chain reaction), northern-southern-western blotting analyses, RFLP (for restriction fragment length polymorphism), STP (for short tandem repeats), AmpFLP (for amplified fragment length polymorphism), Y-chromosome analysis, mitochondria DNA analysis, DOT Blotting analysis, microarray analysis, genomic analysis, VNTR loci used in the CODIS database for forensic identification. These analyses will allow relationships or linkages to specific DNA sequences of Gs-As-Ts-Cs, groups of DNA sequences or even single DNA-letter changes which could occur concurrently with a specific behavior pattern or patterns.'

'And the reason for such high technology is simply because there are approximately ten billion DNA-letters which contain around one hundred thousand genes in every set of forty six chromosomes in the nucleus in every cell in the human body; however only about twenty thousand genes are necessary for human functioning. Monkey's genes are 97% similar to human's genes. The entire human population has 98% of the same genes. Humans thus differ between each other by only about 1-2% of all human genes. Therefore, individual humans differ from each other because of the differences in a few million DNA-letters within about a few thousand genes. Identical twins differ from each other because of differences of a few thousand DNA-letters within a few hundred genes. So measuring these small differences in the DNA-letters in the genes is critical. This is indeed high technology at the leading edge of knowledge. And we will do it.'

The development of the Center and the beginnings of Aaron's research program were progressing nicely. The Fifteenth International Conference on Cellular and Molecular Biology was going to be held at the Hyatt Regency Golf and Marine Resort on the Big Choptank River in Cambridge, Maryland during the first week in October, two weeks from now. Aaron was planning to attend for first three of the five days meeting. This resort was located about one hour south and east of Washington, DC, near Annapolis, Maryland. And because it was only about three to four hours from New York City he had decided to drive. Then he could stop on the way back to see the National Institute of Health people in Bethesda, Maryland. He was looking forward to listening to research reports from the world's best scientists concerning the newest technologies for analyzing genes, gene sequences, and DNA-letter sequences. There was a proposed new technique for measuring certain DNA-letter sequences that contained five successive Gs. And -G-G-G-G-G- sequences were reported to be related to aging via apoptosis mechanisms. He would go and learn. In this new world of playing with genes the methodology changed every month, and he must stay up-to-date.

* * *

The Blue Ravens Security Firm had just signed a contract with a scientific delegation from the National University of Nanchang. Dr. Chang Wu, Director of the Research Center of U. Nanchang had arranged for a delegation of fifteen Chinese scientists to attend the Fifteenth International Conference on Cellular and Molecular Biology which was being held during the first week in October at the Hyatt Regency Golf and Marine Vacation Resort on the Choptank River in Cambridge, Maryland. The contract was for a seven day period which began one day before and ended one day following this conference. The Chinese delegation would fly in and out of the Baltimore-Washington International Airport, less than one hour by surface travel to the Hyatt Regency Resort. The Blue Ravens Security Firm would arrange escorted and secure transportation to the conference, during the conference, and upon return to the BWI Airport. The Chinese were providing a small jet for the international travel.

There was only one problem. When David Dekker requested information from the Chinese government concerning the members of the group, he was stone walled. The Chinese government was less than cooperative about supplying the requested information. The best he was able to determine was that each member was a doctor and was on the university web site as teaching faculty of the National Nanchang University. If there was a terrorist in the group, David would never know until too late. He wrote and submitted an official report on these identification and data collection problems to the President of the Blue Ravens and also to the Central Intelligence Agency. The President said go; and the CIA said that because there would be more than one hundred and fifty foreign scientists attending out of more than two thousand attendees they would also be sending three agents. No trouble was expected. And the CIA would provide photographs of each of the Chinese scientists. That would be very useful. It seemed that everything would work itself out.

As usual Dave spent several hours going through the research data and information concerning the hotel, the conference, scientific and non-scientific programs, important foreign and American speakers, key ranking scientists within the Chinese delegation, routes of travel, face recognition, and made an extensive attempt at identifying potential preventable problems.

Dave decided to call in his team captain for the weeklong meeting, brief him, and go over some potential problems. His name was Johnston Utreker and had been with the Blue Ravens for many years.

Johnston entered Dave's office and Dave motioned for him to sit.

Dave asked. "Are you preparing the team for the Maryland meeting next week?'

Johnston replied. "Yes we are putting together the routine equipment and packing extra weapons just in case. We have not been told that there is terrorist danger, but I thought it would be better to be prepared."

"I agree, better safe than sorry so they say," Dave continued. "I want to discuss the Chinese delegation and this science conference next week in Cambridge, Maryland. We have not had very good cooperation from the Chinese government, but the FBI has filled the gap and I think we will be all right. We have the names and pictures of each Chinese scientist. However it will be fifteen scientists and only eight of us plus me, and I need to leave from the meeting early. The Hyatt Regency Golf and Marine Resort is very large complex of several buildings. I have been going over the Resort architectural plans and this will be very difficult. It will not be possible for us to 'protect' each Chinese scientist on a one to one basis. The best we can do is grouping, but I doubt that the Chinese will cooperate for this. We may have to have a different plan for each day, and be ready to change that plan if something goes wrong or simply requires that we change it. Let us go through some scenarios that I have been considering."

"The entire conference would be held within the Hyatt Regency Resort, including all meals. And there would be special security control at entry and departure routes. General security seems well controlled and reasonably tight. Therefore, a terrorist event would not be high on the list of potential problems. A more likely occurrence would be a switch of people, someone sneaking in and/or sneaking out of the United States (spy games). He will need a couple of Blue Raven agents who are familiar with Oriental faces and mannerisms. There are no super wealthy international corporation CEOs coming, so assassination or high level kidnapping seems remote. American medical scientists take home $50,000 per year; while the Chinese medical scientists take home $5,000 per year. So kidnapping of a Chinese scientist is not likely."

"Almost 20% of the attendees to the conference are women; and two members of the Chinese delegation are women. So, at least one Blue Raven agent will be female (to handle any possible rest room or other delicate problems). I wish that I really had more data on the Chinese delegation to use. But we do not. Maybe things will become more obvious to us when the conference begins. Then we can then rework the thinking of how we can better function. Do you have any comments for now?"

"It would be a good idea to have a quick group meeting late each evening before we go to bed," said Johnston. "I would touch base with everyone who was covering certain Chinese scientists, present a summary of activities of that day, and then we can discuss and plan the next day's coverage."

"Good idea," responded Dave. We can make changes each day in advance where necessary."

* * *

The Sunday afternoon before the conference was to begin, the Blue Raven team assembled at the BWI airport in the hanger for special international flights. Customs and Passport Control were always in place there and they were ready for the Chinese flight to arrive in one hour. Dave re-affirmed his assignment of Johnston Utreker, as Captain of the team. Johnston was a typical clean cut American, middle aged, married with two sons, a solid middle class level headed leader. He had been with the Blue Ravens for 15+ years and had performed flawlessly on contracts with both domestic and foreign groups.

The team had its normal six agents (Mike, Roger, Jack, Henry, Dapaw, and Walter) plus two additional. Betty Hu was a thirty-five year old American-Chinese. She was born in China; her parents moved to Los Angeles when she was eight; so she was about as half Chinese-half American as you could get. Betty was single, served 6 years in the American army, and had been with the Blue Ravens for five years. David trusted her to carefully match and monitor pictures with faces and carefully watch for any switches of "scientists" during the seven day period. This would certainly be difficult to directly assist her.

In addition, one other new team member was added. Do Wong was fifty two years old and from South Korea, but had lived in several countries in Southeast Asia including China. He spoke some Mandarin Chinese. Do was being borrowed from another Blue Ravens team for the week. He would assist Betty in face recognition, monitor conversations among the scientists, and be available in any possible negative male-female cultural interactions with the Chinese and Ms. Hu. All team members knew each other so only Do Wong had to be introduced around and welcomed to the Cambridge team.

Dave had a map of the large Hyatt Regency Resort complex. And he posted it on a wall and went over it for the benefit of the entire team.

Dave said, "This Complex is more than one hundred acres in size and is located directly on the Choptank River which is more than a mile wide at this point. The river enters directly into the Chesapeake Bay which enters into the Atlantic Ocean at New Port, Virginia. Many international yachts will be using the first class facilities in the marina. So you will need to keep an eye on the marina as we monitor our guest scientists. As you enter the complex from route US#50 you have to cross several small wooden bridges which cross over winding creeks that snake through the professional status eighteen hole golf course."

"After following this meandering road through the golf course you arrive at a five building hotel cluster in the center of the golf course and marina complex. The large circular central building in the center is called the Chesapeake Building. It is eight floors high and has an Eagle's Nest restaurant on the top. This building contains several lounges, the more expensive hotel suites, conference rooms, and other connected rooms, three restaurants, two swimming pools, exercise rooms, spa, sauna, games rooms, and other recreational facilities. Four rectangular buildings, each three floors high are connected to the central building and run in four lateral directions out into the golf course and down toward the marina. These buildings are named Heron, Eagle, Hawk, and Osprey, local predator birds. They each contain two hundred and fifty bedrooms and one café-pub in each building."

"The Chinese scientists will stay in adjoining rooms on the first floor in the Heron building is near the river. Our Blue Ravens team's rooms are directly across the hallway from the Chinese delegation's rooms in the Heron building. The in-house security check points, remote TV cameras, and control rooms for the entire complex are located on the second floor of the Chesapeake Building. All of these security points are carefully laid out on this particular map that I will give to Johnston. Now please note. One camera in the Heron building is focused down the hallway where the Chinese scientists and us are located. I am having that camera record every minute of every day for future data reference. I have carefully marked angles of vision for the group of rooms for the Blue Raven team, for the Chinese delegation's rooms, and located other specific areas of rotational monitoring for each day."

"The scientific program changes every morning, afternoon, and evening for all five days. Sometimes there will be ten simultaneous presentations by ten different scientists in ten rooms that would each seat one hundred participants. Sometimes there will be two simultaneous speeches by two senior people in two rooms that would each seat several hundred participants. And sometimes there will be only one "super" talk by a "special" leader in the cellular and molecular biology research field. The latter will take place during the evening in a large ballroom which can hold more than two thousand people. In addition the ballroom can be subdivided into five conference rooms that will each seat four hundred participants. During the week there will even be two sit-down dinners in this ballroom on two different evenings; and this always includes a key note address by a famous scientist. Tuesday night the speaker will be Dr Talbert Sonerberg, Director of the National Institutes of Health, USA. Thursday night the speaker will be Dr Erica Thomason, Finland, 2006 Nobel Laureate in Biochemistry and Medicine."

"So there will be continuous movement between the many rooms at different times of the day and evening, and throughout most areas of the resort complex. There are four café-pubs and four restaurants for dining areas to choose from for each mealtime. There is also the golf course and a boating-sailing marina available for those scientists who run out of scientific energy, and need to break away for a couple of hours and rent some sunshine."

"In general, it is basically impossible to monitor everything or follow fifteen different participants every minute of every day for the five days of the scientific conference; even with a fifteen person team it would be very difficult. The best we can do is to remain close to the Chinese delegation; hopefully they will remain somewhat grouped anyway much of the time due to Chinese-English translation language difficulties."

"If I understand correctly every talk in every meeting will be in English with no translations. When the group splits into smaller groups or individuals we will have to also split and stay with as many of them as we can. And of course we will always have an agent near the hotel rooms where the delegation is staying, to protect against unwanted intruders, camera coverage or not. Therefore, following and watching is about all we do unless/until something negative happened. Does anyone have any questions?"

Betty spoke up, "I assume that you want me to stay with the two women Chinese scientists as much as is possible. If they separate what do I do?"

Dave answered, "Yes, if the two of them split we will try to use one of the male team members to help. But I think that the male Chinese scientists will also split into individuals or small groups of two or three. All we can do is to keep our eye on as many of them as we can most of the time."

Johnston reminded Dave, "Dave requested that I obtain a brief summary from you at the end of each day and make written notes of what you saw happening. We will then all meet in Dave's room, which is the center room in our series of rooms, at 11:00 PM each evening. I will give this brief summary and we can approve or change it to make certain it is accurate. Each of you can make a direct contribution. Then we can discuss the next day's scientific programming and make plans accordingly."

"Johnston is right." Dave responded. "I think every day will be different and we must think ahead and be ready. Are there any questions now? If you think of something later please ask Johnston or me. This is an important international scientific delegation. We have to do it right."

* * *

The private Chinese jet touched down at 4:00 PM on Sunday. All passengers disembarked and went through passport control and customs. They were then loaded onto the private bullet proof bus which had been rented just for this special contract. After all of the scientists had settled into a seat, David Dekker stepped to the front of the bus.

"Welcome to the United States of America. My name is David Dekker. I am the Director of Intelligence of the Blue Raven Security Firm of Washington, DC. We have a team of eight agents, extensively trained in security procedures and techniques. We will be with you the entire seven days, both on the road, going and coming, and inside the Hyatt Regency Golf and Marine Vacation Resort. Let me introduce each of these people to you such that if there is any problem you can immediately approach them and let them try to solve the problem for you.'

He stepped back a little. "Step up here when I call your name such that our guests can see your faces. First is the Captain of our team, Mr. Johnston Utreker. Mr. Utreker has had more than fifteen years of experience with us providing security for American and foreign groups. And you never lost a single client, right John?"

There was just a big smile on John's face.

David continued. "Next is Ms. Betty Hu. Ms. Hu was born in China, and as a school child came with her parents to the USA. She is almost perfectly half Chinese and half American. She is on our team to help us communicate with you about any and all things. None of the rest of our team can speak Chinese. Ms. Hu will have to help us understand each other. The other team members are lined up just outside this window. They will always wear these Blue Ravens name tags on their jackets so you can approach them for information and assistance anytime. We will try to stay close to you but not get in your way, if that is possible."

And he smiled while watching for smiles from the Chinese scientists to determine who did and who did not understand English. Only three Chinese scientists smiled.

He then continued to introduce the other members of the Blue Raven team, one by one. After the introductions he asked if there were any questions from any of the guest scientists. One scientist asked about the geography of the area, Washington and Baltimore and Philadelphia and New York.

Dave was rather surprised because those four cities haven't been moved in the past three hundred years. He was certain that the Chinese had extensive and up to date maps of the United States.

Nevertheless, he took a few minutes and gave a brief history of the central eastern coastline of the USA, and then of the Cambridge area. Betty Hu translated. Everyone was apparently satisfied so they took off for Cambridge, Maryland.

The Chinese scientists rode in the bus while the Blue Raven team rode in two cars, one in front and one following the bus. David Dekker drove his own car as he planned to leave early. Everyone arrived at the Hyatt Regency Resort without difficulties. They checked in and went en masse to the Sea View Restaurant to have dinner. The Chinese scientists and the Blue Ravens team sat at separate tables but near each other. Immediately after dinner they retired to their rooms for the night.

* * *

That evening, after four hours of driving, Dr. Aaron Armand arrived at the Hyatt Regency Resort. He checked into the hotel. Then he stopped by the conference registration desk to pay his fee and pick up his conference badge and the program book. He went to his room, unpacked, and went into the Golf View Restaurant to have a light dinner. He then immediately went to bed. There was a scientific presentation tomorrow at 9:15 AM by a scientist from Argentina. He wanted to be certain to hear about this new technology using laser for analyzing –G-C-G-C-G- and -G-G-G-G-G-

DNA repeats. So he would need to get up early enough to have breakfast and then find the room for this talk.

* * *

On Monday morning the corridors were overflowing with scientists checking into their rooms, registering for the conference, looking for breakfast service, seeking out one of the ten rooms where scientific presentations had already begun, making reservations for a round of golf or sailing for sometime later in the week, and in general orienting themselves to a new and very large resort. The more physically active ones were attempting to locate the exercise rooms, swimming pools, spas, and saunas. And several were seeking to make a reservation for a day tour of Washington, DC on the following Thursday. In general everyone was here for business; but Americans from the other coast or foreigners from outside of the USA, while near the American capital, planned to sacrifice a day of science and play tourist in Annapolis, Washington, or Baltimore.

The Chinese scientists arose early, their biological clocks were backward. They registered for the conference, had breakfast and split into four groups to attend four different simultaneous scientific presentations in four different rooms. Tight security control was already lost. So the team split into four groups and someone went with each group. At least, it was better than trying to go in fifteen different directions. However, before the day was over various members of the Chinese delegation went in various directions and attended other scientific presentations or went walking or went swimming or went to talk with American and other foreign scientists or went to their rooms to check their E-Mails or simply found a quiet sunny spot to work. All scientists, worldwide, are individuals. Most of their "thinking" work is accomplished when they are alone with no other people or other things to interrupt the local brain circuits. So it simply was not possible for eight people to provide security for fifteen people if those fifteen people were scientists. Fifteen security agents would probably not be enough.

The team met every night at 11:00 PM to report in on the day's activities. Monday went rather quickly. All fifteen of the Chinese scientists went in groups of two or four in the morning and attended various talks in the meeting rooms and listened to many scientific presentations. However the afternoon was a disaster. Each scientist seemed to go somewhere by himself or with another scientist from America or a foreign country. They did meet and have all three meals together. So the Monday report card read: morning - all monitored; afternoon – most not monitored; evening – some monitored; no major problems or suspicious activities. It appeared that this was going to be a rather unusual series of written reports.

* * *

The report card for Tuesday was even more difficult as the Chinese group had breakfast together, but then groups of two or three or four went in different directions; some listened to science presentations in different meeting rooms; some went to visit the marina; some walked over part of the golf course; some went back to their rooms to work with their lap tops; one even walked by himself around the premises and went down to the marina and back. They did not eat together at other mealtimes, but ate alone or in their separate small groups. Only that evening did they all meet in the ball room for the Tuesday evening dinner and the keynote speaker at 8:00 PM. So the Tuesday report card: morning – group scattered after breakfast, but all remained on the Hyatt Regency Resort complex all day – most monitored, some were not monitored; no problems or suspicious activities.

* * *

The report card for Wednesday continued with a mixed effort due to a scattering by the various Chinese scientists. Three scientists rented a car and went into Washington, DC, to play tourist. Several of the scientists attended scientific presentations in different meeting rooms in the morning, a different several scientists attended scientific presentations in different meeting rooms in the afternoon. Two scientists played a round of golf in the late afternoon. Three scientists visited the marina during the late afternoon and did a little sunbathing, or watched the female sunbathers. In general the various scientists went their own ways just as did the other foreign and the American scientists. No big deal! They had eaten breakfast and lunch as individuals or in small groups, but met as one large group in the Eagle's Nest Restaurant for dinner that evening. After dinner all but two retired to their rooms. These two went to the Blue Crab Pub in the Heron Building for a couple of beers before turning in sometime after midnight. The Wednesday report card: morning – group scattered after breakfast and did not meet together again until evening dinner; most attended scientific sessions: three went to Washington, DC for the entire day; two played golf in the late afternoon; three went to the marina and stayed there sunbathing all afternoon: others stayed on the Hyatt Regency Resort complex all day; no problems or suspicious activities.

Even with the limitations and handicaps, the week was going smoothly. All Chinese faces seemed to still match the original pictures that were given to them by the CIA. So far so good, they thought. In fact, things were going smoothly enough such that David decided he would go back to Washington on Thursday. He made arrangements to check out after breakfast the next morning.

* * *

Dr. Aaron Armand had attended several of the scientific presentations and was learning, but less than he expected. Either there was not as much "break- through" technology being reported this year, or else there was not that much being discovered. Usually academic scientists report all of their most recent discoveries. But private laboratories frequently held back certain research or details of certain research because of future pending patents for which their companies had applied. So he was pleased that he had planned to go to the NIH in Bethesda and Rockville, Maryland on Thursday morning. He would go after breakfast.

* * *

On Thursday morning David Dekker packed up, left his room and went out to his car which was parked nearby, put his suitcase in the car, and went into the Sailside Café for a quick breakfast. He sat near a corner window overlooking the marina which was filled with lovely yachts, and ordered a mushroom omelet, an apple and coffee. The café was quite full.

Aaron Armand left his room, gave his suitcase to the valet, retained his brief case, checked out and asked for his car to be brought to the front entrance in a half hour. He went into the Sailside Café for a quick breakfast. He sat at a table on the window side of the room where he had a lovely view of the marina. He ordered a mushroom omelet, a pear, and coffee. Relaxing, he looked around. He spotted a big guy with red hair and jade green eyes sitting near the window but over in the corner. He looked closer and saw a recognizable cleft in his left ear. He suddenly ran through a series of emotions from denial to possibly to probably to who else can it be. Should he not say anything, get up and leave, or bite the bullet and go find out? Is he or isn't he? Aaron got up, went over and sat down in the chair across the small two person table. As he put out his hand, he said, "Hello Brother. Have we met before?"

Dave looked up. It was as if he was looking into a mirror. This stranger had his face, his red hair, his jade green eyes, and even a cleft in his right ear; no it was the left ear because he was not looking into a mirror. It was himself looking at him. And he responded, "I don't know."

They both knew immediately that they were brothers and identical twins, possibly the one in the dreams. They suddenly had tears in their eyes. All each could do was to stare at himself across the table. Neither could form words on his tongue, as tears came to four green eyes and rolled down two manly faces.

They both simultaneously stood up and hugged and hugged and hugged. This was their first ever seeing and touching. Normally twins would touch continuously for the first nine months of their existence. Here after forty plus years these two individuals who shared the same genes, but never shared the same womb, were touching for the first time. They just stood there hugging, holding onto each other as if each was afraid that the other would disappear if he let go.

They finally each took a step back, but kept holding hands. They both started laughing. But they couldn't stop touching. If one believed in miracles, one had just happened. Two genetically identical people had just seen each other for the first time, and touched each other for the first time, and smiled at each other for the first time, and laughed at each other for the first time, and had begun a series of firsts from which there would be no end.

After several minutes of trying to gain his composure in this public café with many people staring at the two of them, Aaron began first. "My name is Aaron Armand. I was born to Dr. and Mrs. Mary and James Armand at Manchester, New Hampshire on March 7, 1976."

"I am David Dekker and I was born to Mr. and Mrs. Sylvia and Roy Dekker in San Diego, California on February 28, 1976." David answered.

And they both thought to themselves, 'different names, different birth dates, so there has to be different mothers and fathers; what confusion; but the same faces and bodies.'

They fell silent again for several moments, each trying to believe what was happening, and also trying to gain their manly composure. They carefully blotted their eyes and wiped off their faces with their pocket handkerchiefs. They even had to blow their noses, so embarrassing! They had attracted an audience, but one that seemed to understand because there were many smiles and nods of approval.

Then they sat down and started exchanging life times starting with childhood, teenage hood, young manhood, professions, marriage, wives, children and important family events. Somehow it did not seem possible that each had lived so much, so long, and did not even know that the other even existed. They each had wanted a brother, saw one in those nightly dreams, but couldn't find him to touch him. After more than an hour of talking and exchanging family backgrounds and discussing their lives, Aaron was fairly certain, even without any hard core scientific data such as DNA fingerprinting, that they had to have come from the same Mother and Father. And he did remember that they had each given the names of each Mother and Father and the names were not the same. Dave agreed that they must have a common Mother and Father.

In addition, by sharing and comparing their dreams over the many years it seemed that there were possibly two more of them out there somewhere. If there were two others, where were they? Maybe their dreams would change and help them find the others. And just how did all of this happen? It appeared that Aaron may need his CCGBT to help solve his own personal problem. But where should they begin?

Dave asked, "If we do have other identical brothers, how can we find them? They could be anywhere in the USA. Or even anywhere in the world I suppose."

Aaron thought for a few seconds. "Like us they will probably have different names. But at least identical twins have identical finger prints, identical hand prints, identical big toe prints, and very similar optical retinal patterns. We can use prints and patters, work from there."

"We might be able to seek the finger print data immediately," Dave responded. "As Director of Intelligence of the Blue Ravens Security Firm I have access to certain government finger print records and the means to rapidly search through them. I probably can also search some military files as well. Since the 9/11 tragedy many states now require thumb prints on all drivers licenses. With a little help from my friends I might be able to scan these thumb prints, at least in some of the states that now do this. So we can begin here in our genetic quest. If you can think of any other approaches let me know."

Aaron thought that would be a good start and said, "I always carry here in my brief case a packet of cotton swabs and a couple of vials of alcohol. Please if you will allow me. When we leave let us go into the bathroom.

First you must rinse your mouth thoroughly with water. Then I will give to you two cotton swaps. Be careful to not touch the cotton or you will contaminate with bacteria. With one swab scrape the cotton area on the inside of your right cheek. With the second swab scrap the cotton area on the inside of the other cheek. Place the first swab in vial #1 and the second swab in vial #2. And be certain to place the cotton area down into the alcohol. The cotton on the swabs will have some of your body cells. I will take your body cells to my laboratories at Columbia University and we will run a DNA fingerprint analysis. I will then do the same thing on myself and run a DNA fingerprint analysis from my cells. If indeed we are identical twins this will give us positive proof. Such proof will hold up anywhere, even in a court of law."

They paid their bills and on the way out stopped in the bathroom. Dave did as instructed and gave his inside cheek cells to Aaron to take for genetic analysis. They then agreed to meet regularly but clandestinely. E-mail would work nicely. It would be better if "they" were not yet known to the media. They shook hands, even hugged another time, now in an embarrassing fashion. It was weird to hug yourself. Then they said their goodbyes, and went to their separate cars.

As Aaron was driving toward Washington from Cambridge, he began going through the past hour in his mind. 'It was really weird to talk to yourself, and have yourself talk back to you. He had learned about his own, yet not his own, life which he had not known before yesterday. He learned about his parents, his wife, his children, his security profession, his house, his car, his everything, and all from himself. Every time Dave said something he heard himself. As he was driving through Annapolis, past the US Naval Academy, he recalled Dave's experience in the army in Afghanistan. He thought he too could probably kill bad guys as long as he could see who he was shooting. But to push a button more than hundreds of miles away from the bad guys, and to shoot some rocket that you had never seen, and then to not kill the bad guys but instead to kill a bunch of women and children, he would also have trouble living with that. Collateral damage? He also would change professions after such an experience. He was really a nice guy. I even liked him! And he seemed to have done very well in his professional life. If I had been allowed to choose a brother, Dave would be a good choice. But we need to resolve the genetic problem. Yes! They had the same Mother and Father, but who and how? And where and how did the conceptions occur? They both knew where they were born. They each had different birth certificates for different

Mothers on different days one week apart on the opposite side of the USA, Massachusetts and California. It would be good to know the why, but not so terribly important. The result of what happened of course was them. Down deep, he knew that soon all of these questions would be answered, and that he would soon meet his other two brothers. And that would be a grand affair.'

* * *

Waiting for David at his car was Johnston Utreker and Betty Hu.

John greeted David and started to explain something.

Betty excitedly jumped in first. "There has been a switch with one of the Chinese scientists. I am very sure but not positive. What do we do?"

David asked, "Have you said anything to any of the CIA people?"

She replied, "No. I was going to do so but I thought it better that you told them."

"And then if you are wrong it is my head on the block, huh?"

"No, no, no," she panicked.

First chuckling, then, "What does Do think?" he asked.

Do Wong had not yet had a chance to have a good look, because the man in question seems to prefer to work in his hotel room," she responded. "I only saw him once, but I think that I am correct. He was definitely a new face. There has been a switch."

David said, "I will cancel my leaving and stay here until we get the Chinese delegation onto that Chinese jet at BWI Airport. In the meantime try to get another look at this fellow. Help Do get a good look also. I will talk with the CIA people and try to come up with a plan. Thank you for being so alert. We could easily have missed something as clever as a simple one for one switch among fifteen people. Stay alert, as there may be more than one thing happening here."

John and Betty returned to duty. David went back into the front desk and re-rented his room near the team and the Chinese delegation rooms for two more nights.

* * *

The report cards for Thursday and Friday nights were about the same as each Chinese scientist went his separate way or they moved in small groups listening to various scientific presentations and discussing science in the lounges and cafes. The possibility of a switch of one of the male

110

scientists was carefully noted, a written record was made, and it would be followed up on Saturday when everyone prepared to leave the USA to fly back to China.

The conference simply continued on schedule, but the attendees began to dwindle down. Not everyone stayed for the presentations on the last day. As the crowd diminished, the team found it easier to monitor their clients. The scientist in question was seen only one more time, and only by Betty. Do never clearly saw his face. So it was becoming a problem. How far should the security people, specifically the Blue Raven team and the CIA, go with a one person sighting? It was not a problem for the hotel security as all of the Chinese would leave from the hotel together.

Clever in planning or accidental, either way, the Chinese plane was scheduled to depart from BWI Airport at 6:00 AM on Saturday. Therefore the team and the delegation had to leave the conference center at 4:30 AM. Of course it was still dark at that time. So what to do? It was simple. Give the ball to the big guys and let them play.

David Dekker had written an official report concerning the possibility of a switch by a person with Oriental facial characteristics, believed to be Chinese, with one member of the Chinese delegation. He gave this report to the agent who was the head of the CIA security group at the conference, in front of witnesses, on Friday evening at 7:00 PM. As soon as the delegation boarded the plane the contract would be fulfilled by the Blue Ravens Security Firm, and their problem would end. And just be careful until then?

* * *

So on Saturday morning fifteen Chinese scientists checked out of the Hyatt Regency Resort, boarded the bus, and left the Cambridge area. The Blue Ravens team chauffeured the delegation to Baltimore, to the BWI Airport and to the hanger for special international flights. The Chinese jet was waiting, and so were the Passport Control people.

Dave and John were standing and watching the Chinese jetliner and talking. John spoke, "I am glad that this adventure is over. I really thought we were going to have trouble. I was wrong."

Dave replied, "Don't give up hope; they are not in the sky yet."

And then someone yelled, "There goes someone!" And he was pointing toward the airport perimeter fence behind the back of the bus.

One of the airport guards shouted, "Let the dogs stop him."

Three dogs were released and they brought the fleeing person down in less than a minute. He never got near the fence.

The other scientists who were lined up, looked at the action; but they just continued, one by one, to go through Customs and Passport Control and then enter the plane. Apparently, the fellow that tried to escape had remained hidden in the bus and had jumped out a back window when no one was watching.

The Airport security handcuffed the man. He apparently was not one of the fifteen original members of the Chinese delegation. The Security officials took him into the nearby CIA office. All other members of the Chinese delegation were checked and cleared through a second Passport Control. They then each boarded the plane. The plane took off without the man who had tried to escape. David Dekker and his Blue Ravens team breathed a big sigh of relief and headed for home. Another job was well done.

Two weeks later the President of the Blue Ravens Security Firm received a letter from the Director of the Central Intelligence Agency. The letter thanked the Firm for their alertness in restraining an American citizen, Chinese ancestry, who was on both the FBI and CIA wanted list for stealing some high technology military secrets, and was fleeing the country. He would be put on trial for treason.

# 8 – There Are Three of Us

Columbus did not discover America. In the year of 1492 there were already more than fifty million people living in South, Latin, and North America (the Inca Empire in eastern South America - twenty million people, the Mayan Empire in Central America - six million people, the Aztec Empire in southern North America - eighteen million people, and the "American Indians" of North America - twelve million people; plus the rest of South America). No skulls or skeletons of humans earlier than the Homo sapiens have ever been discovered in North or South America. So these "Homo sapiens - Indians" had to have arrived from Asia crossing over the Bearing Straits to Alaska during one of the ice ages before 1492. Columbus called them Indians because he thought that he had found India. Wrong again. He had discovered a land mass between Europe and India about which most Europeans did not know.

Soon these same Europeans, in an attempt to colonize a land rich in gold, silver, beautiful women, and exotic food, named it America, after another European, and called the native inhabitants American Indians. During the past five hundred years most of these Incas, Aztecs and American Indians have been killed or absorbed by the white Europeans. Of the several hundred American Indian tribes, only a few remain today living on their own tribal land which was "granted" to them by the generous governments of the United States of America. One specific tribe of American Indians was not so completely tamed and today still lives on its native land. They are called the Seminoles.

Seminole is an English word adapted from the Muskogee language in which Seminole meant wild or unconquered one. This referred to several tribes of American Indians living in the states of Florida and Georgia. The English declared that the Seminole Indians came into existence on November 18, 1765, and that they would be allowed to live on the banks of the St Johns River and in the rest of the state of Florida (where they had already been living for hundreds of years).

The Seminoles were more advanced than many other American Indians in that men wore clothing made of leather and deerskin; women wore leather and deerskin skirts, short in summer and long in winter. Both wore deerskin or bearskin coats in winter and deerskin moccasins year around. Feathered capes were worn by socially prominent leaders. Both men and women adorned themselves with many types of jewelry fashioned from shells, pearls, animal claws, and bones. Later, when silk and cotton became available through trading with the white man, the women made intricate clothing designs, even dresses. And the Seminoles lived in huts with a smoke hole at the top. The huts were called chickees and were constructed from tree limbs and palmetto palm fronds, so they were rather permanent, not readily moveable like the standard Indian teepee. The Seminoles usually located in one place and remained there for many years. They did not seasonally migrate like most American Indian tribes did.

These "Wild Ones" did not integrate easily with the foreigners. Their culture was isolated and many hundreds of years old. They fiercely resisted change. Some became Christian. Most did not. And even today many Seminoles maintain their "old ways". Non-Christian Seminoles, as they were labeled, believed in a Great Spirit, plus several good and bad spirits. They believed that there was a delicate balance in nature, and that man was not at the top. When they killed animals for food, they held rituals and prayed to the spirits of those animals such that those spirits would be appeased and would not send diseases to their villages as revenge. All living organisms had spirits which were released when they died. They believed in a Skyworld, where the good spirits went, and a Below-World for other spirits. The Seminoles believed that the supernatural, which no one understood, but which the ultimate in respect must be given, included the sun, moon, and rainbow, and human diseases. So the shaman (doctor) was all powerful and used numerous powders from plants, stones, minerals, bones, horns, special native herb plants, and dance (rattlesnake) rattles.

Even today, several Seminole tribes and villages maintain their famous Green Corn Dance. This event is held in June or July and lasts for four days. The first two days involves a variety of rituals, special foods, crafts making, ceremonial events, stage ceremonies, and many types of dancing. A judicial court is held on the third day and the elders hear cases on infringement of tribal laws, morals, and customs. On the third night an all disease curing corn drink is prepared and, with special rituals, the men drink it. On the fourth and last day certain stage ceremonies, more dancing and all males partake of a hot-cold water ritual competition, eat a special bowl of corn mush, and perform, wearing masks, various types of hunting dances. It was to this last day of the Green Corn Dance, at the Big

Cyprus Seminole Indian Reservation just north of the Everglades National Park area, that the Collingswood family was going. And it was only a few miles from Indian Nest, Florida where the Collingswood family lived, so it was an easy and short drive by car.

Charles and Janice Collingswood were now married and had two children, fraternal twins. The first was a boy with red hair and almond colored eyes and was named Samuel. Second, about five minutes later, was a girl with straw blond hair and jade blue eyes. She was called Sara. For their sixth birthday they were on their way to day number four of the Green Corn Dance at the Big Cyprus Seminole Indian Reservation. Mom and Dad had promised the children they would all go on Thursday, to the big last day, if they finished their routine chores for Thursday and Friday on Wednesday. And yes they did. So they left early for the 20 minute drive, and arrived to find a good parking space up front. The last day of the Festival was the most popular and it would be crowded with knowledgeable and non-knowledgeable, but eager to learn tourists. And indeed all would learn about the Seminoles culture.

They parked near the entrance to a football sized circular area which resembled a giant ant hill that had a flat top. There was a continuous four foot high temporary fence around the entire area, which was designed to keep out non-paying guests and to keep in children who happened to stray away from their parents. This festival was very popular and was attended by families and by children's groups such as girl and boy scouts. There was only one entrance and exit, but emergency exits could easily be made by simply pulling up a couple of the support stakes and pushing the temporary fence to the ground. It was at this one entrance that Charles and Janice Collingswood imposed their ultimatums to Sam and Sara. Charles pulled a map of the festival area from his pocket. And he showed it to the family.

Dad spoke. "These are the rules for today. If you do not follow them we will immediately leave the festival and go home. Is that understood?"

Two sets of big bright shiny eyes looked up at him, not knowing whether to believe him or not. They looked at Mom to check. Dad was not known for his stern ultimatums. In fact he was rather a softie. But, not taking any chances, they nodded their understanding.

He continued. "Please study this map. We are now here at the only entrance-exit gate. And the car is located just outside of it, here. OK?"

They both looked and nodded.

"This fence goes around the entire area. You are not to go outside of this fence." And looking at Sam he added, "and that means not over or under." And he smiled at him.

Sam smiled back but he knew what that meant; Sam was an extremely good "outdoors man".

Dad pointed out certain important places in the festival area on the map. "Look at the very center of the map and then to top of the hill and you see those flag poles. Those are the flags of the state of Florida and the United States of America. Just beyond those two poles is a large amphitheater where stage events are held. We will locate in the center on the top row (row 50) of the wooden benches that form a semi-circle around the stage. Here! From here we can see all the stage and side crafts arena events."

"This morning, starting in one half hour, at 9:00 AM, there will be several different types of dances by girls and women that honor the souls of various animals living in the area such as birds, deer, wild pigs, burrowing animals like the black rat, snakes, and alligators. In the afternoon there will be dancing on that stage by boys and men which demonstrate different type of hunting techniques. Behind the seating area on the lower left, next to the fence, is a marked off side crafts arena where all day today Seminole Indian women will teach how to make clothing crafts and jewelry. You can go there and make your own jewelry if you want to do so."

Sara looked at Mom, got a yes nod, she gave a yes nod in return. It's OK.

"Now behind the seating area on the lower right, next to the fence, is a marked off side crafts arena where during the morning Seminole men will teach how to make hunting spears, bows and arrows. Sam and I will go there and see how good we are at those crafts."

A big smile came from the little big outdoors man.

"Now look here." Dad pointed to the map. "Between the stage and the two side crafts areas are the toilets. On the left side are the girls and women's. And on the right side are boys and men's. Think that you can find them?"

Both children laughed and gave thumbs up signs. They knew Dad was always embarrassed when seen going to that type of a place – he claimed he got sick of the smells – didn't everyone.

Dad continued. "Immediately inside of the entrance to the left is a refreshment area that sells original Seminole foods. They use recipes which are hundreds of years old and all of the food is cooked by Seminole women.

You can buy and eat it here, or buy and take it home to eat later. Next to the food sales is a large picnic area. We brought our own full picnic basket so we will just eat at row 50 center bench, at the top of the stage seating area. OK?"

Each quickly agreed.

"We will later buy some original Seminole food to take home later." He continued.

"One last area that we need to talk about, and that is just inside the entrance and to the right. Near the entrance is a cold water and soft drinks stand. You have some coins to buy whatever you want, but we also have cold fruit drinks in the basket. Further to the right are two small buildings. The first building is the cold water building. The second building is the hot steam building. In the afternoon the Seminole boys and men will challenge each other to see how long they can stay, first in the hot steam building and then in the cold water building. Those with the most perseverance, or craziness, and stay the longest in both buildings will receive grand prizes. The grand prize winners then will be allowed to lead, wearing animal masks, the type of hunter's dance of their choice on the stage, if they have sufficiently recovered from the hot-cold contest."

"Is everyone alright?" All nodded affirmatively. "So let us go up the hill and locate at row 50-center bench, and then you can explore. And don't forget the day's ultimatum. Stay inside the fence, check back to row 50-center bench, regularly. Have fun, stay out of trouble, or we all go home immediately."

Sam and Sara looked at each other, then at Mom, and smiled to themselves. Dad purchased their tickets, and up the hill they went. They sat their picnic basket and small ice chest at row 50-center bench. Mom and Dad sat down to claim the spot while the children took off to reconnoiter the area inside the temporary fence.

The weather was a mild 78°F, and a normal humid day for southern Florida in June. All should go well. No rain was expected. During the morning Sara and Mom went to the Seminole jewelry area and Sara made herself a beautiful necklace and bracelet. At the same time Sam and Dad went to the Seminole hunting weapons area and Sam made for himself a really neat bow and three arrows. The adults, and sometimes the children, watched the morning animal ritual dances on the stage below. There was so much to see that sitting in one place for any period of time was difficult for little ones. So they came and went with ease.

At noon Mom opened the lunch basket and laid out the food on a nearby blanket. Sam and Sara sat on the blanket and Mom and Dad sat on the row 50-center bench.

Sara asked, "Dad, what do you think of my necklace?"

"It is very lovely," answered Dad. "I especially like the turquoise blue of the stones."

Sara asked again, "And do you like Mom's necklace too?"

"Of course," he said. "But I like yours better."

And Sara gave a smile to her Mother and said, "He means that my necklace is better for little girls and that your necklace is better for Mothers. Right, Dad?" And she reached for a chicken leg. And glanced at Mom and smiled.

Dad looked at Mom and agreed, "That is what I meant." He always seemed to need rescuing when it came to saying the 'best' thing for Janice. And he reached for a chicken leg."

But Sam also needed to get approval on his morning work so he asked, "Mom, do you like my bow and two arrows? They had bigger bows but Dad would not let me make a bigger one." And he reached for the biggest chicken leg.

Mom answered, "I think that bow is large enough. You are too young to go hunting for wild boar. That is a good bow to target practice with. And yes, I think that you did a really neat job." And she quickly grabbed a chicken leg. Chicken legs were popular today. But she knew that the entire family was leg oriented so she had prepared a dozen.

Dad asked about requests for soft drinks, took each can for each out of the ice chest, opened them, handed them around, and a picnic lunch began in earnest. They had each worked up an appetite from their morning labors.

After the lunch was finished the females first and the males second visited their respective toilets, then they were ready for the afternoon events.

The first and main event was the hot-cold contest which was open to only Seminole boys or men; and all must wear swim suits. It was sort of the highlight of the four days of the Green Corn Dance festival.

And that afternoon the hot-cold contest produced the youngest winner ever. There were twenty three contestants between the ages of sixteen and thirty five years. Simultaneously all contestants entered in the steam building. After about fifteen minutes contestants started to slowly leave the steam building. Finally an eighteen year old boy lasted thirty three minutes in the steam building. He was declared the winner.

After a fifteen minute break all contestants simultaneously entered the cold water building and climbed into the ice water bath. Within ten minutes, contestants started to leave this building. Finally after forty one minutes in the cold water bath in the cold water building, they had brought in ice so the water was really ice-cold, only one contestant remained. And it was the same eighteen year old boy. His skin was a light blue color, and his lips were white. When he realized that he was the last one remaining in the cold building he stuck his head out the door and started tantalizing some of his buddies to come on in, that the water was really nice. If they brought their colas with them he would convert the colas to 'cold drinks.' He was not only the youngest to win but the first ever double grand winner. And he celebrated with a large cup of hot tea. So the Collingswood family saw history that day. The entire event was a lot of fun and a neat memory to have.

Later in the afternoon Charles spotted the famous Seminole Chief White Cloud playing with some children. Chief White Cloud was ninety five years old; his family said he was closer to one hundred and ninety five years old. Whatever, he had the spring of step and social character of fifty years. Chief White Cloud was famous for many reasons. He had refused to take a white man's Christian name, so the government had to give him his citizenship papers and driver's license in his Seminole Indian name. He was famous for his future predictions of events. And he was also a famous Seminole shaman or medicine man. If anyone wanted something from the Seminole Indian nation they had to clear it through him or legally go around him. All Seminole Indian common land had been legally registered in his name more than seventy five years ago. And that included the thousands of acres of land in south Florida and on all sides of the entire Everglades area. Chief White Cloud was the Chairman of the Seminole Elders (Board of Directors of the Seminole Foundation – legal arm for the entire Seminole Indian nation). He was also known to be a "Conjurer of Spirits." Charles had been trying to catch and talk to him for several months, without success. So very carefully, and with much respect he approached the Chief.

Charles spoke first. "Good evening Chief White Cloud. How is the crab hunting going this summer?"

Everyone knew that the Chief had his own secret hunting mechanism for catching crabs and that he was very fond of crab meat.

Chief White Cloud turned. They exchanged Seminole greeting gestures and smiled at each other. Then Charles was suddenly afraid that he was going to turn away from him and go back to the children. Instead he took Charles by the arm and led him away from the children.

As they walked toward an open and private area, Chief White Cloud spoke. "Reverend Charles Collingswood, you are just the man I wanted to see."

Charles was shocked. Those were supposed to be his lines. Then he noticed the Chief was looking at him out of the corner of his eye and smiling.

Chief White Cloud continued. "I wish to talk to you about some spirits. This time it is not animal spirits, but about human spirits which are suddenly prominent. You need my help. And you need it immediately. Can you come to my house this Saturday night after dark, say around 10:00 PM?"

Charles was shocked again. He knew that the Chief lived alone in a small chickee on a small side road about half way between his church and the reservation grounds. It would take about ten minutes of driving time at most. So, without thinking, he blurted out, "Of course I would be honored to come to you at 10:00 PM Saturday night."

Chief White Cloud dropped Charles's arm, gave a little bow and said, "See you then."

They exchanged a good bye in the proper sign language of the Seminole Indians which had been used for hundreds of years, and still used between brothers.

As the sun started its beautiful red descent the children were becoming tired and hungry again. So Mom took the little ones to the car as Charles stopped and purchased some authentic Seminole food. He then joined them at the car and they called it a full day and headed home. And heads won over the stomachs as both Sam and Sara were asleep before they had gone two miles.

Saturday night came around quickly. Charles discussed the incident with Janice.

He asked, "Why do you think Chief White Cloud wants to see me at his chickee so late on Saturday night, and alone?

She responded, 'You know that I accept both the Seminole way of spirits and the Christian way of spirits, believing in both the Sky Spirit and the Lord - both are up there. But I cannot shed light on what Chief White

Cloud has in mind. I do think that he will talk to you from the Seminole Spirit rather than from the Lord's Spirit."

Charles followed up by saying, "He did say something about human spirits, and my immediate need. It was a little scary."

That Saturday night, Charles arrived at Chief White Cloud's chickee sharply at 10:00 PM. The Chief was behind the house around a small ritual fire that was blazing. He was sitting on a small log and waiting for Charles. As Charles greeted him he bid Charles to sit across the fire from him and on one of the three other small logs located around the fire.

Without wasting words, Chief White Cloud motioned for Charles to remain quiet. The Chief was boiling water in a small pot on the fire. He reached over and picked up a nearby cup and a small bag filled with crushed leaves. He poured boiling water into the cup and placed a small handful of leaves into the water. He swirled the cup for a couple of minutes while chanting a ritual in the ancient Seminole language. He had asked Charles to bring with him a childhood toy that he treasured. He now asked Charles to give him this toy.

The Chief already knew what the toy was — it was a small stuffed alligator given to Charles by his Mother before she died in the house fire of exactly thirty years ago on this day. He held the toy high into the night air and continued singing a Seminole ritual song. The fire seemed to blaze higher. He took the cup and quickly drank the contents in one gulp. Swallowed the liquid and chewed the leaves. He now picked up a small drum, threw Charles's childhood toy into the fire, started beating the drum, got up and started dancing around the fire while he continued chanting and beating the drum. As the toy slowly burned the old man started spinning around. He continued dancing, spinning, and singing while beating the drum for several minutes.

Then suddenly he collapsed. Charles did not know what to do so he did nothing. A few minutes later the Chief came out of his trance, and sat down on his small log as if nothing happened. Charles was eying the remains of his burned toy and was almost on the edge of crying, yet he felt no anger.

After a few more minutes Chief White Cloud spoke in English, his first words to Charles that evening:

**"I have been with your spirits. You have been having difficult dreams during these past years. Those are dreams of your three brothers. Two of your brothers live on this side of the Great American River. One brother lives beyond it. Your brothers are looking for you.**

**If you do not find each other soon you will all die. The first brother that you must find lives beyond the River but you will find him on this side of the River. Tonight I have taken from you your Mother, but I have given to you your brothers. You must find all of them soon, or? Go home, sleep, and dream."**

[At exactly 10:15 on the same Saturday night in New York City, Aaron Armand, in Washington, DC, David Dekker, and in Des Moines, Iowa, William Bassinger simultaneously received a bright flash of green light which temporarily blinded them. Each of the three had to sit down, close their eyes for several minutes until the bright light disappeared. Aaron and David each thought the other was trying to communicate with him. They did not yet understand it was a third brother trying to communicate to the both of them. William just did not understand what happened.]

In shock, the Reverend Charles Collingswood drove home. Everyone was asleep and he went directly to bed and to sleep. He did dream:

'It began with a view of a giant body of water which was beautiful, dark blue and almost lake like smooth. The bright yellow sun began turning to orange and then to red and then to green. The surface of the giant body of water began to roll. Near the center of the view he suddenly saw two figures. The two figures were coming toward him. They were two giant alligators. Each alligator had a man riding on his back similar to that of a person riding a surfboard. Each man was large, muscular, handsome, and had red hair and jade green eyes. He could feel the heartbeat of each man. He could sense that one man was a medical person who was looking for his genes. The other man was a searcher who was looking for his body. He tried to reach out to them so they could find him. He was reaching. And they were reaching.' Then he woke up in a daze. He knew those two men were his brothers, but where were they?

# 9 - There Are Four of Us

During the past few weeks Aaron Armand and David Dekker had progressed reasonably well in the genetic quest of searching for themselves. Using their own biological cells Aaron had run a series of DNA procedures including the PCR, Northern Blotting, and RFLP. So far, all of the data showed that they were indeed very identical twins. Their genes originated not only from the same man and woman, but from their fertilized oocyte and subsequent blastula (cells). David had started searching all fingerprint data bases that were available to him including: FBI, CIA, others in the Department of Homeland Security, Military sources and several private sector sources in which he had to purchase. However, even though he found his own fingerprints in the Department of Defense files, and he found Aaron's fingerprints in a file with the New York State Driver Licenses Bureau, he found no other matching fingerprints.

But their communications had moved from the carefully worded E-Mails to mental telepathy at night when asleep. They now had the capacity to "spiritually communicate" with each other but only during their sleep. It was not a word for word detailed type of message that they could send. It was general concepts, suggestions, pictorial ideas and scenes in color, general agreements or disagreements.

For example, one night last week, Dave explained, using a pictorial explanation, that whenever he searched the state of Florida immigrant fingerprint files he kept seeing the number three. During the online search, suddenly the number three would fill the screen, then the picture would go off, the computer would shut down, and he had to re-boot and start searching again. This happened at exactly 3:00 PM on each of July 3, 13, 23, and 30. Aaron replied to Dave, using a similar pictorial explanation, that at that same time on those same days the electricity shut off in all of his labs. Fortunately the emergency systems kicked in and no damage was done; but it was all recorded by the building's environment management computers. Also he frequently felt spiritual vibrations from the air and water in the direction of the state of Florida. Dave acknowledged a similar feeling of a common spirit from that area of the USA and the feeling of a set of spirit hands seeking him.

They both had separately come to the conclusion that one of their twins was living on the water in Florida near an immigrant community. When he was between assignments, Dave would go down there and start a search.

* * *

Several weeks after the Green Corn Dance festival, the Save the Everglades Foundation was preparing for its annual meeting. The Reverend Charles Collingswood and his wife, Dr Janice Stryker-Collingswood had been living and working in the Everglades National Park area for more than a decade. Janet maintained her teaching position at the U Miami and was deeply committed to her research on the changes in the animal populations within the Everglades. Charles was a true nature lover and had become an environmentalist. Their children also loved it. So they had decided to give the rest of their lives to trying to save this vast natural American resource. The Everglades National Park was the largest subtropical wilderness in the United States. There were than more twelve thousand square miles of land containing ten thousand islands and lakes filled with God's plants and animals; and fortunately not yet man. It appeared to them that since man could not conquer it, man was determined to kill it. This was not unusual in the history of mankind on this planet.

After several years as a member of the Save the Everglades Foundation, Charles was elected President and was in the process of organizing this meeting in his church basement. Janet had taken his position on the governing Board so she was complementing his efforts. The Foundation was not a wealthy NGO. It survived on contributions from individuals and a few tourism related sources. Therefore the meeting would be held in the Reverend Collingswood's church in Indian Nest, Florida. Most of the Board members were from within the state of Florida and would be driving to there for the one day meeting and one day excursion of the Everglades, courtesy of Dr. Janice Stryker-Collingswood.

Sitting at his desk in their moderate sized three bedroom wood frame house near his church, Charles laid back, looked at the ceiling and thought about the problems facing the life of the Everglades.

'The waters in south Florida used to flow freely from the Kissimmee River, just south of Orlando, to Lake Okeechobee and southward into the Everglades and Biscayne Bay, south to Miami, and on into the Atlantic

Ocean and the Bay of Mexico. There were no major obstructions, natural or artificial. This water flowed through saw grass marshes, sloughs, large and small ponds, large and small islands, swamp areas, hardwood hammock areas, and forested uplands. For hundreds of thousands of years this natural system evolved into a delicately balanced ecosystem that became the biological infrastructure of the south half of the state of Florida. Early settlers to the region viewed the Everglades as a worthless swamp filled with mosquitoes and which had to be drained to become useful.

So beginning in the mid 1800s, drainage canals were begun. The construction of drainage canals, the systematic draining of the Everglades and the surrounding areas, and the construction of new railroads, auto roads and cities which infringed into this fragile ecosystem still continue today.

During the past one hundred years the native habitats have been rapidly replaced by canals, roads, and buildings. Seventy years ago the American Congress authorized the construction of an elaborate system of roads, canals, dams, levees, and other water flow control devices in an attempt to protect the Everglades ecosystem and yet let man have his inalienable right of land ownership and property control.

Today this effort has resulted in the loss of more than 50% of the original wetland area. It simply is gone. Alone with this loss is a decrease from 50 to 90% of many species of plants and animals; and the appearance of exotic dangerous pest plants which now choke out native plants. The ecosystem is rapidly being destroyed by humans. The Foundation has data to show and prove such destruction is occurring now. And the Foundation also has data to list the methodologies that humans are currently using which destroy the Everglades. This data must be publicized. Their motto "The Everglades Cannot Become A Neverglades" was a good publicity expression.

On the following Saturday the Board of Directors of the Save the Everglades Foundation met in Charles's church in Indian Nest, Florida, which was physically located on the northern edge of the Everglades National Park. Janice would guide them on an all day tour through the Everglades on the next day, Sunday.

After nine of the ten Board members had arrived, Charles opened the meeting.

Charles as the President of the Foundation officially opened the meeting by saying, "Welcome to Indian Nest and the Everglades. Please let us all be seated. Did anyone have any trouble getting here today?"

No negative response

"I am passing out copies of the past years treasurer's report. Arnold Watts, our Treasurer, faxed it to me last night as his youngest daughter was in an auto accident yesterday and is in the hospital. Look the report over and we can discuss it later. He will try to join us later today. We have four speakers who will talk about their data gathering projects during the past year. They are Dr. Watts Barclay – Heavy metals and industrials poisoning of the water in the Everglades; Anne Brown – Phosphorus and the sugar plantations; Tony Batista – Continued intrusion of housing developments into the area; Dr. Janice Stryker – Recent changes in the animal populations of the Everglades. Are there any questions?"

He paused for a minute, "If not, let us begin with the reports. Dr. Barclay if you are ready, please."

Dr. Barclay, Department of Environmental Studies, University of South Florida, Tampa, Florida came to the podium and began. "I have titled our recent research project - Heavy metals and mercury pollution of the Florida Everglades. This project has been in motion for the past five to six years. It is not finished and this will be only a progress report via the efforts of three of my graduate students and myself."

"We took feather and excrement samples from two types of wading birds, the endangered wood storks and the non-endangered great white heron, and from two types of flying birds, the osprey and the tree swallow which are all located in several places throughout the Everglades areas. All of these birds live locally along the rivers and in the water. The wading birds wade, hunt, and eat the fish found in the bodies of water that are polluted from industrial, agriculture, and urban development. The flying birds use nesting material and eat fish, insects and worms which grow near their nests. "

"We collected feather samples from both young and adult birds. And we measured the concentrations of mercury, cadmium, selenium, manganese, aluminum, lead, copper, zinc, and molybdenum. We traveled to Jamaica and Costa Rica and collected similar bird samples to compare as control groups."

"So during these past several years we have collected more than two hundred bird samplings and we have completed the mineral analysis of most of these samples. By the time we complete the study we will have more than one thousand numbers of mineral levels to compare. Do you have any questions concerning our population base or our methodological approach?"

Hearing none he continued. "Because your interest is in the results, not in the chemical methodology of extracting and quantifying these toxic metals, I will go directly to that. If anyone wants to know about the laboratory methods that we are using, just say so, or I can talk about it with you separately later."

"We found the highest concentration of each metal, especially mercury to be in the wood storks in the Everglades. The very high concentration of mercury is probably one of the key reasons that this bird is on the endangered species list. Mercury is a potent toxin that causes reproduction problems in birds. It is also known to cause neurological problems in humans."

"Recently researchers from the University of Florida reported that the populations of wading birds in the Everglades decreased more than seventy five percent between 1950 and 2000; this paralleled increasing levels of mercury probably coming from coal-fired power plants and city incinerators, via air and/or water during the same time frame."

"And I can quickly summarize our data by saying that all of the metals that we tested were higher in all four birds that we tested from the Everglades area, when compared with the same species of birds from Jamaica or Costa Rica. We will be publishing some of our findings before the end of the year in the International Journal of Environmental Toxins. If any of you want a copy of that scientific publication please let me know and I will be happy to send one to you. Now do you have any questions?"

Charles spoke up. "Why do you think that the wood stork has higher levels of mercury than the great white heron?"

Dr Barclay responded. "Certain species of animals and even some subspecies of animals seem to take up and store more of specific toxic metals. This is one mechanism that ecology researchers use to monitor specific toxin pollutants in a specific environment by knowing which animals are most sensitive to that toxin. Amphibians, especially frogs, and other animals which undergo a metamorphosis during their lifespan, are commonly employed as toxic monitoring animals. They seem to be more sensitive to many toxic substances, especially water borne toxins."

"Another good example from the near past is the American bald eagle. Our national bird is only slowly coming off of the endangered species list, after being on the list for over 50-60 years. Why? Many years of heavy use of the pesticides of DDT and 2, 4, 5 T caused the egg shell of the eagle to become so thin that the bird embryos died of infections before they could be born. Only with the recent 20 years of discontinued use of these two pesticides have the eagles now started to survive and increase their numbers. Why are the eagle's egg shells more sensitive to those pesticides than other birds' egg shells, and why is the wood crane's reproductive system more sensitive to mercury than the reproductive system of the great white heron? I do not think anyone knows. I certainly do not know. The only immediate solution is to remove the toxins from the animals' environment. A major problem in the ecosystem of the Everglades is the increase of metal toxins which are entering into and probably killing a wide variety of animals, especially the wading birds which basically 'live' in the water ten to twelve hours every day."

After a few moments of silence, Charles spoke up, "If you have a pertinent question please speak up. If not, we will have plenty of time for general discussion of all of the presentations this afternoon and for subsequent strategy sessions. OK?

Tony spoke up, "Is coffee toxic?"

He looked around and no one said anything. They all looked at him with puzzled expressions.

"Good," he said. "I worked until early this morning on a case and I need to hear everything Anne is going to say. So may I help myself to a cup?" And he got up and got himself a cup of coffee. That was simply the type of guy that was Tony. He was self made, and as an environmentalist and a lawyer, he dealt with people and pollutants.

And of course it was too late to answer Tony because he already had poured his coffee, added three sugars, and was headed back to take his seat.

Dave just smiled. 'OK, let us move on to the next speaker."

And there was a quick round of applause for Dr. Barclay, plus a shaking of heads and several chuckles for Tony Batista.

Dave stood up and requested quiet, and asked, "Is Anne Brown ready?'

Anne Brown was a forty five year old lifetime environmentalist. At one time her family owned more than fifty acres of land directly on Biscayne Bay in Miami. When she was a young girl her father was killed in an automobile accident, her mother had died one year before, and she was alone without family. The Dade County government, with the encouragement of a local developer, re-zoned much of the shoreline of Biscayne Bay as an industrial zone and planned to build there several large import-export marinas. The Brown's land was included within the new zone. And suddenly little Anne owed several hundred thousand dollars in new taxes. Anne was thus forced to sell her Father's land for much below the market prices – she just got ripped off. So she moved away from Miami to Orlando where she has been a staunch environmentalist ever since.

Anne took the podium and began. "Thank you for allowing me to tell you about my latest studies concerning the new increased pollution from the sugar cane plantations around Lake Okeechobee, just north of the Everglades. I have been collecting data from there for the past fifteen years. I will just summarize some of the more pertinent numbers which I think that you will find interesting."

She looked around the room and realized she was among friends. When one was fighting a farming block that provided many jobs, a substantial inflow of money into an area, and now a new important automobile fuel precursor, not everyone considered her to be "friendly". She had her share of negative receptions when she gave 'local pollution' talks.

"For more than fifty years land developers and sugar cane farmers have been moving into and expanding the sugar cane growing region around Lake Okeechobee in south central Florida, just north of the Everglades. Fifty years ago no sugar cane was grown here, it was mostly citrus trees. This area now grows almost half of the sugar cane in the United States."

"Sugar cane has recently become the major source for the sugars used as the key sweetener for numerous industrially produced foods such as soft drinks, and it is a better source for making alcohol for automotive fuels than corn. It is now in high demand."

"Lake Okeechobee is the second largest freshwater lake wholly within the United States. Sugar cane plants require massive amounts of fertilizer which results in massive runoffs of fertilizer contaminated water after heavy rains, and especially during hurricanes. Because laws were passed to limit the quantity of pollution from sugar plantations onto adjacent lands, several large pumping stations were built to back-pump the run off of the polluted agriculture water into Lake Okeechobee."

"Recently it was determined that approximately thirty two billion gallons of this contaminated water is discharged into the lake every year. Calculations suggest that this is more than 60,000 one-hundred bags of pure phosphate being dumped into the lake each year. Blue-green algae massive growths or blooms have become a regular occurrence in the lake. And the toxins from the blue-green algae are very toxic to human liver, and cause skin rashes, GI pains, cramps, nausea, vomiting and diarrhea. Area Health Department reports of such symptoms in young and old people have increased several hundred percent during the past few years in many nearby communities. And Lake Okeechobee is the major source of drinking water for several million people living near the lake and along the Atlantic Ocean shore such as West Palm Beach, Fort Myers and further south into northern Miami."

"Over the years there have been a variety of efforts by the sugar cane owners, local, state, and national government and non-government organizations, and people living in the area to try to deal with this difficult problem. Most of these efforts have focused on trying to repair the damage, after the fact, caused by the farming and land cultivation."

"A few years ago the Governor of the state of Florida arranged to use two billion dollars of public funds and purchased two hundred thousand acres of sugar cane farmland, closed it down to farming and converted it back to nature. The land that was purchased was located between Lake Okeechobee, the Big Cypress Preserve, and the Everglades National Park. This conversion would occur over a ten year period. Approximately four hundred thousand acres of sugar cane farming would continue south of Lake Okeechobee, immediately north of the Everglades."

"So on the east side of the Lake where population density is high, and where drinking water comes from Lake Okeechobee, the farming would slow and the pollution would decrease; while on the south side of the Lake where population density is low, farming and its run off pollution would continue southward toward the Everglades. And no more back-pumping of the polluted runoff water into Lake Okeechobee. Overall, this means that more of the phosphate polluted water will flow into the Everglades. This is what is happening today."

"What also is happening is that the remaining sugar cane farmers are increasing the density of their plants and the subsequent required fertilizers. Hence this also increases the amount of pollution in the water drainage areas in the northern everglades. And it has caused an increase in the mass of exotic (not native to Florida) plant growth in the area. Many of these exotic plants are very aggressive and simply take over areas where native grass dies out due to the pollution. There is current talk at the level of national and state governments of attempts to construct a green filter system between the sugar cane farming area and the Everglades. More money will probably be spent to try to correct the problem and repay subsequent damage, and not to prevent the problem."

"Now I ask you, will a temporary block of the drainage of fertilizer polluted water prevent the problem? No. Over time the pollutants would leak through. A good example is a similar pollution control mechanism employed in the state of Iowa. In the 70s and 80s most of Iowa's streams and rivers were highly polluted with nitrogen and phosphate from heavy fertilizer applications to the corn plants. Increased density in planting yielded increased profits but also required increased quantities of herbicides and fertilizers. Increased water runoff of both types of pollutants into local streams and rivers occurred. And most of Iowa's towns and cities were using drinking water from local wells or local sources. So an acute problem was rapidly getting worse.

"One solution put into place was to not plant commercial crops within fifteen to twenty feet of any creek or river. The idea was to let a natural green biomass build up and filter out most of the pollutants. This worked for a while. Pollutants did decrease in most of the stream and river water tables. Also the deer population increased dramatically because now they had nesting shelter, water to drink, and plenty of corn to eat. And all for free. However, after fifteen to twenty years the fertilizer and pesticide pollutant levels in the creeks and rivers again began creeping upward. A saturation point had been reached."

"There is another solution now being considered in Iowa. The development and utilization of corn seeds/crops that require less fertilizer could be financially sound and could decrease pollution problems. Researchers in Iowa are experimenting with single gene transfer technology. In the near future we may see gene engineered (GE) corn crops which require less fertilizer."

"So I leave you with the idea that maybe we should support similar research efforts to develop new GE sugar cane crops which require less fertilizer and therefore decrease the quantity of pollution as it drains into the Everglades."

There was a stunned silence. A couple of the Board members looked at each other in puzzlement. What was gene engineered - GE crops?

Finally Board Member Atkins Berrat spoke up. "Thank you for the very interesting presentation and an even more interesting suggestion. Now you have to tell us what gene engineering is?"

Ms. Brown laughed. "Before I read about the Iowa research efforts on corn crops, I had not even heard about gene engineered crops. I knew about gene modified foods, but not gene engineered crops. They are similar in that one gene is transferred into something to change that something. How many times in life did you wish you had a gene to accomplish something like that. I could have used a nice gene yesterday to accomplish something with my fifteen year old daughter; such as when will you listen to me. But since I haven't decided what I would have wanted to accomplish with her, I don't know what gene I would need. Do not get me wrong, my daughter is a good one, just difficult at times."

"Besides," and she chuckled, "I am not sure what genes are available at what prices and at which 7-11 supermarkets these days. Plus I have not seen any discount sales lately. No, I am just playing with you. But I do think such a thing could happen at some point in the near future."

And she got her share of return smiles and the nodding of heads. Everyone had been serious for too long this morning. But this was a serious issue.

Jerry Witherson spoke up, "Will these genes work on wives also?"

And another round of laughter sprang up. None of the problems for which the Save the Everglades Foundation wanted to solve were going to be solved overnight. So, a little humor might be good therapy for so many difficult and serious environmental problems.

She continued. "Really though it is that simple. In the past if you wanted to change the color of your corn from yellow to red, your crossed your yellow corn with purple colored corn. You allowed the chromosomes (thousands of genes) from the yellow corn to mix with the chromosomes (thousands of genes) from purple colored corn just to get that purple gene to mix with that yellow gene to cause a red color to appear."

"Today, you can take that purple gene and inject it directly into the yellow corn cell; it will mix with the yellow gene and directly make red colored corn. It is no longer necessary to transfer thousand of genes. When it is only one gene that you want to transfer, to change the characteristics of something, all you need is just that one gene and a mechanism for transfer. So if any of you know a 'decrease the requirement for fertilizer sugar cane gene,' let me know and we can decrease the fertilizer contaminated pollution into the Everglades. This will make the sugar cane plantation owners happy at the same time as expenses will decrease due to the use of less fertilizer."

Marshal Benter spoke up and asked, "Can you explain the composition of food crop fertilizers, and does sugar cane have a special fertilizer combination? And why is phosphate so bad?"

Ms. Brown responded. "In general most fertilizer combinations always include nitrogen, phosphate, and potassium. For example a home garden fertilizer could be 8:6:9. This would mean 8% nitrogen: 6% phosphate: 9% potassium and the remaining 77% would be none-active ingredients. Each of these components can be used in different atomic forms. For example nitrogen can be in a liquid, solid, or gas form, nitrate, nitrite, sulfated urea, and anhydrous ammonia. The same is true for the other components of fertilizers."

"Various sugar cane clones are currently being tested with different combinations of these fertilizer ingredients. The research shows a wide variation in the requirements for nitrogen, phosphate, potassium, magnesium, manganese, sulfates, etc. for the different clones. From what I understand each farmer selects his own sugar cane crop variety to plant and his own fertilizers, herbicides, and pesticides each year. His aim is to get the maximum yield for the minimum cost from his land. If there were several genetic engineered sugar cane varieties available which had more efficient energy systems, he could decrease his costs with decreased fertilizer application, and there would be less fertilizer to spill over into the downstream Everglades region. I simply think that we need to learn about GE sugar cane and support such research efforts. These sugar cane farms are not going to go away. Commercially they are extremely viable, as they are now a major source of energy for both humans and automobiles. We have to learn to live with them and try to help decrease their spillover pollution."

"And lastly, phosphate is the bad chemical that kills many types of native plants and simulates several types of non-native plants to grow in this region. For example, cat tails is a non-native exotic plant whose growth is stimulated by phosphate. Because of this, it is called the death plant. Where ever you see it growing, there is probably a high quantity of phosphate due to a fertilizer overflow a nearby farmer's field."

She got a nice round of applause. The talking and questions began to fly. So Charles spoke up, "Why don't we take a coffee break and come back for our next presentations by Tony Batista and then Janet Styker-Collingswood in maybe a half hour. OK?"

Half an hour later, after coffee and carrot cake, everyone settled back into their chairs and Charles called the meeting to order again. "This morning the talks were very stimulating. They present a challenge to the next two speakers. Tony, are you ready? Then let's begin."

Tony Batista was an American citizen of Spanish origin living with his wife and three children in Florida City, Florida. Florida City is located in southern Dade County between the ocean and the Everglades. It used to be about ten miles from the Everglades, now it encroaches into the marsh waters of the Everglade area. Construction of draining canals and housing developments have continued in the area for the past forty to fifty years even though many court battles and law suits have come and gone. This is an area that has become famous because the taste of the local drinking water changes every month. If you don't like today's flavor, just wait until next month.

Mr. Batista is a lawyer and he has been involved in several of the legal wars concerning man's development versus Everglades. So he has seen and heard the arguments on both sides – Citizens for Progress versus Save the Everglades. He had enough of the former group and was now fully supporting the latter group. He had been a member of the Board of Directors of the Save the Everglades foundation for more than six years, so everyone knew him. Today he was going to simply give his opinions and ideas which might be of some help for his children's favorite animal, the manatee, which had recently been put on the endangered species list; and during the afternoon he would help identify any legal problems if the Board decided on any strategies or projects to pursue.

Tony began. "Thank you Charles. It is again a pleasure to be with you again and to continue to seek ideas to protect this outstanding creation of God, and the most outstanding natural resource of America, even though Americans do not know it. I live at the bottom right corner of the Everglades. Every pollutant and problem that the Everglades have, I also have - on my property and in my house."

"Most of the legal battles that I have been involved with over the past few years have been in the South Florida Water Management District which involves Broward and Dade Counties. So I will focus there in my talk today. There are two major problems for residents in this area: 1) securing enough drinking water; 2) dealing with water pollution. As the population in these counties has grown well past the millions mark, water shortages have become worse and worse. Regular rationing of faucet water is common every year. And of course heavy summer rains and hurricanes create havoc with the existing canals and pump stations. The area's flood control systems take a beating during hurricane season. And this increase in population has also put similar strains on all of the existing septic and surface water run-off systems."

"As I see it there are three major problems that this massive metropolitan area presents for the Everglades:

1) Drainage canals and construction of houses and industrial buildings deplete the organic peat in the nearby areas and also allow oceanic salt water to penetrate fresh water areas which creates a brackish water region

that drastically changes the bio-habitat which results in the killing of many species of both plants and animals;

2) home, industrial, and city septic exhaust is not processed enough such that when it is pumped into the Everglade waters it contains numerous toxic contaminants such as mercury and petroleum organics all of which kill nature;

3) Buildings, homes, and street water run-offs contain high levels of toxic substances such as garden pesticides, herbicides, and fertilizers. As we know these are very toxic for all native and even domestic animals."

"Today, several NGOs keep an eye on the entire Everglades water basin. When they see a specific something that they think will "hurt" the Everglades in a specific way in a specific place, they try to legally interfere or try to correct and possible decrease the "hurt." Several such law suits have been taken all the way to the US Supreme Court to finally have a legal decision made and implemented. Some of the decisions from these suits have helped and some have hurt the Everglades. So, there is a limited place for the law to assist in the protection of the Everglades. But one can identify the specifics and work out a winning argument. It is no longer enough to say 'they are killing baby seals.' People respond emotionally. The legal systems do not respond emotionally. But legal systems do respond to people. So people pressure is very important."

Tony looked around the room and saw some gloomy faces. He had painted a no-easy-solution picture. Most of the foundation people knew this. But hearing it from one of the key environmental gladiators was rather depressing.

He asked. "Do you want me to clarify or expand any of these ideas? The future will be a continuous battle against man's desire to own property and to use that property as he sees fit, without his destroying the environment near him. The entire American tax structure system is based upon the requirement that man must buy a house and obtain thirty years of tax deductible payments. Then he must sell that house and buy another larger house and again obtain thirty years of tax deductible payments. Then again he must sell that house and buy a larger house and obtain thirty ........; this continues until he can no longer borrow enough money to put down on the next larger house. A house is the single largest investment that most Americans make during their lifetime. The problem lays where he buys that house and how he manages his property over those years. He has to be continuously educated about his private property and its relationship to nearby commons properties, private or government owned."

Jack Roister spoke up, "I see on television that many of the houses on the canals near the Everglades routinely have back yard green visitors. They probably no longer believe green is the true color."

Tony smiled and responded. "Very true, it is almost common to have friends over for a backyard bar-b-q and have an uninvited alligator join the group. This is especially true if it is good old red meat such as bloody steaks that you are cooking. They can smell blood from afar. Also it is not unusual to have a neighbor dog disappear if left in the back yard when you are out shopping. Children and even adults have been attacked on their own property by alligators. Other animals that "float in" are the wood rat, cotton mouse, raccoons, opossums, and a variety of snakes including the poisonous diamondback rattlesnake. In fact several 'save the animals' companies have popped up over the years which, upon call, come to your house and rescue that poor little rattlesnake from your kitchen cabinet, for a fee of course."

Again he called for questions. There appeared to be none for now. There was a nice applause.

So Charles called for his wife, Dr. Janice Stryker-Collingswood to come forward to talk about animal diversity in the Everglades, and support her conclusions with her own research data.

Janice began. "Thank you for allowing me to talk about my life work; secondary to my Charles, Sam and Sara of course."

A few smiles went around the room because most Board members knew that it was she that brought him into the environmental biology fold in the Everglades.

"My graduate students and I have been collecting animal data from the Everglades for more than twenty years. Let me share some of these data with you today. As you know the Everglades contains a variety of microclimates which host a wide variety of plants and animals. In general, there are more than one hundred and fifty species of plants and about ninety species of animals living there. We only study the animals. We perform bi- or tri-monthly evaluations of animal numbers, nesting pairs or new born, health status of young and adults, status of macro-habitats and micro-habitats. We use the following methodology to collect this data. The plant/geological character of the Everglades can be recognized as follows: slough, saw-grass, mangrove, hummock, and pineland. Different animals live within these five environments. We divide the Everglades National Park into five large geographical quadrants. Within each quadrant we select two or three of each of these environments for the study of the animals which are making that environment their homes."

"Let me give some examples:

1) Slough – soft swamp like ground in which we monitor butterflies and dragon flies the snapping turtle, leatherback turtle, green turtle, wood duck, wood rat, cotton mouse, and otter,

2) Mangrove swamp – small trees and shrubs that have an interlacing above ground root system in which we monitor butterflies and dragon flies, the bull frog, green sea turtle, leatherback turtle, roseate spoonbill, brown pelican, white tailed deer, manatee, wood rat, and cotton mouse,

3) Saw-grass – grass like plants which have margins on their leaves toothed like a saw in where we monitor the great blue heron, great white heron, wood stork, several species of butterflies and dragonflies, and apple snail,

4) Hummock – elevated tract of land rising gently above surrounding flat land like a knoll or hillock in which we monitor the green snake, tree frog, tree snail, and diamondback rattlesnake,

5) Pineland – marsh land with standing pine trees; we monitor the diamondback rattlesnake, red fox, white tailed deer, wild pig, and turkey."

"We do not monitor or get near the American alligator or the American crocodile. American Alligators are in abundance in many areas. But there are only few American crocodiles. The National Park Service keeps an eye on them. I really do not like them."

"Using these select groups of animals in each of five environments we get a very good idea if that environment is in trouble, or if just that animal is in trouble. And by comparing the same type environment in all four quadrants we can estimate just how wide spread the environmental insult happens to be at that point in time. We have recorded that a decrease in certain animals can be seasonal (related to a certain time of the year and not related to reproductive changes such as springtime). So we take this into consideration when analyzing our data."

"During these past twenty years I can definitely say that every animal that we have been routinely following has shown a decrease in population. The decrease in numbers is highest in the northern Everglades especially near the Cyprus National Preserve and in northern Dade County. The animals that have decreased the most are the certain species of butterflies and dragon flies, tree frog, tree snail, apple snail, hawksbill turtle, and leatherback turtle. It would appear that many of the toxic chemicals that are entering the Everglades strongly interfere with molecular mechanisms of metamorphosis. So animals that require a metamorphosis cycle in their route to adulthood, suffer the most."

"Also during these past years we have seen the numbers of several animals decrease such that they have now been placed onto the endangered species list. These include the green turtle, leatherback turtle, hawksbill turtle, Atlantic Ridley turtle, cotton mouse, wood rat, wood stork, cape sable sea side sparrow, southern bald eagle, Florida panther, and the manatee. A defined endangered species is a species of plant or animal, that, throughout all or a major portion of it normal living habitat, is in danger of extinction."

"In addition the populations of the green frog, tree snail, apple snail, wild pig, and several species of butterflies and dragonflies have decreased from 50 to 70% during the past ten years. The larger animals are probably more resilient to microenvironment changes. There are at least two reasons for this. A larger body volume seems to allow for a dilution of the toxic chemicals within the body; and mammals in particular have excellent liver detoxification and cellular immune systems that can neutralize and excrete these chemicals before they can do lethal damage within the body."

"So I am in agreement with all of the speakers of this morning. There are a wide variety of toxic chemicals entering, in high quantity, into the Everglades today. Most are probably coming from two directions, north and east. These toxic chemicals are killing many of the animals (and plants) currently living in the Everglades. I do not know how to stop and reverse this process such that even some of the native systems will return toward normal."

"Since money often speaks louder than words, in my opinion, a nice healthy tax on every industrial complex, business, and household that exhausts into the Everglades would be a good place to start. Theoretically, only those who drive on highways pay road construction and road maintenance taxes via gasoline price adjustments. Since everyone pays a monthly septic fee, let that fee reflect a monetary adjustment for the Everglades if their septic flow eventually enters into the Everglades. Then this "adjustment" could be used to try to prevent and correct the tragedy that is currently happening in the Everglades."

And with that she sat down. There was silence for several moments. Then everyone started talking at the same time. Charles let them do so for several minutes. Then he noted that it was noon and suggested that they return to Janice's interesting idea after lunch at about 1:30 PM. So they all adjourned to Spider's Crab House restaurant which was only about five hundred feet down Main Street. There, a sea food meal awaited them.

After the delicious lunch they returned to the church and opened the floor for ideas, strategies and projects which would help the Everglades and it natural occupants.

For the next three hours everyone had a turn to ask questions and give their opinion concerning the problems and potential cures for their "sick baby". Finally they reached a general consensus on three projects.

Charles, as President of the Save the Everglades foundation, recorded that the meetings unanimously agreed upon the following conclusions and recommended the following actions and projects to be undertaken:

1.  To investigate the current research efforts in inserting genes into food crops, especially sugar cane, in attempts to make them grow with higher energy efficiency – lower requirements for fertilizers, and then to support these efforts; - Anne Brown and Janice Stryker would lead this effort,
2.  To initiate lobbying efforts to change the septic exhaust laws in southern Florida and in the area surrounding the Everglades to include an Everglades pollution adjustment tax; - Tony Batista would lead this effort,
3.  To raise monies to try to re-establish some of the animals on the endangered species list such as the green turtle, leatherback turtle, wood stork, and the manatee (the manatee was a mammal like the dolphin and swam with children when acclimated to humans, hence it would be a popular choice for fund raising) - Charles Collingswood would lead this effort.

Along about 5:30 PM the Board of Directors of the Save the Everglades foundation closed their meeting, went to their separate hotels, and planned to meet tomorrow for an Everglades tour led by Janice and Charles. They planned to split the group in half. Charles would provide a land tour in the swamp buggy and Janet would provide a tour in the air boat. In the afternoon the groups would change drivers and vehicles. So everyone got to see "everything" from the land and from the water.

* * *

A few days later Charles and Janice were going over some of the ideas that surfaced at the recent annual meeting. Perhaps Charles, as

President of the Save the Everglades foundation, should attend the Thirty First International Congress on the Environment and Biodiversity to be held at the Convention Center in Chicago two months from now. There would be meetings on all three project areas from both an American and international perspective. He could attend select science and legal research talks about the environment and also rent an interest display booth for the foundation. An interest booth allows a science or environment group to advertise its presence and its current projects to the participants attending the congress. It is quite common for people who share a common interest to "find" each other at such booths at such meetings. There would be two to three thousand professionals from all over the world who were interested and working 0n environmentally related projects. The Save the Everglades foundation could use the exposure, and maybe they would get lucky and identify some substantial monetary assistance for their work.

So two months later Charles found himself sitting at the Chicago Convention Center in booth #163 on Floor #1 in Aisle #12. Over the past three days he had attended several excellent talks on plant and animal population changes related to intrusive pollution into animal habitats. It was the same worldwide. Uncontrolled or non-controlled automotive and industrial exhaust, agriculture and urbanization run-off resulted in pollution of air and waters. The greater the quantity and the higher the toxic character of the pollution run-off resulted in a greater insult to native populations of plants and animals. And of course the greater the insult to the native population groups the greater the killing of nature in general.

Indeed there were several and varied approaches being used by environmental groups to put lobbying pressures on politicians to pass "correct" laws that would assist in controlling pollution damage in many "natural" areas. With regard to the gene engineering project, he just did not understand the science enough to benefit from the scientific presentations about GE modified food crops. He would have to study and learn more about this high technology scientific area.

He was looking through some of his brochures on the Save the Everglades foundation which he had prepared, brought to the Congress, and had been handing out. Suddenly Charles looked up and saw a big broad shouldered guy wearing a grey suit with a blue tie coming down aisle #12. The man had red hair, jade green eyes, a left ear cleft, and was coming down the aisle toward him.

As William came down the aisle he spotted a big guy in booth #163 who was wearing a dark blue suit with a blue tie. This guy had red hair, jade green eyes, and a cleft near his left ear. And he also had his face. What was this?

The guy from the aisle walked over to the guy in the booth and stared. They just stood there staring at each other. It appeared that neither had a tongue as they continued looking each other up and down. It was weird to see an identical picture of yourself without a mirror in front of you. They had both struck the same pose; right hand in the pants pocket, left hand touching the cleft on their left ear, and an expression on the face which said that cannot be me because I am over here. After a minute of staring, and then noticing the attention they were getting from passer-bys, Charles spoke up.

He stuttered, "Are you a doctor or a detective?"

The man answered, "No, are you looking for one?'

William Bassinger, from Des Moines, Iowa, lawyer now specializing in legal problems concerning genetically engineered crops and genetically modified foods, had come to Chicago to attend the Thirty First International Congress on the Environment and Biodiversity. Little did he dream that he might see his suspected but not yet known brother/self.

Then it suddenly dawned on Charles, this person was one of them. Finally, maybe now he would not die as Chief White Cloud predicted. And he was east of the biggest river in the USA. He was ecstatic but also was unsure if it was really true. No, he knew. Bill also knew.

The tears collected in the four green eyes and overflowed onto the four eye lids, flowed down the four checks, and hit the floor. They threw their arms around each other and hugged as if they were long lost friends. But instead, they were identical brothers who had lived for forty two years without even touching one another. And to make things even worse, they each knew the other existed but did not know where he existed.

As a crowd of people started to gather to look at these two big guys with carrot red hair and jade green eyes who couldn't seem to get enough of one another, Charles broke off but kept hold of Bill's hands. As Bill looked around, red faced, and smiling ear to ear, he saw many just people staring at them. And suddenly he understood that they were giving off the wrong public signals.

Bill looked at the crowd, held up their hands, and loudly declared, "See our fingers. We are not married. We are not even engaged." And they both broke out in laughter.

And just as suddenly the crowd laughed, recognizing the two men as identical twins, and began dispersing. Bill and Charles continued to hold hands and walked inside the Save the Everglades booth, sat down on two chairs and began a discussion of their lives.

Only after sitting down did Bill introduce himself, "I am William (Bill) Bassinger from Des Moines, Iowa," and he laughed.

Charles also suddenly understood, and introduced himself." I'm Charles Collingswood from Indian Nest, Florida. What a small world, or is it."

They were both embarrassed, excited, and at a loss to know what to do or what to say. They were identical in every way, and yet they had never met. But they had finally retrieved their masculine composure, and began to talk in fast broken sentences. There was so much to tell and so much to learn. Where to begin!

Charles finally said, "I need a cup of relaxing tea. How about you?"

"No, but I can use some coffee," answered Bill.

So Charles immediately closed the booth and the two "new" brothers went to the lounge area. After a few more minutes of emotional outpouring, they spent the next couple of hours learning about themselves from themselves.

# 10 - The Hunt for My/Our Self-s Continues

Aaron and Dave seemed to have definitely found each other by the unique type of spirit telecommunication. But they were able to communicate only during sleeping hours. And this spirit communication was enough to exchange useful information, so now they need to use E-mail less and less. But they did need to keep the situation a secret. Neither of them had told his wife or family. Secrecy was especially true now that they both could definitely feel two more pairs of spirit hands, sometimes even when the two of them were communicating. The other two were probably their identical twins; there were four of them/us; of this they were certain. But where were they/us; what were they/us doing; did they/we have families; were they/we healthy and all right; why could all of them/us not be brought closer? It was an unusual feeling to be in communication with yourself, and yet not yourself. It was as if there was finally someone in the world that you could completely and totally trust, but you couldn't find him/him. All four of them/us had to be brought together or all four of them/us would go crazy. And it must be soon.

During the past few weeks Dave had made two trips to Florida and visited local government offices which registered and assisted immigrants, but it was of no help because he had no names and only his own face to compare with. He tried to explain that he was looking for his twin brother, but that did not go over very well with whomever he asked. He visited several of the immigrant communities, but the foreign workers did not trust him. They assumed he was looking for renegade or illegal immigrants. He drove and looked and looked and drove and found no one ever resembling a 260 pound, 6 ft 9 inch male, about forty years and who had red hair and green eyes. There could not be very many of these guys running around. Sometimes he would just say, "Have you seen me lately?" Sometimes they laughed. Sometimes they thought he was crazy. Sometimes they just did not appreciate his humor and walked away. He was beginning to wonder if maybe he and Aaron might be a little crazy.

* * *

About this time Aaron had a family tragedy strike. His Father had a bad heart attack and was not expected to live more than a few days. Aaron and Jos left the children with her brother and his wife, Brian and Elaine. Brian was a computer engineer and they had moved to New York City six years ago. They had one little boy, and the three children were close cousins. There should not be any problems there. So Aaron and Jos quickly drove up to the "House" in Manchester.

Upon arrival Aaron could see that everyone was in a state of panic. Aaron had left home at the age of eighteen and never returned. During these past years he had been completely devoted to his Genetic Quest in New York City. He had visited his parents but once every two or three years. So he was now somewhat out-of-date with circumstances at "home." His Father, Dr. James Armand was the backbone of the family in the "House". He had been a family doctor in Manchester, New Hampshire for more than thirty five years. So almost everyone in the community knew him personally, and had the utmost respect for him and the family. Plus he had become the natural head of the Armand families in the New Hampshire and Boston area. If he should go, there would be a big gap for someone to fill.

Mary Armand had never been a healthy lady. She had been barren until at the age of 32 years, they then went "high tech" as she called it to herself. She and her husband had tried to keep Aaron's origin a secret by talking about his natural birth at the St. Gabriel Hospital in Manchester, which was supervised by her husband. Aaron had a legitimate birth, a legitimate birth certificate, a legitimate driver's license, and a legitimate passport. What else did one need to be legitimate? All of the family accepted this except Aaron. No one in the family "talked" behind Mrs. Armand's back because they all loved Dr. James very much. Yet there were the obvious physical differences between Aaron, and his Mother and Father, and even within the family unit. They had tried to overcome this or somehow make up for it, but had always known that Aaron had seen through the mirage. Aaron loved them very much so he also had not pressed his parents about his origin. But suddenly, now things were different?

Aaron and Jos drove up the long drive way toward the "House" The driveway near the "House" was filled on both sides with automobiles. There must have been more than forty cars parked at all angles. Obviously all friends of the family who wanted to 'help' in any way they could. Aaron drove around to the back and parked. They went in the back way and through the side entrance to the kitchen area. Everything and everybody was in an overload as the cook, maids, butler, and several friends of the servants had come to help serve refreshments and soft drinks to the mass of friends out front, in the dining room, the salon, the games room, the veranda, out on the patio, near the stables and tennis courts. Everywhere friends were giving their best wishes and talking quietly.

Aaron immediately took control. He walked directly into the front of the house, into the salon, and with his large physical stature and booming voice, he graciously said. "We sincerely thank all of you for coming and being with us at this very difficult time. I will relay your prayers to my Father as he recovers. But for now it is best that you please allow him to have some peace and quiet so he can better rest."

And Aaron and Jos starting walking among the crowd, from room to room and continued to encourage the many friends to withdraw. They graciously started thanking everyone, showering kisses, hugs, handshakes, pats on the back, and with small nuisances exchanged, he and Jos started moving the mass of friends toward their cars; again they kept thanking everyone for coming and saying that they would let them know of any changes in Aaron's Father's condition. It took the two of them more than a half an hour to 'clear the house'. They then gave all of the hired family members big hellos and kisses, thanking them for all of the extra work and taking care of the numerous family friends. They asked them to please just clean up and go on home for the rest of the day. Finally he and Jos went upstairs to see Dad.

Dad was laying in the master bed in the presence of his wife and Aaron's Mother, Mary, his Father's two younger sisters, Elmyra and Hatice, and his Father's lifetime colleague, Dr. Ashdown. He was asleep. He was very pale and thin as he had been fed only by intravenous feeding since the heart attack occurred 36 hours ago. He did not look good. Aaron and Jos kissed his Mother and the two Aunts. Aaron then motioned for Dr. Ashdown to step outside with him. They stepped into the hallway to talk privately.

The two doctors shook hands and Dr. Ashdown said, "I am very sorry about your Father. Recently he was looking and feeling OK. He had cut back on his patient practice and was trying to adjust into some type of semi-retirement. Of course you know how impossible that would be for him."

"Yes, he is a truly dedicated physician," replied Aaron. All of his patients really adore and love him."

Dr. Ashdown continued, "Over the years he thought that he had become responsible for the health and life of every citizen in Manchester. So, if someone needed his help, he was always there, immediately. This heart attack was a surprise to everyone. But that is often how it happens. I have no idea when he had his last general physical check up. I do not know if he ever had an EKG."

Aaron answered, "Can you give me any idea about his future? Do you hold out any hope that he will recover, improve, and live a longer and comfortable life?"

"You are a doctor so I will not pull punches," Dr. Ashdown replied. "Your Father had a massive heart attack. He had a large embolism in his left atrium. Due to this obstruction his heart is now beating in a very irregular mode. Various blood thinner drugs have decreased the size of the clot, but there has been too much damage to the heart itself. He is too old and fragile for surgery, and of course a heart transplant is out of question. In my opinion he will not recover. I would guess he has only a few more days or perhaps weeks. But it is really impossible to predict with something like this. If he does recover he will certainly be partially paralyzed. Total recovery is not possible."

Aaron asked, "Is there anything that I can do, or that any cardiologist can do to prolong his life? Or is there too much pain involved?"

Dr. Ashdown replied, "He should have been under the care of a cardiologist several years ago. Then this might not have happened. But you know that doctors are their own worst doctors. When is the last time that you had a general medical check-up?"

Aaron ignored the question and instead responded, "I would appreciate it if you did not tell the family that Dad only has a few remaining days. As good Catholic Father Bernardsten would say, 'One cannot and should not second guess God's wishes.' And I agree with this."

"As you wish," responded Dr. Ashdown.

Aaron continued, "I sincerely thank you for everything."

And they turned and went back into the master bedroom.

Dr. Armand had awakened a little and murmured for Aaron to join him at his side. Aaron pulled a chair up to the bedside and sat as close as he could.

His Father's first thoughts were of his son as he said, "How is your work coming?' This was typical as he always thought of others first, and especially his only child, Aaron.

Aaron leaned close to his Father and said, "My work progresses very well. But for now, let us concentrate on your work. And that is for the near future you must strengthen your body such that I can again beat you in snooker."

Aaron and his Father both considered themselves as experts at the pool table downstairs in the games room. Over the many years of playing snooker, the first Dr. Armand was ahead of the second Dr. Armand in games won, at least so the first Dr. Armand's score card showed.

Upon hearing this, the first Dr. Armand replied, "Why I could probably beat you while playing from a wheel chair." And he smiled.

Then Aaron's Father motioned for the others in the room to please leave and allow his son and him to talk privately. The four ladies went downstairs to the salon and ordered their tea.

He whispered, as his voice was fading. He said, "I love you very much. I would have loved you even if you had been my biological son. Maybe that is why I love you because you have become more than just some child to watch grow, mature, and become successful in life. Since your Mother and I could not create our own biology, God gave us you. And you have been more than a Father could expect from his own chromosomes. Now it is time for you to find your own chromosomes, if you so want to do so." He groaned.

Aaron wasn't sure he heard him correctly. Did he hear his Father admit that they did not share genes? Was he going to learn who his 'real' Father was? He had waited for this all his life, but now he did not want to know. Suddenly it was not necessary. This man was his Father. Tears formed in his eyes.

Then Father reached toward Aaron and whispered, "See Jackson McClean." And he closed his eyes and went to sleep.

With tears in his eyes, Aaron just sat there staring at his Father for several minutes, willing him to wake up and repeat what he thought he had just heard. Jackson McClean? Who was Jackson McClean?

After some time, and his Father did not wake up, Aaron left the room and went downstairs to the salon to be with the rest of the family. He told them that Father was now sleeping. He told Mother that she should have someone stay with Father in the room at all times, twenty four hours a day, seven days a week. Perhaps a couple of his clinic nurses could rotate and remain with him at all times. Dr. Ashdown was also having tea and nodded in agreement. He also nodded and smiled at Aaron's wife, Jos. Aaron took Jos's hand, excused the two of them and took Jos into the games room to talk.

After settling into one of the wing tipped Queen Anne chairs, leaning back and sighing deeply, Aaron looked Jos directly in the eyes.

He began, "Father is dying. Dr. Ashdown thinks in terms of days, probably not weeks. But please do not say this to Mother. She does not look very good. Father has had a very long and very successful career, saved a lot of people from pain and death, and he is loved and appreciated for his lifelong dedication to this community. As is not unusual for men like him, he forgot about himself; he forgot that he also lives within a biological entity that requires routine care and maintenance. He had an atrial embolism which did much damage to the left side of his heart. It cannot be repaired."

Jos responded, "He was a true leader and visionary for this community as his participation in community organizations helped bring Manchester into the competitive modern world. He will be missed not only by his patients, but also by the entire community."

Aaron thought out loud, "Yes. He will not be forgotten nor replaced in the family or in the community. And, even though I have not been with him much in the last few years, 100% of my life's foundation was guided and controlled by him. What I have now is because of him. That is why I do not know what to do."

Jos was puzzled. "What do you mean you do not know what to do? About what?"

He thought for a moment and finally said, "A few minutes ago Father confessed to me that he and Mother are not my biological parents. I do not have their genes. I have always suspected this, but to suddenly hear that this is so, it is shocking. I am not sure that I want to know where my genes came from. I have a beautiful, wonderful Mother and Father. If I start looking I might find out my parents are.........less. Maybe it would be better if I did not find out."

Jos responded, "But you know that you have to find out, don't you."

Aaron looked at her and inquired, "Why?"

Jos simply said, "So that the four of you will know your shared parents."

Aaron was shocked. "How do you know about the four of us?"

Jos returned, "Because at night I sometimes hear you communicating with them, and I have heard enough to understand that there are probably four of you that have the same genes. Don't forget, my research training and current research projects deal with genes and chromosomes of twins. You are probably double twins; however that could happen I don't know. And don't feel like I have spied on you. We do sleep in the same bed, remember?" She had joined Aaron's research team two years earlier, and they had been married for eight years. She was well qualified to make such conclusions.

"How can I forget, love." He responded. And he leaned over and kissed her. It was not good to have secrets about your genetic origin from your own wife.

"So how do you want to play it from here on?" asked Jos.

Aaron thought for a moment and said, "We will stay here for a few days and see how Dad does. As you know I can communicate with my other selves from anywhere during night time sleeping. Father told me that the key was a Jackson McClean. I assume that this is the name of the obstetrician-gynecologist that performed what was probably an in vitro fertilization from an anonymous female oocyte donor and an anonymous male sperm donor. Why and how four offspring, I cannot understand. First we must find this Dr. Jackson McClean. I can at least share this information with Dave, and he can look into it. We still have not yet 'found' the other two."

Jos nodded, "Let me know how I can help."

One week later Dr. James Armand died. He went into a coma and did not awaken, so Aaron had no more information concerning his genetics. He knew he could pry more information from his Mother, but now was neither the time nor the place. Maybe later if it really became necessary.

Jos and Aaron stayed three more days for the funeral and to listen to the reading of the will. Then they returned to New York and to their Genetic Quest.

* * *

A few nights later Aaron and Dave had a spirit communication and exchanged their latest experiences. They had been spirit communicating for several years and had met secretly several times so their nightly communication was now accomplished in a semi-sleep state. Therefore, they had much more control and the exchange of information was now strong enough as to be almost like talking over the telephone. Their communication capacities had matured over time.

Dave said, "I found no one in Florida who could possibly be our identical brother, although spirit hands still reach from there."

And Aaron relayed the news about his family. "My Father had a heart attack and died last week. However before he died he admitted to me that my parents are not my true genetic parents, but that they went somewhere and had 'assistance'. He was too far gone to explain how or where, but he did give to me the name of a Dr. Jackson McClean."

Dave stated, "Good, I will start a search for a Dr. Jackson McClean, who is probably a specialist in fertility problems. There cannot be many such specialists with that name in the USA. Should I limit my search to the United States, what do you think?"

Aaron agreed, "My Father would never allow Mother to go abroad for something like this. My guess is everything happened in the New England area, probably in Boston. You might try this area first."

Dave responded, "There are national and international data bases on doctors of all types, so it is not difficult to look both in and outside the USA. I will let you know when I find something.

They both also now felt a definite second pair of spirit hands reaching toward them. Aaron admitted that he did not know what to do to find those hands. There were two sets of spirit hands reaching, but no faces. Where were they/us?

* * *

In a similar fashion, William (Bill) Bassinger, the Iowa lawyer, and Charles Collingswood, the Florida Minister-Environmentalist had met again and had begun to get to know themselves (each other). They also began a spirit communication during nighttime sleeping hours. And like Aaron Armand, the New York City cellular and molecular geneticist, and David (Dave) Dekker, the Washington detective-security specialist, their primary concern was to find their identical brothers. Both Bill and Charles were certain that there were four of 'them,' their dreams had been telling them this for many years. The problem was how to find 'them.' They did not know. Aaron and Dave were already reaching out to their other two brothers. Over the years they had limited success. They could not go public or hire an investigator who specialized in family problems. If the news media found out, the four of them and their families would never have any peace or security. They could just see tomorrow's headlines as – 'Identical

Quadruplets Find Each Other After More Than Twenty Years Searching.' - So the search had to be accomplished very quickly and quietly. It might even be better to not find 'them' rather than risk public exposure. But they just had to keep trying.

# 11 – REX, RED, AND READY

Late one Saturday afternoon there was a little old lady walking down a rather dark corridor in the Museum of Natural Sciences in New York City. She glanced ahead and thought she saw someone on the floor. She slowed down and looked again more carefully. Yes, it looked like a child lying on the floor. It was not moving. Should she call a guard? No, the child moved. She slowly edged closer, watching out for some purse snatcher. As she came upon the child, she saw this red hair. It was a little boy, laying on his back and reading a book out loud. She looked around, and saw no one; and then she saw the boy periodically glancing up as he read. She followed the little boy's almond brown eyes upward. About twenty five feet from the floor was a gigantic open mouth with thousands of very sharp teeth. Above the mouth was a large nose with two nostrils that the boy could crawl into. Then there came two monstrous eyes which were all black. On top of the head she saw small ears, one on each side. Then this green head disappeared. She backed up a couple of steps and looked way up and saw that the head was connected to a green-gray body that just sort of kept going upward and backward. It was the statue of a dinosaur and the little boy was reading to it.

The little old lady said, "Young man, what are you doing lying on that cold floor and reading a book to a dinosaur?"

The little boy looked back over his forehead toward the little old lady and replied, "These days there is global warning on the earth, so soon the dinosaurs will come back. Two hundred and fifty million years ago dinosaurs were the dominant animal on earth, like man is now. There were more ten thousand species living at that time. They ruled everyone and everything for more than one hundred and sixty million years. About sixty five million years ago they started to die. They died because it got be too cold, they were cold blooded you know, and because we killed them. So I am reading St. George and the Dragon to my best friend, Rex. His full name is Tyrannosaurus Rex. St. George killed the last dragon, and she was pregnant, so he destroyed the last chance they had to survive. I want

Tyr to know about St. George's fighting tactics so that next time Rex and his family will be ready when they see St. George coming."

He got up from the floor and stood beside the little old lady. He was only nine years old, had red hair and almond colored eyes, and was a very skinny 5 foot 8 inches, so he towered over the 5 foot little old lady.

He spoke again. "Did you know that birds and man evolved from dinosaurs? There would be no birds today, and we would not be here today, if there had never been dinosaurs. I wonder what will evolve from man when he is extinct."

The little old lady looked up at the lad and frowned. She started to talk 'down' to him. She shouted, "How can you even think that man will become extinct? We were made by God, in God's image, and given the task of populating and dominating the world. And that is just what we are doing!"

She uttered some kind of disgusting phrase which the little boy did not understand, and walked away.

The little boy looked at his Rex and said, "No one wants to understand you guys today. But I love you and I am going to help you."

* * *

The little boy headed for home by way of bus #137W which went north up Amsterdam Avenue to the Columbia University Medical School and his Father's CCGBT. From there he hopped onto the Columbia University shuttle bus which crossed the GW Bridge and down into Palisades Park, where he lived. He had a free bus pass since his Father worked at the CU. He lived about forty five minutes from the Museum, his favorite place to visit. And he did know just about everything in the Museum. But he really was an expert on dinosaurs. As a matter of fact, he was currently the world's nine year old Grand Champion of Dinosaurs.

Last month he, along with thousands of other children around the world, had entered, and he won first prize, in the annual dinosaur contest sponsored by International Dinosaur World. This was an international organization which maintained a huge library and regularly gave On-Line courses in dinosaurology. They had constructed five World Dinosaur Camps in various countries.

There were two in the USA. Each of these Camps contained more than two hundred life size dinosaur statues and numerous exhibits, many of which had robotic dinosaur families. Each Camp had a large hotel, classrooms, laboratories for fossil research, and arts and crafts rooms to construct your own dinosaur. There was also a study room filled with dinosaur books and computer programs from where you could chose a favorite dinosaur, research about it, and present a seminar about its life to the other kids.

The contest had been given only to 9, 10, 11, 12 and 13 year olds from all over the world. And it challenged how much they knew about all types of dinosaurs and the dinosaurs' lives. There was one champion and nine other place winners for each of the five age groups. These fifty winners each won an all expenses paid one week trip to one of the Camps.

Next week, all of this year's winners were going to Palm Tree City, Florida to the World Dinosaur Camp there. Palm Tree City was close to Tampa, Florida. So he would fly from Kennedy International Airport in New York City to Tampa International Airport in Tampa where the Camp bus would meet him and the other winners and take them to the Camp for the week. Southwestern Airlines arranged for all of the flights and monitored the security and safety of the children participants during the flights. It would be an awesome experience.

As he arrived home he found that his Mother and Father were, as usual, working late at the Twinning Center. There was a note from Mom which read that his sister, Hope, would be home at 6:30 PM; and that they would all go out for dinner at the Hi Five Sushi Restaurant at 7:00 PM. It was now 6:15 PM. He was a lover of raw fish so he just smiled and went upstairs to his bedroom. As he went through the door he caressed the attached sign which read:

**Nest of Hype Armand**

**World's Grand Champion of Dinosaurs**

He flopped into his desk chair, opened his PC and put on his latest CD of Dinosaur Rhythm and Blues, sat back and dreamed of next week among the dinosaurs.

* * *

Hype Armand was lying on a bed in seventh heaven. On one bedroom wall were two gigantic triceratops, each were running on four large legs, while on their giant heads each had two long horns with a large head shield between them. They were challenging him. And they would each be more than forty feet long if real. On another wall was a group of raptors from three to eight feet tall, standing on their two legs, short arms out front, and small heads with large mouths full of sharp teeth. They were the most advanced of all dinosaurs because they were very intelligent, very quick and fast on their feet, ferocious in character, and lived in groups and in families. He saw several large and small oviraptors, velociraptors, and also a dilophosaurus. On the third wall were several macronarian Sauropods. He could name each of them: Apatosaurs, Euhelopus, Brachiosaurus, Camarasaurus, and Giraffatitan. They would range from fifty to one hundred feet in length and twenty to thirty feet tall if real. Not one of them would even fit into this large bedroom. And on the fourth wall was a group of various ornithopod dinosaurs. And he named them as: Hererodontosaurus, Iguanodon, Tenontosaurus, Camptosaurus, and Shantugosaurus. All of them would be really huge if real. And finally on the ceiling of the room was a scientific classification of dinosaurs:

Kingdom: Animalia
Phylum: Chordata
Subphylum: Vertebrata
Class: Sauropsida
Subclass: Diapsida
Infraclass: Archosauromorpha
Superorder: Dinosauria
Order 1: Ornithischia
Suborder 1: Cerapoda
Suborder 2: Thyreophora
Order 2: Saurichia
Suborder 1: Saurophodomorpha
Suborder 2: Theropoda

He knew it so well that he could read it up-side down. Wow, he wondered if Dad would let him paint his bedroom walls like this. Probably not. Suddenly he heard his new friends calling for him, so he stopped looking around the room, hopped up off of the bed, and took off out the door. He was late already.

He had arrived at the World Dinosaur Camp in Florida on Sunday afternoon. Most of the fifty winners also arrived on Sunday. He was assigned to a bed in a ten bed dormitory style room, and then explored the area before dinner. After dinner, there was a general get together where all of the winners were given a special welcome and the Camp staff was introduced. And he met other children Dinosaurologists from all over the world. In no time he had a big bunch of new friends who knew "almost" as much dinosaurology as he did. On Monday morning they were organized into two groups of twenty five each and given a general tour of the camp. In the afternoon they were re-organized into groups of five each. These groups would work as teams during the week.

The entire camp was really big and really neat. It was bigger than several football fields, and obviously had been a large forest and pasture land because it was still kind of "wild." There were dinosaurs everywhere you looked. They were all life size and very life like. And he could name most but not all of them. One of his buddies said that there were over two hundred dinosaur statues plus more than fifty robot dinosaurs walking around the grounds. If you were not careful one of the bigger guys could run over you.

Hype caught up with his team as they walked toward their first assignment. The fifty winners were divided into working groups of five children each which would compete for the World Dinosaur Team Championship. Each team had a mixture of ages, sexes, and nationalities. His team included himself as the youngest at nine years of age. There was a pretty ten year Japanese girl named Keiko Matsu, who was really dinosaur smart. It included a dark brown skinned young man named Musina Temasi, of eleven years who was from the Republic of South Africa. From Vienna, Austria, came a twelve year freckled face boy named Heins Glockinstein. His English was not very good, but he sure knew his dinosaurs. And then there was a very tall thirteen year American from Florida, who had red hair, almond colored eyes, and looked like his older twin brother, if he had had one. His name was Samuel Collingswood. So his group was composed of Keiko, Musina, Heins, Sam, and himself. It was a good team as they were all very dinosaur smart. They would win that team world championship.

The group left the hotel area and headed toward the other side of the Camp, a good ten minute walk. The hotel was near the entry gate which was constructed of two hundred feet long Brachiosauri with their long necks entwined at the top. And about one hundred feet inside, just beyond the gate and near Hotel Dino was the famous one, Tyrannosaurus Rex, in all his fifty feet of glory. Just to the right of the gate was the one hundred and twenty bed hotel with a large dining room where the children/students stayed. Continuing about half way around the south side periphery of the Camp was a series of buildings including a Camp Staff Building which contained offices, a conference room, and bedrooms for staff, a library-computer Research and Classroom Building, a Hobbies and Crafts Building, Outdoor Research Projects Building for fossil studies, and a couple of large storage buildings. Everywhere there were statues of dinosaurs of full size, each showing their ferocity. And the north side periphery of the Camp was landscaped and recreated to mimic a one hundred and fifty million year old tropical forest. It was filled with statues of dinosaurs of that era. Every day each group was assigned a work project, and today Hype's group was going to the Outdoor Research Projects Building to watch the staff build and demonstrate robot dinosaurs.

As they walked from the hotel, Hype saluted T Rex, and Musina asked, "Did you guys read Michael Crichton's books or see his movies Jurassic Park and the Lost World. If not they will be shown at 9:30 PM on Wednesday and Thursday nights in the conference room of the Campus Staff Building."

Kieko, who had the quickest wit, responded, "Are not Jurassic Park and Lost World the bibles of dinosaurism. If you come here without reading those books it is equivalent to going to Church without reading the Bible."

She smiled, as a Buddist she was baiting her Christian friends. She added, "Why, I read them to my younger sister when she was six years of age and she loved them."

Musin chimed in, "This is true. If you want to be a dinosaurologist you must read those two books. Just as if you want to be a Christian you must read the Bible."

Sam jumped into this heavy conversation, "Does this mean that if you want to be an ornithologist you must first be a dinosaur and be hatched from an egg before you can understand birds?"

Hype jumped in, "Hey, do you know how many years it took before the Compsognathus became a Archaeopteryx – the dinosaur to bird transition?"

Kieko, Musina, and Heins shook their heads. But Sam, who seemed to know everything, but then he was the oldest, said, "It was less than fifty million years."

Hype was disappointed. Being the youngest he was trying to be one up on his older buddies, and here his 'older brother' zapped him. Sam saw the disappointment in Hype's face, reached over and put his arm around him and said, "I will bet that you and I are the only two dinosaurologists that know that number."

Hype looked up into Sam's face and smiled ear to ear. And he thought to himself, 'This guy is OK.'

Heins changed the subject. Looking at Sam, who was the non-appointed but seeming to become leader of the pack, asked, "Have you decided about your research project?"

"Yes," Sam responded. "I am going to perform research concerning today's last true dinosaur, the crocodile."

"Why do you want to know about him?" Hype asked as he was thinking along the same research lines.

Sam answered, "During the Triassic-Jurassic extinction event, about two hundred million years ago, most of the early Archosaurs such as the Aetosaurs, Ornithosuchids, Phytosaurs and Rauisuchians became extinct. A group of land fauna such as the Crocodylomorphs, Dinosaurs, Mammals, and Pterosaurians continued to evolve. And then during the Cretaceous-Tertiary extinction event, which occurred about sixty million years ago at the end of the Cretaceous period, most dinosaurs became extinct except for crocodylians, lizards, snakes, choristoderans, and sphenodontians. I want to research and try to find out how the crocodyllians survived and why they are todays largest surviving dinosaur."

The other members of the group looked at each other in consternation. Obviously Sam was ahead of them in his thinking. Or at least he was focused, which one must be to perform good research.

Hype was really turned on because he could take cotton swaps and get cheek cells from live crocodiles, but not from dinosaur crocodilian fossils. And he had 'worked' with Mom in the laboratory enough to know that the cotton swab was the first step to DNA/gene analysis and the famous test of DNA fingerprinting. Maybe he and Sam could (later) do a real research project.

"I want to examine the Saurichian and Ornithischian pelvis structures," said Musina. "There must have been major and very important differences that evolved between the two legged versus four legged animals. Today we only have two and four legged animals. Where are the three or five or six legged animals? Multi-legged insects exist; but they did not evolve through the Vertebrata, so they have no spinal chord to support hip structures."

Heins responded, "Changes during the Cretaceous-Tertiary extinction event fascinate me and I want to research this time frame, and look for changes in other life forms such as plants and insects. Did they change and evolve in parallel with dinosaurs?"

"I want to learn about the group or family relationships among the raptors," Keiko commented. "Was the camaraderie just because they had small bodies and needed more bodies for security? Or was it related to a larger brain/body ratio? Was it an inherited or a learned behavioral parameter. There was evidence of herding among several types of dinosaurs; for example the Hadrosaurids or duck-bills. But I am interested in group behavior which possibly involves emotion and long term thinking, not just banding together for immediate protection."

All eyes turned toward to Hype. He blushed, took a minute to regain his composure and said, "I still haven't decided."

But he had decided to go after the crocodile thing with Sam. Sam just didn't know it yet.

Sam spoke up, "Do any of you know anything about why the Tyrannosaurids became dominant in North America but the Dromaeosaurids became dominant in Europe? Heins?"

Heins answered, "I don't know either, but there is a paleobiology group at the University of Berlin that is exploring this question. In my opinion it is just another America versus Europe thing. It does not interest me."

Keiko asked, "Does anyone know if DNA-DNA type of hybridization has been successful using bone free extracts from dinosaur bone fossils of any given Orders or Suborders? The reason that I ask is recently this molecular analysis has confirmed that in the evolution of primates the sequence from old world monkeys to new world monkeys to gorilla to chimpanzee to Australopithecus africanus to Homo habilis to Homo erectus to Homo sapiens is correct. Old world monkeys first appeared about thirty million years ago and Homo sapiens first appeared about one hundred thousand years ago. Is there any similar data on dinosaur DNA for evolutionary sequencing? I know a Japanese Professor that claims such data is being obtained from Ornithisca suborders."

"Yes, I heard the same thing," Sam answered. "I think a group in Australia is studying Ornithisca suborders using molecular technology. We will have to ask one of the Australian students."

Hype's ears perked up but he did not say anything.

And they continued talking "shop" while walking toward the Outdoor Projects Building.

They took careful notes while watching the very interesting demonstration of small robot dinosaurs talking, walking, running, jumping, and playing. They knew that the final team examination would have a couple of questions about robot dinosaurs. At noon, they returned to the hotel for lunch and spent the afternoon in the library and on the computers. Most of the group began their research for their projects. One was still trying to decide.

After studying on line most of the afternoon, an idea finally hit Hype on the head. He wanted to do something related to the last big dinosaur, but he did not want to compete with Sam. In fact he wanted to compliment Sam so that they would have a natural place to later 'collaborate'. From his research he learned that there were four kinds of reptiles that once dominated the earth and still had living representatives here today. The largest of the Orders was the Squamata which included lizards and snakes. The Order Chelonia contained turtles and tortoises. Crocodiles, alligators, caimans and gavials belonged to the Order of Crocodilia. While the Order Rhynchocephalia contained tuatara which was an almost extinct reptile-hipped bipedal carnivore. Crocodilia was the last of the four to have evolved, just before birds and mammals evolved from the dinosaurs. He would give his ten minute verbal presentation on this subject at his scheduled time on Friday morning. And he knew that he would get the maximum points on it.

Wednesday went by very quickly. Wednesday morning 'Sam's team' attended classroom lectures about the importance of the anatomical structure of the hips in the evolution of quadrupeds and bipeds, the size and shape of the brain cavity, the differences in the openings on the face to position the eyes and nose, and the shape of the chest cavities in quadrupeds and bipeds. Wednesday afternoon they listened to lectures on the comparison of evolution based on food sources, carnivores versus herbivores. The team all took careful notes. They were serious about winning that world team championship.

Thursday morning the team worked in the Arts and Crafts Building. They designed and built a wooden model of a new biped herbivore because such were rarely found in studying the evolution of dinosaurs. Most bipeds that evolved were carnivores. The team also postulated a mechanism as to why these dinosaurs might not have survived for very many 'thousands' of years. And Thursday afternoon each team member practiced giving their ten-fifteen minute talks in front of the other team members, graciously accepting criticism, and trying to improve their presentation. Each team member would be awarded points for his talk, which was then added to the overall team total. So this was also serious stuff.

Friday morning came, and all team members were ready. Three sets of talks would be simultaneously given in three different rooms, one talk every ten minutes from 8:00 AM until 1:00 PM. All fifty students would participate as individuals. Each talk would be judged by two Camp staff members and would be awarded points from one to five. So each team could possibly score twenty five points from the individual presentations. A maximum of twenty five points was awarded for the newly created model dinosaur. And from 3:00 to 4:00 PM on Friday afternoon each team would work as a group to complete a twenty five question examination based on the week's lectures and demonstrations, each question was worth two points. Fifty points were available from the team written exam. There were one hundred points total available for each team. In the twelve years of the World Dinosaur Camp Program, no team had scored one hundred points. Sam's team was going for it. And yes ----

**THEY WON ALL 100 POINTS!!!**

The names of Keiko, Musina, Heins, Hype, and Sam would live forever in dinosaur-ville. They were the World Dinosaur Champions. They would never become extinct, at least as long as there was a dinosaur team member remaining on the face of the earth. They so swore to each other. They had a small party with the Camp staff in the Director's conference room. Each received a small trophy of, whom else, Tyrannosarous Rex, neat T-shirts declaring each to be a member of the World Dinosaur Team Championship, certificates of both participation and their championship status in the Program, and free passes to other World Dinosaur Camps anywhere in the world, good for three years. It had been a very successful week by any standard. Everyone went home loving their dinosaurs even more. And Hype found a real friend, who sort of looked like him, and who will turn out to be his first cousin, or brother, depending upon how you count the genes.

* * *

Two young ladies, both had straw blond hair, jade blue eyes and teenage freckles, who looked like twins but were not, were in a deep discussion concerning the World War I airplane that was hanging more than fifty feet above their heads. The first young lady declared that it was a German Fokker Dr.I Triplane. The second young lady disagreed and declared it to be a British Sopwith Triplane. The first lady went on to describe the greatness of the Fokker planes.

First young lady said, "All planes of World War I were made of wood boards and canvas, most were declared flying coffins. But the Fokkers were different. They had some additional wood protection around the cockpit which saved the lives of many German pilots. And for armament most of them had twin Spandau machine guns of 7.92 mm caliber firing forward through a synchronized propeller system. Also the Fokker Dr.I had a rotary piston engine in the unique Oberursel Ur.II 9-cyclinder series which generated 110 horsepower. It had a maximum speed of 103 miles per hour and a maximum flight range of nearly 200 miles. It was the best in the sky in 1917 and 1918. The British and French were just lucky that a production assembly problem allowed only 320 Fokker D.Is to be built, and then the war ended before the Germans could really become dominant in the sky."

Second young lady countered, "Nonsense. The British Sopwiths were the best planes from 1916 to 1918. The Sopwith Triplane, also known as the triplehound, had a powerful Clerget rotary piston engine which generated 130 horsepower, allowed a maximum speed of 117 miles per hour and a maximum flight range of 280 miles. It had the best rate of climb and best maneuverability of any plane in the sky. It was also armed with either one or two 7.7mm Vickers machines which were fixed forward and fired in synchrony. It was the best dog fighting plane in the sky in the last years of the war. Unfortunately, only 140 Sopwith Triplanes were built."

The first young lady came back, "Well in a comparison to which was the best plane, in one to one dogfights, Fokker Dr.I won over the Sopwith Triplane almost 2 to 1."

The second young lady returned, "But that was because the select German pilots that flew the Fokker Dr.I were better pilots. A good example was Baron Manfred von Richthofen who had the largest number of aerial victories at 80 in the last two years of World War I.

Suddenly they looked around and found out that they had become the center of a crowd of tourists. They had been standing on the main floor of the National Air and Space Smithsonian Museum on the Mall in Washington, DC, at prime time, 2:00 PM, looking up at an airplane hanging from the ceiling about 50 feet above them. And as they had been comparing two World War I airplanes, better than any tour guide could do, everyone within hearing distance maneuvered closer so they could hear and learn.

Both young ladies looked at each other, laughed, and then became disgusted with all of the illiterate people who were watching and listening. The first young lady said, "The air conditioning in here is a little too cold for me, let's go outside and sit in the sun for a while and we can continue our discussion."

"I totally agree," responded the second young lady.

So the two young ladies exited on the south side door, purchased hot dogs and colas from a vendor's stand on the sidewalk, and sat down in the sun on the two foot high wall which circumvented the building.

Stefennie Bassinger was the daughter of a lawyer and living in Des Moines, Iowa. She had arrived in Washington, DC three days ago with her school's street crossing guards. The chaperone of the group of twelve students required that they all remain together for the first two days of seeing Washington; then this last day they could go on their own. Stef was a lover of World War I history and all types of World War I airplanes. She thought the idea of flying in a wood and canvas box in an open sky was the ultimate in experiences. You cannot do this today. Convertibles were allowed on the road but no convertibles were allowed in the sky. It was ok. She would talk her Dad into letting her take flying lessons when she got back to Iowa. There was lots of room to play and little competition above those cornfields.

Alice Dekker lived in Arlington, Virginia, just across the Potomac River, fifteen minutes away by the Washington metro system. She also was a lover of World War I history and those flying wooden coffins. Dreaming about flying in one was one thing; actually flying in one was something else. It was just as well that no one can fly 'open' anymore. She just loved the idea of flying; but maybe designing airplanes might be a more interesting career possibility. She came to this Smithsonian building often. And she always looked over the many old and new airplanes, and old and new space vehicles; but she seemed to migrate back to the World War I exhibit area.

The two young ladies had only met a couple of hours ago and already their chemistry was mixing perfectly. They had been exploring the airplanes, satellites, and space capsules when they had settled into that discussion of the Fokker versus Sopwith Camels. It was neat to find someone, who looked like your twin sister, who could even be your twin sister, and who thought like you did. If she could have a sister it would have to be exactly like her. It was unfortunate that they lived so far from each other. Oh well. There was E-mail.

Stef asked Alice, "How did you become familiar with Sopwith Camels?"

Alice answered, "Probably the same way you did. When I was a kid, my Mother and I used to read the newspaper comics together. In this way I was reading adult stuff. Ha. And we read the comics on Sunday morning before breakfast. Peanuts was my favorite comic."

Stef responded, "So you know all about the Peanuts gang of Woodstock, Snoopy, Charlie Brown, and Lucie van Pelt."

And Alice added, "Don't forget Peppermint Patty, Franklin, Sally Brown, Linus van Pelt, and Pig Pen."

"What was your favorite episode?" asked Stef.

Alice enthusiastically said, "I like the Great Pumpkin episode. Every Halloween I waited for Linus to hide among all of the pumpkins in the pumpkin patch all night waiting for the Great Pumpkin to come. And he never comes. Then there is Snoopy, aboard his Sopwith Camel (his doghouse) to challenge a dogfight with and just get shot down again by the Red Baron, of course Baron Manfred van Richthofen. And when they all put on their masks and go trick or treating, everyone gets good things except Charlie Brown who always gets a sack full of rocks. " And she laughed out loud.

Stef joined her in laughing and added, "I like the Christmas episode where everyone is a great skater except Charlie Brown. And Charlie Brown never gets any Christmas cards, cannot get the children to cooperate in rehearsing for the Christmas pageant, can't find a proper Christmas tree, despises the commercialization of Christmas, thinks giving presents is not right, and on and on. Of course in the end, when Christmas carols about Baby Jesus are being sung, he finally approves of Christmas." Again there is smiling and laughter.

And they continued chatting away until Stef finally had to head back to her hotel and join her group for their last Washington meal. The Iowa group would fly out of Washington National Airport at 8:30 AM tomorrow.

As they parted, Stef and Alice exchanged hugs and kissed like long time sisters. Of course they were sisters, as they had the same Father-s, which also meant they were fraternal twins of identical twins and therefore first cousins if not remote sisters; of course they did not yet know this. They would stay in touch and Alice promised to come to stay with Stef next summer, she had never seen fields of corn and soybeans. Maybe Stef could even take Alice for a plane ride, if she had her pilot's license by then. But she had yet to talk her Father into paying for her flight lessons.

* * *

The score was one set to one set. The third and last set was in motion at six games to six games, and the tie-breaker had begun. Today's winners of the Northeastern Regional Tennis Championship for 14, 15, 16, and

17 year old boys and girls at the Arthur Ashe Youth Tennis Center in Philadelphia, Pennsylvania, would soon move on to the national finals. Winners of the ten regional tournaments would play for the American Tennis Youth Championship next month at the National Tennis Center in Flushing Meadows Park in the Queens, New York City. So the excitement was reaching a peak for this fourteen year old girl from Palisades Park, New Jersey and her friends.

The tiebreaker in the third set began with an ace by her opponent 1-0. The first serve by the New Yorker was not returned by the opponent, 1-1. And the tiebreaker rocked back and forth – 2-1, 2-2, 3-2, 3-3, 4-3, 4-4, 5-4, 5-5, 6-5, and 6-6 games. Both young ladies were very cool. Now with the next and most critical serve, and by the opponent, the New Yorker said to herself, 'Come on, I am ready for anything.'

And this was so typical of her life. Hope was not exactly hyper like her big brother; rather she was slow, steady, cool, and always ready for anything. She was slim, close to 6 foot tall, had straw blond hair, jade blue eyes, and hormone initiated freckles on her lovely face. She was ready for school exams at least twenty four hours before the exam. She turned in home work the day before it was due. She had her home chores finished hours in advance. She was always at the door waiting for the others when they were going somewhere, or even sitting in the car waiting for them. No one could remember if she had ever been late for anything, anywhere, or anytime in her entire life. Probably she was just being a little lady by allowing her little brother to come first in the fraternal twin birthing process. Hence she had been dubbed Ms. Ready. And she was ready now.

Hope Armand was ready for a serve down the far left side of the court. Her double backhand was weak so she knew her opponent would try to take advantage of that weakness for this match winning point. Before her opponent served the ball Hope had started her move toward the left and was there to smash that anticipated serve toward her opponent's right hand corner. Her opponent was not ready and did not get to the ball in time as it hit the line and shot past her. The final game winning score was seven-six, and two sets to one to win the match. Her Mother, and her friends, especially her very good friend, Action, who was playing in the finals for seventeen year old males in just a couple of hours from now, went crazy. They cheered for Hope, who was the youngest player in the tournament and was cool and ready to accept her first championship. She headed to the winner's box. There she would receive the trophy. And again she was ready. Before leaving home she had cleared and prepared a special place on her shelf directly above her desk for her first championship tennis trophy.

Hope, Mother, Action and the rest of her friends, some had been her opponents during the five day tournament, were all sitting around a big round table in the Ashe Center's dining area. In the middle of the table was a beautiful trophy that everyone was admiring.

Her Mother, Dr. Josephine Armand, had taken the day off and caught the AMTRAK from the Big Apple to Philly and arrived just in time for her daughter's match. She exclaimed, "Your Father will be sorry he could not see that last match. It was the closest I have ever seen. But my cool daughter likes it that way. Isn't that right?" And she looked her daughter in the eye.

Hope blushed and changed the subject by teasing Action. "We need a second trophy to go beside this one. Maybe in a couple of hours...... " And she glanced up at him from across the table.

He responded with, "I am ready." And they all cracked up and gave a polite applause.

"Well said to Ms. Ready," They all chimed in." Most of the group had been together all week and knew each other. And of course when Dr. Armand arrived she was introduced to everybody. So they were all friends in the cause of winning tennis.

Then with red hair, almond brown eyes, Action added, "You know you were lucky on that last shot. You had started to your left before she even hit the serve. She knew your weakness and you guessed that she would go for it, so you were ready. What if you had guessed wrong? You need to work on your two hand back hand shot, and not rely on guessing. I spend almost half of my practice time on that shot. I will help you learn to follow through with a hook similar to what you use on the single forehand. You need to have over spin to gain speed when the ball hits the court, otherwise you will lose speed and be in trouble for a front court maneuver by your opponent. We can get together the week before the Nationals and practice on our two hand back hand shots. Then you will not have to guess but you will be really ready."

Hope thanked him and glanced up at Mom, who just smiled. Action then excused himself and went into seclusion to prepare himself mentally for his championship match in a little more than an hour.

As the championship match for the Northeastern Regional Tennis Championship for seventeen year old boys began, Action, his buddies, Hope and her friends, and Dr. Armand were all ready. But it appeared readiness was not in question. Action won his championship trophy with two sets to zero; the scores were 6-3 and 6-2. Action was seventeen years and one month, 6 foot 6 inches tall and 210 pounds. He was much bigger and stronger than his seventeen year old opponent and it showed. Action had nine aces to his opponent's two aces. And when you are ripping off ace after ace, your opponent easily gets demoralized and gives up early. That was the name of this match. Hope and Action's crowd of supporters started calling out 'Ace King' every time he hit one. Needless to say Action's opponent was happy to have the match end so he could go home and hide under his pillow.

After their second championship trophy, the entire group went off to a celebratory dinner on Doctor Aaron Armand's credit card. If he could not help with the hard work of winning, the least he could do was to pay for the bodily re-charging energy necessary for the next match. It was T-bone and sirloin steak time, but no champagne for teenagers.

Hope and her Mother returned to New York. The Armands were members of a small SDV Racket and Tennis Club in Ridgefield which was near Palisades Park. Hope regularly bicycled to there and practiced each day for the next month. There was a retired female tennis professional named Ellen Random who had played the professional tennis circuit for ten years before she retired into motherhood and tennis lessons. She was now giving two hour per day lessons to Hope. Hope could smell that National Tennis Championship. And she was going to be ready.

Action Dekker lived in Arlington, Virginia, an inner suburb of Washington, DC. He routinely played the local public courts and also went with his Father to play with a couple of semi-professional tennis players. His Father was the Director of Intelligence for the Blue Ravens Security firm, whose headquarters was in McLean, Virginia. Twice a week each field security agent, including his Father, went to their farm near Frederick, Maryland. The farm was used for shooting practice, physical exercise, special meetings, short term incarceration, and other things. The physical exercise facilities included an indoor jogging track, weight lifting machines, bar bells, boxing-wrestling ring, an indoor swimming pool and an indoor tennis court.

So Action, via his Father's connections, was lucky enough to play tennis (and exercise) year around for free. And he regularly played with a couple of agents who had played semi-professional tennis until joining the Blue Ravens. Obviously eight-ten months of practice for several years was paying off. The previous two years he had entered the national regional tennis tournaments but did not get beyond the Regional's. When he and his fraternal sister had turned sixteen, Dad had purchased for them a good used Ford. They shared it very well. But for this month Alice was letting him have it every day if he wanted to go the farm to practice his tennis. He took advantage of this gesture and went to practice every day. He was going to be ready for the finals.

The week of the American Tennis Youth Championship in New York City was arriving. Action Dekker went north one week early to practice at a friend's tennis club in Woodbridge, New Jersey, which was about forty five-minutes to an hour south of Palisades Park, New York. Action did manage to get up to see Hope on two different afternoons and they practiced together. He tried to show her that by changing the grip for her double back hand shots she could get an over spin on the ball such that it would rebound faster off the court surface. She understood, practiced, and would try to get that shot ready. He did take her back down the street to her house each time after practice, but it was too early and everyone was at work, or somewhere else anyway. So he did not get to meet her Father or brother. He bought and left a yellow rose for her Mother and said to give her the best of regards, and he hoped to see her at Flushing Meadow next week.

Next week arrived and both Hope and Action wished it had not. The Queens was not good to either of them. They both had a very bad week. Hope won her first and second matches, but got beat in a tie breaker on Wednesday in the third match. Action won his first match and sprained his ankle on Tuesday while leading by one set and four to two games in his second set, second match, therefore was medically disqualified. Both were out of the tournament and in their homes by Thursday. But by Friday they were thinking about getting ready for next year.

Hope and Action had become good friends during the summer, and promised to E-mail each other on a regular basis. Washington and New York were close enough that maybe they could even get together to play some tennis. And with all this interaction, neither knew or even suspected that they were children of identical twins which made them brother and sister via the same Father-s, or certainly first cousins and maybe also.............

* * *

It appeared that the children of the four IDENTICALS would get to know each other sooner and maybe better that the gentlemen themselves. Life/lives can be strange.

# 12 – Ever Closer?

Aaron Armand from New York City and David (Dave) Dekker from Washington, DC had continued with their regular spirit communication, but only at night when they were at delta level of sleep. Sometimes when one was not listening/receiving, the message seemed to remain 'suspended' and would be picked up by the receiver a night or two later. Other than a routine exchange of general daily affairs they had little of excitement to communicate about. They still were not sharing with their families the suspected truth of four genetically identical-soul mates from different Mothers and Fathers, born separately in different locations at different times. They had the hard science DNA data from Aaron's labs for two such males, Aaron and Dave, but not for four of them. And they couldn't take a chance that the news media would smell this Pulitzer Prize winning story, and destroy both families, and maybe the two as yet not identified families. So they just remained calm and kept searching for the others.

Aaron had relayed to Dave the last words from his Father when he died a couple of years ago. His Father admitted that he was not Aaron's biological Father and that he could find out about his biological Father from a fertility specialist gynecologist named Dr. Jackson McClean. Dave used all of his Blue Raven security files, government contracts, Department of Health, Education and Welfare files, all private medical files that he was allowed to search, records from medical organizations, MD graduation certificates given by American universities, research journals, patents, etc., and he could not find any Dr. Jackson McClean, Gynecologist. It appeared that was going to be another dead end. But they could not stop searching.

For several years Dave had been looking through state and nationally recorded and documented fingerprints that matched those from Aaron and himself. No luck. And he went to Florida again but had no success in finding one of their identical brothers, even though that pair of spiritual hands continued reaching from there. The other pair of spiritual hands were definitely coming from the west, not the south. But Aaron and Dave could not open a clear communication to either place because of a thick fog which did not allow messages through. The two of them communicated in a complete fog free environment all of the time. It must have been the fact that they had met and touched, body and soul. They knew and accepted that they carried identical genes from the same Mother and Father, whomever and where ever they were.

Charles Collingswood from Indian Nest, Florida and William (Bill) Bassinger from Des Moines, Iowa were also exchanging spirit communications and only during delta level sleep at night. And their spirit communication was open and clear most of the time. Occasionally there seemed to be a delay between the sending and the receiving; but the delay was never more than a couple of days. They also had met and touched, with body and soul. They knew and accepted that they each carried identical genes from the same Mother and Father, whomever and where ever they were. They simply had no hard scientific DNA data to prove it. And they accepted the real possibility that there were two more of them/us out there. But they did not know how to find them/us without exposing the four brothers to the news media. They also did not want any lives ruined.

The four identical brothers had known about each other's existence through a continuous series of dreams, and sometimes nightmares, for more twenty plus years, yet they had only half found each other and did not know where to go to complete the other half. Then another family death opened a window.

# 13 – What Now?

It was a Thursday evening at 5:30 when the Reverend Charles Collingswood was returning from the Everglades and had just turned the last corner to enter the bayou for the last five hundred feet to the Indian Nest's marina. Suddenly a deer jumped into the water just in front of him. Apparently the small deer was running from some predator. As Charles swerved to miss her, he ran aground, lost his seat, and fell to the floor of the airboat. He had already unfastened his seat belt in anticipation of docking. When his boat hit the land he lost his balance, fell forward, twisted, and struck his head and his left shoulder. He was temporarily knocked unconscious. A couple of minutes later, he became conscious but he had a tremendous pain in his shoulder and was afraid of a possible dislocation. He shouted toward the docks, two of his friends heard him, hopped into a small motor boat, and came to help. They eased him into their boat, and took Charles to the one Doctor in Indian Nest who had his clinic only about two hundred feet from the docks. The Doctor examined him and had his nurse take an X-ray of the left shoulder. He decided that Charles did not have a dislocated shoulder, but only had a very bad bruised area on the back of his shoulder. The Doctor gave him some pain killer and bandaged the shoulder tightly. His friends took him home, told Janice what happened. She appropriately panicked. He was almost asleep from the pain killer medicine so they helped Janice put him to bed. And then the friends retrieved the air boat for the Collingswoods.

At the same time on that Thursday evening, suddenly Aaron Armand (medical scientist), William Bassinger (lawyer), and David Dekker (security director) each simultaneously fell down with a sharp pain in their left shoulder. For Aaron and David the pain lasted for about a half an hour and then slowly went away. For William the pain last several hours and lingered through the night. As the pain occurred each had a vision of a man who looked like me/us/them who was riding in an airboat, falling onto the front of the boat, and landing on his shoulder. Each knew immediately that it was their identical brother.

As the pain subsided, Aaron speed dialed to David. They used their cell phones for emergencies. This was an emergency. Aaron began, "Did you just have a sharp pain in you left shoulder?"

David responded, "Yes. It began at near 5:30 PM and is just now going away. Did you have the same pain?"

Aaron responded, "Yes. In addition I saw a man, our look-alike, riding in an airboat and falling onto his left shoulder. Did you have the same vision?

"Indeed I did," said David. "It has to be our brother in Florida. During both times that I went looking for him in that state I did not go into the Everglades area. That boat is the type of airboat used in the Everglades. If you will remember I felt that he was with or near Spanish speaking immigrants. There are several camps of these immigrant workers in south Florida working in the sugar cane plantations and citrus groves. This weekend I will fly down to Tampa, rent a car and look in the area between these camps and the Everglades. My current feelings tell me he is living and working in that area, possibly within the Everglades, because he was alone on that airboat. What do you think?"

"I agree with you. Good luck and be careful. If you find him do not expose the both of you at the same time to the public. When you find him, be sure to meet with him somewhere away from his home. We still need to continue to keep this situation quiet."

* * *

The next day Aaron received an emergency phone call from Manchester, New Hampshire. His Mother had just suffered a stroke and was in intensive care at the Hospital of St. Joseph. She was holding her own, but he should come as quickly as possible. So he cancelled his appointments and postponed his research program for the next few days. Josephine and he left immediately and drove all night to arrive at the 'English Manor House' at 4:00 AM. They got up just before noon, had a light breakfast and drove straight to the hospital. They talked with her cardiologist, Dr. Ronald Halston.

The house servants told Aaron that his Mother was suffering from a bad cold, was taking cold capsules, when suddenly she sat up in bed, grabbed her chest and passed out. They immediately called for an ambulance, which came within fifteen minutes, and took her directly to the hospital. She was put into intensive care hospital ward, and placed on blood pressure and heart monitors. Her body vital signs had somewhat stabilized during the night.

Aaron met with Dr. Halston and asked, "She does not look good. Did she have a relapse last night?"

Dr. Halston replied, "She woke up asking for you and yes, she had another small stroke. I don't think she will last the day. There is nothing more that we can do. I am very sorry."

Aaron said, "If it is alright with you we will remain here with her for the next few hours."

"Of course," Dr. Halston said. "I have scheduled surgery in a few minutes, but I will check back with you after that, probably in three or four hours."

Jos and Aaron settled into the hospital room. They would be here if she should again awaken. However, she passed away that evening. She did not awaken. He was certain that she wanted to tell him about his parentage, she just waited too long. Now he would never know.

* * *

The very next Saturday David Dekker flew to Tampa International Airport, rented a car, purchased a couple of short sleeve tourist style shirts, dark sunglasses, a wide brimmed straw hat, and headed south on route I-75 to Naples. At Naples he turned onto route 41 and headed toward the Everglades and Miami. Within about half an hour he spotted an immigrant campground off to the left of route 41. He stopped, looked around, asked a few questions about work in the area, showed the picture of his 'brother', and got nowhere. In addition, Dave could not 'feel' him here. He got back into the car and drove on. He was getting low on gas so he pulled into the next gas station and had the tank filled. As he paid the young gas station attendant he showed the picture of his 'brother' to the guy.

Dave said, "Have you seen this fellow around here in the past month or so?"

The young guy gave the picture a hard look and said, "Maybe but I am not sure. A lot of people come and go at gas stations. Maybe but I don't remember when."

Again Dave swallowed his disappointment, hopped into his car, started the motor and began to drive away. Suddenly he yelled at the attendant, "Say, do you know where I can rent a swamp airboat around here?"

The young responded, "Sure do. Drive straight on down the road for a half hour and you will see off to your right the Miccosukee Indian Village.

Just beyond the village about two miles, a road goes to the right toward the Everglades and to a village called Indian Nest. They have two airboats there, but I think you rent them with driver."

Dave almost jumped for joy. He could 'feel' him. He thanked the young man, gave him a generous tip, and took off for Indian Nest.

He slowly drove into Indian Nest. It was a small community with near one hundred houses and an abundance of loblolly pine trees and palmetto undergrowth. Mystical Spanish moss was abundantly hanging everywhere. The main street ran south toward the Everglades and there was a small downtown area with a general store, bank, post office, shoes and clothing store, café, pastry shop and a small mall which housed other shops and offices for professional people such as lawyer, realtor, and dentist. It had a single gas station which also sold tires and auto parts. There was a rather large old house on one of the side streets that had a sign in front which declared B&B or by the week rentals. All in all it was a clean tidy little community.

At the end of the main street there was a marina which ran perpendicular. It had one large and two smaller docks projecting out into a small stream leading south into the Everglades. He saw three row boats and one airboat tied up to the smaller docks. The water vehicles had no names, only numbers of the fronts. Adjacent to the large dock was a small building that had signs on the roof that said bait and fishing supplies.

There were only six other streets in Indian Nest. Each was perpendicular and crossed the entry street with orientations both east and west. Each secondary street dead ended into the dense forest. He drove up and back on each one just on the chance that he might see something or someone of use. There was one small church whose sign on the front declared that worship services were held every Wednesday night at 7:30 PM and Sunday morning at 11:00 AM conducted by the Reverend Charles Collingswood. Next door to the church was a small house for the Reverend and family.

Dave's 'feelings' were running strong. The strongest spiritual sensations were coming from that little house next to the church. He parked his car down the street and settled down to wait.

After a couple hours of waiting, and several townspeople walking past and giving him the eye, he decided he should not wait here any longer. His brother might be out of town for the weekend. So he took out paper and pencil and wrote a note which said:

**Reverend Charles Collingswood:**

**I saw and felt your fall when you hit your shoulder on your airboat last Thursday evening at 5:30. We need to talk. Tomorrow, Sunday morning after church services, make an excuse to the family and remain in the church. I will enter through the side door at 12:30 PM. Then we can talk.**

**Your brother Dave**

Dave placed the note into an envelope, sealed it, left it under the front door of the little house next to the church, and took off to find a motel somewhere out on route 41.

That evening Charles and family returned home. Charles found, opened, and read the note. Needless to say he was shocked. They had been actively looking for each other for more than 20 years and suddenly, one accident, and maybe they had found each other. If he had known in advance that an accident could do that, he would have had an accident a long time ago. He thought it best to not yet share this with Janice and the children. He went to bed early but could not sleep that night.

The next morning Charles was very edgy. He was not hungry. And this was unusual because breakfast was his favorite meal. He was nervous and even short with the children. Samuel and Sara just shrugged it off and thought his bandaged shoulder was probably bothering him. Charles gave an excuse and went to the church early thinking his brother might come early. At 11:00 AM the church was full as he began the services. It was not one of Reverend Collingswood better performances. He had much difficulty concentrating. But again, just like the children, the congregation excused his less than average service to the very obvious painful shoulder which was tightly wrapped in a white shoulder brace over top of his black suit. Services ended at 12:10 PM. Everyone left the church by the front door, shook the Reverend's hand, thanked him for the excellent service, and did not drag out the social talk but walked home. Most of Reverend Collingswood flock lived in Indian Nest and within walking distance.

As the noise from the church upstairs quieted down, Dave opened the basement storage room door and walked into the church basement. He was an excellent security man and could pick almost any lock; and the lock on the back door of the church was rather an elementary school challenge for him. He had arrived early, at 8:30 AM. He had brought some breakfast and the Sunday editions of the Miami Herald and the Washington Post, about one thousand pages of reading. In his younger days he had spent many hours on stake outs reading newspapers, drinking coffee, and eating donuts. He wanted to be certain that no one saw him enter the church from the back, and he was curious about his brother's ministry. He wanted to hear his sermon. It had worked out nicely; it was now 12:30 PM and time to meet his brother.

Dave cautiously walked up the back stairs keeping an eye open for anyone who might not be his twin. The stairs ended at the back door so he just turned and entered into the choir room behind the altar. Charles was standing near the altar looking in his direction. He had sensed Dave's arrival. They both looked at each other for a very long time. Yes, the same red hair, the same green eyes, same physical size, small cleft on the left ear, same face, same stature, same left hand in left pants pocket, same.........

Tears suddenly came and fell from four green eyes. There was no doubt, this guy was me. They ran to each other, embraced and kissed and hugged and cried and giggled and laughed, the impossible just became possible. Everything was too much and neither could find his tongue; they just stuttered away trying to express their feelings. No intelligible words could be found. Charles even forgot about the pain in his left shoulder as he hugged away.

Two 42 year old identical brothers saw and touched each other for the first time in their lives. And it happened because one of them fell down and was badly hurt. They were in such a state of shock that they could not express themselves. Finally, after a few moments they regained their composures, and started to talk with some degree of coherence.

Dave began, "Finally, after searching for you for the past, how many years? I am a security professional and I have access to many public, private, and other files with names, faces, fingerprints, and numerous ways to find people, but you were not there."

Charles grinned, "I suppose that Indian Nest is not on those fancy files that you have been using." And he laughed.

Dave picked up on it and laughed also. They were coming back down to earth. And he added, "If you had left just one fingerprint on a public record somewhere, or left your hand print somewhere."

Charles returned, "Did you try looking for your face on the records of the State of Florida driver licenses? If you had found your face you would have found me."

And they broke down laughing again. Suddenly everything seemed funny. And Dave admitted, "To look everywhere for someone for half a lifetime, when I should have been looking for myself; official records of pictures of myself, huh? And I thought I was a good detective. Oh brother!"

And that brought another round of laughter.

"And now thanks to the will of the Great Spirit, we will all live," Charles replied as he smiled.

Dave gave a puzzled look and shrugged his shoulders as if to ask – what?

All Charles could do was to say, "I will tell you later." And he laughed again and pointed up to the sky.

More laughter and these two gentlemen were rapidly aging backwards toward boyhood. Maybe that was necessary such that they could then grow up together.

But they did need to talk long and seriously. And they needed to talk now. Dave had rented his motel room for two nights and suggested they meet there later in the afternoon or early evening. It was settled. Charles would come to Dave at his hotel at 7:30 PM. Dave would purchase and have ready some fast food so they would not need to appear together in public. This double twinning thing had to be kept under wraps.

They reluctantly separated. Charles went home and joined the family who were preparing the back yard bar-B-Q for their Sunday dinner. Usually they had two or three guests who joined them at the outdoor picnic table. The weather was great. But Dave, knowing his security limitations, remained within the church and "spied" on the Collingswood family from inside the church windows. He checked out the wife and children. One cannot just take everything for granted. It was just too good. It had to be true. But his detective instincts wanted more proof. By late afternoon, Dave had confirmed for himself that Charles had a tall slim wife who had blond hair and blue eyes, twin children, a boy with red hair and almond colored eyes and a girl with straw blond hair and jade blue eyes, and that Charles was a good family man, all of this should be true. As it started turning dark he slipped out from the back of the church and headed back to the motel.

* * *

In the conference room of Tanelly, Sherber, Mosely, and Wiggs Law Offices, on Bolton Street in Manchester, New Hampshire, the last will and testimony, and the financial estate trusts of Mary Armand were being read. Mrs. Armand was from an old New England family so there were some legal problems from that direction that was taking much time to declare and settle. There were four claimants in the room that objected to a variety of settlement issues. Two of the claimants were surviving sisters of Mrs. Armand, so it was likely that those protested issues would go to court settlement. The issues of inheritance from her husband, Dr. James Armand, had been settled several years ago when he died.

The 'House' and furnishings, surroundings lands which were agriculture zoned, and most farm related machinery, which she had inherited from her husband, went to their only son, Aaron Armand. Selected house furnishings and specific cash settlements went to various farm and household workers to reward them for their many years of helping to make the estate a live and functional enterprise. Many large estates in the area could not pay their taxes and had sold out. The Armand estate was holding its own. And there were several other little problems such as a small loan for the purchase of milking machines and promises of certain farm machinery to a neighbor. The entire reading took six hours and had run into the afternoon. By 4:00 PM Jos and Aaron were given copies of the will and financial estate trusts and a packet of personal papers from his Mother. They went back to the 'House' to try to relax.

Aaron turned to Jos and expressed his remorse, "everything has happened so fast. Last week she was OK. And now my only known Mother, and Father are gone. And I still did not know who and where my real biological parents are." Jos and Aaron retired to the study and closed the door.

Aaron began, "Now what do we do with the 'House?' I have no desire to return to New Hampshire and become a farmer. It is much too early for retirement. But it would be a lovely place to come for vacations and to eventually come and retire someday. At our pace that will be about fifty years from now. Could we maintain it and not lose it to the tax man before then?"

Jos responded, "I too would be lost if we came here even for vacations. First, we don't have time for real vacations. Second, I am sure that Hype and Hope would become bored in about one hour and ask to return to the city. New York is their speed. Third, we would have to find a first rate live in farmer-estate manager. But even if we found a very good someone, we cannot just walk away and come back in fifty years."

"Yes, I agree." Aaron said, "For tax purposes we should sell the house and lease the farm. If we sold both, we would get killed with capital gains taxes. Let me think about it for a while. The first half of my life was here.

I have a thousand memories. For the rest of the winter let us continue as is. We can make a more final decision in the spring and maybe put it up for sale next summer. The world that we are currently living in is so different from this beautiful world of nature. But our professional work cannot be accomplished here."

And he picked up the packet of his Mother's personal papers and started opening them. Jos left the room to prepare cups of tea for the two of them. Aaron kept opening the notes and envelops with notes and notes within notes. The dates on some of them were many years old. So he opened, glanced, and discarded; opened, glanced, and discarded. Two yellowed sheets of paper caught his eye. One was a legal adoption certificate made out for him to Mary and James Armand on March 15, 1976. The other yellowed paper was a letter head note from a Melvin Jackson Fertility Clinic in McLean, Virginia. The note was dated May 20, 1975. That was about nine months before his birthday. Could this really be true? All these years he thought his Father said Jackson McClean. He had assumed that was the name of the gynecologist who was the infertility specialist that arranged his presence on earth. Could it have been this Melvin Jackson in McLean? He stood up and shouted for Jos.

When she came running into the room he just handed the yellowed note to her and said, "Please read this and give to me your opinion."

Jos looked at him like are you crazy? Glanced at the note and read it; glance at him again; read it again and said, "I do not understand. What is this?"

Then he remembered. He had not shared his Father's dying words with anyone, including his wife. And then he began to cry. He had kept everything about his double twinness from everyone including Jos. She knew that he did not know who his biological parents were. And she knew that there were four identical males. But she had never questioned him, and he had never told her more. And now as he cried, he apologized profusely.

Aaron said, "I am so sorry, sorry, sorry. All of this time I thought that I was protecting you. I thought that I was protecting the children. I thought that I was protecting my three brothers. And all this time I was really only protecting myself. Why? I have a super Mother and Father, family, friends. I should not be ashamed that I was not biologically related to this Mother and Father. I am related by mindset and by soul. I should not be asking for more. No. I must open up and share all, beginning with you and Hype and Hope."

And the two of them embraced and just held the embrace for a while. It felt good to hold each other. And he really needed the assurance that she would forgive him. And now the children must forgive him. He owed them so much in the way of a true explanation about his biology, therefore their biology

And they both sat back down. Aaron looked Jos in the eye and starting telling the untold history of Aaron Armand.

* * *

Two nights after Aaron and Jos had returned, and before he had gotten up the nerve to tell about his genetics to the children he received a spirit dream in color communication from Dave. It went as follows:

On June 9, he was watching a horse race at the Philadelphia Park Racetrack. The race was nearing the final turn. Two stallions, Happy Face and Big Red were neck in neck with a filly named Holly Inn. As they hit the final straight away Big Red pulled away by a full head on Happy Face while Holly Inn had dropped to a half length behind Happy Face. At the fifty yard marker Big Red was still leading and Holly Inn had moved up on the outside to come nose to nose with Happy Face. As they crossed the finish line it was Big Red and Holly Inn nose to nose, a photo finish. And yes, it was Holly Inn who nosed out Big Red to win the Fourth Cup Crown. Emergency Express was the winning jockey again. The betting scoreboard showed Holly Inn's betting odds were six to ten. Next time the odds would change to thirteen to twelve. The dream ended.

The next morning Aaron analyzed Dave's message. His interpretation of the dream was as follows: He was supposed to meet Dave tomorrow, June 10 in Philadelphia at the Holiday Inn on Express Street. Room thirteen was reserved for Dave and room twelve was reserved for him. He knew that the two rooms would have a common connecting door. So no one would see them together. Plus Dave would arrive in the afternoon. And Aaron would arrive in the evening after the dinner hour change in hotel front desk personnel. And if you did not stick your nose out you could never win. This message stuff was fun.

Aaron arrived in Philadelphia by AMTRACK about 7:30 PM, took a taxi to the Holiday Inn, checked into his pre-reserved room number twelve, went up to his room, entered and guess who was sitting in the only comfortable lounge chair and watching television.

Dave greeted him, "Hi little brother. How is it going?"

Several years ago they had compared birthdays. Aaron's was on March 7. Dave's was on February 27. So Dave was older by eight days. Also Dave was three inches taller and several pounds heavier. Therefore sometimes Dave would deflate Aaron's doctor ego by reminding him who the little brother was. They had developed a deep and warm relationship which no one in the entire world knew about them. It was sort of fun having a very unique secret with yourself.

Aaron responded by grabbing Dave by the hand and jerking him up out of the chair. Dave was a very large man. Aaron was <u>only</u> 6 foot 6 inches, 230 pounds. As the floor shook and made strange noises, the two of them exchanged hugs and kisses. Then they each took one step backward and looked himself up and down. They always did this for two reasons. One, they wanted to again verify that he was real and was me. Two, had I yet begun to show his age in places where I show age, or are we aging differently in different places?

Then Aaron spoke first. "I see you have gained weight again. Why do you always gain weight around the waist? Why don't you gain weight where it is important, like inside the skull?"

Dave responded, "Why would I wish for your special types of cerebrosides and phosphosphingolipids in my head. You have enough for both of us."

He was putting Aaron down showing off that he knew the names of two of the many special fats which are present only in the brain. Of course if Aaron asked him what those two fats did for the brain he would have to fake it.

"Maybe then you could become the Director of Homeland Security for the American government," Aaron rebutted.

"It does not take brains to do that; you just have to be friends with the current President. Besides the longevity in that job is only three to four years. Not my balloon." Dave countered.

And they continued to shoot jibes at each other for the next few minutes. After all, they had been together, face to face, perhaps as much as a dozen hours within a timeframe of forty plus years. And they had no other brothers to shoot the bull with during those forty plus years. But now they did.

Dave went first. "I found both of our other two identical brothers. I met and talked with Charles Collingswood, a protestant minister and environmentalist living in Indian Nest, Florida, which is on the northern edge of the Everglades. He is us. His wife is Dr. Janice Stryker-

Collingswood who is an environmentalist professor at the University of Miami and maintains a large research program monitoring the animals in the Everglades. She does her research from their home in Indian Nest."

Aaron was astonished and interrupted Dave, "A few years ago my Hype spent a week at a dinosaur camp with a boy who lived in Indian Nest, Florida. The two boys became good friends. I think his last name was Collingswood."

"There are two fraternal twin children, Samuel and Sara Collingswood."

Again Aaron excitedly interrupted, "Yes, Sam was the name of Hype's friend. Hype called him his dinosaur buddy."

"And they did not know they were first cousins, or maybe even brothers," laughed Dave.

Dave continued again, "His wife is tall and slim, blond with blue eyes. The two fraternal twins are exactly mixed. The boy has red hair and almond colored eyes. The girl is blond and green eyed. Does this all sound similar to our families? And they are a happy, together family."

Aaron was still stunned. "If I had just taken a little more time and interest to Hype's Florida adventure I might have discovered our brother several years ago. But as usual, Jos and I were too busy with our work."

Again Dave continued. "I have all of the numbers such as address, house phone, cell phone, E-mail, etc. I told him about you and gave to him your numbers. I also warned or reminded him about the news media. That is when he told me about our number four."

"When it rains it pours," Aaron chimed in. And he laughed as tears streamed down his face.

And Dave continued. "Our number four, or one or two or three, depending upon how you count us, is named William (Bill) Bassinger. William and Charles met several years ago and have also developed spirit communications, like we have. They are probably the two sets of spirit hands that we have seen over the past years – south and west. William is a lawyer living and working in Des Moines, Iowa. He and his wife are both Iowans from farming families. Her name is Jenny. That makes our four wives named Josephine, Jenny, Janice, and Janet. Jenny is also tall and slim. She is a high school science teacher. And yes they have two fraternal children, Steve and Stefennie. Steve has red hair and almond colored eyes. And Stefennie has blond hair and green eyes."

"In addition, you think you don't pay enough attention to your children, let me look into that same mirror. Several years ago my daughter, Alice, met and spent a couple of days with this Stef in the Smithsonian Air and Space Museum on the Washington Mall. They became good friends and still exchange E-mails as they are both members of the Friends of Snoopy Club. And of course they did not know that they were first cousins, or maybe sisters. Yah!"

"It is my understanding the neither Charles nor William have told anything about us/them to their families. I have the Bassinger's numbers and I told Charles to give to William both your and my numbers. So, if there are only four of us, we may have just found each other. Now the question is who and where are our biological parents?"

Now it was Aaron's turn to tell his latest personal history.

"Before, let me update you about my recent adventure. Last week my Mother died. She died quickly and with a minimum of pain. Jos and I were there. Of course we stayed for the funeral, reading of the will, and tried to settle the household. Some of the house and farm workers had been with the family most of their lives. I inherited most of the estate, but we cannot go to live there, so I don't yet know what we are going to do. Anyway, Mother had a file of collected notes listed as personal papers. These were given to me. I went through them; many of them had yellowed because they were so old. One yellowed note caught my eye. It was a signed contract with a medical fertility clinic. The letter head on the contract read: Melvin Jackson Fertility Clinic, McLean, Virginia. It was dated May 20, 1975. Approximately nine months before our birthdays."

There was a minute of silence and then Dave said, "Are you saying that we all came from the Melvin Jackson Fertility Clinic in McLean, Virginia and not from some gynecologist named Jackson McClean, whom we have never found? Things just seem to get more complex."

Aaron sheepishly replied, "Father told me verbally. Mother told me in writing. What do you think?"

Dave's answer was, "The Jackson Fertility Clinic in McLean, Virgina is three blocks down the street from the Headquarters of the Blue Ravens. I drive past it two or three times a week. The parking lot is always full so they do indeed have a thriving establishment."

Again a few minutes were needed to digest all of this new information. For more than fifteen years Dave had been driving past the place where he had been conceived and did not know it. This time the not possible became possible. Now what should they do?

Aaron suggested, "Let's get all four of the brothers together in the same place and at the same time and discuss what to do. Why don't you plan out a secure arrangement for all four of us to spend a few hours talking about our conception(s), what to do about it/them, and how far do we go in opening up to our families and to the world."

Dave agreed, "Yes, let me make the security arrangements, news media free of course. I will maintain communication with you and with Charles, and Charles can relay the information to William. Give me a couple of weeks. This will not be as easy as one might think. How do you hide four red headed green eyed giraffes in the African grasslands?"

And two of the red headed jade green eyed giraffes again broke down laughing.

# 14 – Run, Pass, or Kick?

David Dekker was sitting at his desk in the Headquarters of the Blue Ravens Security Firm. The sign on the door read Director of Intelligence, and he was now on the other side of that ball game. All of his professional efforts had been to use security systems to prevent entry, movement, and action that he was trying to nullify or control. Now suddenly he was trying to avoid these same security systems and bring together the four brothers, sight unseen by man, camera, or high tech security devices.

George Orwell's book, *1984*, was set in all of America and most of the rest of the world. After the 9/11 (2001) destruction of the twin trade towers in New York City, America panicked and went crazy about security. A complete new national security system was organized, the Department of Homeland Security, which now theoretically brought all anti-bad control systems such as CIA, FBI, Customs, Passport Control, Border Security Guard, and Marine Coast Guard all under one roof. The central businesses and downtown shopping areas, and suburban business-shopping malls in all major American cities were loaded with private security guards and security devices such as cameras and motion detection systems. The streets and select buildings were continuously (24/7/52) under the eyes of various types of security cameras including wireless, color vision, infra red, night vision, motion alert, freeze alarm, and siren speakers. While the interiors of American points of entry such as airports, train stations, road customs, marine customs, etc. as well as most hotels in all cities (even in central USA) maintained micro-security cameras of all types which were the size of your thumbnail and wireless, so they could easily be moved from place to place in a couple of minutes. And this was just physical security. It did not include the many systems to monitor for nuclear, biological, or toxic chemical security problems.

There was another layer of communications security that had been instituted to detect the would be terrorists using encrypted telephones, computers, E-mail, disposable cellular telephones, other wireless headsets, and postal mail which was checked by x-ray, drug tests, radiation tests, and others. Even many outside the city such as farms, businesses, and private companies and factories had purchased and were using security systems to watch for thieves, crooks, criminals, terrorists or any of the bad guys born from 9/11. It had been calculated that if you lived and worked in Manhattan you would have your picture taken at least one hundred times every day. So, Dave needed to develop a plan which would avoid most of these security systems. Now isn't that a good challenge for a security man?

After one week of research and evaluating several different plans, he thought he finally had a solid workable program.

David had begun thinking to himself. 'When trying to beat the system you do it on home turf where you have the advantage of the familiarity of main roads, side streets, harsh and gentle areas of the city, police stations, rush hour street re-route changes, street construction, gas stations, shops, businesses, and parks. Therefore that meant Washington, DC, for him, and of course, them. They would meet in the parking lot of Tyson's Corner Shopping Mall #1 in Tyson's Corner, Virginia which was physically located on the western edge of the Washington Circular Beltway, the ten to sixteen lane divided highway which encircled Washington. The Tyson's Corner Shopping Malls would be very crowded on the Friday afternoon the day after Thanksgiving. That day was the biggest shopping day of the year in America and the double Tyson's Corner Malls had more than three hundred department stores and shops and several gigantic multi-floor parking buildings which should be packed with cars and shoppers. There would be lots of confusion.'

'One must minimize the security cameras, so hotels and shopping centers were out. Everyone would come and go the same day. William Bassinger could do a round trip from Des Moines International Airport to Dulles International Airport in one day. Charles Collingswood could make a round trip from Miami International Airport to Washington National Airport in one day. And Aaron Armand could ride an AMTRAC train from Penn Station in New York City to Washington Union Station and return on the same day. Each entry at a different time in a different place should reduce camera exposures, and certainly eliminated double exposures – two twins on the same camera at the same time.'

'And, I should use the old secure need to know basis. I will send travel instructions individually to each brother using E-mail for William, cell phone for Charles, and UPS post to Aaron. I will initiate the arrangements tomorrow as we only have nine days until Thanksgiving.'

'To William Bassinger: Des Moines International Airport to Dulles International Airport, Northwest Airlines, #2562, lv 8:10 AM, arr 11:21 AM; Return Dulles to Des Moines, Northwest Airlines #2114, lv 7:41 PM, arr 10:38 PM – reservation number 25498731.'

'To Charles Collingswood: Miami International Airport to Washington National Airport, US Airways, #1875, lv 8:37 AM, arr 11:33 AM; Return Washington National to Miami, US Airways, #1376, lv 7:18 PM, arr 10:43 AM – reservation number 99739652.'

'To Aaron Armand: New York City Pennsylvania Train Station to Washington Union Train Station, AMTRACK, #185, lv 8:00 AM, arr 11:04 AM; Return Washington Union to New York Pennsylvania, AMTRACK, #363, lv 7:20 PM, arr 10:12 PM. – reservation number 43743825.'

'I can pick them up one at a time, and then drop them off one at a time, in the Blue Raven's unmarked Land Rover. This LR was special built so it had some extras such as bullet proofing, a four person conference seating-table arrangement inside, 360⁰ security surveillance cameras pointing outward, and the top of the line communication systems inside. It had dark non-see through windows. There was a small kitchen for coffee and snacks. It had been used many times for stake outs and special clandestine meetings. It was perfect for their one day needs.'

The big Friday arrived, and all brothers were in motion according to the plan. Dave first picked up Aaron at 11:15 AM from the Capital Bar and Grill which was on Massachusetts Avenue about three blocks west of the Washington Union Station. Aaron had been instructed to go to this location and wait for Dave. They then drove through the District of Columbia and into Arlington, Virginia. At 12:10 PM, Charles, following instructions, had taken the Metro from the National Airport to the Rosslyn Metro Station, exited on Fort Myers Street north, and was waiting to be picked up at the corner of Fort Myers Street and Nash Street. He was on time and three brothers met for the first time in their lives. The three of them then traveled on to Reston, Virginia. Dave had instructed Bill to take from Dulles a taxi on route #267 to Reston, Virginia; to go to 137 14th Street and then west to John's Café, wait there. At 1:10 PM, they would drive to the front door of this café in a black Land Rover, plate #BR-246, and toot two times. They were on time and he was there waiting for them. All four identical brothers were finally together. What an effort.

The plan was designed such that only one brother would get into or out of the car at any point in time. And each brother would be picked up from a location away from their point of entry to Washington, DC. Therefore at no time were two brothers ever standing outside near each other, so even remote security cameras would not have 'suspicious' pictures to scrutinize. At the end of the day the same security procedures would be observed.

Dave drove to the Tyson's Corner Shopping Malls. He entered parking lot D, went to floor six, removed the 'Do not park – construction' sign and parked in a parking position which was above the commotion and out of line of any surveillance cameras. It was now 2:00 PM. They had four hours to discuss the past forty four years. Where do they begin?

Dave and Aaron turned their seats around so they could the face to the center of the LR, and Charles and Bill moved their seats back and attached a small oblong table in front and between the four of them. It made for a nice and comfortable conference arrangement. Dave turned on the exterior surveillance cameras and the interior infra red lights so they could see out but no one could see in. The coffee pot was turned on and hot coffee would be ready in five minutes. As if anyone needed a stimulant. Because it was his party in his home and because he was the oldest, and biggest, Dave opened the conversation.

Dave said, "Welcome to Washington. Thank you for coming on this short notice. I hope the travel arrangements were not too inconvenient. I tried my best to make our meeting as secure as possible, so it had to be short and fast. In the security world the shorter the exposure time the less the accidental risk for exposure. Tonight I will drop you off, one at a time, near not at, your specific transportations. And in the future I suggest that we all try to use our spirit communications as much as we can, or for something difficult or critical, a UPS special post delivery of a double sealed envelope is very good. A court order is necessary for anyone but the receiver to open such a sealed envelope."

And then everything was stone quiet for several minutes. It was really weird. Each looked in three different directions and always saw himself, yet it was not himself. In each direction it was like looking into a mirror. Three mirrors and three identical men. To the right, left, and straight ahead one always saw the same strong handsome face, red hair, the jade green eyes, that partial cleft in the left ear, and similar facial expressions to this very stressful situation. Me but not me! Tears suddenly appeared in four sets of grown men's eyes. No one knew where to begin. It was scary, but scary positive. But was it real, or another dream? Was a lifetime quest finally over, or was it just beginning again?

The brothers slowly went from Niagara eyes to Niagara noses. Dave only hoped he had enough Kleenex to accommodate the four little giants.

They had been waiting a complete life time for this exact moment to arrive. And now that it had arrived, not one identical brother had thought about what to do or say. Each waited for the other to break the ice. It was like a first date with your first girlfriend. You did not know her; she did not know you; and you each knew that the talking would quickly change all that. But as a gentleman it was only polite to let her go first. So they all sat in a semi-coma state waiting for someone else to say something.

Finally Dave picked up the tension and raised up, reached over, and started shaking hands and making comments and giving hugs and kisses to each brother one at a time, then everyone else partially stood, reached out, and shook hands and gave hugs and kisses and murmured that typical but ridiculous 'nice to meet you', which brought smiles and laughter. That broke the ice. It was necessary to make that physical contact and psychologically acknowledge that they were all biological brothers with warm bodies, and maybe more.

Dave continued, "Certainly we are biological brothers. We can see ourselves in each other, externally. But we don't see each other internally. We each have a different loving Mother and Father, wife and children, profession, life style, and personal history, which we do not know. May I suggest that we each spend a few minutes summarizing our personal histories? Is that all right?"

They each nodded. It seemed like a logical place to begin.

"I am the biggest," and he looked at Bill and grinned, "and I think the youngest, so I will go first," Dave said.

And he began, "I was born on February 27, 1976 to Sylvia and Roy Dekker in San Diego, California. I have no brothers or sisters. My Father worked for the city as a manager in the city water department. I had a good childhood with lots of Spanish speaking sports buddies. We lived in a middleclass neighborhood near the Mexican border. And since I was a lot bigger than most of my friends, they always wanted me on their team, especially basketball. So I grew up where most of my friends went to the military, therefore I went military. I spent four years in a combatant-commandos unit in Afghanistan. Four years was more than enough so I resigned and went to Washington, DC and joined the Blue Ravens Security Firm whose headquarters was in McLean, Virginia. About five years after I joined the Blue Ravens we had some intelligence problems so they created a new division for intelligence gathering on our clients. I became Director of Intelligence and have loved the responsibility ever since."

"However soon after joining the Blue Ravens I fell in love with Janet Simpson. Janet did not know her Mother and Father and had lived in orphanages all of her life. She managed to finish high school and a two year college degree, so she was the manager of the Dorothy Walker Summers Home for Orphans in Arlington, Virginia when we met. Later she got her Bachelor of Arts degree from George Mason University and has been teaching general science to middle school children for the past several years. After two years of marriage we had fraternal twins, Action and Alice. Action and Aaron's daughter, Hope, played tennis together and we Fathers did not even know. While my Alice and Bills' Stef found each other at the Air and Space Museum in Washington and are now 'Peanuts' buddies. Both of our children are in a university. Action is studying Political Science at Georgetown University and will later go to Georgetown University Law School and hopes to enter politics; and Alice is studying Computers and Informational Sciences at George Washington University. How they chose those areas to study, I do not know. But they are doing well, so I know that they will be successful later in their professional lives."

Aaron spoke up next, "I was born on March 7, 1976 to Dr. James and Mary Armand in Manchester, New Hampshire. They had no other children. My Father was a General Physician and practiced general medicine in this area all of his professional life. Both he and my Mother were from a lineage of Irish New Englanders. We lived in a large house on a large estate, as had the previous three generations of Armands. I was the only child and had, literally everything. Eventually I attended Boston College, Harvard University Medical School, and Columbia University in New York City. I received the medical doctorate, MD, and the science doctorate, PhD, and have been fortunate enough to help build a new hospital on the Columbia University campus. This is the first Center for Cellular and Genetic Biology of Twinning in the world. I am currently the Director. The Assistant Director is my wife, Jos."

"I met Josephine Christianson at Columbia University. She is from Denver, Colorado. Jos had a PhD in Molecular Biology and Genetics and was doing post-doctoral research at Columbia during the time that I was finishing my degrees. We had many common interests, fell in love, married, and now work together at the Twinning Center. We live across the Hudson River in Palisades Park, New Jersey. We have two children, fraternal twins, Hype and Hope. Indeed my Hope and Dave's Action played tennis together and we did not put two and two together until several years later. And my Hype and Charles's son, Samuel were dinosaur roommates together about ten years ago, and we just recently learned about it. Sometimes it is hard to see the nose on the front of your face when you are trying to construct a giant orchid. Both children are finishing high school."

Charles looked at Bill and asked, "Do you want to go next?"

Bill responded, "No, I want you to go first. Then as a good trial lawyer I will have the goods on all of you and I will have given nothing. At $1000 per hour I am on my way to paying for my travel expenses."

At first they thought he was serious. Then they saw the smile on his face. They did not know that Iowans had such a sense of humor.

So Charles began, "I was born March 5, 1976 in Atlanta, Georgia to Susan and William Dekker. I was four years old when the house caught fire and my Mother was killed. I never fully recovered as I considered her death to be my fault. Father never remarried and so I was an only child. Otherwise I had a rather full but rather subdued childhood. In my later teens I started going to a local church, developed a friendship with the pastor, and decided to become a minister. My Father said no. So, because I had a love for animals, I went to Atlanta University and obtained a Bachelor of Science degree in Biology and Environmental Sciences."

"Then I went to the Dawson seminary and received my theology certificate. My first ministerial appointment was in a small town called Indian Nest, Florida which is located on a stream which directly enters into the Everglades from the north. There are several tribes of Seminole Indians living nearby with which I am studying their worship/death rites. Working in this community was a young lady named Dr. Janice Stryker. She was an Assistant Professor in the Department of Environmental Studies at the University of Miami. She had a large animal research program in the Everglades which she managed from a small rented house in Indian Nest."

"We fell in love, married, and had fraternal twins, named Samuel and Sara. Both children are in college. Samuel is studying Environmental Engineering at the University of Miami and Sara is working on a Doctorate of Veterinary Medicine degree at the University of Florida. And over the past twenty years, Dr. Stryker-Collingswood has had an 'inexpensive' family team to help paddle her canoes, drive her swamp buggy and air boat, and monitor her live animal traps. And I can confirm that my Sam and Aaron's Hype were indeed good dinosaur buddies some nine or ten years ago; and we also only learned about this connection after Dave found me a couple of weeks ago."

'Well I guess I am last," Bill commented, "or should I say that I hope that I am last. Four of us have been difficult enough to bring together over these past years. Aaron, please don't tell us there might be more of us out there and that we must still look for them!"

Everyone assumed that was more of that Iowa humor. Aaron grinned and shook his head in a direction that meant probably not.

Bill continued, "I was born and raised on a farm in Iowa, as was my wife, Jenny, and my parents, and her parents, and our grandparents, and our great-grandparents and just about all of our friends and professional colleagues. It is a life style that you either love or you get financially (mega-farm mega-acres ownership) locked into the system. We are the Iowa aristocracy. I was born on February 28, 1976 and my parents were Dorothy and Fred Basssinger. I have no brothers or sisters.'

"My childhood was typical for an Iowan which meant farming chores by day and playing sports by night. And I was good at both. I was tempted with an offer to play tight end for the Chicago Bears, but I thought that I was smart to say no and go on to play amateur football at Iowa State University. The first year I immediately broke my leg, so sports were out and studies were in. I graduated from ISU and went on to Drake University and obtained a law degree. Over the past twelve-fourteen years I have specialized in legal problems concerning genetically engineered food crops and genetically modified food. So I will call upon Aaron to come and lecture to us about DNA and genes sometime in the near future, if we can work this look-a-like thing out."

"My wife, Jenny graduated from Drake University and is currently teaching science in a high school in Des Moines. We also have a pair of fraternal twins, Steven and Stefennie. Steve is working on his MD at the University of Iowa. Stef is studying at Drake University in the School of Humanities and Social Studies. And, yes my Stef and Dave's daughter, Alice met and got to know each other on the Washington Smithsonian Mall in DC several years ago. We found this out only a few weeks ago."

Then Bill asked, "May ask a question? Each of us has children which are fraternal twins, boy first and girl second. Is this right?"

Each gave a positive nod of the head.

He continued, "Does the boy have red hair and almond colored eyes?

And there was a yes answer from everyone.

"And does the girl have straw blond hair and jade green eyes with a face that develops freckles during puberty?"

The agreement came with a round of 'unbelievable' from the brothers.

Each identical twin looked at himself across the table and just plain laughed with himself/s. Yep, the odds of the chance that they were indeed identical quadruplets just went up.

And Aaron had the last word. "Not only did our children become friends before we found each other, so did our wives."

And Dave, Charles and Bill gave him a strange are you crazy look.

Aaron continued. "Yes they did. Each of our wives has a special interest and is teaching in science. I just learned a couple of days ago about a certain meeting in Boston which took place a few months ago. It was the Annual Meeting of the American Association of Mothers of Science. During that meeting four ladies by the names of Jenny Bassinger, Janet Dekker, Janice Stryker-Collingswood, and Josephine Armand were on the same panel together. They gave a very well received panel performance and later went out to dinner and spent the evening together. During the meal they discussed the limitations of teaching science to young people. They did not know, nor did they find out, that they all had the same husband!"

And Aaron broke down laughing. Soon the other 'husbands' caught on and smiles and chuckles bounced around the table for several seconds. Did they each have four wives? It was doubtful that the four wives would each admit to four husbands. This was a genetic mess that could never be corrected.

Aaron continued, "So we are almost the last members of our families to meet face to face. It only keeps getting a little crazier doesn't it? Now are we all certain that there are no more skeletons in closets that we have not yet heard about? My feeling is - NO!"

Bill spoke up, "I don't have any empty closets in my house. The five closets that we have are all filled with my wife's clothes. So I know we don't have any skeletons"

The brothers smiled at each other, puzzled, and hoped that this Iowa humor was not contagious.

And the possibility of trying to digest all of these crazy genetic interrelations was mind boggling. But there it was. They only needed for Aaron to perform two more DNA fingerprint tests on the cheek cells from Charles and Bill to confirm that indeed the genetics for the four of them would verify the same genetic mother and father for each. Aaron was certain that it would.

Again they all looked at each other, laughed and shook their heads. The impossible had become the possible.

They were now beginning to feel 'comradely,' even 'brotherly.' Maybe a forty plus year wait wasn't so bad after all. But it was still a lot of years of sibling emptiness. And now they certainly understood that one should not expect to find the same story in a group of books that have the same cover. One simply had to open the book and look more closely.

Suddenly there was some noise outside the car. Dave quickly glanced through the security cameras. The back left camera showed several people coming toward the car. As they got closer, a group of guys split off and sat down on the ground, leaned up against the nearby wall, and took out of their pockets paper and a packet of chopped leaves – marijuana. They were a bunch of young guys, rather hard looking. And they started to roll and light their cigarettes. How long would they be there, maybe an hour or so. This would not do.

These guys were given fifteen minutes to really get the smoke going. Then suddenly four oversized identical red haired green eyed giant things appeared out of nowhere; they charged the young guys by shouting and hollering and acting crazy. One look at these four giant monsters was all they needed. Within about two seconds the group of young guys was in full speed going down the up ramp. The oversized identical red haired green eyed quadruplets broke up laughing. That will be a memory and story that those young guys will be telling for a long time to come.

And Dave, Aaron, Charles, and Bill got back into the car, re-initiated the car's security systems and continued laughing. Their first joint operation was successful, and fun. Risk – No. Who would believe a Washington Post headline which declared that there was an attack by four red headed green eyed monsters from Mars in parking lot D floor six at the Tyson's Corner Shopping Mall on Friday, the day after Thanksgiving which .........

"OK brothers, it is time to think about tomorrow," Dave remarked. "Where do we want to go from here? Aaron, if we are biologically identical quadruplets; how could we have happened?"

Aaron responded, "There are several possibilities. But the most likely one is this. In a fertility clinic an anonymous female donates one ovum cell and an anonymous male donates several million sperm cells. The technician places the oocyte into the middle of the group of sperm cells within a vial containing special growth solutions. Within a few minutes the fertilization of the ovum by one of those sperm will occur. Within a few hours the newly fertilized ovum or zygote will start to undergo cell division resulting in many identical cells, a type of self cloning. This cellular cloning will continue and produce a ball of identical cells called a blastula. The cells are called blastocytes. This blastula will continue to grow for about two weeks and then it starts to change or differentiate into several new additional types of cells and becomes a gastrula with many different cell types. It is the blastula, at about eight to twelve days after fertilization, which is implanted into the womb of the woman and then grows into a child."

"When identical twins happen, they result from the blastula breaking into two masses of blastocytes or two blastulas which continue to grow on their own and eventually form two mature blastulas and then two gastrulas and then two babies. Thus two identical babies are always the same sex. And of course these identical twins are born from the same woman in the same place at one time. With us, we have four identical babies born from four different women in four different places at four different times."

"Just how this happened I don't know. I could speculate. But that would be useless. I simply need more data or information."

"The most logical explanation, as I see it, is that some technicians and or doctors in some clinic made a major mistake. What, I do not know. Why, I do not know. But we are the products of that mistake."

That explanation went around the circle several times. We are mistakes! Ok, so what are we going to do about it?

Bill spoke up, "This is a very strong tort case if we wanted to pursue it. A tort is when a wrongful act, not necessarily the breaking of a contract, results in injury to another person, property, reputation or the like and for which the injured party is entitled to compensation. This clinic fulfilled the contract. They gave the couples, our parents, a baby, us. Subsequently the injury occurred and continues to occur to the lives of identical quadruplets and their four different mothers. And one could easily argue that the injury to the parents and the babies was of such magnitude that compensation, probably of a substantial amount, should be awarded."

Dave asked, "And what would a substantial amount mean?"

Bill answered, "Easily several million dollars, for each of the plaintiffs."

Charles asked, "And we are the plaintiffs. Am I right?"

"I certainly hope so." Bill responded. "In this tort case Plaintiffs would be each parent, each child turned man, probably each wife, and all children. So, if we are counting up to twenty four plaintiffs at around several million dollars each, we are talking about more than a few hundred million dollars."

There were a couple of minutes of silence.

Bill again spoke out, "All of this would require that we could prove from which clinic we came. It is not important whether the problem resulted from correct procedures or a mistake."

Aaron, Dave, and Charles looked at each other with mixed expressions. None of them had been offered several million dollars. Was this real?

"We can do exactly that," Aaron said. "I have a copy of a contract signed by my Mother and a Dr. William Jackson, dated May 22, 1975. The letterhead on the contract is the Jackson Fertility Clinic in McLean, Virginia which is about eight to ten miles right down that road. We also have three living Mothers who were 'serviced' at that clinic and who we could ask to testify, if necessary."

Again more silence. David commented, "Are there any more surprises? And now what do we do? The bottom line is - do we trade anonymity for a few million dollars and extensive publicity? Or do we live within our current incomes and remain in the closet? I think that is a decision that cannot be made by the four of us today."

Aaron agreed, "This problem must be talked over with our families and some kind of joint family decision should be made. After those family decisions have been made we can all get together again and discuss everything. We can each try to explain why each family decision was made in which way, and perhaps then the four of us can make one final overall decision as to what to do."

The four brothers looked at each other, thought for a couple of minutes, and agreed. Thus four brothers who had identical genomes and a common soul, which they did not know about yet, discussed the pros and cons of going public for money. Was it really worth it? And if they lost the case they would have gone public for nothing, yet revealed their existence. But one could do a lot of good with several hundred million American dollars.

William asked "If we took this Jackson Fertility Clinic to court and won, would it bankrupt or destroy them?"

"Yes and no," responded Bill. "If I understand correctly, this is a large established and successful clinic, so they would have to have substantial liability insurance coverage for 'accidents' such as this. We are dealing with babies and potential 'paying' parents. Their insurance company would pay, and we would probably settle out of court. They, and we, would want to limit publicity. Any significant publicity would be bad for both of us. Major publicity could destroy them and be disastrous for us."

Dave added, "And besides, this is not just about the four of us. We each have parents, wives and children who would be caught in any negative publicity. This has to be discussed within each family unit, and then we must meet again to decide what to do. What do you think?"

There was a general agreement. So there was not much left to discuss for now. And it was getting late to have adequate time to catch their return modes of travel.

Dave interrupted the train of thought, "We all accept that we are biological brothers. Aaron is a specialist in DNA fingerprinting and he ran fingerprints of his DNA and my DNA. The results proved, legally, that we are identical brothers. If you will allow he will analyze your DNA to verify whether you, all of us, are identical or fraternal brothers. Then we will have the data necessary and a stronger legal basis to investigate our parentage if we decide to do so. We can talk more about this later. Aaron."

Aaron broke in, "I have with me several small vials which we use to take samples of cells from inside the cheek. Before we separate, if you will give to me such cell samples I will run a DNA fingerprint analysis on them to determine exact parentages. My guess is that we are identical quadruplets. However, these tests will allow us to prove or disprove this. And the tests results will hold up in court."

"Also my Twinning Clinic uses a questionnaire form with all volunteer patients. This has questions about your 'medical and personal life' and about some of your common habits and lifestyles. Our research attempts to correlate units of DNA with behavior patterns using identical and paternal twins. If everything is positive with these DNA fingerprints tests, later I will try to talk you into volunteering for our complete research program. But for now I need the genetic material and the information for our own personal purposes first."

Charles and Bill looked at each other, shrugged their shoulders as if to say – why not? And they took the vials and cotton swab sticks, made the necessary cheek cell recovery maneuver, placed the cotton tips into the alcohol, gave the samples to Aaron, and asked to be informed of the results as soon as possible. They were both excited about participating in a scientific experiment, especially one using their/his own body cells.

It was approaching 6:00 PM, and they seemed to be at a stalemate for further decision making. They agreed to discuss all of the known facts with their wives and children, but not the parents yet. Then they would meet again and continue the discussion, or if there was a unanimous agreement, they would pursue that agreement. So they each touched, hugged, kissed, and said their goodbyes. The conference table was taken down and stored, seats were returned to their original positions, security cameras were turned off, and the LR was restored to its road travel mode.

Dave drove down the ramps to ground level. They did not see the young guys, and quickly left the shopping mall area. First they headed toward Reston, Virginia. They let Bill out at a taxi stand outside of town so he could take a taxi to Dulles to catch his Northwest Airlines flight to Des Moines. Next they traveled to Old Town Alexandria where they let Charles out on a street corner from which he caught a taxi to Washington National to catch his US Airways flight to Miami. And then they went on to Capitol Hill where Aaron hopped out in front the US Capital building, walked down to Washington Union Station and boarded his AMTRACK train to Penn Station in New York City.

Dave let out a big sigh of relief, smiled from ear to ear, pounded four times on the dashboard, and headed back through DC to Arlington and to home. "What a fantastic day I/we had. Today I/we performed a miracle! Now do we dare show the world our miracle?"

# 15 – Anonymity Versus Notoriety - Armand

The forty plus year old problem of trying to find one another seemed to be solved. The four red haired jade green eyed big gentlemen accepted that they were indeed quadruplets, identical or fraternal would be decided from Aaron's DNA fingerprint analysis. Now the problem was one of deciding to remain anonymous, or to sue for big bucks and enter the ranks of the rich notoriety. What would be best for their parents, what would be best for them, what would be best for their children, and how would their friends and work colleagues accept such a change? Each gentleman needed time alone with the family to discuss in detail the pluses and minuses of such changes. Christmas was coming in a couple of weeks. All of the children would be home from school. Both Christmas Day and New Years Day were on Thursdays, so there would be two complete weeks of vacation coming up. The logical thing to do was to get away from the house and go somewhere to relax, play a little, and talk a lot. And the four big gentlemen each had the same and very logical decision making capacity – family decisions were best.

*  *  *

The Armands were all avid skiers. Aaron had gone to northern New Hampshire almost every winter of his childhood and young adulthood to ski. Josephine was born and raised in the snow covered mountains of Colorado. Hope was all athletic, from tennis to basketball to skiing. While Hype could do it all, so he thought. So, logically the Armands made reservations at their favorite ski resort, the Super Pine Ridge and the Big Moose Lodge at the top of the White Mountains in New Hampshire.

Super Pine Ridge was a great location for downhill skiers. It had a vertical drop of thirty two hundred feet, thirty eight cross country and downhill ski trails, and twelve ski lifts including fixed-grip quads, high-speed detachable quads, triplets, surface and wonder carpets. There was an aerial tramway and two large snowboarding areas, one for beginners and one for advanced. And the large club house had three large fireplaces, two dining areas, and a spectacular view of the skiing slopes so you could 'watch' your children if you were not a very good skier yourself.

Within ten minutes driving time was the Big Moose Lodge. It was a large five floor building with only sixty five rooms and family suites. The Armands reserved a fifth floor three bedroom suite for three nights. The suite had a beautiful panoramic view of the snow covered mountain valleys. It had its own wood burning fireplace, large living and dining areas, a bar, and a small kitchen, with snacks and drinks; but most meals were called into the central kitchen and delivered to the suite at meal time. In the center of the living area was the traditional big bear rug, and out of the wall above the fireplace was the traditional big moose head. It was a very traditional New England hunting lodge setting, without the log walls of course. It would be warm and cozy for heart to heart talking.

The day before Christmas the Armands drove from New York City to Manchester to the 'old English Manor House' and held a family Christmas with all of the employees of the house and farm. They brought a car trunk full of presents, at least one for each employee. At the end of the long ride they finally turned into the half mile long driveway up to the 'House' at around 3:30 PM on the evening before Christmas. As they arrived into the circular drive and parked, Hype jumped out and ran to the front door, but the house and grounds seemed deserted.

Hype looked around and shouted, "I don't think anyone is home! I do not see anyone!"

Aaron tooted the car horn, Hype rang the door bell, and suddenly the 'House' came to life. Doors opened and from all sides of the house and people started flooding toward the car. Merry Christmas! Merry Christmas! Everyone was rushing forward. Aaron, Jos, Hype and Hope had not been 'Home' for Christmas in more than five years.

Aaron was now the new 'Master' and the children were young adults. It was a fantastic welcome and it brought tears to his eyes. He remembered that this was his childhood home and it was filled with thousands of positive memories. And, yes, lately he had been delinquent at renewing those memories and the people who helped bring them about. As the car was surrounded with a mob, the Armands slowly got out and got hugged and squeezed and kissed to death.

"Welcome, Welcome, Merry Christmas, Merry Christmas," filled the air from everyone.

The welcome was so sincere that even Jos, Hype, and Hope started feeling guilty of neglecting the 'homestead." They had been so busy with school and friends and New York City that they had not even given New Hampshire a second thought in many years. Tears of happiness filled many eyes.

Aaron decided it was an appropriate time to hand out Christmas presents to everyone; it seemed as if all of the employees were here. So he opened the car trunk and said to the children, "Hype, you and Hope give out Christmas gifts, red-white-blue color wraps for the children, blue color wraps to ladies and red color wraps to men."

Everyone was talking to everyone and no one could hear but Hype grabbed Hope and the two of them starting giving out Christmas gifts to all members of the family household and farming units. Including all members of each family, there were more than sixty adults and children ringed around the car. It was a happy joyous occasion. Currently there were no Armands living on the Armand estate. All held out hope that this might change in the near future.

Five years ago Hype and Hope had been only twelve years old. Now they were tall, handsome young adults of seventeen years. And everyone was filled with shock and wonder about how they doubled their size and maturity so fast. It was a lovely, touching, memorable welcome.

After the presents were passed out, Aaron asked for quiet. When the noise had subsided he said, "We want to sincerely thank you for your loyal and steadfast service to the Armand estate over these many years. You made my Mother and Father successful and happy people. And you helped grow a boy who is becoming a successful and happy man."

The adults smiled at each other. They all knew that he was referring to himself.

"We have not made any decisions concerning the future of the 'old English Manor House'. But I promise you that we will make a decision concerning the future of the estate immediately."

Slowly the crowd dispersed and three of the men took the Armand's suitcases and boxes up to their bedrooms and said their goodbyes. Each family member partially unpacked as they were going on the ski resorts day after tomorrow. As each was tired Aaron said to the household staff, "We are exhausted from the long trip so we will take short naps. If you will kindly prepare tea and some pastries for an hour from now we will be down for tea time." And they each went to their bedrooms.

Upon hearing the request, the house chef, Marion, and her assistant, Anne Marie, started preparing the tea time request to be served in the salon; they also began preparing a light meal for them for later in the evening which would be served in the dining room. Tomorrow evening, Christmas day, they would serve a large dinner for senior personnel and the managers of the estate and their spouses. Preparations for the Christmas dinner were well under way.

A little later as they sat down for the traditional tea time, Aaron (Dad) opened the conversation, "It is really wonderful to return to my childhood home. But I feel guilty that I have done next to nothing to reward or thank the many people that helped me grow up and are the real lifeblood of the Armand estate. If any of you have suggestions please let me know as I must take some kind of action soon."

Jos (Mom) spoke up, "I have a special love for this land and people also. I don't want to see them hurt. You must decide for the estate and for them at the same time."

"Even though I have only been here a half a dozen times, I too have a special place in my heart for the people and the land," added Hype. "And Hope and I talked about walking everywhere tomorrow and reliving our childhood memories. The flowers, shrubs, and herb gardens are sleeping, but the swimming pool, tennis courts, horse stables, cow barns, pig sheds, pastures, woods, Erving and Sider creeks, Mt. Snoco, everything is waiting for us to say good-bye."

Hope slipped in, "Hype and I think that you and Mom don't have time to live in two places. Your hearts are in the Twinning Center, even though your soul may be here. And Hype and I will have to concentrate on our university studies starting next fall for, because who knows how many years we will be studying. We will not be able to come here often. So we sort of thought that this might be our last chance to see it all one more time, before it changes. And it will change whether we are here or not. We understand and must accept this."

Dad responded, "Reasoned and spoken like the bright young lady that you are. And you too Hype."

Hype was a natural high alpha personality and never liked it when his little sister got praise and he did not. Dad was aware of this so added that last comment to prevent any future problems. Although, when necessary, Hope had learned how to put Hype in his place.

Mom asked Dad, "Have you decided whether you can have both the estate and the center?"

"Yes, I cannot," Dad answered. "I accept that I cannot give proper effort in two places, so far away at the same time. Especially with this other genetic problem that seems to be coming to a boil. I will talk with you about this later. But I do have to make some definite decisions soon. Tonight I could feel the employees begging for a decision. Obviously they want us to come here and live; but more importantly they want stability for their families – job security.

The Armand family talked a little longer and then retired to their beds, which always remained empty when they were not here. And they were at that level of exhaustion that they each went to sleep quickly and slept until late the next morning.

On Christmas morning, after they had all awoken, showered, dressed, gone downstairs to the large salon, sat around the big Christmas tree, and had their pastries and coffee, they opened their Christmas presents to each other. They also had brought special presents for the household staff, now down to only two maids, one cook in addition to Chef Marion, who had taken over the responsibility for all household chores, and one major domo who did any and everything that needed to be done inside the seven thousand square foot house.

The weather was pleasant, near freezing but with beautiful sunshine and minor clouds. So Hype and Hope dressed in their snow gear, each took a back pack with a quickly packed lunch, soft drinks and water. As they walked out the door Hype hollered back, "We will be back in the late afternoon. The estate is so large that we will need much of the day walking just to see some of it, especially our favorite places."

Mom responded, "Be careful and I want you in this house before dark."

The two grown children just waved.

But yes, in many places on the estate the woods was so thick that much of it had not been walked on by Homo sapiens in many years, and one could easily get lost in there. So they would walk everywhere that they could, certainly revisit their favorite places, and have lunch out there.

As they passed the tennis courts Hope look mournful, "This was where I learned my first tennis with old Mr. Watson when I was five years old. He was the only one who had the patience to keep chasing the balls that I kept hitting over the fence. I remember one time when I had hit maybe six or seven balls over the fence and he went over to get them. He was gone for a long time. Finally I got tired of waiting so I carefully sneaked over to where he was looking and what did I see? He was laying down where I could not see him, his eyes were shut, and he was taking a quick nap. He was tired from chasing my balls but would not admit it. So I went to the bench and lay down and took a nap too. He did not tell anyone and I did not either. Mom and Dad just thought that we were practicing really hard."

They walked on down toward the horse stables and looked inside. There were only three horses where there used to be ten. The three not so healthy animals looked at the children as if to say please come play with us, ride us. It was obvious that they were not being ridden. They were clean and smelled good. But they looked unhappy.

Hype said, "Did I tell you about the time when I was riding Grey Streak and a stag deer almost ran us down? Yes, I was probably about ten years old when I was riding alone going up Sider Creek. It was clouding up very fast, large black clouds. I knew that I had better hurry home or I was going to get drenched. It started to lightning and thunder. So I kicked Grey Streak and we speeded up a little. The terrain near the creek was rough, so I was watching it very carefully. A sharp barb of lightning and a big crack of thunder hit. And suddenly a large stag, at least thirty points and five hundred pounds, broke from the forest and ran directly at us. I tried to shout but it all happened too fast. I could see him lowering his antlers and aiming for Gray Streak. I started to jump off in the other direction. Do you know what happened? Instead the large reindeer jumped over both Gray Streak and me. I quickly stood up and grabbed the deer by the antlers, swung myself up and onto his back, and rode him all the way back to the house. And we went so fast that we outran the rain and I never even got one drop on me."

Hope looked at her big brother and said, "Can't you ever be serious? I'm surprised that you did not choose a pterodactylus, your favorite flying dinosaur, to ride."

Hype responded, "Yeah, that would have been more exciting. Thanks for the idea; next time."

And they continued walking down to the cow barns and then over to the pig sheds.

Hype couldn't resist, he had to make a comparison. "You know if I was born again, I would prefer to be a cow and not a pig. Pigs smell so bad I don't understand how they can stand themselves. And cows have really big boobies." The hormones were coming on.

Hope gave him an are you are crazy look, turned and walked toward the woods. Hype hurried to catch up as he didn't want to miss anything exciting. He caught up with her, grabbed her from behind, he was several inches taller than her, turned her around and gave her a big kiss on the cheek. She blushed a little and said, "that's better."

And away they went climbing up toward Mt. Snoco to relive the 'good old days' when they were just kids enjoying life and not worrying about how to grow up. That latter growing up time seemed to be sneaking up on them. And they had a great afternoon climbing up and down the steep inclines and down into small ravines, visiting favorite big old oak trees, and crawling out on small ledges where they could see 'all the way to Boston', chasing a couple of rabbits, waving at the birds, and just trying to see everything they had time to see and lock in old memories. They both knew it was going to be the last time. And they were back in the house by dark in time to shower and prepare for tonight's dinner party. They had to remember to not think of this evening as the last meal in the 'House.'

Around 7:00 PM people started arriving. It was a formal dinner so everyone had on their Sunday clothes, dark suits and nice dresses. The dinner table was set with Japanese china, Viennese silverware, German lead crystal wine and water glasses, and three silver candelabras which were Armand heirlooms. The table cloth was another heirloom; it was made of Belgian lace. There were thirteen chairs around the long table. There was one chair each for: Mr. Erwin Nobles, single and the new full time temporary Estate Manager; Mr. and Mrs. Jack Berels, Manager of the Swine Production Unit; Mr. and Mrs. Larry Railsberg, Manager of the Dairy Unit; Mr. and Mrs. Robert Bluesson, Manager of Commerical Crops Unit, Mr. and Mrs. Berry Adverman, Director of Estate Grounds and Maintanence Unit, and of course seats for the four Armands.

Aaron looked around, counted heads and decided that all invited guests had arrived, "Can we please all take our seats so we can begin to taste the great smells that I am enjoying."

All had assigned seats with Aaron and Jos sitting at opposite ends of the long table. Hype and Hope sat across from each other in the center of the long table sides. While the guests sat with the wife to the right side of the husband. This allowed for the almost perfect alternate man-woman seating that was proper in the New England culture. Aaron, being host of the dinner, said a short prayer of thanksgiving for the new Christ child, and the food was served. Marion, Anne Marie, and two temporary assistant cooks had worked several days to prepare this feast for a king. In fact Aaron was their current reigning 'king. The males of the host family, Aaron and Hype opened bottles of a French Chenin Blanc wines. Major domo Oscar poured a glass for each person. The meal then began with raw oysters. Next they enjoyed lobster, swordfish filet, baked potatoes with a cream-cheddar cheese sauce, cranberries, succotash with nutmeg, and three types of hot fresh breads and rolls. For desert, anyone who still had space was treated to the locally famous orange cake with cranberries topped with maple syrup. And as a chaser, freshly brewed Columbian coffee, English or Japanese green tea were the choices.

It was a very lovely and quite proper New England formal dinner; although the children labeled it as boring. They knew that they were supposed to be hospitable to the Armand 'family', but this 'family' was all strangers plus they were old people. Some of them they either had never seen or just did not remember their faces. The atmosphere really did not become warm and friendly. There was a lot of small talk but nothing of a serious nature was approached. In addition the managers did not really know the new estate owner very well, other than as a child. Aaron's Mother had been the responsible person for both the house and farming units for many years even before his Father died. Aaron had not been living in New Hampshire or on the estate for more than twenty years. His current life was in New York City. What was the new 'responsible person – owner' going to do with their livelihood and in some cases their lifetime work – continue it or sell it?

After the meal the guests did not stay very long but left rather quickly. There were no men and cigars in the games room and no women and tea in the veranda. And the Armands thanked Marion and Anne Marie for the fantastic meal, said a few nice things to each other about the house and today's happenings. Then they headed toward the bedrooms to think about tomorrow on the ski sloops. The 'old English Manor House' and the estate was Dad's problem. And he must make a decision soon. But he knew that, and he would do so.

Jos and the children went to sleep immediately. But Aaron could not sleep. Indeed the problem was his, so the solution was his. What, when, and how should he decide the future for these loyal, some life-long, family members?

Aaron went into and out of sleep. 'I cannot decide how to handle this new inheritance. The decision involves the responsibility of twenty one employees and their families and a large farmstead which is currently breeding and milking twenty three milk cows and raising forty seven pigs, of which forty three would soon become pregnant, plus growing corn, soybeans, wheat crops, and the larger apple orchard. It is a very large operation. Fortunately I have found a temporary estate manager to take over. During the past couple years my Mother has not been healthy enough to manage full time. So we employed a Mr. Erwin Gobels to help part time. Mr. Gobels can now take over temporarily full time until I can make more final decisions concerning the estate. It is a sad but happy Christmas. Sad because the Mistress of the 'House' is gone; happy because everyone got to see and fall in love with the two new teenagers of the 'House'. They had not visited for more than five years, and indeed they had transformed from children to young beautiful adults. And everyone put pressure on Jos and I to move back, bring the children and bring everything back to life. All I can say is that no decision had yet been made. But it was a very touching reunion for the 'old English Manor House. I have to make a difficult, but a very kind decision for everyone."

* * *

The day after Christmas day the Armands drove up to the Big Moose Lodge. They would stay only 3 nights such that they could be back in New York City before New Year's Eve. It was only a couple hours of driving time to the Lodge from Manchester, so they arrived about noon. They quickly unpacked, had a light lunch, and headed for the ski slopes.

It was traditional within the Armand family that the first four trips down the sloops were family togetherness. Dad chose the first slope. Mom chose the second slope. And Hype and then Hope, because Hype was a couple of minutes older, each chose the next slopes. After that they were each on their own as to when and where they skied. So the first afternoon was exciting and exhausting. And that evening it was eat and go to sleep, the sooner the better.

The next morning no one was awake before noon. But once awake, and with a high energy sausage and eggs breakfast, everyone was ready for a chance at some of the new slopes which were not here when they were last here, three years ago. So again it was down the hill game.

Hype said, "I am going to try the Crazy Legs Down Hill this afternoon."

Hope replied, "That is not as difficult as the Bora Bora Down Hill. The Bora Bora is more difficult and longer. I am going to do it."

And the typical sibling competition was transferred from New York City to the mountains of New Hampshire.

While both Hype and Hope tried the new ones, Mom and Dad sort of stuck to some of the older, medium incline and not such long slopes.

After the first trip down Mom felt a little dizzy so Mom and Dad sat out on the second downhill and promised to join the kids in the afternoon runs. Hype and Hope took off to the lifts while Mom and Dad went inside, took a couch by the fire and ordered coffee. A few minutes later Mom excused herself and went to the bathrooms. Dad lay back in the couch and watched the beautiful roaring fire. Suddenly at 10:47 on that Saturday morning, December, 27, he passed out. Twenty seconds later he awoke, had a tremendous headache, and a knot on the left side of his head just behind the ear. He knew what had happened so he asked the waiter for a couple of aspirins and said nothing to anybody.

Soon Hype and Hope completed their second runs, had checked their skis and came inside for some energy rebuilding late lunch. They joined Mom and Dad, and together took a dining room table and ordered. The two younger ones had the high energy meal with lentils, two soft boiled eggs, bean sprouts, broccoli, and for desert yogurt with sesame seeds, plus a small sack full of peanuts for later in the afternoon; and the non-alcoholic red bull to chase it all down. Mom and Dad ate a normal meal. And after an hour again resting beside the fire, they all finished off the day on the slopes going with gravity

After a short digestion time Hype announced, "Come on Hope, let's go 'one more time with gravity', I will race you down the Spiral Down Hill."

Hope popped up and said, "And I suppose that you want a head start so that the race will be more fair." And she laughed, went over, grabbed her skis, and headed out the door. Hype was one half of a step behind her.

By the time the second full day had arrived everyone was slowing down a little. Mom and Dad only hit three slopes in the afternoon. Hype did three/three slopes morning/afternoon. And Hope, in order to be one up on big brother did three/four slopes morning/afternoon, and had finished with one of the more advanced slopes. Two and one half days was enough intensive exercise. Of course they did not pace themselves very well because they did not know when they would be coming back to New Hampshire to ski, university began next fall, and the Twinning Center kept the adults busy twenty four/seven.

And Aaron had stalled as long as he could. So during the last evening, after excellent venison steaks, citrus roasted asparagus and peas, maple glazed potatoes, corn bread meal with a hot Alaska for desert, they settled around a blazing red and yellow fireplace.

Dad opened the conversation. "Hype and Hope, I have something very serious to tell you. And I need your promise that what I am about to say will never leave this room. You must not tell anyone, even your best friend. OK?'

They gave each other a look, and then they both gave a verbal "yes sir".

Dad continued. "I am not your Grandfather Armand's son. Or to express it another way, I do not, therefore you do not, carry the Armand genes. Now this is not an inheritance problem. I was legally adopted by them. So I am legally their heir, just as you are legally my heir. Here is the situation."

"Your Grandmother, Mary Armand, apparently, could not conceive, could not get pregnant. As you know this is unusual in the Armand families. Each Armand family has several children. When she passed 30 years of age the families put pressure on her to do something about this no heir situation. So, with the approval of her husband, Dr, James Armand, she went to a fertility clinic in Washington, DC to try to 'correct' this heir problem. This clinic put her on a special hormone schedule and when her body was ready they implanted into her womb a pre-embryo, which then grew into a baby – me. The genes for this pre-embryo did not come from an Armand, they were provided by anonymous donors. This means I do not know who my biological parents are. Therefore you do not know who your biological grandparents are from my side of the family.

Both children did a double take. They looked first at each other, then at their Dad, then at their Mom, and then at the fireplace, then out the window, then down at the floor, and then back at Dad............

Dad continued, "And there is more. I have three identical brothers from three other mothers. One was born in San Diego. One was born in Iowa. And one was born in Atlanta. So what do you think of that?"

Hype popped up, "Are you trying to pull a fancy joke on us. That is not possible. How can four identical babies be born to four different mothers in four different cities. And I suppose they were all born on March 7, 1976." He knew his Father's birthday.

"It may sound unbelievable, but it is true," responded Dad. "And no, each of us was born on a different day, but all just a few days apart."

Hope was puzzled and asked, "Do you know how this happened? And did the genes for you and the other, your, brothers, come from the same source?"

Dad answered, "Maybe yes and yes. We think this clinic made a mistake. We think it prepared several pre-embryos and somehow gave each of four waiting women the same pre-embryo. How four exact pre-embryos came about from one, we do not know. If that is what happened, then yes all four of us have the exact same genetic Mother and Father somewhere in the world."

Jos spoke up, "And it took them more than forty years to find each other. All four of them met for the first time this last Thanksgiving."

Hype quickly jumped in, "That was a real thanksgiving wasn't it, Dad?"

And Dad suddenly had tears running down his cheeks. His son, who had no brothers, understood what brotherhood was all about. He stood up, reached over, grabbed Hype, and gave a big hug and a kiss. Then he reached over, grabbed Hope and gave her a big hug and a kiss. By then Jos was standing and he went over and grabbed her and gave her a big hug and such a long kiss that a couple of coughs were heard in the background apparently produced by a couple of siblings. But by then everyone was teary eyed and it required a few minutes of quiet before Dad could go on with the story.

"So I am sorry, but I do not know my biological parents so we do not know your biological grandparents," he repeated.

"And there is more," he added.

Hype and Hope looked at each other as if to say isn't this enough for one evening?

Dad continued, "My Iowa brother is a court lawyer who specializes in genetically engineered food crops and genetically modified foods. He is a lawyer who handles a lot of tort cases both in and out of court. A tort is when someone does you wrong and badly hurts you physically, psychologically, or your reputation, or your family. He says that if we take this fertility clinic to court we could probably expect to win several million dollars for each person who was wrongfully done to. All total there would probably be twenty one of us including the original parents who are still alive, or now, grandparents, the babies or men and their wives, and their children. So twenty four people, minus my loving parents and minus brother Charles's Mother who died when he was a child, would allow for near one hundred million dollar plus tort case. And I have the necessary evidence to prove that it was this certain clinic which was at fault."

Hype and Hope were shell shocked with the first admissions, now this. Where indeed was Dad going next? They were almost afraid to ask. But of course ask they did.

First Hope asked, "Are you telling us that we could get several million dollars just because this clinic might have messed up? If they paid us all of that money would they go bankrupt and have to close down? If they went bankrupt who would help other women who need help having babies? Would the people that just made a mistake have to go to jail? And…….. "

It is always the truth that first comes from the mouths of babes. But she was not exactly a babe. She was a seventeen year old young lady, tall and slim who had just finished her high school biology course, but as a university choice, she was thinking social systems and management. And these were good questions. If they took the clinic's money, many women who wanted children might not have them, and hard working people might go to jail just because they made an honest mistake.

Dad tried to answer. "Wait. Slow down. According to my brother, William, the clinic would probably have an insurance company that would pay the money, so the clinic would probably not go bankrupt. And innocent people do not go to jail."

Hope responded, "But you don't know for sure, do you? Where is the fairness in all of this. A second wrong doesn't correct a first wrong."

No answer came from Dad. What could he say? Yes. He didn't know for sure.

Then Hype saved him by asking, "I was seriously thinking about majoring in banking and finance in the university next year. Maybe this money would help us get started and we could develop our own bank somewhere, and we could set up a financial consulting division. What do you think, Dad?"

He got no answer, only a dirty look from his Father and his Mother.

And to save face Hype asked Mom, "did you know about this situation before now, or is it all new to you too?'

Jos answered, "I was aware of the possibilities of Father having three other identical brothers because I heard them talking to each other at night. These four men each had dreams of each other for many years, only recently they finally found each other. They can talk to each other at night via some type of mental telepathy which they call spirit communications. You probably know that your Father and I sleep with each other."

And she smiled at Hype and Hope. And they turned a little red in the faces and smiled back. Indeed the hormones had arrived.

"Since they talk to each other at night, while we are in bed, I hear them talking. I do not know what the brothers say but I do hear what your Father says. At first I thought he was just talking in his sleep. Later I began to understand that these conversation were serious and finally determined that they were genetically related family that he was communicating with."

"But the torts law suit idea only surfaced when the four identical brothers met for the first time last Thanksgiving; so all of this legal info is new to me."

Dad answered. "I have been thinking about what we could do with several million dollars. At Columbia U we have the only Twinning Hospital in the world. Identical twins especially have specific and very special needs. Many of them do have spirit communications between them. We four identical brothers can communicate by night time spirit dreams which we have some control over. Recently when one of us was hurt, we other three felt this hurt at the same place on the body and at the exact same time that our brother was injured. There are reports of many mutual, unexplainable communications between identical twins."

"For example, one identical brother lost an arm in an accident. His identical twin felt the pain of this at the exact time that it happened. Several years later, the second twin that still had his arm, believed his arm had been lost, so he stopped using it; and because he never ever used that 'lost' arm, the blood circulation stopped, and it had dried and shriveled up to about one half of its original size."

"There are partially controlled and completely uncontrolled communications that exist between twins, especially identical twins. There are many genetic controls involved in behaviors in normal people as well as in twins which we do not understand. Identical and fraternal twins respond differently in various test situations. Are these controls the same or are they different? We have only begun to understand what these controls are and how to work with them. A second or third Twinning Hospital, perhaps in South America and Asia would help us move more rapidly at discovering the genetic connection to behavior control."

"We could learn more between nature versus nurture. This means that genetics controls some behaviors and our environmental learning controls some behaviors. Behavioral difficulties and diseases could be better controlled and corrected if we knew whether the control was due to genetics or learning processes. If we know the control, then we can prescribe the correct treatment to help that person. And this would be a very good thing."

Again there were a few minutes of silence. Jos looked at Aaron and then at the children.

She spoke, "We always have a problem in getting money for research at the Twinning Center because there is not a deadly 'twinning disease.' The National Institutes of Health has 27 institutes and centers. It is the largest medical-disease research center in the world. The various research institutes include: Cancer Institute for cancers, Eye Institute for eye diseases, Heart Institute for heart diseases, etc. There is no Twinning Institute at the NIH. So to compete for research money we have to try to project a possible DNA linkage of a disease with twinning, diseases such as Parkinson's disease, Alzheimer's disease, or even aging. The NIH does not support research projects concerning DNA linkages in twins to compare left handedness versus right handedness, blue eyes versus brown eyes, aggressiveness versus passivity, IQ levels, capacity for language learning, and capacity for mathematics. We have to use money from the private sector, NGOs and individuals. A few million dollars would help us do a lot of very important research related to DNA control of human behavior."

Jos and Aaron eyes met in general agreement. But nothing was said.

Hype summarized things by asking the critical question. "Are we going to have to choose between anonymity and notoriety? Do we have to chose between a cave and Hollywood?" Again from the mouths of babes it is most succinctly put.

And again a few minutes of silence; it was apparent that no decision was forthcoming tonight.

Then Dad spoke up, "Hope, are you still in contact with Action Dekker?"

Hope answered, "No. We E-mailed for a couple of years, but when he went to the university he discovered that university girls were more fun than high school girls."

Dad responded, "Action's Father is David Dekker. Mr. Dekker is one of my twin brothers. Therefore Action would be your first cousin, or genetically speaking he would be your brother."

Hope could only look at her Father with a - you got to be kidding look. After thinking for a few moments she replied. "I guess you would have never let us get married then, anyway!" And gave him that an - 'its ok I love you' smile. "He was too old for me anyway."

And the conversation continued on for another hour. Around midnight they all turned in because they wanted to get a good start on the road tomorrow for that long days drive back to New York City. No decisions had been made and no words were cut into stone, yet.

# 16 - Anonymity Versus Notoriety – Bassinger

During the Christmas week at the Opera House Theater in Golden Nugget City, near Random, Missouri, Charles Dickens's the Christmas Carol was being played with a cast of thirteen professionals plus a symphony orchestra. On the Wednesday afternoon and evening before Christmas at the Briarwood High School in Des Moines, Iowa, Charles Dickens's Christmas Carol was playing using a team of more than twenty five amateurs. Jenny Bassinger not only taught mathematics, biology, and physics, but was also the Director of the Drama Club which was preparing to perform this play on that Wednesday. Many high schools in Iowa have a Drama Club which regularly performs 1, 2, and 3 act famous and not so famous plays during the school year. In these plays the students have every role from designing and building the set, designing and sewing the costumes, selecting the cast, performing as actors and actresses, and selling the tickets. Mrs. Bassinger loved the close interaction with the students and had been a very good actress, herself, when she was a high school student, a few years ago. Her husband, William Bassinger, knew this, so he had arranged a surprise which would begin on Friday, the day after Christmas. The surprise was a special reward for his wife for the extra work with the Club, for the children, Steve and Stef, for their excellent studies in the university, and for him to tell his family his forty plus year secret that he had no parents, therefore they had no grandparents, and of course to see the professional production, relax, and then get serious.

Steve, Stef, and Dad skipped the Wednesday afternoon performance but were in motion for the evening performance of Christmas Carol. They entered the Briarwood High School gymnasium as the play would be performed on the parallel elevated stage adjacent to the gym floor. They looked around a bit, as they had forty seats from which to choose. Mom was behind the curtain trying to control last minute problems, and make certain everything was all right.

Christmas Carol was written by Charles Dickens in London in 1843. Mr. Dickens was already a well known English writer when he wrote what is now probably the most famous play in history. It is a story of social injustice and poverty at a time when people living in London were either very rich or very poor.

The story revolves around a very rich miserly old gentleman, Ebenezer Scrooge. All of his life all he wanted to do was to make money. He lived in a large old mansion in the center of London and had one employee, a clerk named Bob Cratchit. On the night before Christmas Bob invited Mr. Scrooge to his house for Christmas dinner. Mr. Scrooge responded with a "Bah, Humbug", and then continued to talk about how Christmas was very wrong. People that didn't make their own money shouldn't have money. There were poor houses for the poor to live in, they did not need presents. And they could buy their own gifts if gifts were so important..........

This same day, seven years before, his good friend and business partner, Jacob Marley had died. This night Jacob Marley's ghost returns and tells Mr. Scrooge that he is going to die tonight unless he changes his ways and learns to share his wealth. Early during night the Ghost of Christmas Past visits him and tells him he will die tonight and his ghost will walk forever. Then during the middle of the night the Ghost of Christmas Present visits him and tells him he will die before the sun rises and his ghost will walk forever in the streets of London. And then just before sunrise the Ghost of Christmas Future visits him and tells him he will die immediately and his ghost will walk and live among the London poor forever and ever.

When he does wake up to find out he is still alive he reforms because he thinks he is being given a second chance. He immediately sends money and food to the Cratchit family, sends money to several charities, sends money to his neighbors, sends money to everyone he knows, and even adopts Tiny Tim Cratchit as his own child so that seven year old Tiny Tim will inherit all of his wealth when Mr. Scrooge does die, however that date has now been extended.

Today, when someone hoards his money and refuses to share or spend his money he is called scrooge, the name that Mr. Dickens chose to call the 'hero' of his story.

The Briarwood High School put on an excellent performance of the Christmas Carol that evening. The students and the audience loved it. At the end of the performance the cast received three standing ovations. Jimmy Rotary received the loudest ovation for his portrayal of Tiny Tim. And Mom received her special ovations and several bouquets of flowers. Everyone was happy to participate and to watch another Briarwood HS play. They knew that they could expect another such quality effort next year.

The Bassinger family left the gym and retired to a nearby favorite pub. They went in to celebrate another success for the Bassinger family. A triumph by one was a triumph by all. And this deserved a special prize. So they sat down and each ordered something to drink, colas for the kids and beers for the adults, and potato chips for everyone.

Then Dad spoke, "A salute to our beautiful Mother who has again proved that the Bassingers continue to light up the Des Moines community."

And Steve and Stef both applauded and gave their Mother a congratulations kiss.

Dad continued, "And tonight I have a very special prize for all of us. It is in this envelope."

And he gave the envelope to a surprised Mom. This was not the standard way they celebrated a family success. Something was up.

After opening the envelope she began talking out loud, "I see here four tickets for the upcoming Christmas weekend evening production of the Charles Dickens's Christmas Carol in the Opera House Theater at Golden Nugget City in Random, Missouri. I am also finding four reservations for an American Airlines flight # 1852 from Des Moines, Iowa to Springfield, Missouri, leaving at 8:30 Friday morning. I also find four reservations for Friday, Saturday, Sunday, and Monday nights at the New Ozarks Hotel in Random, Missouri. And there is a short note attached which reads, 'I would be the happiest man on earth if a certain Jenny, Steve, and Stefennie Bassinger would join me for a special Christmas in the South starting tomorrow. PS – I have ordered any and all snow in the area to be delayed for one week or I promised to open a multi-trillion dollar torts case against Golden Nugget City. All my love. Hubby and Dad

Everything was quiet for a few moments. Then Steve spoke up, "My name is Steve Bassinger and I accept."

Immediately Stef spoke up, "My name is Stefennie Bassinger and I accept."

And then everyone looked at Mom. Again Mom stayed cool. The children's looks changed to hurry up, Mom. Again Mom remained cool. "My name was Jenny Strowsky but I changed it to Jenny Bassinger so I guess I qualify to give a decision. Right?"

About that time she had a son who was 6 foot 7 inches tall, 215 lbs and a daughter who was 6 foot 2 inches tall, 120 lbs standing beside her; they were looking down on top of her head.

Mom looked up and grinned, "As always, the babies rule the nest."

And when the babies started to pick up Mom's chair while Mom was still in it she quickly said, "I accept. I accept. Don't drop me!"

And Dad got up and kissed each of them in turn. It was Christmas vacation in the Ozarks. These two college students were twenty two years old and on their two week break so he wasn't sure whether they had made their own plans for the coming two weeks. After all he was only giving them a ten hour notice of his pre-arranged plans. If they had made no plans, there were no problems. If they had made plans they were astute about canceling them and joining the family venture. He knew he would never know. They were good kids.

On Christmas day they woke, opened their Christmas presents, had a light breakfast and then went to the farm to spend the day with Grandpa and Grandma Bassinger. This had become traditional.

On Friday, the morning after Christmas the Bassingers got up early, had a fast breakfast, and hurried to the Des Moines International Airport, and flew south.

They arrived in Springfield at 11:08 AM, disembarked, found their luggage, went to the car rental booth, selected their rental car, loaded and climbed in it, and took off for Random which was about one and one half hours away. On route they found a nice restaurant, had a brief lunch, and finally arrived at the New Ozarks Hotel about 3:00 PM. They checked into their two reserved rooms which were on the fourth floor. Each room had 2 king size beds and a connecting door. Mom and Dad had one room and the children had the other. The children were old enough and mature enough to share such arrangements. After all they were each big enough that they required separate king sized beds anyway.

And Dad called for a rendezvous in the parent's room at the little round table. The table was filled with brochures of the many forms of entertainment available at Golden Nugget City and its environs. So they sat down and starting looking over the entertainment brochures. After half an hour they were ready to propose a program.

Mom spoke first, "Since we are here because of my recent outstanding direction of the Christmas Carol, I guess I am entitled to choose first. Does anyone disagree?"

She knew how to control the show. No one would dare disagree. But everyone might not necessarily agree. Hence the negative question to get the positive answer.

Mom continued. "OK, then Sunday is my day. Sunday evening is the primiere performance of the week of Charles Dickens's play a Christmas Carol at the Opera House Theater. It begins at 8:00 PM so we will need to have an early dinner that evening. Therefore, Sunday morning we can go to the First Methodist Church services at 9:30 AM. They are having church services both Saturday and Sunday this weekend. Next, the Christmas Parade takes place on Golden Nugget City Main Street at 12:00 noon. We can find a restaurant in that area and watch the parade. We can then stroll around Main Street and visit the many shops. In the evening we can eat at the Ozark Gardens Restaurant and then watch a Christmas Carol. Is that all right?"

No one was shocked that Mom had taken over the show. One had better quickly jump in or......?

Dad came back, "And since you guys have not yet made up your minds yet, I would like to see some more live stage shows. How about tomorrow afternoon we go to see McHafies Homestead? Then tomorrow night we can dine at the Total Ribs Steak House."

No one complained, disagreed, or even argued over Dad's choices. So that was good.

Stef spoke out, "I would like to suggest, at 4:00 PM every day there is a Showboat Cruise, Dining, and Dinner Show that leaves from the dock near the Specialty Shops Circle. It goes until 9:00, but it also includes dinner so it might be fun. It's Golden Oldies for Mom and Dad. How about this entertainment for Monday?"

Steve jumped in, "How about tonight we go to the Dolly Pardon Rodeo Show and Dinner? It is supposed to have real cowboys, real Indians, real horses, and real grub. It starts at 7:00 PM." No one complained, so each day was now filled in with a menu of events.

Dad said, "Let us all remember that Tuesday morning we have a flight to catch at 12:30 PM."

The Golden Nugget City area was several miles in size, more than one hundred lakes and connecting rivers and canals, and in the center of three Tom Sawyer National Parks which had twenty five to thirty campgrounds. There were numerous entertainment spots clustered and scattered, most within Golden Nugget City and some nearby. But it was necessary to have a car or motor transportation to shuttle from place to place. It was wise to plan half a day at each place which you wanted to visit. And that is just what they were doing. It was going to be a great adventure.

That evening they headed for the Dolly Pardon Rodeo Show and Dinner. This western extravaganza took place in a large circular building which could have been used for animal shows, auctions, displays, performances, and more. It was cowboy in style and character with the inside center being a large corral containing a soil-sand mixture, about the size of half a football field. It was surrounded on three sides with ten rows of seats which had narrow table sized eating areas for seating in groups. Between the seating area and the lower dirt corral was a six foot high fence to protect either the people or the animals depending on your perspective. At the far fourth end of this corral were located several animal pens and the animal doors to the adjacent barns. The Bassingers entered, found their reserved seats, sat and ordered beers and colas. They had only ten minutes to wait before dinners would be served, the show would start one hour later. In the meantime they were being entertained by a medley of Nashville country western live music. The group, called Country Critters, was performing on a small wooden stage on wheels in the center of the corral.

Dinner was served from several horse drawn chuck wagons which were circulating around the corral near the fence. A group of cowboys and cowgirls took the boxes of food from the wagons and passed them out to the audience. All had a choice of bar-b-q beef or bar-b-q chicken or bar-b-q buffalo meats plus corn on the cob (again), baked beans, cold slaw, two hot buttered rolls, and a small apple cobbler for desert. Additional beers and colas were free.

As it neared 8:30 PM the Country Critters were replaced by the Slaughter House Gang. This group was located on a platform above the animal pens at the far end of the corral. And the music was a little more Denver-like and less Nashville-like. Soon Handsome Jamison Broker, the Master of Ceremonies for the evening took over the microphone. For the next two hours all were entertained by the Blackstone Dancing Horses which performed a variety of fancy trick dance maneuvers, an ostrich race around the barrels, a shooting battle between cowboys and Indians around the circled covered wagons, and a variety of regular rodeo events such as wild bull riding, calf roping, wild horse taming, and long horn steer tackling.

As the show closed, Steve and Dad 'rode' their horses back to the car.

..............

Saturday morning came quickly and the Bassingers got up and went down to breakfast at 8:30 AM, and headed out to the special Ozarks. The play started at 1:30 PM so they played tourist in the area around the Mac Ozarks Theater building and went window shopping. Dad got a little tired walking so he sat down at a wooden bench in the warm sun in a small garden, the other three continued strolling.

On this day, Saturday morning, December 27, at 9:47, William suddenly passed out but remained in an upright position. About ten minutes later he woke, had a tremendous headache, and a knot on the left side of his head, behind his ear. He knew what had happened. When the family returned he asked Jenny for a couple of aspirin, expressing that he had a headache. After taking the aspirin his headache slowly went away, but the knot under his left ear remained.

McHafies Homestead was a popular 'hillbilly' play which performed six days each week in this large theater building which seated almost three hundred people. There was a large slightly elevated stage area which contained several small buildings. There was a paint-less little old house with one door, one window, and a full length porch on the front which was on the left center of the stage. The small chimney was leaking a little smoke from an old wooden stove in the back right corner of the one room structure.

Slightly behind the old house and to the right were several structures. Close to the house was a old wooden outhouse. Next to it and further back was an old shed which contained a broken down tractor, a single blade plow, a corn shucker, and a set of mule harnesses lying on the ground.

The play focused on life in the Ozarks in the 1920s. It was the story of life at the McHafies house on a typical Sunday afternoon. It began when Ma came through the front door onto the porch with fresh baked bread in her hands and hollered for the chl'n (children). "Where are you stupid kids? Bring those eggs here, right now!'

The kids came running from behind the barn and were carrying a basket of fresh eggs from the hen house somewhere behind the barn.

They were both out of breath and shouted, "We were coming when Gursey's old goat came after us. So we had to make a detour."

Ma took the basket of eggs, hollered for Pa. He came from behind the house. Ma gave to him the bread and the basket of eggs and said, "Take these down the road to the new'uns who just moved untu Smith's old house, and then yo'al come right b'k. Ya heer?"

Used to following orders, he just took the bread and eggs and headed down the road, saying nothing.

Some new people moved in down the way so she was doing her neighborly thing to the new'uns. On the way he passed Aunt Alice coming toward the paint-less house. Ma went back inside and Aunt Alice sat down on one of the porch rocking chairs. The children, a boy named Mo, and a girl named Midie, crowded around Aunt Alice.

"Aunt Alice can ya please tell us sum good ol' yarns and tales of the valley," they asked.

Tales telling was the most popular sport in the valley. And everyone was good at it. So during the next hour, with various neighbors coming and going, Aunt Alice started tales telling.

"One time when their Ma and Pa were driving the old wagon to church, Pa steered the old mule wrong while crossing the creek, upset the wagon and Ma got thrown into the creek. Pa went without fresh bread for weeks after that!"

"Once upon a time Jilt Horsman stole Pete Taly's mule and took it home to the other side of the mountain; next morning the mule had gotten loose and returned to Pete Taly's house, and Pete didn't even know it was stolen!"

"And during last Halloween evening, Jep, Cal, and Walley turned over the Haper's outhouse only to find out that Mr. Haper was inside. When Mr. Haper got out of it he chased them boys all the way to the river; he was the funniest naked critter running down the road that you ever saw!"

"And then there was the time when a pretty little widow lady purchased and moved into the Bosen's house out near the apple orchard at Sulley Creek. Every male in the valley was selling apples that October; and you can guess from just where they bought their apples I mean!"

"And one time when Mr. Loses was beating up on Mrs. Loses, their six year son, Fry, went and got his Father's shotgun, loaded it, pointed it at his Pa and told him to get off Ma's land. Pa left and never came back!"

"There was the really neat time when the very pretty and popular Mary Twidle married Jed Mopet. The other young men in the valley did not approve, they had interests in Mary. After the wedding ceremony Mary went to change from her wedding gown into travel clothes to go on their honeymoon. Jed's buddies, Jep, Cal, and Walley, sneaked into her changing room, slipped a big potato bag over her, carried her outside, and stashed her into a wagon harnessed with a mule, which they had hidden behind the church. They then quickly drove away to a vacant house down the creek, and kept her hidden there for three days. No one had seen them kidnap his bride so Jed was going crazy. What happened to his new wife? His buddies then convinced him that the Lord had taken her away because he had stolen some corn from his three neighbors. So Jed went and bought three wagons of corn and gave one to each of his three neighbors. Suddenly Mary was found again in the church. And she and Jed went on their honeymoon. Can you guess who Jed's neighbors were? Yep. Jep, Cal, and Walley!"

After a period of tales telling, Ma and Pa joined the three, partially to protect against stories that might be told about them, and to practice their yarns. So the tales telling continued for another hour or so, more neighbors coming, some contributed to the yarns and some just to say hi and by. Then the Yodeling Five, Ba, Be, Bi, Bo, and Bu, were going through the area on their way to a hoedown tonight. They were convinced to stop and warm up here at the paint-less house. They played the banjo, guitar, accordion, ukulele, and mouth harp. So for the next hour Ma and Pa had a front yard filled not only with stories, tales, yarns, truths, and lies, but also some good ol' Ozarks music.

After the McHafies adventure, the Bassingers drove directly to the Total Ribs Steak House. They entered about 7:00 PM and were immediately seated at a large booth with a round table in the center. There was even enough room for the Bassingers to actually spread out a little. With the size of the members of this family such was not a common thing at most restaurants. Dad began with his usual one and one half pounds of baby beef ribs. The ladies each went directly to the half pound of baby pork ribs. And Steve choose one pound of mature pork ribs. In addition to the ribs they each had a large potato with butter, several vegetable side dishes, fresh hot rolls, and any desert they wanted for each pound of ribs that the table consumed.

Dad began the conversation, "This must be Iowa beef as it is really good."

And before anyone could dispute his statement, Dad was putting it away, from Iowa or not. They had had an early breakfast and a light lunch and Dad was apparently making up for lost time. He again declared, "I understand that vegetables and fruits are loaded with vitamins, but they lack protein. And that all people over 200 pounds require extra protein in their diet. Plus, the three of us only had a total 3 ½ pounds of meat. It would be difficult to split 3 ½ deserts. So, such that we all can have a complete desert, I will order another half pound of mature pork ribs."

And he looked Steve and Stef in the eyes and continued. "As you get older and have children you will learn that it is frequently necessary to make small sacrifices for you little ones." And he laughed out loud.

No one said anything. It was obvious that Dad/Bill had something on his mind. But as a family that understood each other they knew that he would tell all when he was ready. There was more than a simple Ozarks Christmas vacation happening here and now.

After everyone had finished eating their main course or more, they did eat their well earned four deserts, paid their bill, struggled out to the car, and managed to get back to their hotel and to their beds without overdue stomach problems but very little additional conversation.

* * *

Sunday morning began late as everyone needed the extra digestion time. They slept in a little but managed to get up, dressed, and out; breakfast was not really necessary after last night. So they hustled down stairs to a coffee and a donut breakfast; then they were off to the First Methodist Church for the 9:30 morning worship services.

The church was an early twentieth century moss covered grey stone structure. It had a high peaked crown which ran the length of the building and a very vocal belfry above the entry. It was large, perhaps near one thousand people could be seated. And in this particular worship service the church was totally filled and had people sitting in the aisles. It seemed as if the church was one gigantic garden because it was also filled wall to wall with beautiful flowers of all colors. There was a Minister and an Assistant Minister. And at the far end of the single large room, was the altar. On both sides of the altar were the choir pews. The choir contained more than fifty boys and girls and men and women.

The services began with a short hymnal 'The Lord Shall Come.' Then the Assistant Minister said a few words about this day and what happened when a baby was born in an old barn in a little unknown town called Bethlehem in what is today called the Middle East.

Then a small group of children came up to the front and sang several songs: Away in a Manger, Infant Holy-Infant Lowly, Silent Night, What Child Is This. Then the children left the room and the Assistant Minister got up and read from the Bible, St Matthew, Chapter 2, verses 1-14 which describes the birth of the baby Jesus in Bethlehem. Other hymnals were sung such as O Come All Ye Faithful, Angles We Have Heard From On High, Come Thou Expected Jesus.

After brief announcements, the Minister got up and gave his sermon for the service. It was titled 'From life to death to life'. His main theme was that Jesus' birth was but the first step in the life for mankind. Just as we all took a similar step at the beginning of our lives. And look at what Jesus did with his life. We do not have to copy him, but we can accomplish a fraction of the good that he taught to us by reaching out to people everywhere and offering faith, hope and love, as he did. We can only do this if we try. And we only have a limited number of years to even begin to match his efforts.........

After several more hymns, the warm and moving church services finished, the church emptied and everyone started walking slowly toward the Golden Nugget City Town Circle for the 12:00 noon Christmas Parade.

The Parade started on time with the relighting of the thirty foot tall Christmas tree in the center of the Circle. The lights were every color of the rainbow and there were numerous decorations from colored hanging shells to small wreaths to ceramic eggs to numerous toys to a model Santa Clause, his sleigh, and his reindeers. Of course on the top was the star of Bethlehem. And guess who was leading the parade, another, but a real Santa Clause and his sleigh.

However, the sleigh was on wheels and there were no reindeer. There were five horses which had antlers attached to their heads pulling the wheeled sleigh. Some imagination! Oh well. This was compensated for by the more than one hundred elves dressed in red and green (local school children). They followed Santa, performed stunts and handed candies to every man, woman, and child watching from the side of the street. Some of the watching children seemed to have some kind of rapport with the children elves because the small children collected the biggest quantity of candies. And some watching children obviously knew in advance about the parade program because they brought empty sacks to the parade and took full sacks home from the parade.

The parade continued for about a half an hour with many floats, little music groups, clowns dressed in red and green, small entertainment acts, two local high school marching bands...........

After the parade finished, the Bassingers strolled to the nearby Culinary and Craft College to have lunch and look at the crafts. The first floor was similar to an original old European country house and had a small salon around a fire place and adjacent to the kitchen was a small dining area. This is where they had lunch. Currently a baker and candy-taffy maker shared the kitchen and supplied the dining area with sandwiches and pastries. The upper three floors of the interior had been converted into several craft shops.

Currently there were eleven artists actively working on these floors: silversmith, glasscutter, candle maker, potter, chip carver, blacksmith, basket weaver, quilter, stained glass artist, wooden toy maker and an ikebana specialist (Japanese dry flower arranger). Mother loved the quilter while Dad found the chip carver most fascinating. They spent the afternoon there watching the craftsmen work. In anticipation of the early dinner tonight, they each nibbled only a little during the afternoon.

They had dinner reservations for 6:00 PM at the Ozarks Gardens restaurant which was near the Old Opera House. The Christmas Carol started at 8:00 PM. The traffic would be heavy so they had to hurry. Dad drove rapidly, and parked in the Old Opera House parking lot.

They entered the crowded restaurant at 6:30 PM, ordered dinners, quickly ate their food, left the restaurant, and walked down the street to the Old Opera House. They entered the theater at 7:55 PM, almost but not quite late, and quickly took their seats.

The Old Opera House was a lovely five floor building. It had an all white façade with eight marble columns and was copied from the world famous Opera House of Vienna. Like all of the famous opera houses in Europe there was a main floor which seated five hundred people, plus the four levels of balconies, each seating more than one hundred people. Each balcony formed a semi-circle around and above the main floor, such that the ceiling for the main floor was five floors above that floor. The center above the main floor was open. All seats facing a raised stage which was as wide as the main floor seating area. Immediately in front of the stage was a lowered area known as the orchestra 'pit.' The Bassingers had seats on the ground floor on the left side in the fourth row from the front.

As they sat down the orchestra music reached a crescendo, the curtain opened, and Mr. Ebenezer Scrooge, wearing an old black suit, the jacket had short tails, wrinkled white shirt and black tie, walked onto the stage and into his salon. The salon contained two Victorian style arm chairs and a King Edward style small couch, two stands with Victorian lamp shades hanging over porcelain lamps on each stand, a small roll top desk and Queen Ann style chair against one wall. The wallpapered walls were designed with a bunch of parallel straight ruffles green in color, and the curtains were yellow-gold and cut to allow the top part and sides of the window to be closed while the bottom could remain open. It was mid nineteenth century England. As Mr. Scrooge was complaining about all of the noise in the streets, children's Christmas carols, Bob Cratchit entered.

Bob said, "I have finished all of the books for the week. Since it is Christmas Eve, may I have your permission to leave a little early?" It was 4:45 PM.

Mr. Scrooge answered, "NO, Christmas is a bad enough thing and now you think you can use it as an excuse to get out of your work. You must complete your regular fifty hour week or I will deduct those hours that you are not working from your salary. But I will be generous. You may take tomorrow off, Christmas day, without pay of course. But you must be here the day after, Friday, and continue your work. I don't want my work to fall behind just because someone calls this day Christmas."

Bob replied, "Thank you for the day off. I am going out to buy a small turkey to eat for Christmas dinner. Would you be able to join us for dinner tomorrow tonight?"

Mr. Scrooge looked at Bob as one would look at a sick dog on the street and said, "Christmas dinner, Bah! Humbug! It is all a myth created by religious people in order to get everyone's money. Let the poor people live in poor peoples' homes. If they don't have money why should they get presents. If they make some money then they can buy themselves some presents. You come back to work on Friday or don't come back at all!"

And the play continued through three acts where the ghost of Jacob Marley, the ghost of Christmas Past, the ghost of Christmas Present, and the ghost of Christmas Future visited him and convinced him that if he did not change his ways he would die immediately and his ghost would walk forever among the poor people on the streets of London. He believes them, repents, changes his ways, and becomes a generous and nice old man.

The Bassingers all knew the characters and their lines, but seeing it in a real Victorian setting and having music made it much more real. For example the music for Mr. Scrooge in the beginning was loud, rough, and filled with drums and brass. Toward the end this music softened. And during the last few minutes, after his metamorphosis had occurred, the music for him was soft with only stringed instruments playing. In addition each character had a short and moderate music theme which was played when they had the center stage attention or in support of key speaking phrases. Each ghost was represented by a different musical instrument and special sounds. In general it was a very unique interpretation of a play which they all thought they knew, but of course were reminded that there was a rather large gap between the amateur and the professional. It was an experience they would always remember, even if Mom should again choose the Christmas Carol to present at BHS in the near future.

. . . . . . . . . . . . . . .

Monday began with a visit and a little serious shopping for presents in the shopping center of Golden Nugget City. Then they had a nice light brunch in the Vegetarian Luncheon Center.

Later a short car ride took them to the docks to the Showboat Bell Anne. They were going to enjoy an afternoon/evening of music, dining, and dancing on a retired, but nicely renovated, Mississippi River paddle wheel boat named the Southern Bell. It left the docks at 4:00 PM and they made it in plenty of time. They cruised toward the west on one of the many lakes, watched the sun set, and then retired inside to the large ballroom which could seat at round dinner tables about three hundred and fifty people, several people to a table. In the center of the semi-circular grouping of tables was an open dance floor and beyond it was room for a moderate sized orchestra.

The paddle wheel Mississippi River boat was a new experience for the Iowans. They had the Mississippi River on one side and the Missouri River on the other side of the state, both rivers more than a mile wide in some places, but Des Moines was a two-three hour drive to either river. A four hour round trip car ride to enjoy a half day boat ride had not yet appeared on their life agendas. But life should involve new, positive experiences. This boat ride was indeed one of those. And it was a lovely over-the-water red sunset memory.

Upon entering the ballroom, they quickly found their table, took their seats and Dad ordered a bottle of a California Chablis. They sipped their wine and listened to recorded music which focused on the Big Band Sound era. Dinner was served at 6:30 PM. They also brought a second bottle of the same wine with the meal. Everyone received the same dinner which was chicken, brown rice, brussel sprouts, corn, a small lettuce-carrot salad, hot rolls and cold tea. A slice of apple pie and coffee were for dessert.

During the meal the live orchestra entered, warmed up and started playing some of the other Big Band Sound of the 1940s, 50, and 60s. This set the stage as a young couple, Phyllis and Phil, came on stage and began to explain to the full house that, because it was Christmas, they were going to do something special tonight. They actually did this special for the two months of December and January each year.

A little later in the show they were going to have a contest. The orchestra would play famous golden-oldie music from the 90s, 80s, 70s, 60s, and 50s, and the person who could name the song and singer or group would win a monetary prize. So they advised everyone to not leave early. As if anyone could leave from a boat in the middle of a lake.

Steve spoke out, "Is that an old person's joke from the 90s?"

"It probably is," responded Stef. "If you noticed, only the older people in here laughed at it. Do you think such dumb jokes like that will be popular when we become old people?"

Steve replied, "Why don't we just stay young then we will not have to live with such jokes."

And they both laughed and looked over at the middle aged parents who really did not think that the two children were funny at all. So they each sort of ignored each other for a while.

The first round of songs included: Call Me Irresponsible, New York – New York, Amore, White Christmas, It Had To Be You, Lemon Tree, I Am Woman, All Of You, Ticket to Ride, You Don't Bring Me Flowers Anymore, Moon River and several movie sound tracks such as Sound of Music, James Bond's Gold finger, Pink Panther, Riders of the Lost Ark, Breakfast at Tiffany's, Porgy and Bess, and Godfather II. It was a beautiful sample of the musical creativity of America over many years.

The orchestra took a fifteen minute break and went outdoors to cool down; it had become very warm in the ballroom. When they re-entered they had changed several of the instruments. Then the contest began. The lady singer, Phyllis, gave the rules, while the male singer, Phil, watched.

Phyllis said, "OK, let us begin the Classic Rock and Roll Music Contest. The orchestra will play a few bars of a song which was a big hit sometime during the last 50 years of the twentieth century. We will begin the in the 1990s. At each table is a buzzer. If you can name the song and singer or group, push the buzzer. The sequence of who pushes the buzzer first versus second versus third will be noted here on this 'electronic buzzer board.' Now, this is the way the prize system works. From the person who pushes the buzzer first we will ask the name of song and singer or group. If you are correct, we will give the prize immediately. Each prize will be in US dollars, but a different amount for each song. If you are wrong, you will pay to us that same amount of US dollars that you would have won if you had been correct. So think carefully. If you are correct, you win. If you are wrong, you pay."

After a minute of letting the audience digest this information, she continued. "The first two songs will be from the 90s. Each is valued at ten dollars."

The first song was the sound track for Lion King by Elton John. A youngster from table 23 was right there with the answer and grabbed his ten dollars. The second 90s song was We Will Rock With You by Guns N Roses. Again a young lady from table 16 gave the correct answer and received her money.

Phyllis again came on the microphone, "Now we go to the 80s for a couple of golden oldies. Each of these is valued at twenty dollars."

The first song was the Joshua Tree by U2. A man from table 12 pressed the buzzer, gave the wrong answer, and paid his twenty dollars. The second lady from table 27 who pressed her buzzer was correct and won twenty dollars. The second song was Start Me Up by Mike Jagger and the Rolling Stones. A lady from table 44 was correct and won her prize.

Phil spoke up, "On to the 70S for these two songs. Prize money will be thirty dollars each."

The chosen song was Born In The USA by Bruce Springstein. Two people tied for pressing the buzzer, tables 3 and 33. So Phyllis went to table 3 and the woman whispered her answer into Phyllis's ear. And Phil went to table 33 and the man whispered his answer into Phil's ear. They were both correct so they each received thirty dollars. The second song from the 70s was How Great Thou Art by Elvis Presley. An elderly lady from table 17 pushed her buzzer first. Although later it was found out that her grandson was the official buzzer pusher at their table. She was correct, collected her money, and then gave it to the official buzzer pusher for his outstanding assistance. He was a very happy young man.

Phyllis announced, "We go on to the 60s. Each song will be worth forty dollars."

The first song was It's Been A Hard Days Night by the Beatles. Every buzzer in the house was pressed. But a woman at table 9 was first. And yes, she, and probably the entire room, was correct. She almost felt like a fool for winning so easily. Almost. The second song was Walkin to New Orleans by Fats Domino. This one was a little more difficult. Only three tables pressed their buzzers. Table 18 was first and was wrong. He paid his forty dollars. Table 21 was wrong and he paid his forty dollars. Only Table 41 remained. The middle aged woman gave the correct title and singer and won the forty dollars. There was a round of applause.

"And now the senior golden oldies of the evening," said Phil. "These two songs were popular in the 50s. Each is worth fifty dollars. That is fifty dollars to win or fifty dollars to pay. So be careful."

The first song was Rock Around The Clock by Bill Haley and the Comets. Only one table pressed their buzzer. It was table 13, the table of the Bassingers. Dad had pressed the buzzer. Phyllis asked Dad for the correct song title and singer, and he gave the correct answer. He took the prize money, placed it into his pocket, and just smiled at Mom, Steve, and Stef. They didn't believe it. Dad doesn't like music. Dad doesn't even listen to music. How can this be?

The second song was Shake, Rattle, and Roll by Big Joe Turner. This was going way back. For a few seconds no buzzer sounded. The electronic buzzer board was empty. Then suddenly table 13, again pressed their buzzer. The children looked around and there was Mom with the buzzer in her hand. Their immediate reaction was that she was going to purposely lose such that Dad would have to pay with his newly won fifty dollars. Phyllis, in hesitation, came over to the table. Maybe it was a mistake. If a mistake and they did not give a song name or singer it was alright. The contestant was only committed if they gave a song name or singer and was right or wrong. Mom called out her choice of a title. Phyllis jumped up and down. No one had ever remembered Big Joe Turner in all of the previous contests over the years, until now. Shake, Rattle, and Roll was his only big song. Mom graciously accepted her fifty dollars, placed into her purse, and mimicked Dad's previous expression to Dad, Steve, and Stef. And they all broke up laughing.

This could not be happening to them here and now. The world must suddenly be rotating backwards. And when the sun comes up from the west in the morning everything will be straightened out, and life will start again, somewhere. All the way back to the hotel, they were flying. Not one of them had ever won any prize in their lives, and now two in one night. Impossible. Does seeing require believing?

Because they were leaving tomorrow Dad decided that he could not delay any longer. So he called Mom, Steve, and Stef to the little round table in the parent's hotel room for a 'brief talk'.

Dad began, "I have something that I have been waiting many years to tell you, and the time has come for you to hear what I have to say."

Steve and Stef both thought the same thing at the same time, 'This sounds serious, let's have it.'

He had everyone's undivided attention so he continued, "As you all know the Bassinger family can trace their ancestry back several generation to the time of the formulation of the United States of America. I just learned last month that, unfortunately I am not a Bassinger, and you are not Bassingers either. I do not know who my Mother and Father are. So I do not know who your Grandmother and Grandfather are. This is the situation as I currently understand it."

He looked at each one but they had no questions, they were just holding their breaths. So he went on, "The person that you have been calling Grandma Dorothy Bassinger apparently carried me as a baby, but my genes did not come from her or Grandpa Fred Bassinger. I think I am some type of a test tube baby whose genes came from an anonymous source.

Conception or fertilization took place in a test tube in a fertilization clinic in McLean, Virginia. And then my cells were implanted and later I was born to Dorothy Bassinger. Only last month I learned that the same thing happened to three other people at the same time in the same place. What I am trying to say is that I have three identical brothers, yes we are identical quadruplets.

They are Aaron Armand, a medical research doctor in New York City, Charles Collingswood, a minister-environmentalist in Indian Nest, Florida, and David Dekker, a Security Specialist in Washington, DC. We think that we are all offspring from this same anonymous source. We will know for certain as soon as Dr. Armand finishes running the necessary DNA tests to determine this."

Again he looked around to see if there any questions. He continued, "What I am saying is that if all of this is true, in addition we have the legal right to sue this clinic in the range of a hundred million dollars. But to do this we would have to reveal that we are not Bassingers."

Jenny spoke up, "Are you then not the legal heir of your Father of forty two years? You were legally born to your Mother forty two years ago. Emotionally we are all attached just as if we were also genetically linked. This is very unfair."

Bill/Dad spoke, "I am very, very sorry that I did not tell you this sooner. I always suspected something strange about my parents, but they never ever said anything, and I didn't want to hurt them. I love them just like a real Mother and Father. This will not change that. Legal? I do not know if they legally adopted me when I was born. I will have to ask them."

"I have always called these two people Grandma and Grandpa," said Stef. "I cannot change that. But how could they do this to us? I mean hide this secret. Did they think this secret would never surface, that we would never find out?"

"I agree with Stef," added Steve. "How could anyone keep a secret like this for more than forty years? Des Moines, Iowa is a small and close community. When growing up no one could keep secrets, gossip always reveals the non-truths and the truths. Why I can remember sometimes that Mom knew before I did who was my new girlfriend. I am shocked that this 'truth' was not revealed during all of these years. This must be the secret of the century."

"Can't you ask them now?" Jenny asked. "You know your/their secret. Find out if they know your/their secret. And ask their opinion about what they want us to do, keep hiding it, or reveal it? They are responsible for this. It is not your fault."

Dad continued, "Please keep this information a secret for a little while longer, especially from Grandma and Grandpa Bassinger, until we can scientifically confirm that there are indeed four of us. Please remember that there are three other families involved. We four brothers will meet again soon and discuss what options are available. For now let us sleep on the problem and then we will talk about it again before we four brothers meet. And Stef, do you remember Alice Dekker?"

"Of course," Stef answered.

Dad said, "Remember she lives in Washington, DC? She is the daughter on one of my twin brothers, David Dekker. Therefore she is either your first cousin or sister, depending upon how you want to look at the situation."

Stef was too shocked to answer.

They talked for only a few minutes longer. They were all too shocked to think clearly. And then each went to bed to a sleepless night.

* * *

The next day, Tuesday, they were leaving in the afternoon. But Dad's revelation sort of took the fun out of continuing to play in Gold Nugget City. In a rote fashion they got up, had breakfast, drove to Springfield, boarded the plane, flew back to Des Moines, disembarked, walked to their car, drove home to Briarwood, had some snacks, went to bed, and tried again to sleep. The vacation was too long and the unsettling news was too much.

# 17 – Annonymity Versus Notoriety - Collingswood

Charles, Janice, Samuel, and Sara Collingswood were headed for the Amazon River basin for a week of vacation and collaborative environmental research with a Brazilian Scientist, Dr. Pedro Alvares, from the Universidade Federal do Amazonas (UFAM), in Manaus, Brazil. Dr Alvares had a large environmental – agriculture run off research project in the area. Charles and Janice wanted to learn how the research project satisfied the new environmental laws in Brazil, because the project involved sugar cane plantations; this was the major problem that they were fighting in South Florida. They would leave after the Thursday Christmas Day, and would return on Saturday after New Years Day. Charles and Janice were environmentalists with several academic research publications and several articles in environmental magazines. Samuel was working on his Masters of Science degree in Environmental Engineering and was looking around for a good research project in order to fulfill the requirements for this degree. Sara was studying for her Doctorate of Veterinary Medicine so she was always interested in animals other than 'common' animals of the USA. And Janice wanted to compare some of her data with the data from Dr Alvares's project. She hoped to learn some new methods that might help make her work easier and more complete. And Dad had a secret to tell.

They would fly from Miami to Bogota, Columbia, and then on to Manaus, Brazil which was a large city in the center of the Amazon River basin. From there they would drive east in the direction of Itacoatiara, which was on the River and about one hundred miles from Manaus. This region was where a large deforestation project was occurring and therefore the environmental damage was big and growing. They would stay just outside of Manaus in a small three bedroom house, built up on poles, and very near the river. It would be an exciting adventure.

On Saturday morning, the vacation/study began at 6:15 AM at the Miami International Airport when they boarded Mexicana Airlines flight #1737 to Bogota, Columbia; from there they would continue on

Brazil Airlines #3642 to Manaus Airport with arrival time expected early evening.

During the flight, at 11:47 AM on that Saturday December 27, Charles passed out but continued sitting upright. Twenty seconds later he woke up, had a terrible headache, and noticed a bump on the left side of his head behind the ear. He felt the bump, and said nothing to the family because he knew what had happened. Janice thought he had simply been napping. He told her he had a headache. She was the walking pharmacy of the family. She gave him two aspirins; he asked the stewardess for a glass of water, took the aspirins, and tried to forget what had just happened. And he hoped that his brother was getting better.

Later in the day as they flew over the Amazon River Charles started thinking about what he had recently read about Brazil and the river which dominated the entire country.

'The Amazon River is the biggest volume river in the world which occupies almost all of northern Brazil. It discharges more than one hundred thousand cubic meters per second of water into the Atlantic Ocean; this is more than the combined volume of the world's ten largest rivers combined. The Amazon River basin covers more than two hundred thousand square miles which is larger than Alaska, is lightly inhabited (about ten million people), and is currently one of the largest areas of agribusiness in Brazil.'

'Brazil is the world's largest producer of sugar cane, coffee, tropical fruits, and has the largest commercial cattle herd in the world. It also exports large quantities of soybeans, corn, cotton, cocoa, tobacco, forest woods, and a variety of minerals from gold to copper to tin to iron ores. A large percentage of these agriculture and mining products comes from the land in the Amazon River basin which is currently being deforested. The crops are being grown from the land made available by the cutting and selling of hard wood trees and the burning of everything else. This burning is currently producing the largest single source of atmospheric carbon dioxide in the world, and destruction of the largest rain forests in the world by burning them. It is a major contributor to the world wide global warming problem.'

'Of special interest to our Save the Everglades Foundation is the Brazilian cultivation of sugar cane. Several years ago, in an attempt to become self sufficient in energy, the Brazilian government offered large incentives to the private sector to grow sugar cane and convert it to alcohol which could then be used in the transportation industry, biofuels. It was a very successful venture. Today Brazil is energy self sufficient. It does not need to import any oil. All gas stations always have two pumps, one for gasoline and one for alcohol. And alcohol sells at a 10 to 1 ratio over gasoline. Certainly it is cheaper. And it is Brazilian.'

'And now they have begun to develop a similar system with a weed called switch grass. However the billions of tons of sugar cane and switch grass for alcohol production requires billions of acres of land to grow these crops. And where is that land? A major portion is in the Amazon River basin. So a sizable portion of the 'burning of the rain forest' was and is yet encouraged and financially supported by the Brazilian government. In my role as President of the Save the Everglades Foundation, I especially want to learn how the people of Brazil accept this 'rape of nature'.'

'So we will spend our entire stay in the Amazon River basin which had more than thirty thousand plant species, and more than fifty thousand species of insects, fish, amphibians, reptiles, birds, and mammals. At one time it had the greatest biodiversity in the world. However during the past two-three decades this has markedly decreased due to the slash and burn mentality of many local and foreign investors who are only interested in converting the jungle/rain forests into productive agriculture lands.' And he fell asleep.

When they landed in Manaus, Jose Mendes, one of Dr. Alvares's students, was waiting to pick them up.

Jose met and greeted them. "I shake each of your hands and welcome each of you to Brazil and Manaus. I will travel with you much of the time and assist in both people to people language translation and in the naming of the various plant and animal species throughout the basin area. I am studying for my PhD in environmental ecology. We have many plans for you to travel and see much of this part of the Amazon River. And we will spend a couple of days at the project site, which is three – four hours driving time from Manaus."

Charles chuckled and replied, "Thank you for your efforts. Since we are going to be together as a family, why don't you call us by our first names? I am Charles. My wife is Janice. And this big fellow is my son, Sam, and my daughter Sara."

Jose kissed the hand of each lady and again shook hands with the men. And he winked at Sara. Sam saw the wink out of the corner of his eye and made a mental note

It appeared as if they were welcome and, if careful and a little lucky, they would have an interesting and even exciting time. After all, they were here for pleasure as well as work. And meeting interesting new people was a fun part of both. This guy looked like a fun one.

They hopped aboard the minibus named the Gator, which was Jose's name for the medium sized beat up mode of transport. It was a positive omen for the Floridians and everyone would understand the reason for the name before the end of the week. They headed into Manaus on a modern four lane divided highway with palm trees every twenty five feet growing down the center of the highway. From this angle it looked like Miami without the ocean.

As he drove, Jose played tour guide and commented, "Manaus is the capital of the Amazonas State and the largest city in northern Brazil. More than two million people live here in a very modern and sprawling metropolitan city. It is the chief port and hub for a well organized and extensive river transport system. Sitting on the banks of the Rio Negro (meaning Black Water) it is the center of ecotourism in Brazil. Fifteen miles upriver is the famous Negra beach, and fifteen miles downriver is the beginnings of the "uncivilized" rain forest. The city has botanical gardens, zoological gardens, and numerous lovely old European style houses from the early twentieth century when it was the Paris of the Tropics. It deteriorated during and after World War II, but has now almost recovered. The rapid and massive deforestation and the production of commercial crops were speeding up the recovery process as investments from foreigners and foreign monies are rapidly entering the area."

The four Collingswoods made no comments but only looked and absorbed the bright multi-green foliage landscape.

As the Gator entered the city from the west it continued and left the city toward the east. Their pole house was located between the city and the heavy Amazon rainforest/jungle area beginning just east of the city. However, if one looked around one would see every house within one hundred feet of the river was on poles or floats. Regular flooding was obviously a regular problem.

Dr. Alvares thought the Collingswoods would enjoy this location rather than a downtown hotel room. Fortunately he was very correct. So they arrived at their new Brazilian home, which they soon dubbed Stiltsville. They thanked Jose for his meeting them and his "courteous and continuous" explanations of each and all on the ride from the airport. Jose said his good bye for now and departed.

They climbed up into their new home, looked around, picked out bedrooms and fell exhausted into the living room cane chairs and couches.

They checked and there was food in the refrigerator. But the three meals on two airplanes and the stress of travel put everyone into a sleepy mode. Ten minutes of brief conversation and each went to his bed and fell immediately to sleep. Stiltsville would be their new home for the next week.

* * *

Sunday morning everyone was up and ready by 8:30 AM. Manaus was located about three degrees south of the equator, so the weather was continuously hot and humid. Each had down dressed and was wearing light shirts and shorts, tennis shoes without socks, and had caps or hats to keep that tropical sun at bay.

For breakfast they had several bottles of delicious fruit juices, milk, day old therefore toasted bread, three types of cheese, tomatoes, cucumbers, domestic and 'wild' bananas, some unknown jams, and of course a choice of several types of coffee beans. They chose red delta, ground it, put enough in the coffee maker for two cups each, and enjoyed the smell and taste of coffee for the next hour. This was certainly not America, no breakfast cereals, no eggs, no bacon, no skim milk.

Mom spoke up, "Dr. Alveraz is currently in Brasilia and will return this evening, and then will take us to a bar-b-q. So I guess we are on our own today. Does anyone want to call Jose and ask him to play tour guide? He said he would be available anytime we wanted him."

No one spoke up and said yes, or no. So she assumed that it was a not-today-Jose.

Dad added, "We could take a taxi, and this morning tour the historical house area, see sights by land; then after lunch we could see sights by water and try one of the Amazon River boat tours. What do you say?"

Sara agreed, "If I remember from the city maps, that the jump off for the boat tours is near the downtown city docks, and that is in the middle of the historical house area."

Sam added, "I would like to see the museum called Museu do Indio which covers the culture and history of the native people of the Amazon basin. It is also near the city docks."

And then Mom added her ideas, "Ok. Then tonight we have the Brazilian Bar-B-Q. I have a feeling that will be a lot of food, so eat lightly during the day."

Dad called the taxi which arrived immediately and they took for the 'center city' area.

They began walking in the old district. They saw many dilapidated old houses and but most were nicely renovated wooden houses originally built more one hundred years ago. One could understand how Manaus was indeed a Parisian forest city back in those days. In the middle of the old house area was the Museo do Indio. They went in. There were many exhibits of the indigenous peoples. And it did not take very long to see what a harsh life it must have been a thousand years ago.

The Brazilian Indians and early European settlers would have great difficulty in trying to survive in a thick jungle like the rain forest. There were at least twenty thousand species of adversaries against the single species of Homo sapiens. And it sort of helped one to better understand the 'need' to clear the land if it was to be lived on and to make a living on. Man could not live in this forest. The museum allowed one to see the other side of environmental provocation. You did not have to agree with the methods that the locals and settlers were using, but you could see the need to cut, burn or move on. After all it was only three hundred years ago that American pioneers were doing the same thing in clearing the forests to create farmland in middle USA; forests which had been taken away from the indigenous Indians and given to the pioneers by American governments. Was this any different?

As lunch time drew near, the Collingswoods starting asking around for a good Brazilian restaurant which cooked Brazilian food. A short walk down the street they found the restaurant, entered, were seated, and started looking over the menus.

Sara was bravest, "I am going to try something completely new. Why don't each of us try something completely new and then we can share with each other. Or if one of us gets a dish that is too peppery hot we can throw that dish out and share from the other dishes."

Sam said, "I am all for that and I know what I want."

Both Mom and Dad looked at each other, exchanged, 'a how do we get out of this'. "OK, as long as we get to each chose our own first."

So when the waiter returned, Sara went first. "I want Caruru do Paro." This was a pot of shrimp in green sauce, okra, onion, cilantro, and tomato using denfo or palm oil.

Everyone looked at Sam to find out what it was that he knew that he wanted. Sam ordered, "Arapaima with yams, corn and a small green salad." Arapaima or Pirarucu was an Amazon fresh water fish.

He explained, "A Brazilian friend of mine at the university said that this was the best fish in the world and that it must be eaten only when cooked by Manaus chefs. I will find out."

Dad was ready and went next, "If you are having Amazon fish I will too. Let me have a small filet of Tambaqui with Brazilian pico de gallo." Tambaqui was one of the largest fish in the Amazon River, and pico de gallo was also known as vinaigrette which contained green and red bell peppers, red onions, tomatoes, vinegar and olive oil in a separate mixed bowl.

Mom looked around at her family; obviously they had done some homework of Brazilian foods before they left home. "OK." She said, "Since you are all going to eat from the water, I will eat from the land. I would like to order Carne de Sol and Arroz com Coco." Carne de Sol was a dish made from sun dried beef, cassava flour, red onions; Arroz com Coco was long grain rice prepared in coconut milk.

The waiter commented. "Each of you made an excellent and brave selection. What would you like to drink?'

The Collingswoods looked at each other and thought, 'what does he mean when he says we make a brave selection?'

Dad responded, "We just arrived in Brazil last night, so maybe you could chose a nice Brazilian white wine for us. OK?"

The waiter complied and they all waited expectantly. All of the authentic Brazilian dishes arrived promptly, and they each took a deep breath and gave them a try. After a few bites they agreed that they were really starting this Brazilian excursion on a high note. They did make excellent and brave selections. And with the museum tour they were beginning to understand the difference between trying to live on open plains (such as the American Midwest) compared to living in a jungle (such as the Amazon River basin).

As they finished, Dad asked the waiter, "What kind of dessert is your specialty tonight?"

The waiter responded, "We have two super specialties – banana cake and walnut prunes cake."

Sara said, "How about a half piece for each of us?"

They all agreed.

Then Dad quickly ordered, 'And four great coffees, please."

The dessert and coffees came immediately and they continued in the luxury of new smells and tastes.

Finally along about 1:30 PM they were ready to enjoy the water tour. The docks were but a five minute walk. They walked among the old city houses and down to the tour boats, chose the one that went both up and down both branches of the Amazon River, climbed aboard, and settled into seats near the front. The boat was appropriately called the Amazon Queen. At 2:00 PM they took off. It was about two thirds filled with foreign tourists. After a small poll of the passengers was taken, they announced that this afternoon the guide would speak in English and German.

The Amazon (Rio Amazonas) River split into two branches at Manaus. The northern branch was the Negro (Rio Negro) River and the southern branch was the Solimoes (Rio Solimoes) River. Manaus was on the south side of the Negro River so they began their river expedition going up the 'Black River'.

The river banks were one continuous series of numerous shades of green. The foliage was so dense that you could not even begin to see through it. And periodically there were branches of smaller rivers feeding into the Amazon River. Where the tributaries met the big river there were public places of leisure and swimming areas which were popular for natives on weekends. The Collingswoods regularly saw alligators and crocodiles, so swimming could be risky. The Florida crocodiles might be on the endangered species list, but the Brazilian crocodiles were happy, healthy, and having babies.

Dad commented, "Aren't you glad that the American crocodile is an endangered species in the Everglades, Janice?"

Janice responded, "Yes you are right. Crocodiles have a nastier disposition than alligators. If there were hundreds of these guys in the Everglades I would probably be afraid to enter and do my research."

In a short time they came upon the Anavilhanas, which was the world's largest archipelago of fluvial islands. There were more than five hundred small islands in the Negro River, each was covered with brilliant green forest. During the dry season the waters receded and numerous white sandy beaches and millions of long tree roots and trunks appeared above the ground. The rainy season was just beginning so thousands of roots and many of the white beaches were still visible. It was a spectacular sight, especially since the water was black.

Next they turned around and headed down the Negro River, and near Manaus turned right to enter the other branch of the Amazon River, known as the Solimoes River. It was also known as the continuation of the real Amazon River. Just south and east of Manaus they reached the

'Meeting of the Rivers'. At this point the Amazon River split into these two major branches.

The northern branch, which provided the southern port for Manaus, was the Negro River which began in Venezuela and northern Columbia. It was black in color and very warm.

The southern branch was the Solimoes River. It was clear or white, cold, and began in southern Columbia and northern Peru.

The two river branches ran side by side for more than six miles just south and east of Manaus, before they began to mix into one major Amazon River. It was quite a phenomenon to watch. One could actually see the streamlets of black warm water mixing into streamlets of cold clear or white water. Eventually, the black water won, because for the next one thousand miles to the Atlantic Ocean the Amazon River had a brownish color.

Sam could not help but comment, "If white and black Homo sapiens would have blended together so easily and quietly, there would have been many fewer wars through history."

The Amazon Queen continued several kilometers beyond the confluence of the two branches. The Amazon River does not become a nice normal, well defined and banked river like the ones you see in Europe or the USA. Due to the continuous rains from December to September the sides of the river are constantly shifting into small and large water ponds and small and large islands (flood plains). So for much of the next one thousand miles there are fewer commercial ports and even fewer bridges. After traveling a few miles down the one Amazon River, the Amazon Queen turned around again, headed back up the Amazon River to the branching area and took the right branch up the Negro River to dockside in Manaus. It was a fascinating and a very unique afternoon.

From the tour boat dockside, the tired Collingswoods took a taxi to Stiltsville and indulged in short naps. There was a note waiting for them from Dr. Alvares. He said that he would pick them up tonight for dinner at 7:30 PM. It was now 5:45 PM. At dinner they could then discuss his tentative travel ideas for the week.

And exactly at 7:30 PM, Dr. Pedro Alvares pulled up in front of their Stiltsville house and climbed up to the door. Charles greeted him, he entered and the entire Collingswood family introduced themselves and thanked him for the invitation to visit his project. He welcomed them and told them how he was so happy that Americans were interested in what they were doing down here in Brazil.

Looking at Sam, Dr Alvares said, "I thought by now you might be hungry. So tonight we will go to a Churrasqueira, Brazilian Bar-B-Q, for a Brazilian feast."

Each of the Collingswoods looked at each other and Janice said, "And why not. We have been treating our stomachs to a lovely roller coaster ride, why stop now?" And she explained how and what they had been eating.

Dr. Alvares congratulated them. "Usually we have to take Americans to the river and gently push them in and teach them how to swim. It sounds that you have already been swimming and actually enjoy it."

They all hoped into the Gator and took off to the Gaucho's Village Churrasqueira, Bar-B-Q Village, in the Municipal Park of Mindu. The group of six entered and sat at a long wooden picnic table with bench seats. Jose joined them.

For the meal they could chose any or all meats bar-b-qued on a skewer. Their choices included: beef, chicken, tapir, lamb, goat, pig, and several kinds of fish including pirarucu and tambaqui. Many skewers of meat were simultaneously cooked over a wood fire. When one skewer was determined to be thoroughly cooked, one of the three chefs would take that skewer, walk around the tables, and offer each guest some of the meat from that skewer. If you wanted some from that skewer, you said yes and he cut some off and placed it onto your plate. If not, you just motioned to pass. So, one had a continuous choice of different freshly cooked meats and fishes every ten minutes. In addition one could help themselves to portions of cassava meal, corn porridge, sweet potatoes, and a variety of fresh vegetables such as tomatoes, carrots, and small white onions. They finished off bottles of red and white wines. It was a very good day and a fascinating evening meal.

During the meal the group discussed the logistics of the research project.

Dr. Alvares began, "We have managed to bring together the Brazilian government, a German development company, Kruman International Ltd, the Environ Watch World Group, an NGO, and our Department of Ecology and Environment at the Federal University of Amazonas. The project which I discussed with you last year is in full swing. Basically it is an attempt to develop cooperation and understanding between sugar cane growers and advocates of environmental pollution. The plan is as follows."

"The Brazilian government, utilizing the land developmental incentive laws passed some fifteen years ago, are leasing for one hundred years, one hundred and fifty acres of rain forest land located just north of the Amazon River between Intarcoatiara and Parintins. That land is east of here about two hundred miles. The area is a typical rain forest which will be destroyed and experimental genetically engineered sugar cane will be planted. Over the next fifty years, during both growth and harvest the bio-environment within two kilometers in all directions from this area will be monitored for environmental changes. Government, private owner, and environmental research groups will cooperate and share all data forthcoming. The government will tax profits at one half current rates and one half of that tax money; ten percent of the tax will be made available to environmental groups to pay their justifiable research expenses, again over the next fifty years. It is a true partnership of government sector-private sector endeavor. All must cooperate, because if there is no profit everyone loses and no one wins. In other word all of our research is financed from the sugar cane profits."

The Collingswood family members looked at each other wondering who should ask the first question, there would be many. "What a fantastic project."

Janice started, "Have you established your marker plants and animals and are you monitoring them before, during, and after deforestation and before sugar cane planting?"

Dr Alvares answered, "Yes, we have ten thousand acres of land available to us which is currently divided into alternating strips of natural (left uncut) and planted sugar cane. Each strip is ten acres wide by twenty acres deep. Each of the ten by twenty acre strips (two hundred acres per strip) alternates as uncut (non-deforested) and cut plus the sugar cane plants. There will be thirty of these two hundred acre strips alternating between uncut/natural strips and cut/sugar cane plants; this totals near six thousand acres within this experimental project. Also the longer side of the rectangle parallels the Amazon River. And this long side begins one half of a mile from the river."

"First the timber cut is made; then this deforested sector is 'prepared for the sugar cane.' The deforestation crews first cull the commercially viable trees for their wood, such as balsa, teak, sandalwood, rosewood, and mahogany. They then do a cut and burn of the rest. After the burn the land lays idle for two years to allow recovery. During the past three years, almost half of the crop strips have been made ready for sugar cane planting. They will probably start planting in a couple of months. So, we environmentalists have been working for the past three to four years developing a baseline within and on all sides of the area."

Dr. Alvares continued, "Our overall goal is to determine the specific bio-environmental changes which occur during deforestation, during recovery with partial reforestation, and during the planting and growth of 'normal' and genetic engineered sugar cane crops over a period of several years when different combinations of fertilizers and herbicides/pesticides are used. We will be monitoring the uncut/non deforested strips within the rectangle and for two miles on each side of the entire rectangle. It is a large, long term project. I am probably committed to this project for the rest of my life."

Sam perked up, "It seems to me that there is an unlimited amount of environmental data to collect from analyzing this six to ten thousand acres of land. Do you have manpower to monitor for bio-changes over such a large area?"

"No, not to do it thoroughly," Dr. Alvares answered. "As you can see we need people with both botanical and zoological training. Currently we have three environmental research teams each headed by a university professor. Each team works three weeks in and one week out of the forest. A research coordinator schedules a working period and working area for each team, so there is a minimum of overlapping coverage. We change the responsibility of the coordinators every year. Currently I am the coordinator for seven more months. Most of the research teams have four to seven people, usually students or volunteers. I have a team of four. You already know Jose. He is team leader and is well on his way to finishing his research project and completing his PhD, probably in another year. The other two are also students: Evo and Chico are both working on their MS thesis research with me. We are an all male group."

Sam quickly followed up, "Then if you work straight through for three weeks, do you have living facilities on the project site?"

"Yes." replied Dr Alvares. "We have three movable buildings. One is a dormitory that has twenty five beds and sleeps as many people as is necessary. One is a kitchen and dining hall where two cooks provide breakfast, a carry-out lunch for researchers who usually do not return to the hall at noon, and an evening dinner. The third building is a large lounge-study area with a small library and facilities for ten computers and online capacity for each, via satellite. The deforestation workers have their own facilities which are about one mile from us. Food and all supplies are under the control of a manager who purchases the supplies and brings or has them shipped to the project area by boat. We will go there by car and then by boat. The last fifty kilometers is by one logging road, so is very difficult even for four wheels drive vehicles."

Sam maintained control of the questions. "Would you have a place for a foreign student on your research team?"

Dr. Alvares responded, "Of the twelve students working on the project, four are foreigners: German, Austrian, Mexican, and English. And for your next question, yes, we use the English language much of the time. As you know, international science is performed, written, and spoken in English."

Sam could only grin. While studying at the University of Miami he had plenty of Spanish speaking colleagues. So he had picked up some Spanish. And Spanish and Portuguese languages were close enough that he could probably learn the latter if he should come here to work here for a while. Of course he would have to learn to like Jose.

Sara asked, "Will you be directly involved in any of the genetically engineered sugar cane work? I mean that by comparing changes in the loss of plant and animal species you could recommend certain GE sugar cane that caused less or minimal damages. Or will the German company always have the final say about which cane is chosen as best?"

"I only hope I live long enough to be able to have an input into those kind of down the road decisions," answered Dr. Alvares.

So, after again gorging themselves, it had been difficult to say no to someone who was continuously offering different great smelling and delicious tasting meats every ten minutes, they piled into the gator and Jose them drove back to Stiltsville. He told them they needed to leave by 7:30 AM and that they would breakfast at Itarcoatiara.

* * *

By 9:00 AM on Monday they were in the gator and traveling on road AM-010. The day threatened rain, but the road was stabilized and good. They had packed clothes for four days, two half days coming and going and two full days on site. At mid morning they stopped at a small restaurant in Itarcoatiara and had Feijoada, which was the Amazonian national dish of black beans and pork stew. It was the original slave or poor man's food. Why? Because it was not good pork skeletal muscle that was used. It was pig's ears, feet, tails, tongues, eyes, etc, just about everything that the master or free man did not eat when he ate his pork. But it was delicious. The Brazilians, half way through a meal of Feijoada, loved to tell about the pork components and watch their foreign guests swallow second and third times. What the foreigners were not told was that most cooks added some bacon and a couple of leg bones to spice it up a little.

Because the logging road was not in good condition, and the rainy season was starting, they next went by boat from Itarcoatiara down river toward Parintines. It was a private boat under lease to the research group and was just adequate for ferrying small groups of people and supplies from Itarcoatiara to the temporary boat dock near their current triple house, as they called their living facilities. Two miles further down river the deforestation crews had their own dock and housing facilities. Each dock had its own temporary roughed out road from river to deforestation site which was just adequate to carry people and supplies, via a couple of old pickup trucks. The triple house was located almost one and one half mile from the river. The deforestation site began near one mile inland. The water side of the project area had a five mile buffer along its entire length and would eventually be the continuous major research area; but for now it had to be traversed when coming and going to the site proper. It took them another three hours by boat and then walking a small narrow path to finally arrive at the triple house.

So the route was a long and difficult five hours. During that time they saw fewer than a dozen locals, and that was in the restaurant in Itarcoatiara and on a couple of boats passing them in the Amazon River. It was a beautiful forest for plants and 'wild' animals only. It was green-green-green, and filled with a thousand voices each trying to drown out the other. The water provided a constant supply of crocodiles, all colors of fish, giant turtles, pink dolphins, and snakes. The trees were filled with gorgeous flowers, especially the wild orchids, and multicolored parrots and macaws, plus what seemed like a hundred types of monkeys. This was what it must have like before the Homo sapiens. Beautiful! Exotic! Magnificant! And it was unlivable for the Homo sapiens. But now mankind seemed to be winning the survival race.

Dr. Alveras had called and left a message.

**'I am very sorry but I will not arrive until late tonight, so please make yourselves at home. Jose can show you around the triple house area, but I request that you do not go into the forest because getting lost is a common pastime for all of the researchers. We all wear specific GPSs when we enter the forest anywhere, anytime. Because you do not have GPSs you will always need to have an 'escort' when playing in the forest. Thank you. Take care. See you tomorrow.' Sincerely, Dr. A.**

It was mid afternoon and they were tired so a little nap was called for. Charles, Janice, and Sara heard the call and so responded. However the males, Jose and Sam, were too macho for an 'afternoon' nap so they found a big one thousand year old rosewood tree, sat down under it, and talked the afternoon away. It appeared that they were actually becoming friends.

The evening meal was served at 7:00 PM. sixteen people attended, which included two of the three environmental research teams. This week Dr. Alvares's team was off, but he and Jose were there because of the presence of the Collingswood family. Soon after the coffees were finished, most of the all male teams went to the dormitory building to go to sleep. Each had spent all day fighting his way through the forest to do monitoring and counting of specific plants and animals. In this forest, the nature continuously changed. You had to find and memorize natural path-like areas and use them as much as possible. So seven-eight hours of forest trekking per day usually resulted in ten-twelve hours of sleep. This was not a type of work for less than strong people.

After the short naps, the Collingswood family members were still wide awake at 9:00 PM, so Dad enquired, "It is too early for us to go to bed; what shall we do? We cannot go outdoors."

Sara spoke up, "I remember a certain brother of mine who studied about rain forests so that he could give a short oral seminar on the subject when we had free time. Is he ready to give that presentation now?"

Sam replied, "Of course. Gather around my friends and I will tell you a tale of raw terror, where the powerful kill the weak and even eat them, where the tall crowds out the small, the big step on the little, and the ferocious over power the friendly. It was always this way and will be this way forever. It is titled the Evolution of the Rain Forest."

Intrigued, everyone within hearing distance quieted down and moved closer. Including the three Collingswoods there were only five others, even Jose had gone to bed. But for his first lecture in Brazil, eight student learners was a good start.

Sam continued, "The Amazon River basin is home to the largest rainforest on Earth. It is almost as big as the forty eight American states in the USA. It begins in eight different northern and western South American countries. It is a mosaic of ecosystems which include more than one thousand and one hundred tributaries of variable forested areas. About fifteen million years ago the Amazon was a fresh water inland sea. As the

Andes Mountains rose the water was pushed eastward and a massive fresh water swamp and lake-like region slowly grew."

"About ten million years ago the waters worked their way through the sandstone in what is now northeastern Brazil. The water then started flowing eastward. At this time the Amazon rainforest was born. During the Ice Age, three to four million years ago, the world's sea levels dropped and the lake-like area became a river flowing into the Atlantic Ocean."

"Today the Amazon River is more than four thousand miles long. The basin is more than two thousand miles long and covers a land mass of near three million square miles, of which approximately eighty percent is forested. The quantity of fresh water released by the Amazon River into the Atlantic Ocean is so enormous that in the Atlantic Ocean, more than three hundred miles from the river mouth, the water is still fresh, not salty."

He continued, "The Amazon is home to more species of plants and animals than any other terrestrial ecosystem on earth. Almost half of the world's species were or are found here. It is common to find 400-500 species of trees within one hectare of the basin. Just to give you an idea, there are approximately: 300 species of mammals including the only home for the sloths, anteaters, and armadillos; 1,500 species of birds; 2,000 species of amphibians; 2,500 species of reptiles; 3,000 species of fish; and more than 100,000 species of insects including more than 1,500 species of butterflies and 10,000 species of beetles. It certainly has by far the greatest biodiversity of any area on this earth."

"There are four horizontal layers to a rain forest:"

"The uppermost layer is called the Emergent layer. It has the tallest trees, which are more than 200 feet tall and have trunks nearly ten feet in diameter. This layer towers over all other plants and animals in the rain forest. Because of the thickness of the forest, this is the only area that has plentiful sunshine; so it is where the broad leaved hardwood evergreens grow and the predator birds such as eagles, and bats, monkeys, and the butterflies play."

"The next upper layer is the Canopy layer. This is the primary vegetation layer, 100 to 150 feet high that form the roof over the rest of the forest below. This layer is a maze of tree branches and leaves where numerous birds, monkeys, tree frogs, and tree snakes live."

"The second to lower layer is called the Understory layer. Here only a little sunshine reaches so most of the vegetation is of small trees, shrubs, and short plants, around ten to twenty feet tall, most have large leaves.

The animals at this level include leopards, jaguars, tree frogs, tree snakes, and a wide variety of insects."

"And the lowest layer is the Forest floor. This area is dark with only a few plants, other than vine-like plants. Decay of leaves and limbs is very rapid. The animals include numerous small animals and giant anteaters."

"Now if you ask, so what good is a rain forest, you can prepare an open list which would include: major carbon dioxide/oxygen exchanger, major stabilizer of the world's climate, major bio-source for medicines and foods, protection of numerous plants and animals which are on the endangered species list......... "

"And if you ask, why are rain forests disappearing, you can prepare another open list which would include: 95% is from human hands to build agriculture regions for both small and large farms, wood for timber and for home cooking fires, grazing land for cattle, cleared areas for commercial food crops,............."

"And if you ask, can rain forests be saved? Deforestation certainly can be slowed down. In this way much can be saved with government and private sector joint efforts in attempts to develop land policy reforms and law enforcement reforms which allow for a sustainable use of the existing forest, increased productivity of deforested areas, rehabilitation of deforested areas, the prevention of deforestation of protected areas,................"

"In my opinion the use of high technology should be extensively employed to aid efforts to save as much as possible of the current rain forest. I strongly support efforts to improve the productivity of the sugar cane plant and thus decrease the quantity of land needed to grow it. I have heard rumors that, converting sugar from cane for vehicle fuels, Brazil could become the Saudi Arabia of bio-fuels in the near future. Would such efforts completely destroy the Amazon River basin rain forests? No one wants to even ask this question."

There was a short but spontaneous applause from the small audience. Sam bowed low in all four directions. And then for the next hour or so there was a general discussion of forest versus agriculture interrelationships; construction versus destruction. Many were questions, but few answers.

* * *

On Tuesday morning, Dr. Alvares had arrived. The Collingswoods and Dr. Alvares all sat together at a breakfast table. They were anxious to get out there into the forest.

Dr. Alvares began, "I apologize for being late. But this is my team rest week and I simply had off week things to accomplish. I am now yours for the rest of the next couple of days. I understand you had a superb lecture last night."

Charles spoke up, "Yes, he might make a good professor or minister someday." And he glanced over at Sam who was looking at his plate. Nothing else was said.

"Then let us concentrate on the next two days, and hope that we do not get too much rain. The rainy season is upon us. Some days it rains for twenty four hours and we wear all plastic gear in order to enter the forest and monitor our marked locations. Other days it will only rain for a few hours and we again usually wear all plastic gear to be able to monitor our marked spots.'

"What I am saying is if you do not have adequate rain gear, let us know because we are well stocked in all sizes. It becomes a delicate balance because it stays hot and the skin does not breathe through plastic. So we carry small back packs, and take on and off or exchange plastic and light cotton clothes depending on the sky and the protection the trees give us."

"Above the trees it may rain hard for a couple of hours. And the ground will remain reasonable dry. While where we are on the ground the leakage through the trees onto our head may continue lightly for the rest of the day. The forest floor does not receive a lot of light even on sun shiny days. On dark rainy days, a nice big flashlight can be very helpful in trying to spot and identify both plants and animals, and in trying to avoid covered pits. The decaying vegetation is excessive on the forest floor, so it obscures holes or pits. You can learn to recognize them in the light. But during a darkened day they are most difficult and can be dangerous – for broken legs."

"We will break up into two groups. Charles and Sara will go with me. Janice and Sam will go with Jose. Both groups will go in the same direction and stay within a one hundred yards of each other. Jose and I have a ten mile radius, wireless, water proof head phone set, so we will remain in constant communication. Do you have any questions?"

With no question for now, they headed into the forest. Soon Charles was grateful that Janice had insisted that they bring with them their hiking boots. It would not be Everglades swamp grass, but it would have its share of dangerous little guys wondering around on the ground looking for food. And he was in no mood to provide even a small blood sample. All four Collingswoods had lived in 'dangerous' territory much of their lives – the

Everglades. In such places you look before you reach, you look before you step, you look before you climb in or out of a heavily scrubbed area or grassy knoll, and you looked before you moved. You walked slowly, never ran, unless there was an alligator chasing you. So it was automatic. Charles, Janice, Sam, and Sara each activated his/her intuitive defense receptors for danger from any direction at any time. Caution was the name of the game for this real Brazilian rain forest day.

The two groups walked over to the deforested area and began entering the forest there. Even though they were only a couple of miles from the chain saws and large tree and dirt moving machinery, the noise was terrible. And of course this is exactly what Dr. Alveras wanted to illustrate. They walked for five to ten minutes before they even saw a small snake. All larger animals that had a large home range had left the area as soon as the machines and their noise arrived. Humans could not live next door to that noise. And two years later most of the larger animals had not returned. But the vegetation was something else. Brilliantly spectacular was all one could say.

You could not begin to see the tops of the trees; they were just up there somewhere. And as they were looking up the sun broke through the clouds and everything sort of lit up, like turning on a forty watt light bulb in a very large room. It was like from not seeing much to seeing many things reasonably well. The further they went into the forest the more sounds were heard. First it was small bird calls. Then numerous multicolored parrots and macaws began to talk. Next monkeys started making their presence known with continuous chatter. Then on the ground animals seemed to add their voices to the symphony. A monstrous anaconda snake, a good twenty feet long, slithered along about six feet from the group. Also the flowers appeared and got thicker and more colorful as they walked further from the deforestation area.

Suddenly Dr. Alvares got very nervous. Sara had disappeared from his view. He looked around for a couple of minutes, fighting down panic; then he heard some commotion off to his right and ahead about thirty paces. He hurried in that direction and what did he discover? Sara had brought with her a large bag of unshelled peanuts and she was sharing them with the monkeys. Boy did they love her. And obviously she was having a ball. Indeed, peanuts were an international food for monkeys everywhere, tame or wild. Then he suddenly saw several flashes of light coming from off to the right even further. As he moved in that direction he saw Dad taking flash pictures of daughter playing with the monkeys. And he remembered that the Collingswood were not normal Americans. They had lived on, around, and in the largest marsh/swamp area in the United States. He could probably learn some defensive trekking from these Americans.

And the other group of Jose, Mom, and Sam were seeing similar biological patterns. The further one went from the deforested area the more nature had either not left or had begun to return. The environmental problem was not one of chemicals or other toxic pollutants; it was noise and soil run-off. Whether the same plant and animal flora would re-establish themselves later was unknown. It was good that Dr. Alvares and his teams had flora data of the area before the deforestation crews started arriving and cutting and clearing the land.

As Jose and Sam were walking side by side Sam commented upon the lack of large mammals. And as soon as he said this he heard some pig-like noises off to the left. They stopped and Sam slowly and carefully moved in that direction. Within about forty paces he saw a large male tapir coming toward him. He looked beyond this guy and saw four other tapirs, one medium size, probably mommy, and three smaller, about three quarter grown, siblings. The big guy came rapidly toward Sam. Sam stopped. The big guy stopped. Sam took a couple of slow steps forward. The big guy took a couple of slow steps forward. This was repeated by Sam. And it was repeated by the big guy. They were about twenty feet from each other. Both stared into each others' eyes for several minutes. Neither one blinked. Then they seemed to come to some kind of understanding because first the tapir blinked, then Sam blinked, and they both turned around and slowly walked back in the direction from which they had come.

Jose and Mom had been watching this 'standoff' from afar, not knowing what they would do if the tapir had decided to attack. They looked at each other. And Mom gave Jose that what did you expect from my son look. She remembered the old days in the Everglades when Sam had a standoff with the crocodile that had protected them from the two big alligators. Sam was special.

Both groups walked for a couple more hours and began to observe what primitive wild nature, untouched by humans, was all about. It was spectacular to look at, but to live in was questionable. They met for lunch. After lunch they all walked a couple more hours in a different direction but the two groups remained in parallel. There really were no sufficient adjectives or adverbs to adequately describe what they were seeing. It was simply marvelous in every direction. There were unlimited and brilliant colors from the flowers and the birds; unlimited noise from the parrots and monkeys; unlimited smells from the dying and decaying branches and leaves. It was one of the few places in the world where mankind had not entered, so it was truly natural. - UNTOUCHED BY HUMAN HANDS - Dad took enough pictures such that they would use them to wallpaper one living room wall back home. Near 4:30 PM they decided they had developed a 'feel' for the forest and headed back toward the triple house.

It took an hour to get back. So they hurried to the showers, put on fresh clothes and joined the others in the dining area. You would never guess what was being served. Yes. It was Feijoada, pork remains and black beans. However because this was a special night and there were special guests, pork remains were not used. Instead they bar-b-qued an entire pig and served the pig (skeletal muscle) and black beans side by side, along with the other unusual corn, kale, cassava, peppers, and a variety of fresh fruit. Coffee and a special torta de banana, banana cobbler, was desert. And then it was on to bed for a good sound sleep by all.

* * *

Wednesday morning everyone was up and ready to go out to the forest early. But it was raining very hard, so the Collingswoods hesitated. They decided to wait a while and see if it would ease up some. They had a good outing yesterday and, with the heavy rain and the dark day, they would probably not expand their knowledge base very much. The student teams also decided to wait for the rains to ease up. So they turned on the computers and opened web sites for rain forests and the Everglades, comparing plant and animal species, endangered species, reasons for and types of pollution, relationships to local sugar cane plantations, sugar cane genomes, etc. After lunch it was still raining hard so they decided to have a small group seminar discussion on plant genomes. Dr. Alvares, Charles, Janice, Sam, Jose, and the three other fellows in the room who knew nothing about DNA and genomes joined in. Sara recently completed a course in Molecular Plant Genetics last year so she was the starting point. And before coming to Brazil she had gathered some online data about the sugar cane genome. So many of the ecologists sat around a large table and Sara began to talk about DNA.

Sara led off, "I have some course learned knowledge and online information about genomes that I can share with you. Let me begin with the human genome, which as you know was completely sequenced just a few years ago."

254

"The human genome is coded on twenty three pairs of chromosomes. It has more than thirty million base pairs, the DNA letter code. The human genome carries the code for near 100,000 genes, of which around twenty percent code for functioning proteins; all of the rest code for punctuation, regulatory molecules, spacer regions, coordinator regions, control regions, multiple duplicating regions, and functional and non functional junk. Many of these protein coding regions are even found in multiple copies. So the critical functional codes are found in 20 to 30,000 of the 100,000 genes in the 46 chromosomes. This is a very messy set of genes to allow its host, Homosapiens, to now dominate all of the life forms on this earth."

"Plant genomes also vary widely, over a ten-fold range. Wild plants have smaller genomes. Domesticated plants have been crossed or bred so often that most plant cells have high polyploidy. This means that they have many extra copies of the same chromosome or parts of the same chromosome, or many copies of the same gene or parts of the same gene. In other words they have a lot of excess DNA that they probably do not use. Therefore, it is very difficult to elucidate and sequence plant genomes. Within the scientific classification for plants, the Andropogonese includes maize, sorghum, and cane. They are similar in gene composition, but the DNA has not yet been fully sequenced. So today, we do not know the genome of any of these plants. However, sugar cane and sorghum are most closely related."

"Different sugar cane strains have 40 to 150 chromosomes depending upon which domestic strain you examine. It has high polyploidy, three to ten copies of some chromosomes. So there is really no such thing as a natural, native sugar cane plant in existence today. Sugar cane and most commercial crops have been extensively cross bred such that 'native strains' of most commercial crops do not exist. At least, the sugar cane DNA is being sequenced and the entire genome should be available in the near future. And that is about all I know about the genes of the sugar cane plant. Does anyone have any questions?"

"What I have learned is that we, during the past hundreds of years, via agriculture specialists, have extensively cross-bred, re-bred, un-bred, up-bred, down-bred and on and on, food crops. Today there is no original food crop that can be called pure, original, or virgin anywhere in the world. Wheat, corn, soybeans, sugar cane, grapes for wine, and all crops being grown and harvested today have thousands of different genomes, probably most of these genomes are not even functional. This is why Mexican corn is very different from American corn, or Russian wheat is very different from Brazilian wheat. And sugar cane? Of the more than 50 varieties of sugar cane being grown today, no two varieties have the same set of genes. The variation may be as much as 20 to 30 percent. And keep in mind that the genes from the five major ethnic groups (species) of humans vary by less than 3 percent.'

"Therefore, we humans have not cross-bred, re-bred, et.al. nearly as much as have our foods that we eat. Only the future will allow us to find out if this is good or bad for human evolution. Will plant genomes and animal genomes cross-bred someday? We are animals you know!"

And with that Sara sat down. There were only a few questions. Sara was really over the head of most of the students. The group was ecology oriented and did not know much about this molecular DNA stuff. But it was fascinating, and most students knew that they had to learn about this molecule which carried the code for all forms of life that exist on this planet.

As the evening dinner approached the group prepared to re-enjoy a repetition on last night's meal. They would finish the left over pork and beans. However they would open new bottles of Brazilian wine to drink,

So they sat around talking and turned on the television. This was New Years Eve and CNN-Bra-1 was carrying the New Years events from around the world as each region hit their 12:00 o'clock. These midnight events in the Pacific Ocean began in the morning hours in Brazil. So the New Year celebrations had already begun in many countries when the TV was turned on. With the excellent satellite reception one could not escape civilization here deep in the jungle. Man's science and technology was now all powerful and had penetrated everywhere on earth. Dinner was not also spectacular because everything had to be cooked over a stove. Brazilian foods were best when cooked over an open fire. The rains had ruined their last day in the rain forest.

* * *

On Thursday the Collingswoods had to return to Manaus as they needed to catch their return flight early on Friday morning. They were all up by 8:00 AM and had breakfast together. Dr. Alvares told Sam he would be welcome to join them in their research if he wanted to do so. And Sam responded that he would request a leave from school to be allowed to come and collect data for a MS thesis. However, the two of them would need to E-mail specific research ideas back and forth so he could draft up a good thesis proposal. If that could be soon accomplished, he could probably return at the beginning of next semester in February or March. And they concluded it with the gentleman's handshake. And Sam turned to Jose and slowly held out his hand to shake. He really didn't want Jose's kissing slobbers all over his hand. Jose was a bit of a character, fun, but it was wise to keep an eye on him. He knew that his sister would not return with him so things would be all right.

The Reverend Charles Collingswood, President of the Save the Everglades Foundation, headquarted in Florida, USA, and his wife, Dr. Janice Stryer Collingswood, environmental biologist, learned what they came here learn. It had been a very positive experience.

As they sat around the breakfast table Charles summed it up, "We wish to sincerely thank all of you for your time and showing to us that nature and agriculture can work side by side to protect native plants, animals, and people. We can develop systems that will provide a livelihood for people and also protect those same people and their neighbors. But it must be done openly and under the cooperation of the people themselves. A proper marriage is where the result is a win-win situation, both sides must be happy. I understand that both the takers and the givers must be consulted before any project is initiated. Again, thank you for showing us one way to accomplish this difficult task."

Goodbyes were said all around. Dr. Alvares did give hugs and kisses to each Collingswood. The females were kissed on the hands and on the cheeks. The men were kissed only on the cheeks. That was the true Brazilian way. They placed their belongings into the boat which would take them to the gator which was waiting for them at Itacoatiara. And then Jose would drive them back to their stilthouse. The entire return journey was rather quiet. The memories were circulating around and around. They saw and did so much in one week. This certainly was a trip that they would not forget. And yet there was one more not forgettable 'conversation' to happen.

They had lunch at a restaurant near Manaus, arrived for the last night at their Brazilian home, carefully told Jose goodbye, repacked for tomorrow, and got ready for bed when Dad called them all to the table. He had something he wanted to tell them. They sat down. Sara glanced at Mom. Mom shook her shoulders. She did not know either.

Dad opened up, "I have some very difficult news to give to you, my lovely wife and my delightful children. Your grandparents, Susan and William Collingswood, are not your grandparents. They are not my parents. Yes, I was born to Susan Collingswood before she died in that terrible house fire when I was a little boy. Grandmother, apparently, could not conceive, so she, apparently, went to a fertilization clinic and had a pre-embryo implanted into her womb. I am the result of that process. My genes, therefore half of your genes came from anomalous ovum and sperm donors. I do not know who those donors were. And I will probably never find out who were my genetic Mother and Father. I am very, very sorry Janice that I never told you before this. I probably would never have told you if another thing had not recently happened. So there is more."

And Mom looked at Sam and Sara. All three were getting nervous. You just find out your husband, or your grandparents, is not your husband, or your grandparents, and now he tells you that this is just the beginning of his difficult news. What could be next?

Dad continued, "For many years I had dreams of events, happenings occasionally nightmares. Always these dreams involved a boy or a man who looked like me. And usually the dreams involved some place where I had never been. So eventually I felt that this person who looked like me was my brother. And then a few years ago I met him. His name is William Bassinger. He is a lawyer and lives in Des Moines, Iowa. We have developed a telepathic form of contact; we call it a spirit communication. It only occurs at night when we are asleep. And we do not have complete control of what is seen and said. But we can send 'messages' to each other. This is not uncommon in identical twins, which is what we are, I think. Anyway, there was always another set of spirit communications which I, and Bill, could partially understand, but it was as if the reception was coming through a fog bank.'

"A couple of weeks ago a second brother found me at the church in Indian Nest. He had seen me in some of his dreams and knew that I lived near a marsh-swamp like area. He and Bill and a third twin saw me fall in the air boat when I hurt my shoulder. They each shared my pain at the exact time when it happened. That is how David Dekker located me. He is a security specialist and lives in Washington, DC. David informed me of this other brother whose name is Dr. Aaron Armand. He is a DNA/Gene medical researcher who is director of a twinning center hospital in New York City."

Immediately Mom and Sam looked at each other and nodded. Sam went first, "Does he have a son named Hype Armand?"

"Yes," Dad answered. "He is your dinosaur buddy of the past. And biologically or genetically, probably he is your cousin, or even your brother."

Sam and Mom again looked at each other but what was there to say?

Dad continued, "And there is more yet. We are probably four identical brothers, identical quadruplets. Aaron is currently performing DNA fingerprint tests of cell samples from each of us to determine if we are identical or fraternal. That information should be available anytime. We think identical. And we think this fertility clinic made a major mistake by placing the same pre-embryo into each of four women. But we do not know how this happened. Anyway, Bill thinks that if we want to do so, we could sue the clinic because of this mistake. And we are talking about a law suit in the range of more than one hundred million dollars."

'Yes, this was a monster.' Sam was thinking. 'Dad was telling us that he did not know his Mother and Father, therefore we did not know our Grandmother and Grandfather. And that he had three identical brothers. And what if they sue the clinic that brought him/them into the world this - family? – They/we could make several million dollars.'

Janice was thinking, 'Charles's Mother is gone. His Father is in his seventies and not in good health. I don't believe there would be a crisis in our immediate world if word of the four twins got to the news media. And several million dollars could be used to stimulate a lot of sugar cane genomic research which could be used to reduce environmental pollution from sugar cane growth and that would save some of my Everglades children from extinction which would................'

While Sara, who was very tired, thought, 'There are too many complexities here. I think I will go to bed and think about this for the next few years. It has been a long week.'

So there was a general agreement that this problem situation would be brought up again in a couple of days after they had thought about it and had recovered from this 'vacation'.

* * *

On Friday morning they were up early and the taxi was waiting. They hurried around as they were going to take the Mexico Airlines flight #1327 at 9:05 AM to Mexico City and then American United flight #2933 on to Miami. They made all of their flights on time and without any delays. After landing at MIA they went straight to the car, drove directly home, and went immediately to sleep, for the next forty eight hours.

# 18 – ANONYMITY VERSUS NOTORIETY – DEKKER

The first inhabitants of the Pocono Mountains in eastern Pennsylvania were a dozen or more native Indian tribes including the Delaware, Iroquois, and Shawnee. The Dutch were the first Europeans to establish settlements there in the mid-seventeenth century near the famous Delaware Water Gap. A few years later the English and Germans arrived and drove the Dutch out. Over the next one hundred years the area developed with permanent residences, hotels, inns, boarding houses, cabins, bed and breakfast establishments. As New York City and Philadelphia grew, this nearby area of mountains, forests, fast flowing creeks and rivers soon became known as 'Pennsylvania's Playground'.

During the prohibition era in the 1920-30s, the resorts of the Pocono Mountains developed a Puritan concept of life and did not permit alcohol, prostitution, card playing games, or gambling of any kind. On Sundays one was not allowed to play golf, tennis, cricket or any team sports. And in the mid-twentieth century, the Poconos of eastern Pennsylvania became the "Honeymoon Capital of the World". While toward the end of the century, vacation and retirement communities and select city life such as theater and musical productions entered the Pocono Mountains. There were already numerous types of sports, available from downhill skiing, golf, cross country hiking and skiing, caving, white water rafting, water carnivals and holiday festivals. It was a breath of fresh air for people living in the large cities in the area.

David, Janet, Action, and Alice Dekker had reserved four nights at the White Wolf Mountain Lodge and Inn near Stroudsburg, Pennsylvania, which was in the heart of the Poconos Mountains. This was now the outdoor vacation center for New Yorkers, Philadelphians, Baltimoreans, and Washingtonians. Like his brothers, David wanted to "come clean" with the family. He thought that a couple of days of fun and adventure would soften the atmosphere so he would get the benefit of any doubts when he told them who he was or was not and who they were or were not. So he was pre-conditioning them with three days of white water rafting, kayaking for Action and Alice, antique furniture and accessories hunting, vineyards and winery roaming, and possible a day of caving if they still had some energy on the last day. It was all available within a one hour drive from Stroudsburg. Because David had an assignment in Washington, DC during the New Year's holiday period, the Dekker's had reserved the week between Christmas Day and the New Years – in on Friday, December 26 and out on Tuesday, December 30.

Because of Dad's irregular work arrangements the children rarely got to take real holidays when schools were usually out during school breaks. But it was nice to live at home while going to the two universities; that way they could see him during non-holidays, this time was an exception. Action was still playing tennis regularly. But his studying left him no time to practice for national competition, so he just played hard ball with his buddies. He was finishing his BA in Political Science at Georgetown University in Washington, DC and had applied to Georgetown University Law School for this fall if his grades held up. He was running with a GPA of 3.68 out of 4.00; and he thought his Father had enough "friends" in the Washington, DC area that he would have a good future in law, government, and politics. Alice was hard science oriented and had finished pre-engineering and entered the Department of Computer and Informational Sciences at George Washington University in Washington, DC. Her GPA was 3.89 out of 4.00. Therefore both children were attending excellent universities and doing very well; and Mom and Dad were going to see that they continued doing well.

The Dekker's children lived at home just across the Potomac River in Arlington, Virginia. Both universities were fifteen to thirty minutes by bicycle, bus or metro. This allowed them to remain as an intact family for a longer period of time, and helped Mom and Dad pay private university tuition costs. Even though both children had scholarships, university expenses were more than one hundred thousand dollars per year for the two of them. Adding Dad's salary from the Blue Ravens and Mom' salary from the North Arlington Middle School together covered those university costs, but there was not much left over. And the Washington, DC area was an expensive area to live in. Those 'kids' needed to study hard and do well to justify such educational expenses. But Mom and Dad thought the sacrifice was worth it. The two of them had never had such opportunities when they were young, and they were all on the same team. Both Action and Alice knew about their Grandparents, or lack thereof, so they appreciated the support and paid back in kind. It was a hard working and loving family.

Stroudsburg was about a three hour drive from Washington, DC. By leaving home early and going against the rush hour traffic they made good time and arrived around noon, had lunch, and checked in near 2:00 PM. The White Wolf Mountain Lodge and Inn were separated buildings, both on mountain ledges and the view of the tree covered mountain valleys was magnificent, even though the deciduous trees were leafless at this time of the year. Both buildings were large wooden chalets which had high open entries filled with ceiling to floor glass windows facing the south such that there was always plenty of sunshine. The main floor of the Lodge contained a large lounge, bar, and small restaurant, plus two large fireplaces. The upper six floors had three and four bedroom suites, with in room food services and fireplaces. While the Inn was a long rectangular eight floor building with motel like rooms, each room had a balcony facing the south. The Inn also contained one lounge with fireplace, a cafeteria style eating area, and a games room. It was more average family oriented and less expensive. The Dekkers had two double rooms with a connecting door in the Inn. Each room had two King sized beds, with standard vanity and vanity mirrors, small table with two chairs, a television, and no fireplace.

After going up to their fourth floor rooms and unloading their suitcases it was planning time. They needed to decide which event and where they would go to for which day. There was one car and four people; and they would need to drive somewhere each day. The family sat around the small table in the parent's room and watched the sun go down from the glass windows on the balcony. The sunset was early due to the short December days and a few dark clouds. Still it was lovely to actually see a sunset. Living in Arlington, which was street to street high rise buildings, they rarely saw a real sunrise or sunset.

Dad opened the conservation, "As always when we vacation, the first day we must be together. For tomorrow I have made reservations on an eight person raft to go white water rafting at the Lehigh River Gorge. Starting time is 10:00 AM. We will have to leave around 8:30 AM to be certain that we find the location and get property attired. The weather will be mild, sunshine and 55°F. You will need a warm shirt, shorts, tennis shoes and a windbreaker type water proof jacket. I know that you each brought these because we discussed the need to have such gear in this area at this time of the year. You can wear baseball caps because of the expected sunshine but they will probably give us helmets to wear. The trip will be rough, many twists and turns, and plenty of water. Fortunately none of us wear glasses or contact lens. We will stop to take a break along the down route and they will provide us with lunch. It should be a lot of fun, but there is a degree of danger, so do not relax too much. Mother and I have done this several times, but that was before you two showed up."

He hesitated to see if anyone had a response or question.

Action questioned, "This will not interfere with my whitewater kayaking lessons on Sunday and Monday will it? I really need to take those lessons."

Dad responded, "No. That was previously arranged and is still on the agenda. I know that during the past couple of weeks you have increased your rowing practice on the Potomac River near the Great Falls Park rapids. And that the extra practice was in anticipation of this trip, and for Jane."

The big guy Action actually blushed.

"And I realize that you need to take the whitewater kayak course so you can become certified and then try those challenging advanced runs up in New York State," Dad continued. "I know your competitive nature and your need to keep up with a 'certain young lady'. As you phase out of tennis you can phase into whitewater kayaking. In my opinion this new challenge will be good. I completely support you."

Again Action blushed and thought to himself, 'Does he mean the challenge of kayaking or the challenge of Jane. He seems to really like her.'

"I like the whitewater rafting idea for tomorrow," said Alice. "I think it will be fun. But Sunday I will go with Action and watch his kayaking lessons. Maybe I will join him and maybe I will not. It depends on the weather. I am not sure that I want to try those Eskimo rolls. Probably I will just take my laptop and play on the keys. I have some surfing to do for a new research project."

Action spoke up, "You don't learn the Eskimo roll on the first lesson." And he gave a couple of chuckles.

Alice just ignored him. Action had always been the bigger, braver, stronger, and more athletic like. She loved her computer and all associated electronic systems. She never understood why Action got some brains to go with his brawn. It really was not fair. But, he was a good big brother to have around, most of the time, or when you needed him.

Dad spoke up again, "Sunday then, while you guys go to the whitewater kayak lessons, your Mother and I will visit the antique outlets in the area. You know that for a long time she has been looking for two European end tables to match her Italian coffee table. And I am certain that she will find other things that will blend into our 'antique' furnished house in Arlington."

And he looked at her and grinned and threw a kiss. Day one vacation was no time to open past disagreements. But he was proud of their house furnishings which most Americans only saw on some British Sherlock Holmes re-runs. When his friends visited they always told him how lucky he was to have a wife who knew what quality was; his house did not have typical American pseudo-plastics. But he was never sure whether she was being put up or he was being put down. Anyway, antiquing they would go because this was a good area for to hunt for European antiques.

"And Monday we will visit a few wineries but adjust our schedule such that we can return and watch Action pass his final exam for his kayaking certificate. I think that is for the late afternoon isn't it?" Dad asked.

Action answered, "I think the final is given as a practical on another nearby gorge. But we will have to check."

"Unless you would rather we watch both days," Mom spoke up.

Action raised his head and looked up, said nothing, but thought, 'Here I am 6 foot 8 inches tall and 226 pounds and Mom still thinks of me as a child.' He made eye contact with Alice who was also just looking up into the air.'

So Dad asked, "Are we all right with the three day program? Alice, you are welcome to join Mom and me for the antiquing or wineries if you want."

Alice responded with the same head and eye motion that her brother had just used. Alice was one of those 'kind' that liked being with herself;

"Then we leave from here at 8:30 in the morning for the whitewater rafting fun," Dad finished.

Around 7:00 PM they went downstairs, had dinner, retired back to the rooms, and went to bed early to get ready for the excitement of a wet tomorrow.

* * *

On Saturday morning the Dekkers were up at 7:30, grabbed a quick breakfast, jumped into the car and were off toward Lehigh River Gorge. As predicted it was a beautiful sunshiny day. The early morning sunrise over the mountains was gorgeous. It was a lovely drive. They arrived at the parking lot which was not at the top or the bottom of the run, but somewhere in the middle.

The Gorge was completely hidden so you really did not know top from bottom. There were continuous shuttle buses from the parking lot to the up for the start or to the down area for the finish. And the buses ran back and forth continuously. They parked the car and took the up shuttle bus to the start location. They arrived about twenty minutes early so they had a chance to look around a little. The starting point was just a ledge which jutted out of the side of the ravine. It was all rocks, looked ferocious, sounded terrible, and the raft looked very small for eight people.

Dad gave the orders, "The raft has four rows of two seats each. So, Mom, because you are not super brave you sit second row on the right side in front me. I will sit right side, third row Alice sit left side, second row beside Mom. Action, sit directly behind Alice on the left side in the third row and beside me. The other two tour tourists are men. So one guy can sit on the left side in front of Alice, and one male guide can sit first row on the right, in front of Mom. In the back row the other tourist can sit on the right side behind me, with a second male guide sitting directly behind Action. In this way the Dekkers will be sandwiched between the four men. The run is classified as a medium class III; 14 years old and up only, are allowed on such runs. Therefore, some extra precautions are normal. Everyone will be given a vest life jacket which you put on over their windbreaker jackets. And they also require that you wear a water proof helmet. So put your baseball caps inside your jackets. Think positively. There is no need to be afraid. We are all together. If you have any questions, we can ask the guides."

The two guides arrived, Routher and Joe. They introduced themselves, looked around at the group, and suggested that they start boarding.

Each person put on his gear, which was checked out by the guides, assumed his assigned seat, and took his paddle and tested it out with a few strokes in the water. The two guides looked around. Confirmed that everyone was ready; and they signaled to the controller. The controller at the start looked up and down the ravine, gave the signal that the run was clear, the water chute gates near the top of the ravine were opened, a rush of water blasted down toward them, and they pushed off. Before they could change their minds, say nea or yea, they were swept down the ravine.

The first experience was a mass of cold water rushing toward them and the raft trying to outrun it. This was going to be an unforgettable experience. They had been told that the Zombi Mans Run on the Lehigh River Gorge was a mixture of two repeating phases, very fast rapids and slow calm flat water, each phase would last ten to twenty minutes in duration.

Obviously the start was going to be all rapids. And they began their ten minutes of breath holding. It was so noisy that you could not even hear yourself think let alone hear the guides shouting instructions to paddle here and not to paddle there.

Indeed it was up and down, around corners to the left and then around corners to the right and then back to the left and back to the right, rocks up here and boulders down there, raft going forward, sideways, and backward all at the same time it seemed, twisting and turning, lurching and pitching, and always the water whirling around them. They thought that they were going to be on the water, but found out that they were in the water more than on the water. You just had to close your eyes, maybe pray a little, and hope that this fast rapids phase would hurry up and become a flat calm phase.

And suddenly that is just what happened. You looked up and found that you were gliding on water like glass. The sound stopped first, which left your ears ringing. Then the flying water and boulders disappeared. The sideways, backwards, and circular motions stopped. And as you went in only one direction, forward, you automatically stopped paddling to breathe. A fantastic experience, but it was a very wet experience. Yes, the slow calm flat water was like a glass surfaced lake. What a difference – night and day contrasts.

And just as you were getting comfortable and beginning to enjoy the gentle journey and the sunshiny weather, you heard this loud sound. The sound came closer and closer. It was the next fast rapid phase. And again, before you could ask about the noise, you were in the noise, and the noise was in you. Wham, before you could hold your breath you were thrown forward and then backward and for survival you automatically began holding your breath again.

You suddenly rocketed down between rising ledges of stone slick with green algae; and began the twisting, turning, half upsetting to the right, half upsetting to the left, bouncing off of this boulder, bypassing the large rock but hitting the next boulder, dipping around a whirlpool here and up over a water covered ledge there, and always getting more and more cold wet. Sometimes you saw what was in front of you, sometimes you saw what was in back of you, sometimes you saw to the left, and sometimes you saw to the right, and sometimes you saw to the left and right at the same time.

Always your forward momentum was such that you would not recognize a lion standing on a boulder and laughing at you.

As you sort of began to accept that life is one super up and down merry-go-round, the noise stops, the turning stops, the dizziness clears, and you realize that all trees are still growing upward, and the leaves are still closer to the sky than the ground. The water turns from white to blue, the sun stands still, and you are still riding inside a raft.

After a couple of minutes, once the hearing returned, Dad looked around, counted three other Dekker heads and said, "How is everyone doing? There are still four Dekkers on this raft so I guess so far we are doing OK."

Mom, Action, and Alice all gave thumbs up, so he assumed no one wanted to quit and go home yet. Not that they could even if they wanted to do so. Probably after a couple of more fast rapids they would be old veterans at whitewater rafting.

Alice spotted some movements in the nearby woods and pointed, "Look there. Why it is a herd of deer enjoying the last remnants of autumn green grass. I count five or six."

And one of the guides spoke up, "There is a feeder station for deer and other animals where food and shelter is made available during the cold winter months. They are migrating in that direction."

And before Alice could ask more questions she heard the noise approaching from beyond the front of the raft. So she turned around, they all tightened their grips on their paddles and braced themselves for the next rapids.

Several of the sharp turns in certain fast rapids phases had scary names and this next phase was called the 'devils handshake' because it twisted into a pig tail double curve. As the raft went into the rapids everything was going good. About half way through, suddenly Mom partially stood and at the sharp point in the double curve she fell toward the water. Dad lunged for her, caught her, settled her into her seat, but then he lost his balance and completely fell overboard. He immediately bounced off of a large boulder and was washed into the front of the raft. The raft chased him for several minutes as they both bounced from rock to rock.

Suddenly Dad's helmet came off; he hit a large boulder head first. He went unconscious and went under the water. He was probably unconscious for about twenty seconds at 10:47 ET on that Saturday morning, December 27. Luckily the cold water woke him up, the life jacket brought him to the surface, and he managed to partially control his down the rapids movement. Being a big strong fellow he was able to successfully arrive at the bottom of this rapids phase, move into the calm flat phase, and work his way over to the shore. As the raft completed the rapids phase the guides paddled the raft over to him at the bank and tied it up.

The all got out of the raft and gathered around Dad. He was exhausted and already laying on the ground in a semi-conscious state. The guides, trained in emergency care for just such emergencies, examined his head.

The guide Routher said, "I am going to carefully clean off the blood with a cotton gauze and alcohol. If I hurt please let me know. As first look I think you scraped some skin off your head when you hit that boulder." And Routher began cleaning the blood from around Dad's hair near the cut area.

Dad responded, "Yes it does hurt a little, but the dizziness is now gone. I can see everyone clearly."

Routher responded, "It looks like you are going to have a nice baseball sized lump behind that left ear just below the cut area."

Dad reached back to feel this area and said, "I need to put some ice on this as soon as possible. Is there ice at the lunch stop?"

"Are you sure that you can go on to the break point, Dad?" asked Action.

As the guide looked Dad over and remarked, "It appears the head cut and bruise seem to be the only obvious injury."

He performed the usual eye contact, sound localization, balance, and swallowing tests. Dad passed all of them successfully. But he certainly did have a large lump, still bleeding a little, on the left side of his head just under the ear.

Alice asked, "Are you sure that you want to continue the run?"

And Dad's response was, "And why not?"

[They did not know but would learn later, at exactly 10:47 (Eastern Time) on Saturday morning, December 27, an Aaron Armand, while sitting in a large arm chair in a lodge in the White Mountains in New Hampshire, suddenly passed out for about twenty seconds, developed a tremendous headache, and soon had a large swelling on the left side of his head behind the ear. At exactly 9:47 (Central time), on Saturday morning, December 27, a William Bassinger, while sitting on a park bench in the middle of Golden Nugget City in the Ozarks, suddenly passed out for about twenty seconds, developed a tremendous headache, and soon had a large swelling on the left side of his head behind the ear. At exactly 11:47 (Brazil time), on Saturday morning, December 27, a Charles Collingswood, while sitting in an airplane flying over the Gulf of Mexico, suddenly passed out for about twenty seconds, developed a tremendous headache, and soon had a large swelling on the left side of his head behind the ear. Later, these gentlemen would spirit communicate, and exchange wishes of good health.]

The two guides radioed to their controls at the top and the bottom of the run, reported what had happened, the results of the physical examination, and were given permission to continue on to the mid way point for lunch. They would have a doctor there which would give a more thorough examination of Dad and decide if he should continue for the rest of the run. They had gone through three rapids and had only three more to pass until the mid way stop, about another twenty minutes. The most difficult rapids were behind them, so they all hopped back in the raft, again sat in their assigned seats, gave Dad a larger helmet, and off they went.

In about twenty minutes they hit their next rapids, but were now whitewater veterans and psychologically ready. Even though each Dekker was worried about the Daddy Dekker, between the concentration required for the rapids and the fact that he was big enough to take care of himself, the problem sort of melted from their minds until the end of this fast rapids phase. And in the next flat water phase Dad was chatting as if nothing happened so things were 'normal' as they completed the first half of Zombi Mans Run on the Lehigh River Gorge.

It was near noon when they reached the mid way rest area. They stopped, de-rafted, walked around for a few minutes to retrieve their land feet, and then sat down at several picnic tables and chairs where box lunches and cold drinks were ready. Each chose to sit in the sun, not under the umbrellas. They needed some drying time. So they opened their lunch boxes and sat in the winter Pennsylvania sunshine.

The doctor had arrived. He gave Dad a more thorough examination. The doctor decided that Dad had indeed suffered a mild concussion, but he would live. He placed an ice pack over his left ear and the giant nodule that had sprouted. He then gave him some pain killer pills.

Then the doctor said, "I want you to have a head X-ray at the emergency services at the Tobyhanna Hospital on route I-380 this evening before you go home and go to sleep. I strongly suggest that you let some other family member drive you back to the White Wolf Mountain Inn tonight and possibly drive again tomorrow if your headache continues. If you should have any problems tonight here is my card, my clinic is only about fifteen minutes driving time from the White Wolf Mountain Inn." And he handed his card to Mom.

So they sat back, continued to dry out, and ate their lunch. To smooth things a bit Routher added, "You are lucky in the sense that the weather is indeed lovely for late December – early January. Usually the deer have already gone down to the feeder stations by this time, but you saw them. They seemed to not be in any hurry. So the cold winter is still some time away. Your stay here with us should be in good weather."

Action replied, "Thank you, we will be with you for the next two days and I need good weather to take try for my kayaking certificate."

And that opened the door to a conversation of white water kayaking on the Pennsylvania and New York rivers; which was best; why which was best; which was easy; which was difficult and why? The conversation even stimulated Alice to reconsider tomorrows kayaking experience with her big brother.

Then the discussion began about whether and or how they should finish the run. They could quit here and return to the parking lot to the car.

Mom was first, "I think we should just call it a day. It has been really great. I have enjoyed it and will always have a fantastic memory. But if we continue for two more hours, and where we cannot leave the run you should suddenly need some medical help, what would we do? You are too big for us to carry up the side of a ravine."

Dad looked around and saw that the doctor had left. So he hollered toward one of the guides, "Hey, about how long would it take to get an emergency helicopter here to the Gorge?"

"We can have one here within fifteen minutes," Louther responded.

Dad continued, "How long would it take for that helicopter to get from here to the nearest emergency service clinic or hospital?"

Again Louther answered, "That would take about fifteen or twenty minutes depending upon the type of anticipated emergency we are talking about. If you are thinking a neurological emergency, then twenty minutes would be about right."

Dad looked at Mom and said, "See I could be in a hospital being taken care of before you guys could carry me up that ravine wall. So there."

"Dad, don't be silly," Alice joined in. "We have had our fun and we don't need to risk your brains just to have more fun." And she chuckled.

Action joined in, "Hey, it is OK. If Dad wants to have a muddled brain, that's fine. Then maybe we can program him to fill up the gas tank in our old car more often, Alice. Now we seem to always ask him when he is broke" And he chuckled.

Mom was beginning to pick up on the train of thought. "Do you think that if he lives with a homogenized brain that it would interfere with his income earning status?"

With zero university education, David Dekker was only the Director of Intelligence for the Blue Ravens Security Firm which was responsible for the safety and lives of VIPs as they traveled in the USA.

And finally Dad defended himself, "Look, that little old 5000 pound boulder just got in front of a 300 pound ex-combatant commando, and you see what little it did to me. I have a small bump on the side of my head. What we need to do is to go back up to that boulder in the devils handshake and find out how many pieces it is now. I will bet you that it is broken into at least ten pieces or it simply has a very big hole through the water side."

They all laughed out loud. And then they suddenly realized that they had lost. Dad was going to finish the afternoon run. Argument was usually futile with him anyway.

The second half of the run was not quite as much fun or exciting. There were several challenging rapids but the fun had sort of been taken out of the day with the accident. They all agreed, except for Dad, that he was very lucky and that he should not push his luck. So they finished the run, gave everyone a super thank you, especially for the medical services, and took the shuttle bus up to the car. Action drove to the hospital and they had Dad's X-ray taken. The hospital doctors declared that he just had a mild concussion; this was probably due to his hard head as it could have been much worse. They placed another ice pack on his head lump and prescribed a bottle of pain capsules. All climbed into the car and Action drove them back to the White Wolf Mountain Inn. No one felt like a real dinner, so Mom went downstairs, purchased some sandwiches and drinks, brought them back to the rooms, and they settled into a TV movie evening.

* * *

Sunday morning they all piled into the car, Dad was feeling alright so he drove. It was going to be another cool crisp day. They took Action and Alice to the Pocono Whitewater's Kayak School. Day 1 of the lessons was for basic kayak training. While the lessons on day two included a kayak maneuvers test, a short kayak carry over a small forested mountain trail to another whitewater ravine, and a second practical down a fast rapid run. Action hoped that this would allow him to develop the confidence to challenge some of the more 'dangerous' runs up in New York State, in Canada, and even in Switzerland. After Mom and Dad had let both children off at the Kayak School, they took off for their first antique dealer, the Old Red Barn Inn.

Alice found a nice table and chair that appeared to be waiting for her, so she sat down, opened her lap top and said."Yesterday I was all excited about joining you for today, Action. But now that today is here, I have changed my mind. I will play cheerleader for you. If you need my help just let me know."

And she settled into her own mental world within a few seconds. Obviously she was not going to take any kayak lessons. She had enough cold white water to last her for a long time. And her research was super fun. Action waved goodbye and went up the hill.

Action went to the school office to check his registration. He was registered for the 10:00 AM class, but the instructor had some car trouble and he would be late; therefore the lessons would begin at 10:30 AM. He had about forty five minutes to wait. So he walked up to a grassy knoll which had a lovely view down into a Big Mole Valley, so he lay down on the grass. As he relaxed he began to wonder just how he had gotten into this kayaking binge. And then he remembered her and last summer. A memory he could not forget.

'It all began at 8:30 on a June Sunday morning when I decided to ride my bike from our Arlington, Virginia house over to Georgetown University to see if the grades for my spring course Introduction to International Law were posted yet. I was beginning to lean more and more toward the international arena so this grade was very important to me. The traffic was zilch so I was moving rapidly down Military Road, turned left onto Chain Bridge, crossed the Potomac River, entered Georgetown, and turned again left onto MacArthur Boulevard.'

'As I flew down MacArthur Boulevard, near the Georgetown University overlook, with the Potomac River and old Canal down on his left, I heard a shout for help off to my left. I immediately I hit my brakes, jumped the curbing with my bike, and ran onto the sidewalk on the left side of the road. I heard the shouting again and spotted someone down near the ten foot wall from which the ground dropped away into the old Canal and then on down toward the Potomac River. That person was struggling with a kayak which had slipped down over his head and was sliding, bodily, toward that wall and the water. From the road to the top of the wall the distance was only about fifty feet; it was a good forty five degree slope and the wet ground made the climb up from the old Canal treacherous. And that person with the kayak was losing the battle. In a few more seconds he would be in the water. I hopped off my bike, and in three strides I had one hand around the arm of the sliding person, with my other hand I grabbed the kayak, and the two of us slowly worked our way up to the sidewalk near the road.'

'Finally the kayak was firmly established lying up against a tree; and the kayaker was firmly sitting of the flat curbing of the sidewalk. We began to catch our breath and looked at one another. Neither of us knew what to say.'

'The kayaker was female, tall, slim, very pretty, and in her early twenties. And I was immediately attracted to her.'

She looked me in the eye and said, "Thank you. May I buy you a cup of coffee. There is a very nice coffeehouse on the corner near Chain Bridge"

'And with the kayak over my shoulder and the young lady pushing the bicycle we headed up to the corner. After parking both the kayak and bicycle near a window so we could keep an eye on them, we entered the coffeehouse and sat near the window. When the waiter came we ordered two coffees. And a new world began.'

After a few moments of silence, finally she spoke, "My name is Jane Bergman. And I want to sincerely thank you for rescuing me back there. I was on my way to a cold bath and maybe worse if you hadn't slid down the side of that bank like a leopard and grabbed me."

'And we sat there for a minute or so simply absorbing all of what had happened so quickly.'

"My Father is a diplomat and I have gone kayaking in several countries but this is the first time that I have really been in kayak trouble."

I asked, "How many countries have you lived in?"

Jane answered, "I have lived in Argentina, Japan, Ireland, and right now my parents are in Switzerland. I usually go back and forth, living in my parent's house when I am here. I am currently going to summer school at Georgetown University; that is why I am here for the summer."

After a pause, she continued "I am in my third year majoring in linguistics."

I said, "I am still curious. Did you learn kayaking?"

She responded, "Yes. When I was sixteen years old my Father gave to me a kayak as a Christmas present, and then purchased a membership in a local kayak club. For the next few years I went kayaking every weekend that the weather allowed. My older brother said that my kayak was the best boyfriend that I would ever have. And unlike boyfriends, it would never give me any trouble or let me down. But what he didn't know was that if it did let me down that you would be there to pick me up."

'And then she quickly looked away as her face turned crimson. I thought that color looked good on her'.

And then she added, "By the way, what is your name?"

'Now it was my turn to be embarrassed. I had been too interested in her and forgot my manners. So I quickly made up for lost time.'

"My name is Action Dekker. I live across the Potomac in Arlington, Virginia with my Mother, Father, and my twin sister, Alice, who is a computer freak. My Mother is a school teacher at the North Arlington Middle School. And my Father is the Director of Intelligence for the Blue Ravens Security Firm. They are the largest and best private security company in the USA. I am currently in pre-law school at Georgetown University and hope to enter GU Law School this fall. My GPA is 3.6. My sport is tennis. But I have always wanted to learn kayaking."

'Actually I had never seen a kayak up close until twenty minutes before. But it was only a small non-truth, because I was looking for another sport to play. My interest in tennis was diminishing, so kayaking could be that new sport.'

And Jane asked, "Are you a good player? And would you like to play some mixed doubles tennis next Saturday morning at the GU tennis courts? My regular partner went home for the summer. So I am in need of a good partner. We would be playing against two very excellent players who have played in several tennis tournaments. Each has won at least one regional championship."

"I also have played in regional tennis tournaments but never won one," I responded. 'So there was no way I could say no to such an open challenge from such a lovely lady. I simply rearranged my previous plans for that next Saturday.'

And I remember how I responded, "Only if you let me buy this coffee; and if you teach kayaking."

'And that was my very clever maneuver.'

And the male spider suddenly found himself in his own trap. What he did not know was that after making love the female spider ate the male spider.

'That next Saturday it had been tennis, which Jane and I won of course. The next day, Sunday, I got my first kayak lesson in a calm water area just below the massive rock rapids called the Great Falls on the Potomac

River. And the rest of the summer was spent for tennis on happy Saturday mornings and kayaking on happy Sunday afternoons.'

And then he heard the call to his group to come and begin their lessons at the kayak pier. So he went in pursuit of his future. But he enjoyed the new challenge tremendously. If he wanted to keep up with Jane, who had several years of experience on him, he was going to have to concentrate and run fast or do the fast run.

The kayak is a small human powered boat which has a covered deck and a one person cockpit covered with a spray cover. It is propelled with a double-bladed paddle held directly in the hands of the paddler. For thousands of years it was used for mostly of the transportation and hunting by the natives of northern Asia, North America, and Greenland. Today it is generally associated with recreation. There are many types of kayaks. Today, Action would be learning from the whitewater kayak.

The morning of this first day of lessons Action remained most of the time on the flat calm water. He learned the necessary terminology about the parts of the kayak, about the associated equipment, how to use various strokes for in the water and out of the water maneuvers. He also learned rescue procedures and certain rolling techniques. He practiced until he perfected the wet exit, bracing skills, straight line paddling, angle paddling, and changing of positions while paddling.

After lunch Action was skilled enough so that he moved on to learning eddy turns, peel-outs, ferrying, ruddering, surfing, the famous Eskimo role, etc. And during the latter part of the afternoon he took and passed the necessary skills tests. So tomorrow, he and two others, who also passed the tests, would make their run on a low degree of difficulty rapids for forty five minutes. If successful, they would then exit the water, lift and carry the kayak for about an hour while following a trail over a mountain ridge which had lots of trees and rocks, re-enter another rapids area, re-launch the kayak, and proceed down a more difficult rapids at their own speed until the end of the skills and endurance examination. Usually the last rapids took a continuous two to three hours.

So it was indeed an evaluation of a person's capacity to kayak down unknown whitewater runs. Those who passed both days were awarded the American Canoe Association accreditation certificate. This certificate would allow one to attempt about eighty five percent of the whitewater runs within the USA. The most difficult runs, such as in upstate New York, first required an ACA refereed and certified experience on several lesser difficult runs, and then with success he could move up to the big ones. Jane was already qualified for the big ones. He needed to hurry so they could travel together to the big ones.

And where was little sister, Alice, during the physical exercise of her big brother? She was in her own mathematical world of allegoric reactions and interactions.

Mom and Dad, on the other hand, were checking out as many antique dealers as they could in the two short days. A one half hour drive took them to the Old Bright-Red Barn Inn. This was a very large red barn shaped structure with lots of open exhibit space scattered over three floors. It sold classic-authentic-unique antiques. They had a wide variety of American classical antique furniture including living, dining, and bed room sets, light fixtures, grandfather clocks, player pianos, nickelodeons, victrolas, gramophones, tavern bars, apothecary cabinets, iceboxes, jelly and spice cupboards, and on and on.

Janet commented, "This is all very nice but it is not what we are looking for is it?"

And Dave replied, "I was thinking exactly the same thing."

They had walked and looked for two hours but just did not find anything that they wanted to buy. So they hopped into the car and moved to the next antiques dealer on their list.

Their next stop was called the Fierce Golden Medusa Head Antiques Mall. They stopped and entered the main corridor entryway and looked around. It was indeed a large covered mall arrangement that advertised many quality antique dealers. Each dealer had from five hundred to one thousand square foot of display space in separate rooms all of which opened onto the main corridor. And each dealer seemed to be exhibiting antiques from different areas of the world. They strolled through shops that exhibited Egyptian, Greek/Hellenic, Holy Land, Roman, Byzantine, Islamic, and Chinese coins, vases, statues, icons, jewelry, and more.

Janet pulled Dave aside and said, 'I don't like most of these antique things. They are just not my cup of tea. Let us go on."

This was a fascinating antiques mall, but again it did not have what they were looking for at this time. So they left from antiques number two.

It was lunch time and Dave was still recovering so he was eating light; he had skipped dinner last night because of his head injury. From any injury or physical problem his stomach always seemed to recover first. He was not sure whether his head had recovered. But his stomach felt fine. So they spotted a nice little restaurant on the road, stopped and had sandwiches and colas. After lunch they took out their antique dealer notes and began making afternoon plans.

Janet said, "I am getting tired of walking. It is already after 2:00 PM. We need be back at the Lehigh River Gorge around 4:00 PM to pick up the children. It gets dark early you know. So let us get organized."

Dave agreed, "Our first priority is European antiques. It is more probable that we can find your end tables with such an antique dealer. I too do not want to walk through two or three more malls. Look over your list and see if you find anything that looks European."

Janet carefully checked her list and responded. "There are several but they are more than a one hour drive, I think."

Dave also looked over the list and spoke up, "Here is a place called Victorian Red Rose Antiques."

"Where is it located?"

"It looks to be about thirty minutes from here, and it is back towards Stroudsburg and closer to the Lehigh River Gorge area."

"Then why don't we give it a try. Are there any other European sounding names in that direction?" She added.

Dave spotted another. "Here is one called the Commonwealth Antiques. But it might be too far."

"OK. Let us give the Victorian antiques first chance and then consider the Commonwealth antiques if we don't find something first in Victorian antiques."

Dave finished by saying, "I have a feeling that we will find lots of nice antique furniture at Victorian Red Rose Antiques, and that we will find your two little stands."

"I agree," she returned. "But if we don't find the correct ones we could continue antiquing tomorrow."

And she gave her husband that I love you smile. And he knew he was being reminded of who wore the pants in the family.

So they climbed into the car and headed out again.

They drove until they found the Victorian Red Rose Antiques, parked the car, entered the building, met by a little, lovely gray haired woman who was dressed in Victorian style clothing.

Dave glanced at Janet and said, "Yes, this is it. I can tell from the look in that little old lady's eye that she knows what we want and will find it for us immediately."

"I want to look first. Let us ask her later," Jane responded.

Dave just nodded and they started looking around. The first thing that caught their eye was a sign beside the entry door that read 'Fine European Furniture, Antiques, and Collectables'. They again looked at each other, grinned and began to check out this rather moderate sized family establishment which had been dealing in European furniture for more than fifty years. And it did have a wide variety of European, not just English Victorian antiques. They thoroughly enjoyed strolling through Europe of a couple hundred years ago.

Jane could even name most of the lovely and some just old pieces of house furnishing such as: Queen Anne armchairs, a 19th century three seat sofa, a Victorian chaise lounge, eight English spoon back chairs, an old wing inlaid armchair, Victorian wing-tip arm chairs of differing design, a birthing chair, a nursing chair, a drop arm sofa, an 18th century oak coffer, a Victorian mahogany, a King George III bow front chest of drawers, a matching pair of 19th century small French bedside cabinets, an Edwardian pearl inlaid display cabinet, a Victorian rosewood buffet, spindle back dining chairs and matching table, a set of six Victorian dining chairs with Hepplewhite design. They spent more than an hour just looking and walking and sitting and talking, pretending they were guests in some medieval castle in Europe. On their salaries it was all just a dream.

Sitting in a large wing tipped Queen Anne armchair, Dave spoke up, "We are lucky. I'm certain that if we were rich our house would be filled such wonderful furniture. And then we would need to buy a lovely large Victorian stone house in Georgetown to go with the furniture. It really brings the past back to life. I never cared much about history. But sitting here in this old, hand carved and beautifully preserved, chair, I feel very comfortable. Hand carving is an art almost extinct. No one knows how to carve in hard wood, like oak or hickory anymore. And the time it takes to carve such furniture, people don't want to pay the extra costs. Machine made is always cheaper. Plants and animals are on the 'expect to become extinct in the near future' list. Wood carving artists and hand carved furniture are already extinct."

Janet looked Dave in the eye and said, "I love you. You know you can really be philosophical sometimes. You are always surprising me."

Dave responded, "It probably has something to do with the recent homogenization of my brain." And then they both laughed out loud.

Jane walked back to her favorite aisle and toward the pair of 19th century small French bedside cabinets. She asked, "Do you think these will match the Italian coffee table if we put the table in front of the camelback couch on the living room wall under the large window? And we could place the two cabinets, one at each end of the couch? By moving the two wing-tipped Victorian chairs to the opposite wall the room would be in excellent balance. With the other two arm chairs we could then seat seven people. What do you think?"

Dave did not have the capacity to visualize such things like Janet did, so his response was, "I had that arrangement in my mind also, so I agree with you."

And Janet turned away, smiled, and walked toward the front of the building. "Let us talk with the Victorian Lady and see what shipping arrangements are available."

She asked, "Do you ship to the Washington, DC area?"

The lady replied, "Yes we do. Shipping costs are based upon distance, but this summer we are offering free shipping within one hundred and fifty miles."

They got out the maps and calculated a distance of one hundred and forty two miles to their house in Arlington, Virginia.

"You are in luck. Shipping will be free."

Dave commented, 'Well I guess that settles it. What else can we do? We have no choice but to purchase those two lovely cabinets and have them shipped. They will arrive in five days. I will not be home then, but you will, so?

And Janet was ecstatic as she had been looking for something like these for several years. Good things happen to those who have patience or something like that. They paid with credit card and gave the shipping address. With smiles they walked out of the building, climbed into the car and quickly took off to pick up the kids. Because Janet was happy, Dave was happy.

They arrived at the Lehigh River Gorge shortly after 5:00 PM. Action and Alice were waiting. They picked them up, headed out, and each told of his successful day. So they decided they should celebrate. And this time Alice had spotted the restaurant that was the logical place for a festive occasion. Near the White Wolf Mountain Lodge there was an International Pancake House restaurant. And after the money that they just dropped today, Mom and Dad totally agreed that this was a place they could afford. Besides, after prime ribs, pancakes were Dad's number one favorite. So, with a champagne free celebration, substituted with a standard wine, they ended a happy, successful day.

Near the end of the meal, after the waiter had removed all of the dirty plates and had brought four fudge-lime sherbet desserts with coffee, Dad starting looking around the table and started meeting everyone eye to eye. They were sitting in a corner in a round booth and away from the crowd. They sensed something was up. They could tell that Dad was getting serious. Did he really have something important to talk about, or was his homogenized brain acting up again? Each grew quiet, stopped eating, and stared at him.

He began, "I have something to tell you. It is a secret that I have been keeping all of my life. And now it is time that I share it with you. You must never tell anyone what I am going to say or many people will get hurt. I do not know who my Mother or Father are. Therefore you do not know your Grandmother or Grandfather. Grandmother Sylvia Dekker, apparently, purchased a pre-embryo in a fertilization clinic, had it implanted into her womb, carried and gave birth to it. I am the result of what she purchased. Apparently, she and her husband, Roy Dekker, do not know from where this pre-embryo came. The sperm and ovum were given by people they did not know, and the security arrangements are legally protected with special coding; this means I, we, will never know who my genetic Mother and Father are. Sylvia and Roy Dekker were very good to me and gave me lots of loving. But I always sensed that they were not my 'real' parents.

As I was growing up, and even to a lesser extent today, I have been having dreams of me in strange places. These were places that I had never been to nor even seen. Only during the past couple of years have I been able to put the dreams and my feelings into perspective. The guy in those dreams was my brother – four brothers to be more exact. Yes, I am an identical quadruplet. Last Thanksgiving the four of us finally all got together for the first time in our lives. They are all nice guys. I liked and enjoyed their company for the few hours that we had together. This was the first and only time in forty plus years that we had even seen each other."

And Dad looked around to see if they were each still with him. By the three puzzled expressions he knew they were.

Jane spoke up, "Why did you not tell us before?"

Dad responded, "I had been suspicious for a long time. I had been investigating the possibility of identical twins for the past four-five years. I had been accumulating data or evidence about what I assumed was a genetic impossibility, a double identical twin situation. First I found one 'twin' and I was finally able to find the 'other two twins'. They were living in New York City, New York, Des Moines, Iowa, and Indian Nest, Florida.

But I only really believed it when we were all together in the same room at the same time. There were actually four identical men, each large in size, each with red hair, each with green eyes, each with a cleft in the left ear, and possibly produced from the same pre-embryo. DNA fingerprints are currently being made to confirm that we have the same DNA and are legally genetically identical."

Jane asked, "I think there is more isn't there?"

Dad smiled and said, "Yes. Since there are four men, this means there are four families, wives and children are involved. One of my brothers is a lawyer; another is a medical researcher of genetics and twins; the other is a minister/environmentalist. They think that the fertility clinic must have made a major error during the implantation procedures. We do not know what. To our knowledge there is not nor ever has been four genetically identical babies born to four different mothers in four different places at four different times, who grew up separately, and only found each other in adulthood. They think that we could take this fertility clinic to court and sue them for several hundred million dollars. But to accomplish this we would probably have to reveal our secret. The news media could make all of us into freaks. So think about all of this for a few minutes, and give me your questions and opinions."

There was indeed several minutes of thinking. No one really wanted to go first. Was the quadruplet thing good or bad? What difference would it make?

Finally Mom went first, "This does not change anything. When I told you that I did not have a Mother or Father you did not reject me. Do you think that I will reject you now that you don't have a Mother or a Father? Are we going to pretend that the children do not exist because they do not have any of four grandparents? Don't forget I still have my home children and my house children. Those orphans that I grew up with are even more precious to me because they did not have parents. Loss of parentage is not loss of the world. Love may begin with parents, but it does not end there. And love also begins outside of parent-child relationships. Do Action and Alice love each other more or less than we love them? In fact I have seen much stronger brother-sister love relationships than parent-child love relationships. Not all parents love their children like they should. You do not need a Mother or Father for me to love you. That is ridiculous."

And some tears started to form in some eyes. As Alice and Action looked at Dad they tried to get their thoughts translated into word.

Action finally spoke up, "It is OK Dad. I still love you too, even if you don't know who you are. It is all right to be a Father without ever having been a son." And he gave Dad a big grin.

"Yeah," agreed Alice. "Who needs grandparents when you have the greatest set of parents in the world? Besides, I'm sure that none of my university buddies have a Dad that can break a 5,000 pound boulder into dust with one ten pound head."

Dad looked around. Everyone was grinning from ear to ear, but with obvious tears. And he didn't know what to say to top off his clan.

After it appeared that each had given his first thoughts, Dad said, "Let me summarize this genetic conference. You guys still love Mom and I even though we don't have parents? OK. It's a deal. We will continue to love you even though you don't have grandparents. Is that a deal?"

Mom spoke up, "We can think about this and discuss it again can't we?"

"Of course," said Dad. "We four identical brothers will meet again in a few weeks and discuss everything again and try to develop a plan to move forward with. "

They all chuckled. It was a good short break from Washington. They finished their desserts and headed back to the Inn for a good night's sleep.

* * *

On Monday the Dekkers completed their vacation as planned. Action finished his kayaking school and received his ACA certificate. Mom and Dad were successful in their search through the vineyards and wineries. They found several excellent wines at reasonable prices. And Alice went with Mom and Dad, sometimes in the vineyards, sometimes in the wine storage caves, sometimes into the wine sellers' chalets, and sometimes in the car with wireless on-line. Each Dekker finished up his last day of vacation and sort of started thinking about the new year which would begin Thursday. Both the identical quadruplets and the several hundred million dollars seemed to have been forgotten.

* * *

They arrived home around noon on Tuesday, had lunch, and then each member of the Dekker family went in his/her own separate way.

# 19 – Resolved?

Aaron had finally completed a series of DNA fingerprint tests which proved (legally) that all four were identical positive. Each of the four brothers was linked by his genes but of course not by life experiences. Aaron had sent a series of written tests and data forms to each brother. Each filled out the material which listed his behavioral characteristics and life choices such that Aaron could start compiling data for his nature versus nurture books. And now each brother had to make a very difficult decision. Each had excellent rapport and numerous positive life experiences with his 'Mother' and 'Father'. Each loved his Mother and Father. And each was certainly emotionally linked to his parents. Which was more important, genetic linkage to his brothers or emotionally linkage to his parents? They each had to consider the possibility that each might have to chose between the two types of linkages. Emotions are always subject to change. In general, genes do not change. Most normal children are linked both emotionally and genetically to their parents. The four brothers were not normal.

Just what did each have to lose and what did each have to gain by declaring that each was not a descendent or from the direct lineage of his Father? What would each Mother and Father lose or gain by declaring that each son was not in lineage of his Mother or Father? And what about the emotional stress on the identical quadruplet's children when such 'lack of lineage' information became publicly known? Was their Father a bastard? Were they bastards or only bastard's children? And then were their children bastards of bastard Fathers?

During the past few months each family had several discussions about this situation. Was it important to them to try to correct the official records, or would everything be better off if just left alone? There were indeed many possible legal problems such as inheritance rights. Eventually, each family came up with their own answers.

* * *

The genetically linked quadruplets had been spirit communicating and exchanging E-mails regularly for quite some time. They were becoming emotionally linked and badly needed to confront the place where this tragic problem began. With the only evidence available, they had focused on the Jackson Fertility Clinic in McLean, Virginia. It appeared that this evidence came from only one source, the personal papers of Mary Armand, Aaron's Mother. Those papers also provided data to prove that James and Mary Armand, who were both now deceased, had taken out legal adoption papers for Aaron Armand. This implied that he was not their genetic offspring; otherwise such would not have been necessary. The other three brothers, William, Charles, and David, had not confronted their 'parents' concerning their genetic relationships. So they did not know if they were genetically linked to their parents or had been legally adopted. This could become another problem. Whatever, the group decided to take the easy way out. First they would confront the clinic. And then, if not satisfied, they would talk to their parents.

Therefore, Aaron Armand, William Bassinger, Charles Collingswood, and David Dekker found themselves dressed as Mardi Gras Indians, complete with masks, in the very crowded dining room at the House of St. Louis hotel on Bourbon Street, during the peak of Mardi Gras on February 26, Fat Tuesday. They were waiting for Dr. Anthony Jackson, MD gynecologist, co-owner of the Jackson Fertility Clinic in McLean, Virginia, and son of the previous owner of this clinic Dr. William Jackson. They had agreed to this clandestine meeting to protect the identity of the four male identical quadruplets probably produced in this clinic.

* * *

In 1699 the French Canadian explorer Jean Baptiste Le Moyne Sieur de Bienville landed just south of what is now New Orleans. He named the little peninsula Pointe du Mardi Gras. The Fort Louis de la Louisiane was built on this spot in 1702. And nearby in a settlement called Fort Louis de la Mobile the first Mardi Gras was celebrated the following year.

Mardi Gras means literally Fat Tuesday in French. Such celebrations were held in ancient Rome. They have been associated with the ancient Jewish Passover. Now they have been recreated in the new world several hundred years later, most extensively in Rio de Janerio, Brazil and New Orleans, Louisiana. They represent a celebration during the period between Epiphany, or the 12th night, and Ash Wednesday, which is the Wednesday before Easter Sunday. It ends at midnight on Tuesday night, the night before Ash Wednesday.

New Orleans was established in 1718 by Jean-Baptiste Le Moyne. By the 1730s the Mardi Gras was regularly celebrated there. In the 1740s, a carnival and elegant dance balls were introduced. Then early in the nineteenth century the celebrations diminished. It was not until after the American Civil War, in the 1870s, that New Orleans began to grow again and revitalized the Mardi Gras celebrations. The colors of purple, green, and gold were established as official colors. A Mardi Gras song was completed and played. A Mardi Gras flag was designed and flown all over the city. Floats, marching bands, and entertainment units developed an extensive multi hour parade complete with prizes. Many private Krewes (clubs) were established and were responsible for sponsoring and building the many floats; they competed viciously for the best float prizes. And King Cake parties became common. These were parties with small cakes which contained small toy babies inside. They represented the gifts from the three wise men who visited Baby Jesus when he was born. Again there was much competition for the best King Cakes. Ninety five percent of the Mardi Gras festival was accomplished by volunteers; it was held on the streets without monetary charge; hence the title of the 'Greatest Free Show on Earth' was attached.

* * *

The Mardi Gras festival is currently held throughout down town New Orleans. But the heart and soul of New Orleans and New Orleans jazz music is Bourbon Street. Bourbon Street is a small narrow one lane wide pedestrian only (original) street of the city. The street is only a few blocks long and has fifteen to twenty open air restaurant/bar/jazz haunts. Bourbon Street is one continuous, twenty four hours a day, jazz festival. A different live jazz group in a different bar every one hundred feet. Bourbon, beer and Creole spicy food is the way of life on this famous street. David booked a suite at the House of St. Louis Hotel where the brothers and the representative of the Jackson Fertility Clinic would hold a critical meeting concerning the brothers' births.

* * *

During the first couple weeks after the first of the year, each of the four brothers had completed a couple rounds of family discussions concerning

285

the genetic problem. And they had become so good with their nightly spirit communications that they continuously exchanged opinions concerning the problem. It was interesting in that they had only partial control of the communication that they were sending. One brother could not 'talk' with just one other brother, each always heard everything. If brother A did not like the opinions of brother C, he could not tell this to brother B and brother D without brother C hearing him. So each 'discussion' was very positive. It required each brother to see only the positive attributes of each of the other brothers. Without disagreement there was only agreement!? The final unanimous agreement was to meet and talk with the owner of the Virginia clinic.

So the lawyer William from Iowa was to contact the owner and request a meeting and an explanation for 'their presence on earth.' The security expert David from Washington would design a clandestine meeting of this owner and the four of them. The medical researcher Aaron from New York would bring the two 'legal' documents and prepare a medical argument to counter or challenge whatever this owner might say. And the minister from Florida would pray that everyone would come out a winner from the meeting.

William Bassinger of the law firm of Jansen, Peterson, Birmingham, Bassinger and Associates wrote the following letter:


***Dr. Anthony Jackson***
***Director of the Jackson Fertililty Clinic***
***1512 Dolly Madison Road***
***McLean, Virginia 22150***


***Dear Dr. Jackson:***

*I am writing to you about certain fertility procedures that your clinic performed on Mrs. Mary Armand, Mrs. Dorothy Bassinger, Mrs. Susan Collingswood, and Mrs. Sylvia Dekker on or near July 20, 1975. Each of these women received a pre-embryo implant from your clinic near that date. Nine months later each of these ladies had normal healthy baby boys who have now grown up and have families of their own. Of concern is that it has recently been established that each of these men are genetically identical quadruplets. How could this have happened if each of the above mothers received a different implant on different days? It could have happened if each of the above mothers received the 'same' implant on the same or different days; or other explanations may be possible.*

*The sons of these four women would like to know what happened concerning the implantation procedures to their Mothers at or near July 20, 1975. They ask that you please check your documents and record books and inform them of the specific procedures and events on those implantation days, specifically with regard to any irregularities that might have occurred. They also ask to talk with the key physicians and laboratory personnel that were involved during the implantation procedures on their Mothers. If you cannot give to them satisfactory answers to these questions, they will initiate a torts law suit against you and your clinic in the neighborhood of 500 million dollars.*

*I respectfully await your immediate response.*
*Sincerely,*
*William Bassinger, Esq.*


Four days later William Bassinger, Esq. received the following letter:


*Mr. William Bassinger, Esq.*
*Jensen, Peterson, Birmingham, Bassinger, and Associates of Law*
*564 Grand Avenue*
*Des Moines, Iowa 50371*


*Dear Mr. Bassinger:*
*Thank you for your enquiry concerning the successful fertilization procedures performed on Mrs. Dorothy Armand, Mrs. Dorothy Bassinger, Mrs. Susan Collingswood, and Mrs. Sylvia Dekker by the Jackson Fertility Clinic on or near July 20, 1975. We have opened our files and are investigating the procedures and events which occurred at that time, almost fifty years ago, with these women; we will be happy to meet with you at your convenience, and share the results of our investigation. However, during that time my Father, Dr. William Jackson was the Clinic Director; he died three years ago from liver cancer. The Chief Technician was Mr. George Wilson, who died several years ago. So there are no key clinic personnel from that time who are available to talk with you directly. I am sorry.*

*Sincerely*
*Anthony Jackson, MD*

When William received the response letter he immediately spirit communicated with his brothers. Then David asked William to set up a rendezvous with Dr. Jackson and his lawyer for five weeks later on the eve of Ash Wednesday in New Orleans. It would be the peak of the Mardi Gras festival. Everywhere would be very crowded and everyone would be wearing masks and costumes and partying and partying and partying. William did as requested.

David gave specific instructions via spirit communications and registered postal mail to his three brothers. Each of them was to cut closely or shave off his red hair and don wigs from dark blonde to brown in color and to also color their eyebrows accordingly. They would each wear contact lens, brown in color. Aaron would wear wire frame glasses. William would wear a mustache and slightly bushy eyebrows. Charles should wear a Catholic collar, large black frame glasses and prepare to act as a priest. And David would wear a beard which would match his brown hair wig. Each would bring face masks that only covered around the eyes, so each could eat and talk with his mask on; and each could wear any type of costume he wished.

Each would travel separately, and make his own plane and hotel reservations for the two nights prior to Ash Wednesday, Monday and Tuesday nights. Everyone would then leave New Orleans on Ash Wednesday and return directly to his home. David reserved a suite at the House of St. Louis Hotel directly on Bourbon Street in New Orleans for the same two nights. No brother should stay at this hotel during those two nights. William had informed Dr. Anthony Jackson that they would all meet in suite forty four in this hotel at 2:30 PM on February 24, the Tuesday afternoon before Ash Wednesday on February 25.

Thus the four identical brothers were sitting there on February 24, Tuesday noon in the large crowded dining room of the House of St. Louis Hotel on Bourbon Street having lunch and discussing the upcoming meeting. The streets were packed with partying people and the numerous beer-bars and pubs with jazz music kept the noise at a maximum. Apparently David, because of his Afghanistan experience which involved direct killing, ordering others to kill, and causing collateral damage involving several women and children, was the natural leader of the four, even though he was the least educated. Also today his professional responsibility involved protecting peoples' lives during much travel. David looked around at these three weird masked strangers, which were his identical brothers, but under their neat disguises.

David spoke up, "Did anyone have any trouble with their travel or does anyone need any help with accommodations? I know I put pressure on you with all of these disguises, but we could not again meet in the Blue Raven's Range Rover at Tyson's Corner Malls in Virginia. Why? Because the Rover will only hold four normal people; it will not hold four larger-than-normal plus two normal people. In addition when trying to avoid surveillance never use the same tactic twice, especially if it is successful."

And they all chuckled and relaxed as they remembered their first collaborative venture when the four red headed green eyed monsters from Mars chased the poor little marijuana users down the up car ramp.

And he continued, "Has anyone been here to the Mardi Gras before?"

Charles spoke up, "Yes, when I was in Atlanta University a group of we biology majors were working on a project just north of here and to the east of the Mississippi River but on the Jordan River. The area was badly polluted so we were trying to determine what and how. We were here during this time of the year. Because we were five guys, we decided to visit Bourbon Street during the Fat Tuesday. However, we were not regular connoisseurs of alcohol. We entered the Street around noon, and ate Creole food and drank several quarts of beer until dark. At dark the fireworks began from the huge river dikes which hold back the Mississippi River and the Gulf of Mexico, Bourbon Street is twenty feet below the water level. The dikes are only about three to four blocks away from the Street toward the Gulf. We five guys lay on the grass on the dike, looking over the water, drinking our beer, waiting for the fireworks, and went to sleep. We not only slept through the entire fireworks but we also slept through the entire night. The next morning when we woke up to the fireball sun, our heads were pounding such that we did not know where we were."

"And what did you do?" asked William.

Charles returned, "We were each given a quart of beer 'by friends who knew' and were told that if we drank more beer it would cure beer headaches."

"And it did the job didn't it?" replied David.

"Yes. Within an hour we could even see good enough to recognize each other."

David verified, "In the army we used that cheap headache cure almost every Saturday night, or should I say Sunday morning. I know it very well."

And the four of them remembered their school days when they competed with their buddies in that game, not always successfully.

David continued, "I know that we have been exchanging ideas over the past couple of months, and I know that these ideas have fluctuated with more family discussions, is it possible that we could each sort of summarize where each of us stand on the issue of anonymity versus notoriety?

Hearing a general ok – yes – yeah, he suggested, "Iowa Bill, I think you are not only the biggest of the four of us, though not the oldest by one day. Would you care to go first?"

William agreed to begin, "I am in sort of a hot spot. Jenny, Steve, and Stef have accepted the situation but they tend to blame my Father and Mother for keeping something like this secret for forty plus years. The children in particular have begun to not want to see their Grandfather or Grandmother nor to go to the 'family' farm house for dinner on Sundays, a tradition that we have maintained most of the past thirty to forty five years. I also do not know if I have been legally adopted by my parents. I have not tried to corner them and they have not volunteered any information. You have to realize that this 'family' farm is two hundred and fifty acres in size with an excellent commercial base. It grosses several million dollars every year. And it is valued in the more than several hundred million dollars. My 'family' has lived on this land for more than one hundred years. I would be stupid to do something to alienate my parents such that my wife and I, and my children, do not benefit from this 'family' farm when my parents pass on. Unofficially I am the fifth generation of Bassingers to work this land. Steve will be the sixth generation. So I am sort of stuck between a rock and a hard place."

David said, "Yes that is a real problem. Aaron, do you have a similar problem?"

"No. My parents did legally adopt me," Aaron answered. "I have a copy of that legal adoption paper with me. And, right now, only Josephine, Hype and Hope know about the four identical quadruplets. Just the opposite is true for us. As a family we never lived, only visited, my family estate every few years over the past twenty plus years. We do not have any long term friends in the neighborhood. So the children see no problem with whatever we decide. Jos and I can even see the possibility of using several million dollars to expand our research base in our Twinning Center. We could ask many scientific questions with such private money; questions that we cannot ask with government monies because twinning does not directly relate to a disease. That is what we are thinking right now."

David responded, "It seems we have one point for anonymity and one point for notoriety."

No one laughed! It was a serious problem. This was going to be more difficult than anyone thought.

"My situation is again very different," spoke Charles. "You know that my Mother died in a house fire when I was four years old. After that my Father and I became real pals. However at twenty two years of age I had finished the university and entered the seminary. At that time my Father sort of disowned me, fell in love with a twenty one year old girl, married, and eventually had two 'legitimate' sons. One of his sons is younger than my children. My Father's wife pretends that I do not exist, and I think my Father wishes that I did not exist. So I do not have solid emotional nor genetic links with my Father. Janice, Sam, and Sara have visited my Father in Atlanta twice, and he has never been to our house in Florida. So we have no strong feelings either way except to say that, yes, if we had a few million dollars we could pursue our efforts to help protect the environment from the increasing world-wide pollution."

David explained his point of view. "You will remember that I was born from Caucasian parents who lived in a Mexican-American neighborhood in San Diego, California. Like many of my Spanish speaking buddies I left home at the age of eighteen years. When I completed my army years I went directly to the Washington, DC area, found a super job, and never left. I have been back to see my parents once every few years. However, during the past decade my Father has been drinking heavily and taking various kinds of drugs. He lives on a major drug trafficking route from Mexico to the three big western California cities. And with so many of the wrong type of buddies, all drugs are easy to come by. My Mother is rather sickly and is aging rapidly; she has given up on life and we don't expect her to live very much longer. The last time I went to see them was more than four years ago, even though Mom and I talk frequently by telephone. My emotional linkages have badly degraded over the past few years, and I guess I do not have a genetic linkage."

"I really do not know where this leaves us," David continued. "Certainly we are divided and we all have good solid legitimate reasons. Does anyone want to add anything or ask any specific questions? It is near 2:00 PM, so if you are ready we could go on up to room 444 and wait for Dr. Anthony Jackson and his lawyer, Ms. Janley Davis. We can continue this conversation later."

There did not seem to be anything else to talk about for now. After the meeting they would spend this evening together, again discussing the problem and maybe make some decisions. So they left the dining room and went upstairs to await the clinic people.

* * *

At 2:30 PM the Jackson Fertility Clinic people arrived for the 'meeting of the century' for these identical male quadruplets. Each was introduced to each. The brothers did not remove their masks or their crazy costumes; while Dr. Jackson and Ms. Janley Davis, the Clinic's lawyer, were dressed in business suits without masks. At the end of the meeting, three hours later, no one had altered their 'uniforms'.

William Bassinger had issued the invitation so he began first:

"Thank you for agreeing to come so far to meet with us. Bluntly, we want you to help us solve the problem of the birth of four identical boys to four different women in four different cities at four different times in 1976. These four women all received pre-embryo implants in your clinic approximately nine months before these four births. These/we four boys did not even know each other for the first forty plus years, and only recently 'discovered' each other. DNA fingerprinting tests have been completed on all of us, and we are legally identical quadruplets. What we want from you is a possible explanation as to what happened in your clinic that might have caused this very unusual situation. What have you found from the investigation of your records?"

Dr. Anthony Jackson responded, "Thank you for the invitation to fascinating New Orleans at the peak of Mardi Gras. I have often thought about coming here at this time, but I could never find the time. I was only twenty eight when I starting taking over the reins of the clinic from my Father who suffered for more than nine years with a malignant hepatoma. But it is a delight to see you four big strong, professionally successful, and happy family men who originated from the efforts of my Father's and my Grandfather's clinic. They would be happy to see the true fruits of their lifetime efforts."

And the four fruits gave strange looks to each other.

Opening his briefcase and taking out several folders Dr. Jackson continued. "We have completed the review of our records for a Mrs. Mary Armand, Mrs. Dorothy Bassinger, Mrs. Susan Collingswood, and Mrs. Sylvia Dekker in May, June, and July of 1975 with regard to their pre-fertilization hormone programs, the subsequent implantation of pre-embryos, and short term follow up before they were released to go to their homes to have their babies (you) in their local hospitals with their local doctors. According to our records Mrs. Mary Armand was using hormone program B and at 9:00 AM on July 28, 1975 was implanted with pre-embryo NG-1536. Mrs. Dorothy Bassinger was taking hormone program D and at 9:00 AM on July 28, 1975 was implanted with pre-embryo TL-7498. Mrs. Susan Collinswood was on hormone program D and at 2:00 PM on July 28, 1975 was implanted with pre-embryo SK-3371. And Mrs. Sylvia Dekker was using hormone program A and at 2:00 PM on July 28, 1975 was implanted with pre-embryo RR-8122. All four women did very well. No one had any bleeding or pain. In a couple of weeks each developed 'pregnancy like feelings', which is normal, and was subsequently released to their chosen local obstetrician several weeks later. Our follow up showed that one normal baby was successfully delivered by each lady."

Dr. Armand spoke out, "Let me recap. According to your records each woman had a different pre-embryo implant on the same day. If this is true it does not explain how each woman gave birth to the 'same genetic' baby boy about nine months later."

Dr. Jackson responded, "I agree with you. Let me also inform you about the special report which was attached to the original records. This is a special report written and dated on December 4, 2001. It was written by Mr. George Wilson, who was the Senior Technician during those months in 1975 when the previously referred ladies were being serviced. It is his signature which is on the transfer forms for all four of the pre-embryos that were implanted into the previously referred to ladies. Unfortunately he was killed in a traffic accident on December 5, 2001. I will now read this special report from Mr. George Wilson:"

**"*Special Report Concerning Pre-embryo Implantation on July 28, 1975***

***Jackson Fertility Clinic, McLean, Virginia***

***December 4, 2001***

*I am very sorry but I have been living with this error of judgment on my part for the past 30 years, and I must tell somebody or I can no longer live with myself. Since I retired last year I have done nothing but think about this problem.*

*Between March, 1961 and September, 1994, I worked as a technician at the Jackson Fertility Clinic in McLean, Virginia. Between January, 1973 and January 1998, I was the Chief Technician at this clinic in charge of in vitro fertilization, growth of blastulas, and preparation of blastulas or pre-embryos for implantation into hormonally prepared women. During this latter twenty years I prepared more than five hundred blastulas which I know to have produced normal healthy babies; my live gifts to the world. However during the week of July 20, 1975, a strange thing happened. I was growing four blastulas in preparation for implantation on July 26, 1975.*

*Two days before, July 24, 1975, there was a heavy electrical rain storm which knocked out the electricity in the area around the clinic for several hours. The clinic's emergency electrical systems kicked in late. The electricity was off in the pre-embryo incubators for almost twenty minutes. I did not discover this until the next morning of July 25, 1975. Of the four blastulas that were growing in the four 10 ml Falcon flasks, three had died. In the fourth flask I found four small blastulas, but they tested healthy and were growing very well. I reported to Dr. William Jackson that the pre-embryos were not ready and needed more days of growth. He trusted me and readily agreed that the implantations could be delayed for two or three days.*

*I separated them and put each one of the four small blastula into four different Falcon flasks, grew them for two more days, labeled them with the original numbers of the dead blastula, and provided each of them for implantation to each of the four ladies on July 28, 1975. I told no one about my switching of blastulas or labels, and no one else was involved.*

*A year later I checked the numbers and learned that the implantation of each blastula/pre-embryo had produced a successful healthy baby. As always I did not learn the names or addresses of my new little ones. My mind cannot handle that kind of knowledge. Sometimes my blastulas fail and the babies do not live. So I want to remember them as living blastula numbers and not as real people. However in this case I was afraid all four would fail. I am happy that each lived. I only hope that the four IDENTICALS never find each other. If they do, this special report will help explain what happened during the week of July 20, 1975.*

*Written and signed by Mr. George Wilson"*

[And the room remained quiet for a few minutes. Everyone was seeing this from a different perspective.]

"Do you have any questions?" asked Dr. Jackson.

And there was dead silence again for several moments. The brothers looked at each other and then sort of nudged Aaron into saying something. He had been digesting all of this, looking for flaws or double talk, seeking a non-logical sequence or false event, but it appeared to be an honest confession of a psychologically bothered man, who was now dead. What he had heard could account for the fact that there were four genetically identical babies born to four different women in four different locations on four different days. Each woman had simply been implanted with the same/similar blastula or pre-embryo and then had gone home to grow and give birth to that baby. It is amazing that the four 'babies' even found each other.

Finally Aaron spoke up, "Dr. Jackson, do you think that the events and procedures that Mr. Wilson alludes to could account for the situation of the four of us sitting here today?"

"Yes," Dr. Jackson answered. "It is a most logical explanation for four identical quadruplets and their separation for half a life time. I am very sorry, but I think that this is the truth."

And Aaron again asked, "When you implant the maturing blastula into a woman, at what day post fertilization of the sperm-ovum do you routinely use?"

Dr. Jackson replied, "We routinely use nine to twelve days after fertilization. After day fourteen it is too close to the beginning of gastrula formation. Implantation of a gastrula frequently results in non growth or loss of the pre-embryo, spontaneous abortion."

So Aaron said, "For the procedures used in your clinic during the week of July 20, 1975, the initial fertilization procedures for the blastulas must have been near July 14, 1975, because the routine implantation time had been scheduled for July 26. The death of the three blastulas and the splitting of the only living blastula apparently occurred on July 23. At that time there was probably around a few million cells in that single surviving blastula. When this living blastula split into four blastulas, each probably retained a few hundred thousand cells. If all of the cells doubled in number every two-three hours, each remaining blastula would be a few million cells by the new implantation date of July 28. So it is probable that the four, each containing approximately three to five million cells, maturing blastulas would have been implanted. Is it not routine to have a maturing blastula with several million cells when it is implanted? The four surviving maturing blastula that were implanted would have much smaller than normal."

Dr. Jackson agreed, "You are correct. I agree with you and your numbers are perfect. Routinely a maturing blastula of several million cells would be implanted. Why the smaller maturing blastula was implanted into each of your four Mothers, I do not know. And I do not know how we can find out as the Chief Technician that was involved is no longer with us."

None of the other brothers had questions, it was just too technical. It appeared that Aaron agreed with the explanation that Dr. Jackson presented; it would logically explain the identical quadruplicate state. The bottom line was that a highly qualified and experienced technician made a bad judgment which resulted in their sharing of chromosomes and genes; and souls?

They talked for a little while longer. It appeared that the clinic people had been honest. They made a mistake via the wrong decision of their technician which resulted in the four way problem. The six of them were amiable in their discussion; no animosity surfaced. Soon Dr. Jackson and Ms. Davis expressed their thanks for the kind hearing that was given to their explanation of events which occurred in their clinic during the week of July 20, 1975. The clinic's lawyer had not said one word. They shook hands and graciously left the hotel room. The four identical quadruplets remained.

* * *

The fellows took off their masks and wigs, down dressed to become comfortable, and started a re-hash of the technical aspects of the last hour. First Aaron spent several minutes giving his brothers a biology lesson. Once they were all comfortable with 'how we got here,' they now needed to discuss the anonymity versus notoriety thing.

Where do they go from here? Dr. Jackson was honest and open. 'Yes, we did it. We made a mistake. And we are sorry.' Can one ask for more than that? Legally, yes!

Lawyer Bill started, "During our discussion just now, I positioned myself so I could watch the lawyer Ms. Janley Davis. I had previously checked up on her background. In 1989 she received the Bachelor of Laws degree from Duke University and was number one in her class. So she is very bright. For the past nine years she has been employed full time by the Jackson Fertility Clinic. This implies that the Clinic has probably been having some legal problems over the past few years. As you know we tape recorded the entire meeting using a speaker from the ceiling light fixture. I have now turned this recorder off. So everyone is free to talk."

"While watching Ms. Davis I could tell that she suspected that we were recording everything, that is why she was very quiet; and I think she had coached Dr. Jackson to say the minimum. Our recording will not serve as court evidence; it is only good for us to know what and where such evidence is stored. Also you may have noticed that they gave to us no copies of the material that they read to us. We would have a very difficult time obtaining copies of those private medical patients' records and the specific procedures used in their clinic. It would all be protected by copyright laws and medical restriction laws. In addition, we will never find out the names of the anonymous donors of the ovum and sperm for our common blastula. We will never know who our genetic Mother and Father are. In addition, I think that she also recorded the proceedings via a tape recorder inside her briefcase. So any type of audio intimidation or the obtainment of certain hard facts will be very difficult if not impossible."

Bill looked around to see if everyone was following what he was saying. He had everyone's eye and ear.

He continued, "If we should decide to take the Jackson Clinic to court on tort charges, there will be only one judge making the decision. They have prepared the grounds for this. Why? They have taken the first step in admitting that they were at fault and apologized. They made no attempt to cover up. Also, forty years ago may be pushing the statute of limitations for such problems. Don't forget. In a torts case it is not the contract that is in question, the Jackson Clinic fulfilled the contract to provide babies to these four women, our Mothers. They were successful in these contracts. We are living proof of their success."

"The case must show injury to a person, property, reputation or the like, and prove that the injured party is entitled to compensation. A single, usually very experienced, judge will decide this. And Ms. Davis has carefully prepared the field for battle if we so desire."

And he looked around again to be certain all brothers were together. "One last thing, if we do go to court, I am certain that Ms. Davis will leak this 'four identical quadruplets found after forty plus years' to the news media. So, in my professional opinion, the anonymity will disappear on day one, and we may or may not be very successful on the notoriety side. So let us think through the situation again and talk about it."

Aaron asked, "Are you saying that we may lose the court case?"

Bill responded, "No, I am not saying that. I am saying that we now have a whole new ball game. Before this meeting we assumed that they were the big bad guys who did not know what they were doing and made a big goof. Now it is obvious that they are only little bad guys, they did know what they were doing, all four of us are living proof that the Chief Technician knew what he was doing. We are big, strong, healthy guys who are successful in life. We even have strong, healthy offspring who are moving toward success in life. Are we supposed to expect more from this clinic?"

Aaron answered, "Yes, they could have informed our Mothers that they gave each of them the same pre-embryo, so they would know what to expect. Our Mothers still do not know about the four identical quadruplets. Yes, I understand. Only the technician knew and he did not tell anyone until 40 years too late. I suppose he is the one at fault."

"And he is dead," Bill returned. "We cannot take him to court. We cannot sue him. We can only sue the clinic. And do not forget, this technician was not only successful with us; he was successful with several hundred other test tube babies like us. We would have much difficulty proving him incompetent."

Dave spoke up, "Are you suggesting that we do not try to take the Jackson Clinic to court because we might lose more than we will gain?"

"No, I think that if we go to court, the first thing that will happen is that the Jackson Clinic will inform the news media. Having brought to the world four identical quadruplets which are successful is not necessarily bad publicity for them. With the proper public relations spin they could even milk this for positive publicity for the clinic. I doubt if any other fertility clinic, anywhere in the world can claim such success. If we were all small physically and mentally, we would have a better chance for compensation. The judge will certainly take all of these factors into account when he judges our tort case."

And Bill continued, "My feeling is that we would win a torts case against the Jackson Clinic, but that the judge would not award millions of dollars. I do not know if we are even talking in the hundreds of thousands of dollars range. And we must definitely prove injury. So, each of you, please make a list of our injuries, to ourselves, to our family, to our property, to our reputation, or to others such things."

Dave spoke up again, "I have another question for anyone, perhaps Aaron. I have been reading about the lives of twins. There are several books about twins, but none about quadruplets. If I understand correctly; there are identical twins who lived together all of their lives; there are identical twins who were separated at birth and lived separately most or all of their lives; there are fraternal twins who lived together all of their lives; and then there are fraternal twins who were separated at birth and lived separately most or all of their lives. Is this correct?"

Aaron responded, "Those are the general patterns in twinning, yes."

"OK," Dave continued. "From my reading I understand that identical twins who lived together all of their lives had extensive communication systems from spirit, to verbal, to hand signs, to facial expressions, etc. Identical twins who were separated at birth and lived separately most or all of their lives had some extra communication systems, but not so extensive. While fraternal twins regardless of upbringing had almost no special communication systems. Now we, I guess, fall into the category of identical twins who were separated at birth and lived separately most of our lives. Yet it seems to me that we have very good extra communication systems, our spirit communications are very good. We are also learning to communicate with our eyes and hands. And I think that if we were together more we would also develop additional means of communications. As of now we have lived separately but can communicate almost as if we lived together much of our lives. How do you explain this?"

The minister-environmentalist Charles spoke up, "I have been wondering about that too. And I believe it is related to the soul that we share. I believe that the soul enters the newly fertilized ovum. Therefore the cells in the one blastula, which had split into four blastula, would all have the same soul. The soul does enter very early during embryogenesis. Also the production of four from one was caused by God, lightening. He had his reason for doing this. So I think He gave us extra communication skills to be certain that we would find each other. This would partially explain the many dreams over the years and why we now have better communication systems than would be expected from identical twins living separately. I think that all four of us may share the same soul."

And there were puzzled looks all around. No one said anything. Obviously each IDENTICAL had his own concept of God and Souls. And this just was not the time to begin such an open ended discussion. So each remained quiet; no one responded to this new concept. What is a shared soul? How and when does a soul arrive? How can a soul be shared?

Finally Dave said, "I suggest that we each talk with our parents. Except for Aaron, we do not know if we have been legally adopted by our Mother and Father. We now have evidence that each of our Mothers did have a pre-embryo implantation at the Jackson Clinic in McLean, Virginia on May 28, 1975. Bill, if you would please make three more copies of the tape of this meeting we could use this to help 'remind' our parents about the events on that date. Maybe after such a private meeting, we could again talk with our children to give them the complete truth, and then we four could meet again or simply spirit communicate, whichever appears to be necessary. What do you think?"

That appeared to be a good idea, and they agreed. Then the subject was switched to 'smaller' talk. After all this was only the second time in forty years that the four of them had sat down together, so there was lots of catching up to do.

# 20 – Specific Gene Stem Cell Therapy for Diabetes

The following year Aaron Armand was feeling very tired. He was working his usual ten to twelve hours days and many weekends, but this was normal. He did not consider himself old therefore he should not be getting tired so easily. He had a couch in his office and he began use it to take afternoon short (fifteen to thirty minutes) naps. Over the next few weeks he began to lose weight, but was eating normal. He began to have blurred vision, urinated many times during the day and at night, was always thirsty. He even seemed to have less energy after eating high energy granola bars and drinking coffee or cola, both contain caffeine stimulant. Then one day Jos was working with Aaron in his office.

They were side by side, heads together, and going over some key numbers when she stopped, looked at him and said, "Aaron, open your mouth and breath into my face."

He did this and she responded, "You have acetone breath. You smell like my nail polish remover."

Aaron looked at her and said, "Are you certain?"

When she nodded his response was, "Oh no, then I have diabetes! I don't have time for diabetes!"

Jos looked him in the eyes and said, "Your eyes are very blood shot. Are you thirsty all of the time, and go to the bathroom more than normal?"

And the two looked at each other, nodded, and Aaron went to the telephone and called one of his colleagues, Dr. Peter Jacobs, Professor of Endocrinology at Columbia University Medical School and Presbyterian Hospital, and asked for an appointment as soon as possible.

The next morning he went to the Department of Endocrinology and was examined by Dr. Jacobs, who was a typical serious physician with Italian metal rimmed glasses, bright blue eyes, and a very bald head. After the general physical exam and medical history questions Dr. Jacobs spoke, "Aaron, yes you probably have number two, diabetes mellitus. You have the general symptoms from lethargy, to blurred eye vision, to mental fatigue, excess liquid consumption and excess urination. We need to run the appropriate blood tests. Even though you may know them, by law, I must explain them to you anyway." And he explained the procedures.

Aaron gave his approval and signed the permission forum which would allow the hospital to test his blood for diabetes.

They took a routine blood sample then, and would test for the normal routine sugar level. Then he went home and would return tomorrow morning without eating anything after 8:00PM tonight. The nurses would then give him the glucose (glucose is the major blood sugar) tolerance test as follows:

They would immediate take another blood sample and test his fasted blood sugar level. He would then drink a lemon flavored drink containing a total of 75 gram of sugar. They would take blood samples ½, 1, 1 ½, and 2 hours later. A normal non-diabetic person would, at these times, have levels near 180, 160, 130, and 120 mg sugar per 100 milliliter of blood plasma (liquid part of the blood when all of the cells have been removed). A diabetic person would have, at these times, approximately 400, 350, 300, and 250 mg sugar per 100 milliliter of blood plasma. Why?

Immediately after eating, blood plasma levels of sugar will go above 120; this is normal after eating a meal containing carbohydrate-sugar. But immediately insulin is released into the blood and the insulin activates certain insulin binding receptors (special docks or parking places) on cell membranes which open the sugar doors and allows sugar to leave the blood and enter into body cells, again immediately. Good insulin action should decrease the high levels of blood sugar completely down to fasting sugar levels well before two hours. Normal fasting or pre-meal levels are near 100 to 120 for normal people.

The next day Aaron returned and gave his 'fasting' blood sample. Then he immediately took the glucose tolerance test by drinking the lemon flavored sugared drink and giving the required blood samples every half hour. A couple of hours later the test results were complete. All tests of blood levels of his glucose indicated he had chronic diabetes, the common form of diabetes in adults.

If he did not receive therapy soon he would have acute heart and eye problems. All body muscles, including the skeletal and heart muscles, require insulin to open the sugar entry doors. So walking, breathing (diaphragm muscle), and running each require insulin. The liver and brain do not require insulin for sugar entry. So long term damage is slower to develop there.

Dr. Jacobs gave Aaron the bad news and continued, "As you know Type I, juvenile diabetes, is usually found in babies and young people. It results from a loss of the insulin gene or insulin gene function. Either way children with this type of diabetes do not have blood insulin. If insulin is injected after a meal, everything works perfectly normal and such self controlled injection systems are routinely available for Type I diabetes. All over the world millions of children are using self insulin injection systems without major problems."

"You have Type II, chronic diabetes. This is commonly found to be high in older or in fat people who perform little exercise, or it may occur within family units. The exact cause is not known, but there are genetic linkages. Type II is a very different problem when compared with Type I."

"Insulin is produced from the insulin gene only in the beta-cells of the pancreas. It is produced as a large molecule which is then cut into three proteins. Two of proteins are sewed back together; the third protein is discarded; and the new double protein is finally secreted into the blood as the active form of insulin – so insulin production is complicated. It is also secreted upon a high blood sugar signal – no sugar, red signal, no insulin secretion; sugar above 120, green signal, secretion of insulin."

"Insulin has two other brother protein molecules called insulin like growth factor I, ILGF-I, and insulin like growth factor II, ILGF-II. These also bind to some, but not all receptors on all types of cells. And there are five types of these insulin binding receptors, all of which bind insulin, some of which bind the ILGFs, but not all are associated with sugar entry doors. Some of the insulin binding receptors-ILGF binding receptors are involved in cell growth programs not sugar entry. So, again there are more complications in the overall action of insulin function. Insulin is involved with sugar entry into body cells and body growth. Both systems are critical for children, but the growth is not so critical for adults."

Aaron asked, "So you are saying you do not know what causes diabetes II; you do not know what or where is the molecular problem located; you do not even know which cell to examine, beta cells, heart muscle cells, skeletal muscle cells, brain cells. Do you at least recommend some type of therapy for diabetes II?"

Dr. Jacob smiled and answered, "Of course. First we will challenge your insulin response system to see if injected insulin will lower your high sugar levels at a normal rate of decrease. We will evaluate your physiological responses to see if you then have normal drinking and urinary desires, normal vision, normal energy levels, and no physical or mental fatigue. In other words, with normal insulin are you now normal? Will supplying the insulin by direct injection give proper signaling? This is where we will begin our therapies. This testing will require about a week. But you can continue to work and just walk over to our clinics during the day for injections and blood sugar measurements as a control."

"Are you then thinking single gene therapy using stem cell carriers?" asked Aaron?

"So you have heard about our research," responded Dr. Jacob. "Good, I will give you some of our recent research publications and you can read about it and understand it better. Yes, if you pass all of my tests I will probably recommend this therapy to you."

Aaron responded, "No. I have heard about this experimental therapy but I do not understand it. In our research we begin by simply taking adult interior cheek skin cells using a cotton swab. Then we directly extract the DNA and make a variety of DNA tests such as DNA fingerprinting. I know very little about intact cell studies, and I know almost nothing about stem cells. I know this area of research is moving very fast. I have a feeling that if I learn about it today that by the time you get ready to try this therapy on me it will be out of date."

OK. Let me brief you about stem cells and then about single gene therapy," replied Dr. Jacob.

"First what are stem cells? They are cells in our body which have the potential to become other types of cells or even become complete humans. During the first few days of the pre-embryo growth all blastula cells are stem cells."

"This is about all that I know about stem cells," replied Aaron.

Dr. Jacob replied, "Then let us start there. There are three types of stem cells: totipotent, pluripotent, and multipotent. Totipotent stem cells are found in the days one to three in the blastula; each of these cells can develop into a complete person. Pluripotent stem cells are found in the days five to fourteen in the blastula; each of these cells can develop into one of several hundred types of mature body cells if properly treated. Multipotent stem cells are found in aborted fetuses and in adult stem cells from within our own bones; they can develop into a few types of mature body cells if property treated. Do you have any questions?"

"So from the three types of stem cells you chose the type that will work best for the therapy that you need to do. Thank you. I did not know any of this?" said Aaron.

"Dr. Jacob continued, "Now there are more than one hundred stem cell lines, most of which have been developed from aborted fetuses. Use of and the growth of stem cells have been going on for more than fifty years. Many scientists have taken individual cells from such sources and grown many types of sub-stem cells. Some of these are currently being used to treat a variety of diseases such as various immune diseases, cancers such as leukemias, and neurological damages and diseases; much cloning therapy is accomplished using stem cells."

Aaron asked, "For your patients what do you use?"

"We get our best results with the multipotent or adult stem cells taken from the hip bone of our patients, said Dr. Jacob. "Let me explain this."

"With multipotent stem cells there are three types of stem cell transplantation systems in use today. First is autologus where the source of the cells is the same person as being treated. We would take stem cells from your hip, treat them and then give them back to you. The second system is called allogneic and it uses stem cells taken from an 'immuno-matching' donor – someone who has a very similar immune system as yours such as a family member. The third is called syngenic and it uses stem cells taken from your twin, if you have one."

"In all of these transplantation systems you take stem cells from the hips, multipotent or adult stem cells, is that right," asked Aaron?

Dr. Jacob replied, "Yes. The concept is to use stem cells which would give the least immune response such that we do not need to use a group of anti-immune drugs for the next many years."

Aaron said, "I understand that you would take the multipotent or adult stem cells from my hip, treat them, and then give them back to me to cure my diabetes. Now how do they cure my diabetes?"

"Good question," said Dr. Jacob. "If we inject these cells directly into the pancreas in the region of the (insulin secreting) beta cells, the so treated stem cells would have a greater than fifty percent chance of growing into beta cells that can synthesize and secrete insulin. The stem cells become beta like cells."

"However our research goes one step further. We use single gene therapy with the stem cells. As you probably know you cannot inject a gene into a cell, you need a gene carrier mechanism. So we use virus XO5 that carries the insulin gene into the stem cells. We then inject the treated stem cells, which are carrying the virus XO5 insulin gene, into the beta cell region in your pancreas. This increases the percentage that the newly injected stem cells will indeed synthesize and secrete insulin. But the procedures are still experimental. We usually do this to children with Type I diabetes. We do not often give it to an adult with Type II Diabetes. Now we would consider doing this only if the tests prove that you have Type II diabetes. The alternative is to use regular self injections of insulin, usually after every meal, for the rest of your life."

Aaron sat still for a few minutes digesting all of this new knowledge. Finally he replied, "So if the tests prove that I have Type II diabetes my choices are taking multipotent or adult stem cells from inside my hip bone, giving them a virus with an attached insulin gene, and injecting those so treated stem cells into the beta cell region of my pancreas, OR self injecting myself with insulin every time I eat a candy bar. Is that correct"?

Dr. Jacob concurred. "That is essentially correct."

Aaron continued, "If I remember correctly, single gene therapy was working very well several years ago with several diseases. In cancer therapy they were synthesizing viruses which would infect only cancer cells. And they placed into the virus a gene/drug which could block a function in the cancer cell and kill it. In the first experimental trials there was much success in killing the cancer cells, and since the virus did not infect the normal cells the therapy caused minimal side effects on the patient. But after injecting the same virus several times over several months of therapy the patient's body developed anti-bodies to the virus and killed the virus and destroyed the cancer gene/drug. So a new virus with the same single anti-cancer gene had to be synthesized and given to the patient to be certain that all of the cancer was killed. In theory it was excellent, but in reality the human body eventually developed immunity against the viruses, killed the viruses, and interrupted the single gene therapy. Now such therapy is very expensive. Every new virus carrying an anti-cancer gene costs a few hundred thousand dollars, and several such viruses may be needed to complete the killing of one cancer."

Dr. Jacob thought for a minute and nodded in agreement, and then replied, "That should not happen here because the virus that carries the insulin gene remains inside the stem cells. It does not get into the blood like the virus carrying cancer drugs. The body will not 'see' the virus. It is already hidden inside the stem cell. So the body's immune system should not see it and make anti-bodies against it. The body's immune system 'sees' only foreign 'things' which enter into the blood. We rarely need to give anti-immune therapy to patients who have received the virus carrying insulin gene inserted into a person's own stem cells which were then injected into the beta cell region of that person's pancreas."

Aaron thought for a minute or two and said, "It sounds good to me. Let me have some of your team's research publications so I can learn more. Maybe we can use stem cells and single gene therapy in some of our research projects someday. I want to learn more about them."

* * *

Two months later Aaron went into experimental single insulin gene stem cell therapy. Samples of his bone marrow from the inside of his hip bone were removed, his multipotent stem cells were prepared, the virus XO5 carrying the insulin gene was infected into the stem cells, and the so treated stem cells were injected inside beta cell region within his pancreas. Within a couple of days his elevated blood sugar levels decreased. The blood sugar levels remained between 100 and 120 mg of sugar per 100 ml of blood for the next few days. So he stopped taking any insulin injections, but kept the diabetic injection kit in his desk drawer. So far so good.

But diabetes was a disease to be controlled every minute of every day; it would not be totally cured. So it still required careful regular monitoring of blood glucose levels to guarantee that the insulin was working properly. Aaron would do this for the rest of his life.

After it appeared that his therapy was working, even though he would need a couple of more pancreatic injections of the virus containing single insulin gene stem cells, he was pleased with the long term outlook. And he started thinking about his family, the other three identical brothers. Since this disease had genetic overtones; it did run in families. The only 'genetic family' that he knew about, having no known mother or mother, were the identical quadruplets. If he had diabetes Type II, maybe they might develop it or already have it as the symptoms were rather subtle, except for the acetone breath of course.

* * *

As the months went by each family had accepted the situation for what it was; each wife had three extra husbands and each child had three extra fathers and several extra brothers and sisters as well as cousins. This was not necessarily a bad thing. So communication became more open and they spent time together, but only two families at a time. Twins were not so unusual, triples more rare, and identical quadruplets very rare indeed. So they limited themselves to twinning situations or each brother vacationing with one other twin brother and his family at a single point in time. This arrangement worked out extremely well.

During this time, Aaron spent much effort in explaining to his brothers about diabetes, its genetic linkages, procedures for diagnosis, and options for therapy. He even sent to them documents describing the disease and talked directly to each one explaining about the need for continuous control and that there was not a complete cure of this disease, called diabetes Type II. He finally received responses from each of them, one by one such as: 'leave me alone I will have a check up!'

Bill, the Iowa lawyer was the first to respond. He had been having the lethargic, excess water drinking and urination symptoms for several months. So he went to an endocrinologist at the Des Moines General Hospital, took the glucose tolerance test, and failed the test. He had diabetes Type II. His endocrinologist did not perform the type of advanced therapy that Aaron had access to, but he was willing to collaborate with Aaron's doctor if possible. Aaron talked to Dr. Jacob. The response was of course. In fact, if the two of them were identical twins he could even use Aaron's virus XO5 single insulin gene multipotent stem cells as they would be immunologically identical. The Iowa doctor sent a sample of Bill's stem cells to Dr. Jacobin in order to legally confirm that the two men were identical twins. They were, so Aaron's insulin gene stem cells were sent to Iowa and Bill's therapy began immediately. It was successful.

A short time later Charles spirit communicated and said that he also had a couple of the symptoms for diabetes. He went to the Division of Clinical Endocrinology at the University of Miami Medical School and Hospitals for the glucose tolerance test. He did not fail but he did not pass. He had elevated fasting blood sugar levels but they dropped at a rate of a pre-diabetic. So he will return to Miami every six months to take the test again. In the meantime he would watch his diet and exercise more. He thanked Aaron and would keep him informed of his pre-diabetic state.

And last to reply was the biggest of the brothers who had a job that required him, in order to keep his job, to continue his three hour physical exercise program twice a week at the Blue Ravens farm up at Fredrick, Maryland.

Dave chided Aaron, "If you had previously come to work for me, and joined with me for my twice weekly exercise, you would not have a dietary sugar problem." He knew that Aaron no longer exercised on a regular basis.

And Aaron responded, "That is because you have a high fat meat diet. You should eat what your wife cooks, not what restaurant chef cooks."

Because Dave was on the road much of the time he ate at restaurants much of the time.

They had really become buddies over the few years that they had 'known' each other. Such an exchange of remarks had become commonplace.

# 21 – NATURE VERSUS NURTURE

During the past couple of years Aaron and his brothers met as twins, two at a time, with their families and got to know each other better. In general, people did not pay very much attention to one set of identical twins, so they successfully went 'public' in this way. Identical triplets or identical quadruplets attracted too much attention. So they played together as families with twin fathers. They quickly learned that the brothers and family members were extremely compatible. Several of the wives and children knew each other before the husbands/dads did. And it was sort of fun to play with two big red haired green eyed Fathers, and not just one running around with them. Because of the remarkable physical identicalness, it was not unusual for a wife to be saying something confidential to her husband, when half way through the private revelation she would discover that she was talking to her brother-in-law and not her husband. Often a child would ask a private question of his Uncle instead of his Father. But that just made it more fun. There really were no family secrets between the four families.

During these years Aaron had tested his brothers with several standard knowledge, preference, attitude, behavioral, and decision making tests. He documented the personal histories of each brother. And he had just finished accumulating, analyzing, and organizing the large amount of data. He now needed to sit back and document it into a double format. He would publish some of the data in medical research publications and he would design and write two books. The medical research publications would be heavy with science and loaded with technical terminology and new theories. Of the two books, one book would tell the personal story of the identical quadruplets. The second book would describe the similarities and differences as related to nature versus nurture. Nature referred to all phenomena controlled by genes and chromosomes. Nurture referred to all phenomena controlled by environmental learning throughout life. Phenomena include physical and mental characteristics, behavior and decision making, and all aspects of life as we know it on this planet. Of course he would never use any real names.

**Obviously the four of them were predominately products of identical nature; however each had had a very different nurturing.**

So late one evening, after he had completed his clinic rounds, he sat down at his office desk, opened his computer, brought up the data on the identical quadruplets, and started organizing it in his mind:

'I now have the necessary data, and enough confidence I think, to begin to start looking into some physical diseases such as diabetes, cystic fibrosis, Alzheimer's disease, Parkinson's disease, Prader-Willi syndrome, Angelman syndrome, muscular dystrophy, Huntington disease; psychological diseases such as violence, sadistic behavior, weapons usage, over aggressiveness; and human emotional relationships such as husband-wife, parent-sibling, boss-employee, and interfamily-family interrelationships; and especially decision making during major crises or under duress.'

'When the problem is only related to the genes, today it is possible to cure. But tomorrow, as the specific gene or genes are identified and their function is understood, it will be very probable to treat that problem with specific gene therapy. However, if the problem is only related to environmental causes, then these causes must be identified and removed or minimized within the mindset and life style of that person. Unfortunately, many problems are related to genes malfunctioning because of environmental problems.'

'Many scientists and physicians use this rational when they explain how one develops diseases, such as cancer. Nature or genetics indicates **predictability or potential** during life and **susceptibility** of obtaining a specific disease; high risk versus low risk. However many diseases require an **environmental insult** such as disease initiators like viruses, toxic chemicals, or obesity. In this way even a person with a genetic low risk may develop a disease if the disease initiator is continuously present in that person's immediate environment.'

'My personal area of experimentation is in trying to identify the interrelationships of human decision making. Why will this man never pick up a gun, yet this other man has no trouble killing many people with any automatic weapon? Why will this man beat up a woman, yet this other man would never even consider hurting a woman? Why is this father or mother the dictator of the family, yet this other father or mother is first and always a team player? Why does this person have no personal friends, yet this other person is gregarious to the extreme? Why does this woman need facial cosmetics and stylistic clothes to be comfortable in public, while this other woman prefers a 'clean' face and pays no attention to clothing styles?

Why does this person cheat and lie during many aspects of life, yet this other person would never consider cheating or lying about anything? Why does this person choose to play sports, yet this other person chooses to play musical instruments or sing? Why does this person choose the outdoors for leisure, while this other person chooses reading books for leisure? Why does this person love all types of pets and animals; yet this other person does not like any kind of household beasts?'

'And there are the opposite doubles in behavior/decision making patterns such as: aggressive versus passive personality, hyperactive versus low activity, talker versus listener, impatience versus patience, leader versus follower, rapid forward versus slow forward, mathematics wiz versus mathematics dunce, rapid language versus slow language learning, mechanical orientation – yes or no, nature orientation – yes or no. All of these doubles have multiple gene connections, probably gene packets which are involved. We have already identified several twins which are opposite in these behavior/decision making phenomena. So we have a good start analyzing possible gene packets which may be accountable for some of these opposite doubles.'

'The most difficult area of all is long term problem solving. Are all of these decisions simply a result of nature and nurture, and does this relationship not change with aging? How does a personal tragedy affect short term versus long term decision making? How does a professional tragedy affect short term versus long term decision making? How does a physical injury tragedy affect short term versus long term decision making? – and on and on'

'Now we four brothers carry the exact same genes. You only have to glance at us to see the exact same tall, large, strong bodies, the same handsome masculine face with Nordic clean shaven features, the exact same red hair and jade green eyes, cleft on the left ear, the same strong hands, solid body, and big feet, the exact same lion like movements when in motion (not fast but controlled, single directed, and confident). In fact we are so identical that when we picnic with our families we often confuse our wives and children, as well as ourselves. Ha! OK! So that is one result of each of us having the same sets of genes.'

'As children we each had a good, warm and loving home. Each parent thought himself/herself to be lucky to have a cute little boy and gave to him/us everything that they could. Our childhood and schooling were positive, except for Charles. Charles's Mother died in a fire when Charles was only four years old. He blamed himself and carried that burden all of his life. He turned to God to find help. He eventually left the big city, isolated himself in a small community in Florida and dedicated his life to helping both humans and animals. We other three have remained in the big city, and probably will for the rest of our lives.'

'And the rest of us also chose giver, not taker, lifestyles. I focus on trying to determine relationships between genes, behavior, decision making, and certain unsolved diseases. William devotes his legal world to working between the consumer, farmer, and the industry in the development and implementation of new and better food crops and foods, and new gene relationships. David spends every day determining ways to protect people from potential assassins and terrorists. And Charles gives every day to his flock, and tries to referee between the polluting farmers and city dwellers and the life blood of nature. We are givers, not takers. And we are each very successful in these very different professions. Plus we each took very different roads to get to the profession which we each choose for ourselves. Genes?'

'Each of our IQ scores was between 140 and 150, so we are intelligent but not brilliant. Devotion and hard work were common assets to all of us in finding and becoming a success in our chosen careers. Each of us is a medium alpha personality; we are not dictatorial, but we do influence group and family decisions by discussion and consensus, not by decree. In fact we each have wives who are physically similar and have very strong personalities. So each of us is lucky; this helps each of us maintain a consistency in making joint decisions regarding the children and future life problems. In other words, each of us has a democratic approach to behavior and decision making. Even with our large physical size, we never attempt to intimidate people. In fact, our good friends know this and frequently take advantage of our sort of pussycat character and talk us down in arguments.'

'We all grew up in a sports playing environment, not vocal or instrumental music. And today we each listen to different kinds of music, and have stopped playing sports. It is possible that the current lack of exercise by William and me during the past few years may have led to our developing diabetes; whereas Charles is outdoors most days rowing, canoeing, and walking through the Everglades, and David is required to perform regular exercises twice a week as a job requirement. Charles is in a pre-diabetic state while David has no symptoms, yet. Obviously we are genetically susceptible to this disease. We certainly need to follow a physical exercise program for prevention of diabetes'.

'And we each chose tall, slim wives with blond hair and blue eyes. They all have professions involving the teaching of science. They all met at Mothers for Science meeting a couple of years ago and did not realize that they shared the same husband.' And a big smile appeared on his face.

'Each has become a good strong lifetime partner. And we each have two fraternal twins as children, boy and girl, born in that order. Each boy has carrot red hair, almond colored eyes, is now near or over 6 foot 6 inches in size, over 200 pounds, strong alpha personality, is studying in a university for his chosen profession, and will be obviously be successful in life. Each girl has straw blond hair, jade blue eyes, near or over 6 feet tall and 120 pounds, strong beta personality, studied in a university for her chosen profession, and is also successful in life. Each child has chosen a different profession to enter. How those choices were made is not obvious. But they each chose universities based upon the professional offerings of that school and the family budget. However, no one is following in his parent's footsteps, so to say. The one possible exception is my son, Hype, who has begun medical school. So, each of we identical quadruplets have been successful, so far, in our family lives. And I would judge that each of our family members is currently successful. This is very important to the family unit.'

'One thing still puzzles me. Usually it is common for identical twins to have their own special communications such as hand signs, facial expressions, and secret words; and they can frequently send telepathic information for short distances. But most such communications occur during the waking hours; at night time they do not routinely communicate. And such special communications occur only between the two of them. In addition they rarely dream about each other. So they have a special communication, but it is not nearly as sophisticated nor as powerful as we four brothers have. I cannot explain this.'

'Currently each brother has only a couple of close personal friends but many family friends, prefer to vacation at outdoor locations, but do not socialize at large cocktail parties and social dinners. Only I do this for fund raising purposes concerning the Twinning Center. We are big fans of professional sports, but not pop music. Our wives are socially oriented only when it involves professional organizations. And the children are each following their own noses and play sports, are computer oriented, hang out with their friends, and listen to numerous all-flavored CDs or DVDs. Each family regularly attends church. So it appears that we are all rather focused on our personal lives. Maybe that allows for some of the success.'

'OK. These are the broad general similarities for us identical quadruplets and our families. Let me think through some of the general differences.'

'Each of us that are working in the city, William, David, and myself, wear suits or sports jackets and slacks to work every day. But we each prefer different styles, colors, textures, accessories, neckties, shoes, hats, and brand names. Some of these preferences are based upon each brother's income and some are related to each brother's professional responsibilities. Charles has no such set daily requirements; so his dress is more causal; but he does preach to his flock in a coat and tie. We all have very rather different life styles, different types of houses, different model cars, different types of house pets, and different ways to invest in savings and retirement systems. Certainly none of us has facial rings or body paint!"

'Now in thinking about aging, retirement, and dying. I have always been concerned about the concept of several people sharing the same soul; and therefore sharing the same death? If the splitting of our common blastula did occur at eight to twelve days post conception, and if a Christian soul entered the few days old blastula, then there was one soul present when the blastula split into four. Now does that mean that we four brothers have and share that one soul? Or did that soul split also and we each have our own soul? If we each have our own soul, then I assume it leaves each of our bodies when each of us dies. If the latter is true then retirement would be important only until our own personal death. But if we each have one fourth of a soul, and we share the rest of that soul with each other, what happens if one brother dies before the other brothers? Can a person even live with part of a soul? Or will all brothers die at the same time such that the soul becomes whole when it goes whichever direction? If the latter, death is not possible to contemplate for the four of us, let alone to understand.'

# 22 – RELIGIONS AND SOULS

The Reverend Charles Collingswood had spent much of the past several months doing his homework research. He thought Aaron was correct when Aaron had postulated that the four of them had come from the same blastula. What he then understood was that the four of them did come from the same blastula when the blastula split from one to four blastulas at eight to twelve days after conception or fertilization. And if the soul entered the blastula at a few hours after fertilization, it must have been there when the blastula split into four. Therefore the identical quadruplets would be sharing the same soul, or would they? He needed to learn more about souls and spirits in world religions, and especially in Christianity. So this afternoon he went out onto his screened-in mosquito-free porch, opened his lap top, took out his study notes of the past few months, and starting re-thinking through his recent homework:

'There are at least five major religions (several million followers each) and more than 100 minor religions in the world today. Some are several thousand years old. Some have come and gone. Some are recent. But each believes similarly and yet differently in the concept of the soul/spirit, how it was created and how it continues to live after bodily death.'

'First of all, what is a religion? A religion is any system of beliefs about a deity, usually involving rituals, a code of ethics, and a philosophy of life and death.'

'Let me begin with non-religion or Paganism.'

* * *

PAGANS AND PAGANISM

'The general consensus of the concept of Pagans is that they are someone who does not believe in an established religion, and are usually involved in more than one God. There are many interpretations of Paganism, all are internationally accepted or not accepted. Many of the ancient religions can be considered Paganism, for example:

Druidic religion is based on the ancient Celtic upper class beliefs,

Asatru religion follows the ancient pre-Christian Norse religion,

Wiccan religion is a pre-Celtic religion,

Neo-paganism could include Kemetism (ancient Egyptian), Hellenismos (ancient Greek), Religio-Romana (ancient Roman) and other traditional religions.

* * *

'There are seven general definitions of Pagans:
- Pagans consist of Wiccans and Neo-pagans
- Pagans are people to be hated
- Pagans are ancient polytheists
- Pagans follow Aboriginal religions
- Pagans follow non-Abrahamic religions
- Pagans do not belong to any main religions of the world
- Pagans are Atheists, Agnostics, and Humanists


There are probably more than one billion Pagans or non-believers in the world of seven billion people today.'

* * *

HINDUISM – 4000 BCE*

'About 6000 years ago Hinduism began in the Indus Valley in India. It is the oldest religion which continues as a main religion today. It is the belief in the unity of everything. It recognizes one supreme God, Brahman. It can also be viewed as a triad – one God with three persons: Brahma is the Creator, Vishnu is the Preserver, and Shiva is the Destroyer. And another interpretation of Hinduism is of henotheism in which there is recognition of a single supreme Deity and also several lesser gods and goddesses in various forms.'

'Hindus believe in a repetitious transmigration of the soul; the transfer of one's soul after death to another body. This produces a continuing cycle of birth, life, death, re-birth, re-life, re-death, and on for many lifetimes. Karma is the accumulation of one's good and bad deeds. Karma in your current life determines how you will live your next life. Through pure thoughts and acts one can each time be re-born at a higher level. If one continues on these tracts he can achieve enlightenment and oneness with God. Hinduism is not only the oldest, but it is the third largest religion in the world today. There are nearly one billion believers.'

* * *

JUDAISM – 2000 BCE*

'Near 4000 years ago Abraham made a divine convent with the God of the ancient Israelites to believe in and follow one God. Later another Israelite, Moses, led his people out of bondage from Egypt and received the Law (Ten Commandments) from God. Then Joshua led these people into the Promised Land; Samuel established the Israelite Kingdom; Saul became the first King; the second King, David established Jerusalem as the capital of Israel; and the third King, Solomon built the first temple to God. This temple was eventually destroyed and the Israelites or Jews were scattered throughout the world. Most of the Old Testament of the Bible relates the history of the Jews.'

'The Jews believe in one Creator who is worshipped as the only and absolute ruler of the universe. It is only He who monitors the lives of people and gives rewards or punishments. The Torah was revealed to Moses by God and cannot be changed. However God can communicate to the people by various prophets. The sacred **Tanakh** corresponds to the Jewish Scriptures and is referred to as the Old Testament by most Christians. It has three books: the sacred **Torah** is given in Genesis, Exodus, Leviticus, Numbers, and Deuteronomy; the sacred **Nevi'im** is Joshua, Judges, Samuel (2), Kings (2), Isaiah, Jeremiah, Ezekiel, Hosea, Joel, and Amos; the sacred **Ketuvim** contains Psalms, Proverbs, Job, Song of Songs, Ecclesiastes, Ruth, Ester, Lamentations, Daniel, Ezra, Nehemiah, and Chronicles (2). In addition the Jews have the sacred **Talmud** which was compiled in 450 BCE by the "Men of the Great Assembly" and contains many stories, laws, medical knowledge, moral choices, and advice for daily life. Today the Jews call their God by many different names including YHVH, Yahweh, Adonai, HaShem,…… Jews believe that they are the chosen people; they do not believe in the original sin of man; they believe the Messiah will come to them in Jerusalem, Israel, by entering through the East Gate, the Lion Gate; they believe at that time there will be a resurrection of all of the Jewish dead; and they believe that God's temple will be built again.'

'Although there are only about 15 million Jews today; they have had a tremendous impact on the world throughout history. One example is that both Christianity and Islam, the two largest religions in the world, originated from, and are based, on Judaism.'

* * *

BUDDHISM – 550 BCE*

'Nearly 2,550 years ago Siddhartha Gautama, the first known Buddha, established what today is called Buddhism. It is a train of thought that transcends the concept of a single personal God. It avoids the religious dogmas of theology; yet it covers both the natural and spiritual. Because of the suffering caused by destruction in life, believers vow to cultivate compassion and learn ways to protect the lives of people, animals, plants, and minerals. They attempt not to kill, not to let others kill, and not to condone killing of any kind anywhere in the world.'

'Buddhists believe in reincarnation of the soul and that one must go through cycles of birth, life, and death. After many such cycles, if a person releases his attachment to desire and the self, he can attain Nirvana. In general Buddhists do not believe in any type of God. They do not believe in the need for a special savior, prayer, or in eternal life after death. However during the many centuries Buddhism has integrated many religious rituals, beliefs, and customs into its thinking, depending upon the geographical area where it is practiced. It is no longer as homogenous as it was 2,000 years ago. Today, Buddhism is the fourth largest religion with 365 million followers.'

* * *

CHRISTIANITY – 20 CE*

'About 2000 years ago Christianity was started by a Hebrew named Jesus. Jesus, born of Joseph and the Virgin Mary, disagreed with the Jewish Rabbi, modified many of the currently accepted concepts of Judaism, traveled around Judea, and gathered twelve disciples. He taught his concept of his God to the people, performed miracles, quoted many parables of life such as 'love thy neighbor' and 'turn the other cheek', claimed to be the Son of God sent to earth to save humanity from its sins, declared that those who repent before God would be saved and their souls would join him in Heaven. He was convicted in the Roman Courts in Jerusalem, crucified, arose from the dead and told his disciples to go forth and spread his teachings. They did as is evidenced in the holy **New Testament of the Bible**.'

'Because Jesus based many of his ideas upon Jewish laws, most of the core ideas of Christianity and Judaism are similar. Christians accept the sacred Jewish **Tanakh** as the holy **Old Testament of the Bible**. Hence the Ten Commandments of Moses are also the supreme holy laws used by all Christians. However there are two major differences in which Jews and

Muslims do not accept. One is that Christians believe in the original sin (Adam, Eve, the snake and the apple), and that Jesus died in man's place to protect man from that sin. And two is that Jesus was fully human and fully God, and as the Son of God is part of the Holy Trinity: Father, Son, and Holy Spirit. Most Christians believe in Heaven, Purgatory, and Hell, where the soul will reside after bodily death. But the requirements vary within each type of Christianity, of which there are numerous Christian groups today.'

'There are over 30,000 Christian religious organizations in the world and about 2,000 such organizations in the USA. There are seven major Christian denominations and sects today. In order of size they are: Roman Catholicism, Eastern Orthodoxy, Protestantism, Anglican Communion, Pentecostals, Oriental Orthodox, Assyrian Churches, and others. Needless to say the religious dogmas, various liturgies, rites, rituals, ceremonies, formalities, observances, and protocols vary between and within the many Christian denominations and sects today. Christianity is the largest religion in the world with more than 2 billion followers.'

* * *

## ISLAM – 622 CE*

'1,350 years ago Islam was founded by Muhammad the Prophet in Makkah (or Mecca). It is the newest of the major religions, yet it follows the faith and teaching of Abraham, Moses, David, and Jesus. Muhammad simply claimed to be the last in this long line of prophets. Muhammad's role was to clarify, formalize, and purify the faith by removing ideas that had entered in error. Muhammad accepted the sacred books of both the Jews and the Christians. In addition the sacred **Qur'an** contains the words of Allah 'the One True God' as they were given directly to Muhammad from his God. The sacred **Hadith** is a collection of Muhammad's sayings from his teachings.'

'Muslims follow a very strict monotheism which has one Creator who is omnipotent and merciful. They believe in Satan who drives people into sin; the souls of sinners and unbelievers of Islam will spend eternity in Hell. Muslims who repent and submit to Allah, will be forgiven and their souls will go to Paradise. They honor those previous prophets, but believe that the concept of the divinity of Jesus is blasphemous and they do not accept it. Today Islam is the second largest and fastest growing religion in the world with more than 1.5 billion followers.'

* * *

'Now let me try to put some of this together. The world's five major religions all believe in the concept of a soul and its continuation after the death of the human body. The two major religions of Hinduism and Buddhism believe that the soul re-cycles many times through several bodies. The three major religions that are based upon the teaching of Abraham, including Judaism, Christianity, and Islam, are similar in that they believe that each single human body has a single soul, but upon the death of that body that soul goes to a special place where only souls can go, it does not recycle. These latter three religions believe in a single omnipotent God which creates the soul, places it into a person after conception while that person is yet in his mother's womb, and then sits in judgment of the life of that person at the time of his/her death. For a good life the soul is rewarded with heaven. For a bad life the soul is punished in Hell.'

'There is not a consensus about just when the soul enters the body, except sometime after conception. It could enter immediately, after a few minutes, a few hours, a few days, or a few months. Biologically, I guess when there is a body available to enter. So we must define a body. Before the days of science and the discovery of cells, tissues, organs and the like, a body was probably a living thing which could reproduce itself.'

'If I understand Aaron, immediately after fertilization or conception, not before, only a newly fertilized ovum or zygote can grow into a living person. Therefore a zygote must be the recipient of the soul. Hence the soul probably enters immediately into the zygote or certainly during early blastula. So, on days eight to twelve of blastula growth, when our blastula split into four blastulas, the soul was probably present. If this is true, we four identical brothers must share the same soul. Or were four new souls newly created and placed into each new blastula after the one split into four? How does this work? And what does all this mean? And if one of us dies, will we all die?'

'However such thinking leads to many other problems. Aaron is a Catholic, Bill is a Presbyterian, Dave is probably a Catholic by his Mother being Catholic, and I am a member of the Church of Holy Mary, but I do not know what my mother was when I was born. So probably our mothers do not share a common church denomination. I do not know what religions our fathers were. Or are our soul(s) related to our biological/genetic parents and their religions? Well at least I think we are all Christians. Why do we know so little about the origin of the soul, when every Sunday at church we focus on where the soul will go when we die?'

'I think that the Catholics somehow consider their God higher or better or something, so I really do not understand whether the soul for a child from a Catholic mother comes from the same source as the soul for a child from a Protestant mother or an Eastern Orthodox mother. I guess we could be from two Catholic and two Protestant blastulas.'

'But then again, if our genes came from an unknown donor whose religion we do not know, and as babies we were carried in women whose religion we do know, what does this mean? Is our soul based on the unknown donors of our ovum and sperm, or the 'mother' who carried us?'

'In addition, our common blastula was formed in a test tube, not in the womb of a woman of an Abraham based religion. We do not even know if our parents, donors of the sperm and ovum, were Christians. And if a soul entered our early blastula while it was still in a test tube, which Abrahamic soul entered, Jewish, Christian, or Muslim; or which type of Christian soul? Do we four guys share the same or different Christian souls? Or is there only one Christian soul? Can someone live with two souls or only part of one soul? What exactly is a multi-soul? What will happen to the others who share the soul if one soul-mate dies? Can the rest of us live with a partial soul? How does this all work?'

'There are many passages in the Bible that refer and support the idea that a life/spirit/soul begins in the mother's womb, and most international embryologists agree with this concept.'

"And the Lord God formed man of the dust of the ground, and breathed into his nostrils the breath of life; and man became a living soul" – Genesis 2:7.

"For He satisfies the longing soul, and fills the hungry soul with goodness" – Psalms 107:9.

"He did stretch forth the heavens, and lay the foundation of the earth, and form the spirit of man, within him" – Zechariah 12:1.

"You created every part of me, you put me together in my mother's womb: I will praise thee: for I am fearfully and wonderfully made: marvelous are thy works: and that my soul know right well: Your eyes saw my substance being yet unformed." - Psalms 139:13, 14, 15, 16.

"Before I formed you in the belly I knew you, before you came forth from the womb, I knew you" – Jeremiah 1:5.

"For what man know the things of a man, save the spirit of man which is in him? Even so the things of God know no man, but the Spirit of God" – I Corinthians – 2:11.

"And the very God of peace sanctify you wholly: and I pray God your whole spirit and soul and body be preserved blameless unto the next coming of our Lord Jesus Christ" – I Thessalonians 5:23.

'These Biblical passages support the concept of the spirit/soul forming in the 'man' within the mother's womb. However no specific timeframe for that formation, except 'within the womb', is apparent. And no specific description a soul's heaven or waiting place is given. Why?'

'So indeed these Biblical quotes support the beliefs of Abraham and his descendents, Jews, Christians, and Muslims, that God created man and spirit/soul and put them together while yet in the mother's womb. Now does each of these religions claim the same God and the same soul formation, or does each religion claim a different God (different names) and a different soul formation?'

'This of course now raises the area of questions about mixed religious marriages. First let me compare within Christianity. A Catholic is required to be baptized in the Catholic Church after birth, receive religious teaching from the Catholic Church, marry in the Catholic Church, give any children he/she has to the Catholic church, regularly confess his/her sins to a Catholic Priest, and have a Catholic priest say a eulogy over his/her body when he/she dies – all of this must and will be done only by 'qualified' priests of the Catholic Church. If these are accomplished by other priests in other churches it has minor religious meaning and your soul can not or will have difficulty entering heaven; maybe it will not even be able to find heaven; it could get lost. If your spouse is of a Christian denomination other than Catholic, this is not important enough for the journey of your child's soul, and you must give your child to the Catholic Church for the sake of your child's soul.'

'The Eastern Orthodox Church has the same mindset, via similar restrictions and requirements. Most forms of Protestantism do not have such possessive restrictions. So from this "only my church knows the real pathway to the real God," the concept is created that there is more than one God, more than one soul, and/or more than one path of judgment, and perhaps more than one heaven and more than one hell, within Christianity. This is all very confusing.'

'Now when one begins to compare marriages and children within the three mixed Abraham derived religions, Judaism, Christianity, and

Islam, the confusion is multiplied several fold. If your mother and father are from different Abraham derived religions, from where will the soul of their child come and where will it go; will it have the soul of mother's or father's religion. If the father is Muslim, the mother is Protestant, and the born child is raised as a Muslim, would the child's soul go to a Muslim heaven or a Protestant Heaven?'

'Can someone be born from a Jewish woman and live as a Christian with a Christian father; if he does will he have a Jewish or Christian soul? Jews believe that Judaism is transferred through the Jewish woman, not the Jewish man.'

'If you are born a Christian, presumably with a Christian soul, and then later you change and become a Jew or a Muslim, what happens to your soul when you die? Does it change? What happens to a baby's soul when that baby is born to a Protestant woman who does not know who Fathered the baby?'

'Since Judaism, Christianity, and Islam are all based upon Abraham's God, can one assume that today these religions all share Abraham's God, or do they each have a different God? Different names are used for worship. Or are sub-Gods involved? Where do I turn to find out?'

'Do priests, ministers, rabbis, or imams have the power to change the status of the soul? I know they can exorcise bad souls; how about wrong souls? How about inserting a new good soul?'

'And one can go on and on seeking unknown answers to numerous questions about spirit/soul interrelationships.'

'One can even make the situation more complicated when one compares Abraham derived religions versus non-Abraham derived religions. If a Hindu woman married a Catholic man, would their child have only one soul one time for a waiting place, or one soul for continuous recycling? If a Christian woman married a Buddhist man, would their child not be able to follow Buddhism because they would have only one non recyclable soul.'

'You can only begin to imagine the variety of questions concerning the spirit/soul if you start to ask about various combinations and mixtures of Hindus, Catholics, Buddhists, Protestants, Jews, Muslims, Eastern Orthodox, and non-believers. Where is the scientific enquiry into the concepts concerning spirit or spirits and soul or souls?'

'Why are the so called intellectuals of the world not studying this problem? Are they afraid of what they might find? Is there a religious conspiracy to prevent such research? Do those in the KNOW think that it is better that the common people do not KNOW. The church successfully maintained a RESTRICTION of KNOWLEDGE for almost two thousand years. What do we know, today, about religion and death-soul relationships, that we did not know two thousand years ago? And what have we learned about death-soul relationships since SCIENCE began, five hundred years ago? What are we afraid of?'

'I guess it is better to just BELIEVE and NOT QUESTION. Isn't that what is called FAITH?'

* * *

**'Where are the medical scientists who are studying theology and "AFTERLIFE"? And where are the theologians who are using science to better understand God? Why do our universities not encourage and support disciplines of scientific theology or theological science? Who is afraid of what?'**

*BCE – Before Common Era (internationally accepted) – equivalent to the Christian BC

*CE – Common Era (internationally accepted) – equivalent to the Christian AD

# 23 – Final Decisions?

Aaron and Jos Armand were in favor of suing the Jackson Fertility Clinic for several hundred million dollars and using the money for the Center for Cellular and Genetic Biology of Twinning. It would greatly stimulate the Center's activities and seemed appropriate to use identical birthing money to study identical birthing. But the New Orleans meeting and William Bassinger's synopsis made them reconsider. They were still seeking a large gift in the neighborhood of seventy to eighty million dollars and allow this person's name to be placed on the finally completed new hospital building; so far no luck.

Aaron sat at his office and started thinking. 'If we attempted and won a law suit for around several hundred million dollars, split between Bassingers-6, Collingswoods-5, Dekkers-6, and Armands-4, that will be about 4 ½ million dollars each. If you remove the lawyer's fees and capital gains taxes there would be maybe two or three million dollar per person as a victory, and we will lose our anonymity. Even if we put together the six million for Jos and me it would not help very much. We cannot take the children's money. We need another seventy five million dollars or more to complete the CCGBT. At the moment a loan of fifty million dollars is being arranged for the Center until such a time that a donor can be identified. This loan has to be paid off within ten years using patient fees and other Center income. Annual income is projected to be near twenty five million dollars per year; annual net profit is projected to be near two million dollars per year. With interest on the loan that will put us into trouble very soon, unless we can find several small donations in the range of ten to fifteen million dollars each. So the six million dollars from Jos and me will be almost meaningless.'

'I am at a loss as to what to do. There are two other groups at Columbia University Medical Center that are working on new specialty centers – an Eye Care Center and an Orthopedic Center. Both of these Centers have begun, like the CCGBT, within current existing hospital and laboratory space at the Medical Center. As they progress they will each try to find a large donor to help each of them with a new building, or they could try 'to buy out' the growing CCGBT if we cannot meet expenses and pay off our loan. There is always someone looking over your shoulder and eying your system, and only too happy to "inherit" your hard work.'

'I do have one other option, my family estate in New Hampshire. I currently have two different real estate agents looking for buyers for the estate. I was wise to not advertise openly, only through channels. So far I have had no flack from the estate's neighbors.'

'And I have three potential buyers already; two from corporations and one from a family. The AHP Corporation is a well known conglomerate in the energy field. They are planning to have the estate re-zoned into plots of five-six acres in size and execute a single family housing development. The houses will each be three to five thousand square feet and have a country flare. In addition they will build a small New England style village in the center. The AHP are talking in the range of eighty to eighty five million dollars for the entire estate.'

'My second possibility is with the large import-export container shipping company named VLTN Trans-World Shipping. This company is thinking of having the estate re-zoned into smaller plots, half to one acre, and build single family houses near two thousand square feet in size. They will have two areas for three floor town houses in which each area would include a club/party house, tennis courts, swimming pool, and other commons facilities. They are also planning to build a large shopping center which would be available to the public. With such density I can see why they are throwing out a big number, one hundred million dollars. Of course this number is contingent upon their getting the zoning that they need. In my opinion they will not be successful. The county zoning board will never allow such high housing density in this area. And I really do not want that either.'

'And my third possibility is with the Hamsteders. Orvil Hamsteder has been the CEO for a high tech Silicon Valley company named TECGO for fifteen years. He is retiring and wants to return to his roots. He grew up in a farming family in New York State, so is looking for a fully developed estate in the northeast where he can just walk onto the land and start farming. He is a young 66, but understands that age can creep up on one very quickly. The Armand estate is just perfect. And he is offering near fifty five million dollars.'

'I have had my family estate on the market for the past four months. And I will have to make a decision within the next six weeks. If I do not, I will have to co-sign for that 50 million dollar loan for the CCGBT. I need to have another rendezvous with the family; and I had better do it this weekend here at home and not next month at some nice resort.'

So the following Sunday evening, Aaron, Jos, Hype, and Hope went to Hype's favorite sushi restaurant, Koyoto Sushi. Uncooked or raw seafood may sound terrible, but such food can be delicious and very addictive. There were several sushi restaurants in the area so they enjoyed this Japanese style of cooking or non-cooking often. This time Aaron reserved the special secluded small round conference table in the back, as he wanted the privacy for heavy decision making. Hype would not sit at his favorite place in his favorite restaurant, the sushi bar, this time. It was fun to sit at the bar and watch the Japanese sushi chefs prepare the many different types of this very special Japanese food, sushi and sashimi.

On this Sunday it was all you can eat for fifty dollars each. And this included one flask of sake each. They had eaten sushi often enough that they each had their favorites. Mom ordered first: miso soup with tofu (bean curd) and green onion; tempura (pieces of meats dipped into a flour batter and deep fat fried) with swordfish, shrimp, squid, and several vegetables such as carrots, and mushrooms; dessert would be banana bread. She was not a strict sushi fan. Alice went second: miso soup with fried bean curd; nine Norimaki sushi which was sea food or vegetables on large thumb sized balls of rice enclosed with dried seaweed – shrimp, eel, octopus, ocean perch, tuna, cucumber, and cooked egg; and for desert she would have daifuku cake.

Next was Hype who ordered nimono soup which was made of dried sardines, twelve Nigiri sushi, which was sea food and vegetables directly on thumb sized balls of rice – eel, squid, shrimp, octopus, swordfish, tuna, carrots, mushrooms, cucumber, and sweet potato; for dessert he chose azuki shiratama (cold sweet dumplings). And last Dad ordered oyakodon soup (chicken and egg soup); six sashimi (raw or uncooked meats without rice) and five Nigiri sushi and five Norimaki sushi – sea perch, ocean bass, shrimp, squid, octopus, tuna, cucumber, carrots, and mushrooms; three large swordfish temaki nori which were seaweed cones containing rice and a special selected sea food, one for each family member; and for desert he chose diagakuimo (candied sweet potatoes).

All of the food for each person is served to the table at the same time. Therefore, food sharing or food trading is correct, right, and fair in this family style Japanese meal. However one is required to ask before you take from your neighbor. Each ball of rice is a two mouth size for smaller people and a one large mouth size for bigger people. So trading is accomplished in terms of my rice ball for your rice ball type of negotiations. It adds to the fun of this 'different' type of meal.

Now there are two additional 'culture' components required to enjoy a sushi-sashimi meal. First you must eat with chopsticks. No silverware is given. In front of you is a small shallow dish in which you pour a small amount of soy sauce. You add a small amount of wasabi (horseradish) to the sauce and mix to your own specifications, not spicy hot and lumpy or spicy hot and smooth, very spicy lumpy and smooth, etc. Then you chose from the sushi that you ordered, which is now sitting on the table in the tray beside you, and gently sit one sushi into your sauce. You let it sit there for three to thirty seconds; next you eat the entire sushi (ball of rice and seafood topping) in one mouthful. The real secret to such eating is to try to not let the spicy horseradish hit your tongue. The chef always hides a small amount of extra-horseradish directly underneath the seafood topping. It takes about one meal to learn how to manipulate your mouth such that your tongue does not get spice burned. Not only is it delicious, it is fun.

The second cultural component is a special method used to keep warm when eating cold (room temperature) food in cold weather. The soups and the tempura are eaten hot; otherwise all sushi, sashimi, and temaki are eaten cold. How do you stay warm in the cold areas of Japan in the winter with this diet? You drink hot sake. Sake is liquor distilled from rice, similar to Scotch whiskey distilled from grain. Sake is served in a small carafe which holds about three-four drinks. Each person receives one serving of one carafe. Now sake is 40-50% alcohol. It is poured into a small cup (two swallows in size) and drank – while boiling hot. However you never pour your own sake. Your neighbor must pour your sake for you and you must pour his sake for him. In this way you never drink alone. And you drink small amounts throughout the meal because the hot alcohol goes from mouth to stomach to brain very fast. At the beginning of a meal, the unwritten rules are sip slowly, eat rapidly, and talk slowly. Later in the evening the rules change and become drink rapidly, usually with the second or third carafe of sake, eat slowly, and talk rapidly. Sake enhances both the meal and the conversation. After three hours of dinner the one carafe eighteen year olds, the two carafe adult Mom and the three carafe adult Dad were feeling very good. So Dad ordered a pot of good strong black American coffee. He did want everyone to understand the multi-million dollar situation about which that they needed to make some decisions.

Dad opened up the discussion, "The meal was fantastic. It is a good thing that we do not live in Japan or we would be pigging out on sushi every night. Thank you for introducing us to sushi, Hype. That was about ten-twelve years ago at Sushico restaurant down on Broadway and 34th, if I remember it right."

"All right. Let us turn to some serious talking and thinking. As we all know I am an identical quadruplet. Several months ago my three brothers and I met with the people from the fertility clinic where 'our' fertilization procedures happened. As I reported to you, they were very open and honest, we think. And they pretty much orally confirmed that they were indeed the 'guilty' clinic. They explained it away by saying it was an error made by a senior technician who died several years ago. The clinic director is also no longer with them, so we have to take their story as truth. My brother, lawyer William feels that to sue them would be most difficult because all of the patient data and laboratory files would be legally impossible to obtain. He thinks that if we sue the clinic we might win a small award, and then again maybe not. If we won a court award of a few hundred million dollars for the twenty eligible people, after lawyer's fees and taxes we would take home less than maybe two or three million dollars each. And of course the world would know about the four closet bastards and their families."

"Does anyone have any questions here?"

After a shaking of heads, he continued, "Now the other problem is the CCGBT. We have not found a donor which is willing to give somewhere around seventy to eighty million dollars for the continued construction of the Center. Within six weeks I will need to co-sign a loan for fifty five million dollars to allow the construction to continue. And I will be required to pay back about seventy million on this loan within ten years. The money must come from Center operations. The projected income says that we will not be able to do this. So any potential monetary award from any fertility clinic lawsuit will not help us nearly enough."

And again, one by one, he looked each in the eyes. He saw both concern and a little fear in their eyes. After all, not very many Dads borrow several million dollars to build hospitals; most hospitals are not for profit organizations. They require large donors to build and to maintain such establishments. And if Dad did not pay it back in ten years what would happen to him, and to us? Would we have to pay it back? If he was taken to court or to jail, would they go too?

Dad began again. "I have decided to sell the Armand estate. The last time that we talked about living there, or trying to run the farming affairs from New York City, I heard three negatives. So I placed it on the real estate market several months ago. There are three potential buyers. 1) AHP is an energy conglomerate which wishes to develop it into a middle-upper class New England style community. They are offering eighty million dollars. 2) VLTN Trans World Shipping plans to develop it into a middle class housing with both single family and multiple family housing. They are talking about one hundred million dollars contingent upon their obtaining the necessary zoning to develop the area to that density level. In my opinion that will never happen. 3) A retiring CEO from TECGO, a Silicon Valley high tech firm, wants to buy it and take up his family's root; his parents were New York State farmers. He would maintain it as a farm, for now. He is offering fifty five million dollars. So what do you think?"

Hype, always the fastest thinker and never shy, went first. "I think you did good Dad. I vote for number one, the AHP people, because the money is enough for the CCGBT, the area would remain classy, and we could have one of the neat big houses for both nostalgia and vacations."

Mom looked at Hope and nodded for her to go next, so Hope said, "I like the AHP group also because I want to see the area remain open and not be all swallowed up like the VLTN people want to do. Is it possibly to delay or control the development of the land up near the House area? Maybe we could keep the animal husbandry units functioning for a couple of more years and help everyone find new jobs." She was ever the little socialist.

Mom spoke up, "If you sold the family estate would you need to co-sign a fifty million loan for the CCGBT?"

"No." Dad answered.

"Good, then I like the idea of selling it, and Hope has a good idea concerning perhaps selling it in two phases. First they could develop maybe two hundred acres, and leave the twenty acres around the house and barns. We could farm that for a few years, and then let them develop that area last. In the meantime we can help the current employees find other work. We could slowly downsize each year."

Dad responded, "I hear each of you. I agree. I will take each idea into serious consideration. First, I will talk with the AHP group and see how they feel about two hundred acres up front and twenty acres in five years. Isn't that what you are suggesting?"

Hope and Mom both shook their heads with an affirmative smile.

Dad continued, "After you calculate in sales taxes and realtor's fees you need to drop the eight to ten percent from the offers. By doing this it leaves the TECGO CEO's offer less than fifty million dollars. That is less than we need. And the VLTN proposal of a high density housing development does not make me happy either. The AHP proposal is good. I like the openness concept. And after taxes and fees the financial offer would drop to near seventy five million dollars, which is adequate for the CCGBT construction."

Mom asked. "What about our income taxes? This would be very large capital gains in our annual income for this year. Probably at least half of it would go to Uncle Sam as personal income taxes."

'I have checked into this," He said. "We will donate it to the Mary and James Armand Center for Cellular and Molecular Genetics of Twinning. Easy come – easy go."

And he smiled as he looked at the three of them when the title of the Center hit them. Yes, it was fair that the Center be named after Aaron's parents. He is here because of them. It is their money. What more can parents give to their child; his life and his lifetime work.

So a decision by the Armand family was made. They would not be going to court.

* * *

Ever since William Bassinger explained the identical quadruplet situation to Jenny, Steve and Stef several months ago, all three had blamed William's 'parents', the wife's 'in-laws', or the children's 'grandparents' for keeping this knowledge secret for the past forty plus years. And William was undecided as to how to approach his emotionally linked Mother and Father.

When he and Jenny were married, almost every Sunday they would drive to the farm, attend the 'family' church, have a Sunday dinner, and spend most of the day with family and friends. After the children arrived, the Sunday on the farm became more difficult and dropped down to once a month. And in the past few years the drive to the farm seemed to get even longer. William had become a partner in the law firm therefore he had more responsibility and more work. Jenny had now taken on more administrative extra-curricular activity projects, like the Drama Club, which took up some Saturdays and Sundays. And now both Steve and Stef were away at their universities studying on week days and weekends. Since their Golden Nugget City venture they had managed only two Sunday dinners on the farm. Somehow the summer had flown by without seeing the older Bassingers; and here it was approaching Thanksgiving. William knew they would be expected for a full Thanksgiving meal; and a full day on the farm. So he talked with the younger Bassingers and asked them to keep cool and quiet about the identical quadruplet situation. He would try to talk to 'Grandpa' alone sometime during the day.

The younger Bassingers arrived with the other Bassingers and gave and got many kisses and hugs. There were thirteen people for the big Turkey dinner. This included the two older Bassingers, the four younger Des Moines Bassingers, and Grandpa's lawyer brother Paul who had served as William's professional role model. There was also Uncle Paul's wife and son, John, who was near William's age. John was now a dentist and had married his high school sweetheart Clara; they had three children, one boy and two girls. William could only hope that he could get his Father alone sometime somewhere during the afternoon. It might not be as easy as he originally thought.

Because the Bassinger families were all descendents of Amish/ Pennsylvania Deutsch (German immigrants), family reunion dinners were major affairs. This dinner was served at 2:00 PM, beginning at the half time of the annual classical Detroit Lions and whichever opponent's football game from Detroit. The dining room table had somehow expanded to seat fourteen people, so it easily seated the current thirteen Bassingers. An extra plate was always ready for a neighbor or nearby friend, who had no friends with which to celebrate this holiday; or if one of the Bassinger children brought with him a friend. This was the proper Lutheran way.

So at 2:00 PM the entire family sat down around the large table. The eldest, William's Father, Fred Bassinger, led the prayers, and then everyone started passing the bowls filled with vegetables and platters filled with meat around the table. This was family style serving in that everyone helped himself to the food as it was passed around the table. There were seven large bowls and three large platters filled with hot food that circulated for the first five minutes. The bowls contained corn, green beans, candied yams (sweet potatoes), mashed potatoes, green peas, cranberries, carrots, black eyed peas, and gravy made from beef broth. The platters were piled full of white turkey, dark turkey, white meat chicken, and small sirloin steaks. The only seasoning was salt and pepper. A couple of baskets of hot rolls and hot biscuits circulated, and had to be replaced several times. Also there was unlimited water and ice tea, with or without lemon, to drink. You simply helped yourself as the food moved left to right around the table.

The cooking workload was not terrible as each Bassinger woman cooperated in bringing two or even three vegetables and maybe one of the meats. So no one person was exhausted from the massive food preparation needed to produce such a meal. And since almost everyone sitting and eating was over six foot tall, and most of the guys were well over two hundred pounds, no food went to waste. Even the three farm dogs might have to fight for any food throwaways.

The conversation buzzed around all types of topics as the men tended to sit together at one end of the table and the women tended to sit together at the other end. This was WASP tradition. And it was yet commonplace as women seemed to have more to say to women and men have more to say to men.

So at Grandpa's end of the table there was a mature farmer, two lawyers, a dentist, a budding engineer, and a budding doctor. Here the topics ranged from the continued war in Afghanistan, to the continued Israel-Arab conflict, to the continued pollution of American fresh water (Were the farmers really at fault?), to the use of single genes to change the character of farm crops, to the question of whether Iowa will again go Democrat in the Presidential elections next year, to the hope that the University of Iowa will win the Big Ten Football Championship this year, and other manly and worldly things. William and son agreed only on the Iowa for Democrats and the Big Ten Football Championship plus a trip to the Rose Bowl. The two of them would plan to go.

And at the Grandma's end of the table the discussion focused on domestic affairs related to family problems, house related efforts, new cooking recipes, the children's future, and 'gossip'.

After the main courses, you could choose between or among pumpkin pie, cheery pie, apple pie, tunnel fudge cake, and cheese cake. And of course there was coffee and more ice tea or water to drink.

Outdoors the wind had picked up and the day had become rather cloudy and cold; and it looked like snow was on the way. So the regular outdoor activities such as playing tag football or horse shoe pitching would have to be postponed until next Thanksgiving. The NFL game had finished and the Detroit Lions lost as usual. So conversation wound down rather early. Soon the ladies of each family packed into their cars the good leftovers of the foods that they had brought to the dinner. They then packed much of the remaining food and placed into their cars. The children assisted in the carrying. And they dragged their husbands away from certain life and death decisions via illegal counsels, shoved them into the front seat, encouraged them to start the car, and pointed toward their home. Laughs and shouts, hugs and thrown kisses, come and see us soon, and the Bassinger families departed until next time, except for one family.

Toward the end of the dinner Stef was in the kitchen helping Grandmother put away some of the dishes which had been washed and dried. When Stef gave her Grandma a kiss and said, "I have missed you."

And Grandma, with a tear in her eye already, responded, "And I missed you too. You used to help me cook dinner. And now you are so busy that you only cook in your Mother's kitchen and bring it here for us to eat. I think it tasted better when you made it in my kitchen." And gave her a sweet smile and kissed her back.

Stef looked her Grandma in the eye and said, "Are you my real Grandmother?"

"What do you mean?" Grandma responded.

"I heard that my Dad was not really your son, therefore I must not be really your granddaughter." Stef answered.

Grandma took Stef by the hand and went into the living room where the rest of the family was preparing to leave. The group looked at the two of them and sensed that something was wrong. Grandma sat Stef on the couch. She motioned for the others to sit down. And then she motioned to her husband.

She said, "Now is the time, Fred."

Fred nodded his head and left the room. Everyone was quiet for the 5 minutes that Grandpa was out of the room. When he returned he motioned for all to come and sit around the dining room table. He sat in his head chair, William to his right, Jenny to his left, and the children next on each side. He lay a large envelope down in front of him on the table.

And Fred Bassinger began to purge his soul by revealing his forty plus year old secret.

"Dorothy and I were married when we were teenagers. We lived down the road in an old house which is now gone and I worked for my Father here on the farm. There was a lot of work and I loved it. We tried to immediately have children. After several years we did not have any, my Father was getting old and was not well. He kept putting pressure on us to have an heir in order to continue the eighth generation Bassinger family as land gentry. So we went to see some doctors in Des Moines. They ran some tests and said if we really wanted a child we should go to this clinic in Virginia. We went to Virginia and they ran some more tests and said that they could help us. They said that we could have a test tube baby. This was a new medical procedure that had only become available a few years before.

We agreed. Dorothy went to this clinic and remained there for more than two months. They told us that an anonymous couple, who we would never meet and never know, would donate the necessary genes, the new baby would grow for a couple of weeks in a test tube, and then they would place it in Dorothy's womb. She could then go home and have the baby. It would be ours. No one would know and we did not have to tell anyone. So that is what we did. And we had the most beautiful baby in the world, and then the most wonderful child, and then the best Iowa football player ever, a super lawyer son, and now the best Dad with the most beautiful wife with the smartest and most super children,..........."

And the tears began to pour down his face. He stopped, looked at his William, Jenny, Steve, and Stef. He looked over at Grandma and she suddenly broke down crying. He could go no further. Grandma also began to shake and rock. Everyon began to shed tears, got up, went to the oldsters, put their arms around them and tried to comfort their Father, Father-in-law, and Grandpa, or Mother, Mother-in-law, and Grandma. The emotional outbursts continued for several minutes. But they each knew the right thing had been done.

Grandpa Fred had never got over the guilt of doing something so unusual, and not saying anything to anybody. It was being dishonest. He felt this dishonesty with his new son, his friends, his neighbors. In the beginning he had great difficulty looking people in the eye when he talked about his son. As the years went by he wanted to tell everyone. But he was afraid that if he told Bill, he might lose his love; so he postponed, delayed, and tried to forget what happened in Virginia in 1975. But he could not forget and the guilt was slowly eating at him and killing him. But now it was out. The people he loved knew. And that was all that mattered. He suddenly knew that his loved ones would still love him. And he was at peace with himself for the first time in more than forty years.

Dorothy spoke up, "Open the envelope."

Fred obeyed, opened it and said, "In here are several legal papers that I want to give to my lawyer son. First is your official birth certificate at the First Methodist Hospital in Des Moines on February 28, 1976. The second is your official adoption papers dated March 15, 1976. Your Uncle Paul helped with this. We took the birth certificate and went up to Minneapolis, Minnesota to some friend of his. We rented an apartment, established Minnesota legal residency, and then Dorothy and I and my brother Paul officially registered you as our adopted child and the right and only heir to our land and property. Minnesota knows this but Iowa does not. I could not have done it without Paul's help."

"Therefore you are legally ours by birth and adoption laws. If anyone ever found out that your genes came from Virginia, I would go back and blow up that confederate city of Richmond again, first time since the Civil War. Here is your baptismal certificate from the Delis Lutheran Church. Here is your first America passport which we never used. There was a lot of anti-Communism activity in the seventies, so many people living on farms, not in cities, obtained passports for all family members. A couple of our friends were arrested on suspicion of Communist activities. So here is your unused and outdated passport which gives Dorothy and I as your parents. And here are your school grade cards for first grade through tenth grade; we never did find out what happened to years eleven and twelve. I guess you must have graduated."

Both children smiled and at the same time they reached for the school cards. They both wanted to know how 'bright' their Father was in school. Grandpa laughed, blocked their reach, took back the cards, and gave them to his son. Everyone was accepting and digesting the truth so the room atmosphere was becoming mellow.

Grandpa continued, "There are also several childhood certificates for such things as swimming awards, boy scouts, summer camps, little league baseball honors, etc. And last here are a bunch of pictures from your school years which shows you in action in sports and school, with boyfriends and girlfriends."

With that last comment Jenny quickly reached for the photographs. Again, Grandpa was too fast. He blocked her reach, pulled them back and gave them to his son.

He said, "It might be better if William screens these pictures before they become community property."

And everyone could see that Grandpa was regaining his sense of humor and therefore slowing re-acquiring his composure.

Grandma finally spoke up, "Please forgive these two old people for keeping this secret for so long. We just couldn't find the right time to tell you. And indeed we had only one fear, and that was that we would lose you. The longer we waited the more there was to lose. So each year it became more difficult. Again we are sorry. We should have told you a long time ago. But we did not. And we are ashamed for not doing so."

And again there erupted another round of emotional outpouring between the older-middle-younger Bassingers. Each was trying to atone for many years of hidden secrets, suspicions, and fears. Now acceptance of the truth seemed to be settling into each of the Bassinger family relationships; and it was obvious that the emotional linkages had won over the genetic linkages.

It was obvious that the Bassinger family was not going to court.

.............................................................................................

Several months after the New Orleans revelations the Collingswoods were still having trouble accepting the new facts of life. The problem was not related to anonymity, Charles parents were not part of their current world – Charles's Mother was in heaven and Charles's Dad had started a new life with a new wife and real children. And they knew the goods and bads of every citizen in the small community of Indian Nest, Florida where they had lived for the past twenty years. So the concept of suddenly being publically labeled bastards would not be a major personal problem for them. The problem concerned the possibility of having several million dollars which could be used in their professional pursuit of rescuing and saving the Everglades National Park in southern Florida. So almost every week or so for the past several months they spent hours trying to come to some conclusions about what they really and honestly could do and could not do with such money.

Charles, still the President of the Save the Everglades Foundation, had thoughts along the lines of: - 'attempting to establish physical blockages and re-routing of the fertilizer and herbicide runoff from the growing sugar cane plantations into the Everglades. The worst of the pollution run off was coming from the sugar cane plantations east of Big Cyprus National Park and north of Highway 41 which ran east and west and was located just north of the Everglades. The State of Florida had spent billions of taxpayer's dollars buying up land in the area and converting it to state park land, but it had only slowed down the expansion of the plantations and the increase in the pollution run off. Will a green filtration system of canals and bio-filters prevent the runoff southward into the Everglades? It certainly will help. But the accumulated polluted water has to go somewhere. And those heavy summer rains and hurricanes raise havoc with drainage canals and their pumping systems. The discharge would have to go into the ocean far out to sea because of the population density along the Florida southeastern shore.'

'There are now almost two million people living between West Palm Beach and Miami. And that was the other part of the reason for the dying of the Everglades. This large population increase over the past one hundred years has created massive pollution problems from housing developments, industrial developments, the road systems that service these developments, and the inadequate septic systems everywhere. Even drinking water is now limited and rationed in many of the urban areas. Proper and extensive blockages and re-routing of the pollution run off would certainly help, but how much and for how long and at what expense. It probably would require billions not millions of dollars. Even then where would be the guarantee for success?'

Charles's wife, Dr. Janice Collingswood, a wild animal life ecologist who had spent most of her professional life within the Everglades, was thinking along different lines. She thought, 'control of pollution entering the Everglades is necessary but it cannot and will not be accomplished in my lifetime. And it will not prevent continued losses and even extinction of several species of my animal children. During these past twenty five years I have witnessed the decrease of almost every species that I have been following. In particular is the loss and/disappearance of several species of butterflies, dragonflies, green tree frog, trail snail, apple snail, hawksbill turtle, leatherback turtle; while I have now placed all of these and the Atlantic Ridley turtle, cotton mouse, wood rat, wood stork, cape sable sea sparrow, southern bald eagle, Florida black panther, American crocodile, and manatee on my personal endangered species list. Perhaps the money could be spent on attempting to re-start some of the lost species by purchasing new animals and establishing new habitats for them which are further away from polluted areas. But I know in my heart that this would only be temporary. If the pollution is not stopped, history will just repeat itself and in twenty to thirty years these re-started animal colonies will probably also disappear.'

Charles's son, Samuel was finishing his MS and would soon start his PhD program at the University of Miami in Environmental Sciences. He had completed his MS thesis research in Manaus, Brazil. His research project involved the development of a large sugar cane plantation in the middle of the virgin forested area in the Amazon River Basin and the monitoring and evaluation of changes in the neighboring wildlife populations.

Samuel was thinking, 'I will use this Brazilian data here in Florida and apply my new knowledge to the sugar cane plantation – Everglade problem. I am aware and following closely several TMDL (Total Minimum Daily Load) studies in the plantation and high population regions near the Everglades. Such studies scientifically measure the level of gases and toxic in-organic substances and organic substances in the water, growth of key grasses, and species versus quantity of both invertebrates and vertebrates in the water and on water associated land. TMDLs are a more sensitive measure of environmental pollution than the monitoring of animal numbers. It can also be used to help identify specific pollutants at specific entry points into the Everglades. But what could be done with several million dollars in trying to protect the Everglades today, I certainly do not know. These Everglades' specific diseases have been occurring over many years, and the cures will also take many years. I expect it to be my life-long work.'

Charles's daughter, Sara, was studying for her Bachelors of Science Degree in Veterinary Medicine at the University of Florida.

Sara was thinking, 'After I graduate I will establish my vet practice in the Miami – Everglades area. In addition to providing a regular medical service for small animals, in order to have bread money, I will work with my Mother and brother in studying disease susceptibility in both domestic and wild animals which are living in the polluted versus non-polluted areas, assuming that I can find enough non-polluted areas to serve for the control studies. If the research looks promising, I will then study for my PhD in Veterinary Medicine from the UM. But today I have no idea how to spend millions of dollars on survival mechanisms for the Everglades.

So after several weeks of discussing how four to five million dollars could be used to decrease pollution in southern Florida, no current methodology or solutions seemed apparent. Money would not solve this problem.

Finally, Charles spoke up, "America has finally woken up to the American and worldwide problem of manmade pollution and destruction of the environment. We have recently been receiving more and larger donations in the Save the Everglades foundation. We have collected more than one and a half million dollars in the past year. So, if this continues, and I think it will, the Board of Directors will begin accepting grant applications to support environmental improvement projects for the Everglades next year. Maybe Janet can apply for funds to re-start some projects concerning endangered species. I know she would receive a fair project review." And he looked at his wife and winked.

So the Collingswood family would not be going to court.

* * *

Dave, Janet, Action, and Alice Dekker were not terribly interested in the promised millions of dollars from a lawsuit against medical people who did not deliberately try to hurt them. One night they sat down together and tried to make a list of the harms, hurts, insults, deprivations, damages, and losses that having a big, loving, successful Father had caused them. So if the Jackson Fertility Clinic had not been there and not helped Dad's Mother, then there would be no Dad, no happily married Mom, and maybe no Action and Alice. Therefore the Clinic was not all bad. And if the other families wanted to go to court they would not say no, they had little face to lose, and of course one can always find a way to spend that kind of money. In addition, Janet never knew her parents, while Dave's parents would not be hurt by any revelations of bastard children.

Janet opened her Bible and started reading,

"Do not take advantage of a hired man who is poor or needy, whether he is your brother or stranger." Deuteronomy 24:14;

One man gives freely, yet gains even more; another man withholds unduly, yet comes to poverty; a generous man will prosper; he who refreshes others will himself be refreshed." Proverbs 11:24-25;

Jesus looked and loved him and said, 'One thing you lack, go and sell everything that you have and give it to the poor, and you will have treasure in heaven, then come and follow me." Mark 10:21."

With this line of reasoning the Dekker family also would not be going to court.

# 24 – End or Beginning

Aaron Armand became dead at 4:44 on Tuesday, July 4, 2022.

Late in the afternoon Hope and several of her friends were sitting on the banks of the Hudson in Riverside Park watching the final construction of the fireworks to go on display this evening, a regular July 4th event. The group was talking and having fun when some fireworks accidently exploded and several rockets came up the hill toward Hope's group. One rocket swerved and struck Hope directly in the face. She screamed and rolled over in agony. However she kept her cool enough to reach for her cell phone and hit quick dial for Mother. Mother answered, Hope screamed that she was hit in the face by a fireworks rocket and she was at the Riverside Park at 110th street. Mom immediately called for an ambulance and the police; then she called Aaron who was working with a couple of patients in the CCGBT. Jos told Aaron what had happened, told him she was at a friend's house up in Ridgewood, New Jersey, so it would take an hour or more for her to get to riverside Park. He agreed and said he would go immediately and directly there.

As he ran down the steps of the Twinning Center building, and en route he opened his cell phone and dialed a friend, a Professor Hampton at Presbyterian Hospital who was a burns specialist. Just as Professor Hampton answered Aaron ran into the street. He had come late today and had parked across the street. A large delivery truck came roaring down the street as the driver apparently wanted to get home to take his children to the evening fireworks display. The truck hit Aaron directly and flipped him high into the air. He lit head first on a nearby stone wall, immediately broke his neck. By the time an ambulance could reach Aaron and get him into the Presbyterian Hospital he was dead.

An ambulance was already present at Riverside Park in anticipation of potential fireworks accidents. So Hope had quickly been taken, upon her request, to the Presbyterian Hospital. She and her Father arrived at the emergency services entrance at the same hospital at the same time. Although she was alive; her father was dead.

Jos had left her friend's house and was on her way to Riverside Park when, within two minutes, she received two phone calls from the police, one about her daughter admitted for emergency care at the Presbyterian Hospital and the second about her husband who was dead and was being held in the surgery unit at the Presbyterian Hospital. She pulled the car over and just sat there and cried for several minutes, finally got herself under temporary control, and drove directly to the Hospital. On the following Saturday the New York Times obituary page had a short note as follows:

*FAMOUS Dr. AARON ARMAND KILLED BY HIT AND RUN*

*Dr. Aaron Armand, MD, PhD was killed Tuesday afternoon, July 4, across the street from Columbia University Medical School by a hit and run truck. Services for Dr Armand will be held today, Saturday, July 8 at 2:00 PM at the St. Patrick's Cathedral on Madison Avenue in Manhattan. He will then be buried at the True Hope Cemetery in Englewood, New Jersey.*

*Dr. Aaron Armand was the Founder and Director of the Mary and James Armand Center for the Cellular and Genetic Biology of Twinning, which is located at the Columbia University Medical Center and Presbyterian Hospital in New York City. It is the only such research hospital in the world which studies the relationships between human genes and human behavior. Dr. Armand's dedication to this area of medical research was such that he sold his family estate in New Hampshire, established the Twinning Center, and named it after his parents. His partner in his life's work is his wife, Dr. Josephine Armand, who is Deputy Director of the Twinning Center. They have twin children. Hype Armand is a pre-med student at Columbia University and is considering following in his parent's footsteps. Hope Armand is a student in the Division of Social Sciences and Humanities at New York University. Dr. Aaron Armand was a self driven medical researcher in his pursuit of knowledge of the relationships between chromosomes-genes-DNA and behavior traits and decision making in identical twins, fraternal twins, and non twins of all ages.*

*Dr Armand's published quotes include, "We accept the concept that we are a product of nature versus nurture. But which is more important for which part of ourselves as we grow up? What we do, where we go, how we live, who we live with, and how we think, which of these questions are controlled by our genes, which are influenced by our genes, and which are independent of our genes but only learned from watching others around us? As we age can we see our Mother or our Father in ourselves, or do we grow independent from our parents? How and Why?"*

*The Twinning Center is dedicated to finding answers to such questions. The Armands ask that you do not send flowers but that any donations should be sent to CCGBT@yahoo.com.*

On that Saturday, July 8, during the funeral services at the St. Patrick's Cathedral, a rented car was parked across the road on Madison Avenue. A gentleman and a lady were watching. It was hot and sunshiny outside, but they were wearing light jackets, hats, and sun glasses while sitting in the car's air conditioning. No one even noticed them. The sat there through the entire service. As the funeral hearse left to go to the Cemetery in Englewood, New Jersey, they looked at each other, nodded, and drove back to Kennedy International Airport.

* * *

Mr. William Bassinger became dead at 4:44 PM on Tuesday, July 4, 2022.

In March, 2022, William Bassinger started feeling very badly. He could not seem to recover from his winter 'cold'. And he was seeing blood in his urine. So in early March he went to a local friend of his, Dr. Chad Bekter, a General Physician at the Methodist Hospital. After an hour of a complete and rigorous physical examination, plus an EKG, an EEG, and an ultrasound exam and Cathode Axial Tomography (CAT Scan) in the lower gastrointestinal tract, and blood and urine samples taken for a large series of laboratory tests, William went home, not back to work. He did not go to work the next day, but the following morning he returned to Dr. Bekter to hear the results of his lab tests. The initial results suggested that he might have cancer. So Dr. Bekter referred him to Dr. Michael Higgins, an Oncologist.

He went to Dr. Higgins that same afternoon, who had his lower abdominal area evaluated with a live time 3-dimensional CAT Scan. The Radiologist, Dr. Stanley Overton, showed to Dr. Higgins the malignant region in the urinary bladder. The cancer had already spread into the surrounding lower abdominal muscles and was not operable. The only choice was immediate radiation therapy followed up by chemotherapy. But both of them knew that this was only prolonging the situation and giving

Mr. Bassinger a few more months instead of a few more weeks to live. He went home that afternoon and told the family. There had not recently been a cancer in the family, so no one knew how to think or what to do.

And the doctors were correct. He had advanced carcinoma of the urinary bladder, not a common cancer and one which was not very curable. The family had to try for a cure so he was immediately given a single series of combination chemotherapy, radiation therapy, and a second round of combination chemotherapy; then a one month break from all therapies to let his body partially recover. In May he was given another series of radiation therapy treatments, another single series of combination chemotherapy with a change in two of the five drugs. And it was not enough; he died in the hospital where he had lived the last month of his life. Services were held for him at the Methodist Church on Sixteenth Street on the following Saturday, July 8, 2022; and then he was buried in the Freeman Cemetery outside of Des Moines which was near the family land and where several of his ancestors were buried. On the obituary page of the Des Moines Register was a picture of William Bassinger and a note:

### *FAMOUS GE LAWYER IS BURIED ON FAMILY LAND*

*William Bassinger, Esquire, Senior Partner of Bassinger, Albreit, Lansom, and Watmeyer Law Firm and Associates, died on July 4, 2022 at the Methodist Hospital where he had been undergoing treatment therapy for urinary bladder cancer. He was loved by a large community of Iowans who knew him personally and professionally. He was from a long line of Iowa farmers, fourth generation since 1931. The turnout was overflowing at the First Methodist Church where he had been a member for more than many years; and the funeral caravan from Des Moines to the Freeman Cemetery was several miles long and the normal 1 ½ hour drive took 4 hours. Mr. Bassinger leaves behind his wife, Jenny who teaches at the Briarwood High School, a son, Steve who is a medical student at the University of Iowa, and a daughter, Stefennie who is finishing her degree in Humanities and Social Studies at Drake University.*

*Mr. Bassinger was one of a handful of lawyers in the Midwest who specialized in the now mushrooming field of SGFs (single gene transfers) in food crops. This field has grown, according to the Iowa patent register, from 15 SGF patents in 1990, to 590 patents in 2000, to 1875 patents in 2070, to more than 5000 such patents today; and there were 364 law suits involving SGFs in Iowa in 2020. Mr. Bassinger will be sorely missed for his professional judgments and his rock solid approach to this new and terribly technical area of law. He will be sorely missed by family, friends, and colleagues.*

During the church ceremony there was a rental car parked on the side of the road facing the front of the church. Sitting in the front seat was an elderly gentleman. He was wearing a hat and sunglasses. Sitting beside him was a younger woman. They both wore sweaters while sitting in the air conditioning of the car. They did not talk nor get out of the car but carefully watched everything from their car. After a while, apparently they had seen all that they wanted to because they did not join the funeral caravan to the cemetery. Instead they returned to the Des Moines International Airport.

* * *

Charles Collingswood became dead at 4:44 PM on Tuesday, July 4, 2022.

It was becoming late in the afternoon. Charles was dressed in shorts, tee shirt, and tennis shoes and had gone out by himself in the air boat to check on some live traps which were in the Everglades about three miles from Indian Nest. It was cloudy and starting to get dark early so he was trying to hurry to get home before a possible rain storm hit. He was walking across an open elevated knoll when he felt a sharp pain in his right calf. He knew immediately that it was a rattlesnake bite, even though he did not hear the warning rattles. So he started to run toward the boat to get to the first aid box which contained a snake bite kit. As he hurried he stepped into a hole, turned his ankle, and fell into a nest of young rattlesnakes. The mother was there and promptly bit him on his left thigh. As he tried to crawl to the boat he dropped his cell phone into the deep grass, looked around and could not find it, and passed out.

Around 7:00 PM Janice began to get worried. She knew that Charles had gone out in the boat earlier, she had already tried his cell phone which did not respond, but it was turned on. So she called the Everglade Rangers and the Florida State Highway Patrol. The Rangers arrived by car fifteen minutes later. The Patrol Officers arrived in a helicopter twenty minutes later. Janice gave the Patrol Officers the code numbers of Charles GPS unit. The helicopter quickly identified the unit on radar, and immediately took off toward the exact coordinates. They found Charles in five minutes flying time, searched for the medical problem, saw the snake bite marks and assumed it was rattlesnake, injected him with anti-rattlesnake serum, hooked an oxygen mask over his face and took off to the Miami City Hospital. They had notified Janice who, with police escort, was on her way to the hospital. They arrived there at 7:42 PM. It was too late. The double bites and no anti-serum for four hours were lethal. He had died almost immediately on his beloved home-ground – the Florida Everglades.

Charles's funeral took place the following Sunday at his church in Indian Nest. A minister friend from a nearby church performed the service. The Reverend Charles Collingswood was very popular and loved by everyone, especially the Seminole Indians, in the small community and surrounding area. Not only had he been the only Man of the Cloth in Indian Nest, he was also a staunch environmentalist, as was everyone living in the northern Everglades region. With church members, Indians, environmentalists, towns people, and personal friends his little church was overflowing with people and flowers. The entire community felt the loss, but they were all aware of the danger of rattlesnakes everywhere, even around their houses. So his death unleashed a general fear that it was necessary to set out snake traps within the village. The Sunday newspaper, the Everglade News printed on page one the following story:

### THE ENVIRONMENTALIST REVEREND CHARLES COLLINSWOOD PASSES AWAY

*The Reverend Charles Collingswood of Indian Nest passed away on July 4, 2022 after being bitten by two rattlesnakes while working in the Everglades near his house. Mr. Collingswood, President of the Save the Everglades Foundation, was assisting his wife, Dr. Janice Stryker-Collingswood, by checking on several of her live specimen traps which are a routine part of her lifelong studies of the animals of the Everglades. He was alone when checking the traps, was struck near a rattlesnake nest, fell and could not call for help. When the Florida State Police helicopter medics found him, it was already too late.*

*The Collingswoods have lived in Indian Nest for the past twenty five years and devoted their lives to trying to prevent the destruction of the Everglades caused by the increasing pollution from the north and east. It is the largest natural water habitat in North America. Mr. Collingswood and his Save the Everglades Foundation successfully brought to the world's attention the story of the destruction of the Everglades. The Foundation provided data documenting the types of pollution from nearby sugar plantations, city coal supported thermo and electrical generating plants, industrial exhaust, city septic exhaust, and urban encroachment into the Everglades via canals, roads, housing and industrial developments.*

*Mr. Collingswood has two twin children. Samuel is working on a PhD in Environmental Engineering. Their daughter is finishing her DVM at the University of Florida. She then plans to return to the Miami-Everglades area and began work on pollution and diseases in small animals in the polluted areas. Including his wife, environmental ecologist Dr. Janice Stryker- Collingswood, Charles is succeeded by a family team of environmental researchers who plan to devote their lives to trying to save the Everglades. God bless them. Any donations for Mr. Collingswood should be sent to the Save the Everglades Foundation@ aol.com.*

During the church ceremony there were two strangers sitting nearby in a car. They were simply watching the proceedings. Neither person got out of the car. The man was wearing a wide brim hat and sun glasses. The woman sitting beside him also wore a sun hat and sun glasses. The two of them did not participate in the services. As the church services were winding down the couple drove away and returned to the Miami International Airport from where they had come.

* * *

David Dekker became dead at 4:44 PM on Tuesday, July 4, 2022.

The Blue Ravens Security Firm had booked a five day security contract with three Australian sheep ranchers. It was not understood why they wanted security for their vacation in America's capital, probably to show to their friends back home that they were important. Each rancher had more than twenty thousand head of sheep on his ranch, so they were indeed wealthy ranchers and could afford this unique business expense. They would meet with an official from the Department of Agriculture while they were here, that made it official and legal and a business expense, hence tax deductible.

David Dekker, Director of Intelligence for the Blue Ravens, had finished his research on these gentlemen and could find no significant threats for their safety for their four day stay. He judged the situation to be one of low risk. He had two new recruits that needed to 'get their feet wet' so he was going to assign them to a four person field team. And he would monitor the team in action a couple of times during the short duration.

The three Australian ranchers arrived on Saturday evening, July 1, 2022, and they were picked up at Dulles International Airport by two team members in one of the Blue Ravens eight person bullet proof van and two team members in a Ford Preview. They were taken to the Marriott Hotel in Arlington, Virginia. The group relaxed on Sunday trying to adjust their biological clocks. And on day two, Monday, the ranchers were taken to the Department of Agriculture Building at 14th Street and Independence Avenue where they spent the entire day. Since things seemed to be going well they remained in the District for an evening dinner. Day three, Tuesday, July 4, everyone went sightseeing on Capital Hill. In the morning they toured the U.S. Capital Building, had lunch in at the bottom of the Hill in the National Gallery of Art, and then headed for the White House as they had tourism passes for the 4:00 PM tour.

David had been busy on Sunday and Monday, thus he had not had a chance to monitor the new team members. So today, Tuesday, he finished early and caught up with the entire group while they were waiting in line along the fence surrounding the Ellipse just south of the White House. The line was about four-five people deep and as many as two hundred people were waiting for the late afternoon tour. All of the tourists wanted to hurry and complete the White House tour such that they could find a good place to view the July 4 evening fireworks. The fireworks would be nearby on the Smithsonian Mall between the Washington Monument and the Lincoln Memorial. They would begin at dark and would last several hours. Currently there was a multimedia live show performing on a large temporary stage near the Monument. The noise from the show was LOUD.

David was standing apart from the group and watching everyone in the waiting line. Suddenly everyone heard a helicopter approaching. Yes, it was the Presidential helicopter bringing the President of the United States from Andrews Air Force Base to the White House. The First Family usually watched the fireworks from their ringside seat on the south balcony of the second floor of the White House. The balcony and window there allowed one to look directly out at the Washington Monument. As the helicopter landed in the Ellipse, additional people crowded up to the fence. They wanted to see the President as he exited from the helicopter. The President stepped down from the helicopter and slowly walked up through the rose garden next to the White House. As he did so, he waved to the crowd; they waved back and started shouting, cheering, and taking pictures.

Apparently the President thought he saw someone he knew or he was just going to shake hands. Whatever, he suddenly started toward the fence and the crowd. The FBI and House Security officials rapidly rushed toward him. This was not correct protocol. As he neared the fence, David noticed a big heavy man in a trench coat forcing his way through the crowd and shoving his way up to the fence toward the where the President was coming. David's commando instinct kicked in, he could smell trouble. He immediately rushed toward this big guy. David reached out toward him just as the man brought out from under his coat an Uzi machine pistol and pointed it at the President. David's old close quarters take down technique was still functioning well. He quickly tackled the man. The man's gun went off. Bullets sprayed in several directions and the crowd went crazy in trying to flee.

All of the government security personnel were on the inside of the fence; none of them were in a position to help David. Two of his own Blue Ravens team members finally managed to assist David and they brought the potential assassin totally under control. Only one person was shot. David had three bullets in his body; two in the chest and one in the left thigh. One of the bullets severed the ascending aorta above the heart such that the bleeding was immediate and massive. Before they could bring one of the White House medics and ambulance to the outer fence location where he was laying and bleeding, David Dekker died. He saved the President's life by giving his own life. The next day the Washington Post headlines read:

***ASSASSIN MISSES PRESIDENT BUT
HITS SECURITY SPECIALIST***
***In the late afternoon an attempted assassination of the American President by a Terry Stihl was prevented by a private security specialist yesterday. Mr. David Dekker, Director of Intelligence for the Blue Ravens Security Firm, had previously served as a combat commando in Afghanistan. He was at the right place at the right time and used those military skills in preventing the assailant from getting off any shots from his Uzi submachine pistol toward the President or any other person in a crowd of more than five hundred people. He redirected the gun into himself and received three lethal shots to the abdomen and legs. Two of his Blue Ravens Security team, who were there on another assignment, assisted in capturing the killer***

*until White House police could arrest him. It is not known what Mr. Stihl's motives were for his attempted assassination of the President. Mr. Dekker was the coordinator of a private security group which just happened to be in that location next to the White House when the President was going from the just landed Presidential Helicopter to..............................*

*Mr. Dekker leaves behind his wife, Janet Dekker and his twin children, Action and Alice Dekker. Mrs. Dekker teaches at the North Arlington Middle School. Action Dekker is attending Georgetown University Law School; and Alice Dekker is studying in the Department of Computers and Informational Sciences at George Washington University. Mrs. Dekker declared that David was the greatest Husband and Father in the world.*

Funeral services were held the following Sunday, July 9, at 2:00 PM at the Arlington Church of the Holy Cross in Arlington, Virginia. Because of David Dekker's previous military service and because of his giving his life to prevent the assassination of the President of the United States he was buried with national honors in the Arlington National Cemetery only a few blocks from where he lived and worked most of his adult life. He was the big bear that was very well loved by his family, friends, and associates. His kind of human being is not replaceable.

At the top of the hill about two hundred yards above where the mixed forces military unit was placing the body of David Dekker into the ground at Arlington National Cemetery there were two strangers, a man and a woman with binoculars, who were watching the proceedings. The weather was warm with sunshine. Both of them had on hats, light jackets, and dark sunglasses. At the end of the official ceremony and after the playing of 'taps', the two looked at each other, nodded their heads, turned around, walked further up the hill to their rental car and drove back to the National Airport.

* * *

Later in the week of July 4, 2022, four different and separate coded cell phone calls were made by four different men from each of the Kennedy International Airport in New York City, the Des Moines International Airport in Des Moines, the Miami International Airport in Miami, and the National Airport in Washington, DC to Jamaica. Each call later traveled from Jamaica via a coded land line to Rio de Janeiro; from there a gentleman passed the coded words by cell phone to Darwin, Australia;

from there the message went by coded land line to Shanghai, China; from there it went by coded land line to Istanbul, Turkey; and from there it went by coded cell phone to four cities in Switzerland: Bern, Zurich, Geneva, Lausanne, and also to Rome, Italy. A single telephone call was made from Rome, on a scrambled land line to a remote telephone in the Bavarian mountains near the German and Austrian border.

# Epilogue - Soul Maestros

September 4, 2023 was the annual meeting of the Founders of the Multi-Soul Company. All were members of the International Society of Scientists as Believers. To be a member of the ISSB one had to have a doctorate in a medical science area, a doctorate in theology, and be actively performing research in the scientific evaluations of religious doctrines. They were meeting in Hitler's secret Eugenics Library on the fourth level underground at Kehlsteinhaus (Hitler's Eagle's Nest Retreat) near Berchtesgaden in the Bavarian Alps. There were seven elderly men wearing dark colored business suits and sitting at a round table: Edwin (American Methodist), Dietrich (German Lutheran), Antonio (Italian Catholic), Haruhide (Japanese Buddhist), Mhotep (Egyptian Muslim), Elisheva (Israeli Jew), and Bhagyalakshmi (Indian Hindu).

The American, Edwin, opened the meeting, "Because I was responsible for the last set of **IDENTICALS** in the eighth experiment in this series, I am pleased to report to you that it went extremely well. There were no major problems. One 10 day old blastula was split into four blastulas again by using the S4 virus. At 12 days each blastula was transferred into a hormonally pre-prepared woman. --- **They came as one, became four, were carried separately, born separately, raised separately, grew up separately, but left as one.**"

"So our methodology has now been successfully used for different time frames over more than fifty years with all types of **IDENTICALS** including twins, triplets, and quadruplets. And I am also happy to report that all clinical fertilization technicians were bought off for less than five hundred thousand dollars. Oh! A nice addition, this time one of our **IDENTICALS** pursued research concerning 'nature versus nurture'. The results were very interesting. Such data should help us with our future research efforts. --- **I think we are ready to continue on to homogenous creed production projects and various heterogeneous creed experimentation projects!**"

Bhagyalakshmi spoke up, "Yes, with the increase in inter-ethnic marriages the multi-ethnic soul is now coming into more demand. All of our religions teach the same thing – one is associated with a warm body for only 80 to 100 years, but one is associated with a soul for eternity. So if you can buy a good, clean soul from us, you can lead whatever kind of life that you want before you die."

And he looked around and smiled before continuing, "But a more complete understanding of the composition of souls would be very helpful, especially the heterogeneous creed variety. Indeed, most of our experiments have focused upon one very semi-homogeneous creed – Christians."

"I agree." Antonio added. "Some of our first experiments were not well designed with regard to enhancing our knowledge of the DNA/spirit/soul interrelationships. We know that the spirit or soul enters immediately after fertilization occurs; but we don't know exactly which hour of which day, or exactly how that entry is controlled. Also, is it related to the religious preference of the male or the female? At least we can control this as we select both the female donor and male donor for every experiment. But this question needs to be answered soon. The Jews believe it is related to the female. I think they are wrong. I think that it is related to the male."

**[The brilliant and simple secrete of the Multi-Soul Company is as follows: The technique or methodology employed allows one to analyze various combinations of ethnic/creeded groups. Example – Oocyte from ethnic woman A, sperm from ethnic man B, and implantation into 'mother' C. Hence, Jewish oocyte, Moslem sperm, and Hindu 'mother'. Where does the soul from such a baby/adult go?]**

Dietrich added, "There are also the questions – Does the soul, itself, have gender? Are there female and male souls? Is the soul composed of coded atoms or genetic units, such as DNA, RNA, or proteins?"

Elisheva commented, "And because each of the major religions concur that there is a unique soul in each living adult person, there must be more than one soul available during the early blastula stage of the embryo. And it seems probable that once a certain soul enters, that same soul remains there for the duration of that person's earthly life. We have no data that souls do or do not change bodies during the physical lifetime. Some Christian priests claim to exorcise bad souls; but can they replace the exorcised soul with another soul, or introduce a new soul?"

"Yes, I wish to congratulate us," Haruhide said. We are doing well. We should focus on designing many more experiments, setting them into motion, and then choosing additional younger monitors for each experiment. Many of us will probably have to watch the overall results for some of our experiments from up there." And he pointed upward and smiled. "Plus, before coming here today, I checked our list of clients.

According to my records we already have more than one hundred clients who have requested single or multi-souls, each has deposited into our Geneva bank account the advance payment of ten million Euros. It would appear that a new price near twenty five million Euros per soul may not be unreasonable. And we can change the price anytime we want, because 'we are the only soul factory in town,' as they say." And he chuckled.

This also brought another round of smiles and general agreement. If anyone deserved to get rich and have their souls go up there, they were on the top of the list. After all, they had spent a lifetime in both the laboratory and in their specific religious establishments. No one knew more about eugenics, chromosomes, DNAs, spirits, and souls than they did.

Edwin spoke out again, "I think that we should consider using a research design somewhat similar to this last time, but use only three gene/person groups, more restricted living conditions, and twenty to thirty year periods. I suggest that we go into large scale production with the homogeneous creed projects using the Abrahamic groups of Jews, Christians, and Muslims, both single and multi-souls."

"Yes," Dietrich quickly followed. "And we could simultaneously use a similar research design for heterogeneous research projects mixing the Abrahamic and the non-Abrahamic groups of Hindus and Buddhists. Certainly the mixture of non-cycling souls and cycling souls should be very interesting."

"Don't forget the evaluation of single and multi-souls with gender variation," added Antonio. "We need Catholic genes/female and Muslim genes/male, Protestant genes/female and Hindu genes/male, Muslim genes/female and Buddist genes/male, Hindu genes/female and Catholic genes/male, and on and on. What do you think?"

Conversations continued around the table for a several minutes.

Dietrich finally asked, "Antonio, do we have enough oocytes and sperm in storage to initiate many multiple experiments at the same time?"

"Absolutely, supply is no problem," replied Antonio. "In fact we have more than 220 oocytes and 600 sputum of sperm in the two liquid nitrogen storage tanks in my labs. And we have good 'creed' and 'religion' mixtures among the donors, thanks to our Gynecology and Urology colleagues in New Delhi and Tokyo. So we have adequate oocytes and sperm in storage to design up a variety of homogeneous and heterogeneous combinations, both for production and experimentation. However, we have only three Fertility Clinics currently functioning with identified surrogate mothers or 'want to be mothers': Washington, Rome, and Tokyo. So we would need to establish some additional Fertility clinics, depending upon the production or experimental design. We have a large number of Abrahamic donors. So, I agree. We might want to set up several new creed production clinics for Abrahamic souls, perhaps in additional Christian cities such as New York, Paris, Berlin, and..............

**<u>MULTI - SOUL COMPANY MOTTO</u>**
**WORLD WIDE RELIGIONS AGREE ON ONE CONCEPT:**
**WE ARE ASSSOCIATED WITH A WARM BODY FOR 80 TO 100 YEARS,**
**AND THEN WE ARE ASSOCIATED WITH A SOUL FOR ETERNITY.**
**CHOOSE WISELY!**

In the year 2020, secret life insurance policies had been established for four American Identical Quadruplets.

On July 23, 2025, the fiftieth anniversary of the fertilization occurred which produced the zygote which became the embryos which developed into these four American Identical Quadruplets. On this latter date special individual bank drafts, each valued at 25 million US Dollars, were sent from four Swiss banks to a certain four beneficiaries as follows:

- Bern to Josephine Armand
- Zurich to Jenny Bassinger
- Geneva to Janice Collingswood
- Lausanne to Janet Dekker

Each special individual bank draft was immediately cashed without difficulty.

# GLOSSARY

**blastula** – group of identical growing cells (blastocysts) between days 1–14 after fertilization of an ovum by a sperm and before differentiation into embryo like cells

**cell** – smallest living life form which can grow and reproduce itself

**chromosome** – rod like structure in the nucleus of cells that house the genes

**conception** – fusion of ovum and sperm to create a zygote

**differentiation** – anytime a cell changes from one cell type to another cell type – stem cells change into nerve cells or into muscle cells or many other types of cells

**diploid cell** – any cell which has a complete set of chromosomes (46)

**DNA** – chemical structure of genes

**DNA fingerprint** – DNA is extracted from a cell; it is cut into thousands of pieces; these pieces are separated and measured; the result is called a fingerprint of DNA and is unique to every human

**DNA letters** – smallest chemical unit which provides the genetic code (only 4 letters - G,C,A,T )

**embryo** – a fertilized ovum develops sequentially into a blastula, gastrula, embryo, and baby

**endometrium** – the lining membrane of the uterus or womb which carries the baby; the tissue lining connects to the umbilical cord during pregnancy

**fertility** clinic – a medical facility where couples go to seek assistance on reproductive problems

**fertilization** – fusion of oocyte and sperm to create a fertilized ovum or zygote

**gametes** – two half cells, such as an oocyte and a sperm, each of which have half of the normal number of chromosomes/genes (called haploid); they must fuse to produce a complete cell which will then have the normal of chromosomes/genes and is called a zygote (called diploid)

**gastrula** – group of growing and differentiating blastula cells between days 15-24 after fertilization of an ovum by a sperm, they begin to form cells of the early embryo

**gene** – sequence of DNA letters which code for special functional proteins inside of a cell

**genome** – complete sequence of all of the genes on all of the chromosomes in a single cell (human genome is the complete sequence of all genes in the human cell; functional plus non-functional genes)

**haploid cell** – any cell which has half a set of chromosomes (23)

**meiosis** – a phenomenon when one cell divides into two cells without doubling it chromosomes (one diploid cell becomes two haploid cells)

**mitochondria** – energy units in a cell that convert consumed sugar into the body's energy molecule which is called ATP

**mitosis** – a phenomenon which one cells doubles its chromosomes and then divides into two cells (one diploid cell becomes two diploid cells)

**nucleus** – a round structure in the center of a cell that houses the chromosomes/genes

**oocyte** – female reproductive haploid cell within the ovary which underwent meiosis and can travel to the uterus; it can fuse with a sperm

**organs** – many types of tissues which 'glue' together to form a specialized body functioning such as liver, kidney, lungs, brain…..

**ovum** – a female haploid cell (after traveling to the uterus) which can fuse with a male haploid sperm cell; this produces a fertilized ovum or zygote (diploid) which can grow into an embryo and become a baby

**sperm** – a male haploid cell which can fuse with a female haploid ovum; this produces a fertilized ovum or zygote (diploid) which can grow into an embryo and become a baby

**tissue** – many types of cells 'glue' together to form a tissue; e.g. muscle tissue, fat tissue, connective tissue, nerve tissue (brain)

**zygote** – new cell produced by fusion of oocyte and sperm to produce a diploid cell